THREE CHEERS FOR WAR IN GENERAL

For Army Reservists throughout the country, weekly meetings and a two-week tour of duty every summer are often a big joke, a chance to dress up in Army uniform and play at being soldiers.

For members of the 229th General Hospital, Reserve meetings were just that—a big joke. Their chances of being called to Active Duty were nonexistent, they thought.

But the Pentagon thought otherwise.

THREE CHEERS FOR WAR IN GENERAL, the hilarious story of what happens when these weekend soldiers are activated, will delight every one who has ever put on a uniform!

'Soldier, soldier, come from the wars,
Did ye see no more o' my true love?'
'I seed 'im runnin' by when the shots begun to fly—
But you'd best go look for a new love.'

—Rudyard Kipling

ONE

The purpose of the Reserve Components is to provide trained units and qualified persons available for active duty in the Armed Forces, in time of war or national emergency and at such times as the national security requires, to fill the needs of the Armed Forces whenever, during and after the period needed, to procure and train additional units and qualified persons to achieve the planned mobilization, more units and persons are needed than in the regular components.

(Aug. 10, 1956, ch. 1041 70 A Stat. 10)
(United States Code)

The 229th General Hospital was, militarily speaking, under the Boston Subsector Command, under the Eleventh Army Corps, under the 1700th Hospital Sector. It was a good safe unit to join, if one were forced to be a member of the Army Reserve: in the event of a war in, say, Ceylon, a general hospital would likely be stationed in the vicinity of Keokuk, Iowa, with not much chance of getting closer to Ceylon than, perhaps, Jersey City. Many of the members of the 229th General Hospital appreciated this safety factor and gladly served out their six-year military obligation listening to first-aid lectures, typing pay vouchers, and leaving weekly meetings early to take advantage of lower-than-civilian prices in the PX on such items as stainless steel razor blades, contraceptives, and cigarettes.

When the unit was at full strength (one hundred and fifty men, one hundred officers, twenty-five nurses, five WACs for clerical duty), it supposedly could maintain a fully equipped hospital with three hundred beds. Under the correct circumstances, each bed could accommodate one patient. At the moment, the unit was down to about half strength on its male personnel. It didn't much matter as long as they met fifty times a year.

In the fall, winter, and spring, the Boston Army Base opened its doors to the men and women of the 229th General Hospital for weekly Thursday night drills. Theoretically, the men used these weekly drills to "become acquainted with the

7

procedures, professional and administrative, of the organization and maintenance of a medical complement under military conditions." In fact, as Specialist Fourth Class Eros Winter claimed, all they did was screw around for two hours, have a few beers and then go home. Whereas officers had maybe three beers.

The summertime meant two weeks of on-the-spot training, actually manning a hospital. One of the drawbacks of this training was having to leave for camp at five forty-five in the morning.

"It's too damn early for human beings to be up," one of the enlisted members of the 229th commented at 5:31 on the morning of August 12.

"You're no human being," shot a lieutenant, in civilian life a clinical psychologist. "You're a soldier. Fall in!" And the taped trumpet from the Army Base loudspeaker pounded tattoo at the starched and khakied civilians who scrambled to fall into formation.

"Companee, ATTEN-HUT!" It was futile command. The men were in no condition to come to attention. They had simply dragged themselves into a semblance of three ranks and put their feet together.

The rumble of buses and trucks and the smell of exhaust fumes filled the air. The sun was up but hidden behind the six-story half-mile-long Boston Army base. "THREE PACES FORWARD . . . HAOU!" and the men took a vague three paces forward to let a Trailways bus, complete with travel toilet section, roar by their rear, filled with sleepy Reservists from another unit on their way to two-week summer encampment.

"REEPORT!" came the command, instantly hushing the whispers in the ranks. "Professional complement present and accounted for," was the automatic reply of Platoon Sergeant Chesley Jackson, nicknamed "Cameroons" because he always regaled anyone who'd listen with the story of how his mother was kidnapped and brought to the States from the Cameroons for white men's pleasure. (She escaped.)

"Administrative complement all present and accounted for," chorused Skippy Dennis, the sergeant in charge of the clerks and office personnel. In civilian life he was a decorator. He had all his fatigues tailored so that they bagged just ever so slightly at the knees. Some of the officers who didn't know better thought Skip Dennis was smooth. He did give snappy

8

salutes, his right hand always meeting his temple at just the right angle, and his snap down to his side was executed with true military precision. "What a pleasure," thought Colonel Gayle Beauregard, commanding officer of the 229th, "to see such an elegant presentation."

Doctor-Colonel Beauregard was a moderately successful, politically oriented dentist, very much concerned with the issue of fluoridation. He had felt for some time that he could be a prime mover of sorts and was growing increasingly tired of looking into people's mouths and concerning himself with the problems of gingivitis, pyorrhea, and that dentist's friend—drift. ("It's somewhat less than desirable in *my* social schema," his wife had once told him.) Being a Gemini, he believed all the palmists that had ever told him there was something special in being a Gemini; thus it was that, while brushing up and down, side to side, and round and round one day, he realized that fluoridation was made to order for the ambitious dentist. With this as his major concern he ran successfully for selectman in the town of Brookwood, south of Boston, promising to "rid, much as the Pied Piper of Hamelin, all the caries in all the mouths of the town." He was swept in on a Republican tide, and led his victory cavalcade to the banks of the town reservoir, where he dribbled in the first token, symbolic dribblings of fluoride. His constituents cheered and went home to brush after their meals.

Colonel Beauregard had white hair, crew-cut extremely close, and a tight, evenly cropped moustache. He was five foot five and took consolation in the knowledge that Alan Ladd had filmed love scenes while standing on top of an orange crate so that the audience would not realize his height. Beauregard was good at compensating.

It was thought that he was a great colonel in the Army Reserve as well. First Army Headquarters believed it. Boston Subsector Command believed it. Eleventh Corps believed it. They all believed in the cocky little dentist as a military commander. So they put him in charge of the 229th General Hospital. "We'll run a tight ambulance," he had said with a smirk below his moustache when informed of his command.

He had run the pumice wheel in private over his teeth the evening that he was to be installed. (He had always had a damned annoying little problem with tartar that he traced to his saliva. It was lucky that he had such easy access to a pumice wheel.) There had been a military band for the occa-

9

sion even though it consisted of only ten pieces. General Byrd from Fort Devine pinned the silver eagles to the epaulets of the now full-Colonel Beauregard, stepped back and saluted. The new colonel braced to attention as only a little man can brace and threw the neatest military salute back. "Congratulations and—carry on, Gayle," said General Byrd, using his first name for a special touch of intimacy. Colonel-Dentist-Selectman Gayle Beauregard smiled a full smile. Not one trace of tartar showed in the smile and he felt that he had done his job well.

He had been anxious to leave his wife that early morning of August 12th, even though she made great pre-summer-camp breakfasts, with the emphasis on Aunt Jemima, and had been the best hygienist that he had ever employed. He had so admired her efficiency some years back (especially with the X-ray machine), that he decided the expedient thing would be to marry her. She stayed on without pay after they were married, performing prophylaxis, giving the special X rays, organizing the League of Women Voters on behalf of fluoridation, pressing his uniforms and polishing his silver eagles. She did it for love: love she felt especially equipped to give in view of her dental hygiene background.

Colonel Beauregard thought of the day of the eagle-pinning as he watched Sergeant Dennis salute. He had practiced the very same salute at home before his wife and children until they assured him it was correct. They had read and digested all of his Army manuals.

"HOSPITALLL!" came the cry deep from his throat. The Colonel squeaked at the last drawn-out syllable. His lungs didn't have the staying power for really effective command.

"HOSPITALLL," came the echo from the section leaders.

"AT EASE . . ." And two hundred and seventy-nine members of the 229th General Hospital shot their left legs out from their bodies and their hands behind their backs, left hand grasping right hand in the attitude of parade rest. AT EASE was something that was well understood by the 229th.

"I'd like to speak to you a bit informally, men," the Colonel began. "And I'd like to quote General Earle F. Dealer, our Chief of Staff, who has said"—here the Colonel produced a small blue notepad and read from it—" 'We live in a world atmosphere of revolution, protracted conflict and risk of nuclear war, a world from which violence is not eradicated and wherein danger is situated only minutes away.' This is

10

why you go to summer camp and why we take you away from your homes, your jobs, your loved ones, for two short weeks every year. Don't you men and women think that this is the least you can do to preserve the freedoms that we all know and enjoy?" He was warming to the subject and discarded his blue notebook. "I'd like to see the man—or woman—who would step forward and tell me that he—or she—is not willing to devote this brief interim to the cause of freedom."

"HOORAY!" ventured a married law school conscript, carried away by the Colonel's oratory. His name was immediately taken down by the platoon sergeant. The Colonel ignored the outburst, as colonels must, confident that the offender would be handled by noncoms in their own private way. He wanted nothing to do with lower level punishment, preferring to drone on about peacetime patriotism and the dangers of being caught unawares.

Across the railroad tracks that ran the length of the Army Base the men could see activity aboard the three Norwegian trawlers that were docked there. Watching the sailors was much more interesting than listening to the Colonel's canned speech, which many of the old-timers could deliver themselves. They became so fascinated watching the dark spots of men move along the decks that most of them missed the Colonel's final word ". . . let me hear the enthusiasm of all of you who are ready to do a bang-up job this summer at Camp Cannon."

Three Trailways buses pulled into the gates of the base and parked in single file directly behind the assembled men of the 229th. Three bus drivers in gray uniforms got down and huddled beside the lead bus. The troops began to chatter. At least they were going to Camp Cannon by bus, instead of in deuce-and-a-halfs, the huge Army trucks that bounced and jostled and made it impossible to ride comfortably.

One hundred and fifty duffel bags, not yet sorted for distribution to the three storage compartments, were piled behind the third bus. Beside the duffels were about two hundred civilian suitcases, flight bags, and miscellaneous luggage that the troops were allowed to carry for use in their off-duty hours. This impressive pile was guarded by the baggage detail, five enlisted men wearing fatigues and combat boots and baseball-brimmed field caps. The detail was usually chosen from the most inept of the unit personnel: either new men, or

11

men noted for their exceeding clumsiness, ugliness, or maverick tendencies. Naturally they took longer to do the loading than any other five men in the outfit.

Colonel Beauregard again strode to the front of the assembly and brought the ranks to attention. "It's important to look deeper than your suntan shirts, men," he said. "Important—before we move out—to give some thought to your duties and what you leave behind. Chaplain Papps will say a few words to you."

The chaplain stepped forward. He was a Methodist with the rank of captain and had one continuous eyebrow across the bridge of his nose. He had tried plucking the hairs that grew in gay profusion in that area, but had given it up as vanity after some of his fellow officers put a dozen packets of Green-Grow Grass Seed under his pillow one night. "If God had wanted me to have two distinct eyebrows," he reasoned, "he would have seen fit to leave the bridge of my nose naked and bare."

Chaplain Papps wore his dress khakis tailored, which meant that they conformed to the rather ample contours of his body instead of hanging loose like everyone else's. He was very much aware of the secular aspects of his calling. His congregation was located in Athol, Massachusetts, a small town in the western part of the state whose citizens were terrorized during King Philip's War and later suffered even greater apprehensions when they thought the Episcopalians were getting some sort of foothold in the Berkshires. He read the *New York Times Book Review* each Sunday and often quoted Walter Kerr in his sermons; he was known to criticize with perhaps too much fervor the literary notices in the Methodist monthly *Together*.

"Thank you, Colonel Beauregard," began the Chaplain. "Gentlemen, and ladies . . . we haven't known each other too very well in the few years I've been with the unit. That's a condition I'd like to change as of this summer session. I haven't been too sure how, as a distinctly Protestant preacher, to approach the problem of being chaplain to Catholics, Jews and Protestants alike. Perhaps you don't like what I've got to say to you. You don't have to like it. I'm here as a spiritual guide in a greater sense than just one denomination or faith or creed." He was warming to his subject and his long white hair, now cut short around the ears for the military, drooped in a long forelock across his eyes. The wind blew coldly up the artificial canyon created by the structure of the Army

12

Base. It made Papps think of himself as John Brown, God's Angry Man, hair blowing in the wind, passionately devoting himself to a cause. He had never had much opportunity to prove his passion in Athol, Mass. It was one reason he continued in the Reserve.

"Do you men really know the reason for going to meetings one night a week? Or for this two-week training every summer? There may be those among you who think the infantry soldier is obsolete, that we have enough power with our ICBMs and the like to destroy any enemy. Gentlemen," and here he paused to look over the faces of the men in their starched tan summer uniforms, "we have faith that our cause is just. But do you realize that the estimated death rate on the *first strike* made by a nuclear foe of this country will be twenty-two million dead? Twenty-two million dead." He paused for effect. "With another thirty million estimated wounded and displaced. No transportation, no communication. Disease and anarchy rampant." The Chaplain stood practically at attention. There were many of his sermons he wished John Wesley could have heard. "Our conventional forces already have battle plans that will see them thousands of miles away. Who is to preserve law and order at home, gentlemen? Who is to prevent this anarchy and chaos? Men like yourselves. Men like the 229th General Hospital. Men of the Reserve with faith in God and their country. I'd like you all to join me in a two-minute silent prayer . . . I don't care who or what you pray to . . . that this need may never arise. But if it does, as it does for your brothers who die fighting now in Vietnam, pray that we shall have the strength to see it through." The crowd couldn't resist being told to join in silent prayer. Even the three bus drivers near the pile of green duffel bags lowered their heads. At last they all had something to pray for.

After a minute or so had elapsed (the Chaplain knew it was a minute, he had always prided himself on being able to judge the appropriate length for silent prayer), the stillness was broken by the low whine and separation of gears that accompany a racing change in a sports car. Necks turned surreptitiously, then the pious atmosphere shattered completely as a small red MG, convertible top lowered, hurtled through the gates, past the startled cops who had signaled a halt, and roared full tilt toward the buses. Driving was a redheaded girl, hair blowing wildly behind her, whose eyes looked toward her

13

passenger, a soldier who was trying to grab the wheel of the car. She pressed the accelerator to the floor in order to frighten him enough to make him quit his attempts. The troops scattered as the car bore down upon the Colonel's jeep. A young officer leaped from the driver's seat of the jeep and drove behind the Chaplain who couldn't believe the chaos wrought upon his goodwill. "May it find that big junkyard in the sky," he whispered to himself, the effectiveness of his sermon now totally lost upon the scrambling men.

The redhead jammed the wheel to the left and crashed on the brakes, whipping the small car around the jeep and narrowly missing it. Then she blasted directly into the center of the pile of duffel bags, scattering them in all directions and finally, plowed to a halt in the mound of civilian luggage. Suitcases snapped open, their contents caught by the wheels and spun off to the rear or side. Once-clean shirts, their cardboard askew, lay amidst ties, summer suits, paper-back books, Alligator jerseys, chino pants—all the off-duty comforts that the men of the 229th cherished. A full bourbon bottle split on the pavement. The nose of the MG was tilted down toward the ground, the tail elevated about two feet on top of a random duffel, the wheels still spinning. "You bastard, Winter!" the redhead was screaming at her companion. "You've ruined my beautiful car!"

The soldier leaped from his perch next to her, pulled his seat forward and, from the well, extricated his own duffel bag and a small flight carryall from which protruded the shaft of his squash racket.

"Thanks so much, Marylynn the Lush," he said. "See you in two weeks. I'll probably be in about this time in the morning. How would you feel about picking me up?"

"Screw you, and the Army, too," she snapped, violently reversing the MG, grinding into first and heading for the gates.

"My sentiments exactly," said Eros Winter, Specialist Fourth Class, Medical Corps ER11341082, as he turned to report.

"Get on that baggage detail, Winter," said his platoon ergeant. "I don't care if your uniform gets so dirty you can never wear it again. And I don't want to see your face until we get to camp. Understand?" The Colonel was furious. The Chaplain was irate. They both made mental notes to keep their eyes on him when they cleared Massachusetts and the last vestiges of civilian life. Winter merely saluted and walked in the direction of the strewn duffels. He was too tired and hungover to protest his assignment.

Eros Winter was a squash hustler. He knew that he could give away points in a handicap, even as many as four or five, to an A player and still win a match for money. It might go into overtime, but he'd win it anyway. He had a knack of anticipating which side an opponent would move to, which type of shot an opponent would hit—corner, or drop, or lob, or smash, or Philadelphia Boast—and he'd be there to tuck it dead against a crack. He probably could have been national champion, if he didn't like to play for money. But the money game was the only thing Eros Winter could count on—that, and the fact that he really didn't know what he was going to do with himself now that he had flunked out of medical school.

"Nobody flunks out of medical school," his father had told him. Which meant that *his father* hadn't flunked out of medical school and was now a society diagnostician.

Dr. Winter was most concerned with the right thing to do. Being a diagnostician he attributed everything but the right reason to his son's failure, refusing to believe that Eros Winter hated medicine. But Eros Winter *did* hate medicine, although he loved his father.

"Everyone should be allowed to do what they do best," he insisted. "I play squash best. Let me work it out of my system."

"Bum!" his father yelled at him. "Bum and failure and disappointment! At least if you played tennis a bum could make good. But *squash*. A Moslem sport. A trivial sport. A nothing sport." It was then that the diagnostician recognized his son Eros's need for military service.

So Eros Winter became a private in the U.S. Army Reserve, pleased somehow to be going south for the winter, to San Antonio and Fort Sam Houston for training as a medical corpsman. Eros Winter's obligation was just beginning. Six months' active duty, followed by five and a half years of weekly meetings and two weeks' training in the summers. "But anything's better than two or three years in," he reasoned. "A piece of cake."

There was no declared war at the time. Oh, a few scares. But nothing serious. The Marines had been in Lebanon, but that was all over; Castro was in Cuba, but was behaving himself; the Berlin Wall was an established fact, and the political

15

situation in Vietnam had become cloudy; but still, nothing to worry Eros Winter. His career in Texas was uneventful, distinguished only by a dose of mild gonorrhea that he had caught in Nuevo Laredo from his regular, Inez, who always let him go twice for the price of one. "Now I know why," he brooded, refusing to return below the border again. Like so many of his buddies, he missed the East. It was difficult for him to hustle in Texas.

When he returned, he was a civilian, still undistinguished, still wondering what to do with himself. Even now America was only remotely concerned with brushfires around the world: border incidents in Korea, Viet Cong infiltrations into South Vietnam. All Eros Winter knew was that he was a civilian and he had to go through the motions of one Reserve meeting every week and two weeks' training every summer, and that it was a pain in the ass.

Thus, the summer following his return from active duty he didn't want to go to summer camp in the worst possible way. His touch around the corners of the court, his soft drop shot, had returned almost to peak form, and enough suckers had forgotten his game to replenish his checking account. But he was twenty-four years old and living with his parents; so his father had a say in his activities, and said. The night before summer camp, during one of these sessions, Eros stormed out of the house with his squash racket, Army duffel and uniforms, determined to make this last night as palatable as possible. He made a date with Marylynn Marcionette the Lush.

Marylynn was a redhead. Eros had a kind of thing for redheads, but found it very tough to find good-looking ones. True, Marylynn was a lush; but she was a high-bouncing one, not too long in the breast department, yet with fine legs, light soft complexion and a darker tinge of chestnut to the redness of her hair. He made the mistake of taking her drinking that night, and she naturally had to test his manhood before she let him take her home. It was a ritual with her which Eros, most of the time, felt was worth it. She got him in a one-sided brawl with a crew-cut forty-year-old, whom he had mistakenly thought he could take. "Snap, snap, snap, snap," went the buttons on the high school letter sweater-jacket of the forty-year-old. "Wzzzzz" went the man's right hand and arm, fingers stiff and extended toward Eros's unprotected Adam's apple. "Thwack" went the side of his hand against Eros's throat. "Gurgle" went Eros, and blacked out, still gurgling.

16

"Snap, snap, snap, snap," went the buttons into place again, and the stranger moved into the night, fingering the raised felt letter on his jacket.

Marylynn the Lush finally got him, bruised and cut, back to her apartment; Eros made her set the alarm for five o'clock. Then, because he was beginning to be possesed by the thought of the Army in the morning, he insisted on polishing his brass caduceus, emblem of the U.S. Army Medical Corps. Marylynn did his brass belt with the other end of the cloth he used. Then Eros gave her the back of his hand.

"What did you do that for?" she asked.

"That, my dear Lush, is for introducing me to forty-year-old Black Belts!"

She began to protest and looked awfully angry. But Eros, adept at keeping an opponent off-balance on the squash court, pulled her to him and kissed her once, very hard on the mouth, holding her lower body tightly against himself. Then he kissed her long and softly, releasing his pressure on her body. Then Eros turned her around, gave her a little push toward her bedroom. "Move out smartly," he said, as any good specialist fourth class would have done.

"COMPANEE, ATTEN-HOOT!" bellowed the first sergeant. He saluted the section leader, who in turn saluted the adjutant, who in turn saluted the Colonel, who said, "Carry on, and file onto the buses in the prescribed manner. It is now 0645 hours and we are fifteen minutes behind schedule, thanks to Specialist Winter. We shall not be fifteen minutes behind schedule for the next two weeks. MOVE OUT!"

The men were marched to their assigned buses, a contingent of officers for each bus. "Column of files, from the right. FORWARD," came the command to file onto the vehicles. The baggage detail pushed the last duffel into the compartments beneath the floor and climbed aboard.

The Colonel was transported by jeep to the gates, where he disembarked and switched to his own big black Buick, driven by the first sergeant. He took Mobil maps of New England and New York State, opened them on his lap, and signaled the sergeant to start.

With sputters and coughs, the buses, three in all, left the Army Base, turned left by the South Station rail terminal and headed onto the expressway leading north. In the rear of the third bus six men were singing a song that one of them had

17

written. They were hard core Reservists, enlisted men from the ranks of students, lawyers, businessmen, and they chorused their own Caisson Song:

> Plug cesspools, can preserves,
> We're the men of the reserves . . .
> Taxpayers, we'll put it to you . . . !
> Swill some beer, not too hard,
> When you're serving in the Guard,
> State's Righters, we're loyal to you!
>
> For it's serve, serve, serve,
> Six whole years in the Reserve,
> Sign in, and bug out for home . . .
> Get a quarterly check,
> Have your congress stack the deck,
> Taxpayers, right up your kazoooo!

They loved the song and would spend the five-hour ride up to Camp Cannon writing new lyrics. It was 0715 hours and the way the sun looked, red and glowing in the early morning, it probably would be a beautiful day.

TWO

"Living on the ground like goddam animals," thought Eros Winter, contemplating field training, "makes me want to vomit." He didn't even feel like looking out of the window at the New York Thruway which flashed under the wheels of his bus. He gripped and ungripped the handle of his squash racket, trying to squeeze something beneficial out of the long ride to Camp Cannon, trying to squeeze some sort of comfort from the familiar feel of his hustling instrument. "What really makes me want to vomit," he decided, "is those Bloody Marys before we pulled out." But Winter, luckily, was a great swallower. He found this much easier than vomiting, despite the convenience of the Trailways traveling john.

Private First Class Eldor von Liebert was also a good swallower. A recent addition to the 229th, he had disciplined himself to be able to sleep on any sort of public conveyance. But twice already he had been awakened to find his seat partner shuffling a deck of cards and trying to play a private solitaire on the back of a previous week's *Time* magazine.

"Would it bother you very much not to shuffle those cards?" asked Eldor von Liebert. "I'm trying to sleep." There were very few hard-nosers in the 229th and the traveling companion put the cards away in the top pocket of his suntans. He was very quiet from then on and forced himself to re-read the sections on the World and the Cinema.

In time the bus stopped at a friendly Savarin Restaurant. This annoyed Winter. Especially at nine in the morning, after a sleepless night. "Why must they have ice cream and Pie Man's Patties this early in the day" he asked himself, since there was practically nobody Eros could speak to in the unit whom he enjoyed speaking to. Besides, the other men considered it a real treat to stop at the highway restaurants on the thruway. Eros Winter made straight for the men's room to wash his face.

Like Eros, Eldor von Liebert didn't like stopping once the trip was under way. He thought it was great weakness to have to buy food before they reached the base. "Obnoxious," he thought to himself, seeing the long counter ringed by soldiers ordering hamburgers and shakes "to go" in never ending profusion. He stood up extra straight, hoping someone would notice his example and brace up a bit. He went to the men's room and took the urinal next to Eros Winter. Winter was leaning against the wall in front of the urinal, trying to coax some sort of definitive action out of his member. "Every time I go to piss and there are people around me waiting," he explained, "all the haltenpissen muscles actually tighten up and . . . nothing." Eldor felt embarrassment, since he had none of that self-consciousness. About bodily functions. "Ahhh, there we go," said Eros in final satisfaction. "Once the bastard starts, it doesn't shut down. Thanks for producing the noise."

"Excuse me?" said Eldor, finishing.

"The noise," said Eros. "You know, the pissing noise. Psychological. Huplo's Syndrome, from the *Journal* of the Southern Medical Association. When you hear someone else, it starts the ol' ball rolling for yourself. Like when you're a kid and your mother runs the water in the sink. Makes you think: *piss, piss.* It always works for me."

Von Liebert thought that Specialist Fourth Class Winter had a voice that implied breeding. Certainly different from the others in the unit. He decided to introduce himself.

"I'm Private First Class von Liebert," said Eldor, "assigned to the 229th just recently as my permanent unit."

Eros wiped his hand on his suntans and thrust it toward von Liebert. "*Enchanté,* Baron," he said, smiling. They were satisfied with each other's handshakes. The dry palm test; the firm grip test.

"My first name is Eldor. I *am* German. Not to disappoint your scheme of things, indeed my father *is* a Baron. But all our lands are—or were—in Prussia. And after the war—you know," von Liebert shrugged. "Everything that was ours is now part of the East German state. So we now live in Munich. Very nice, actually." His accent was slight but noticeable, with the studied lisp affected by many Germans of good education.

Eldor von Liebert was in the United States to train in the various departments of the New England Cooperative Bank before returning to his father's firm in Munich. The Baron von Liebert was seeking firmer ties with some American companies attempting to broaden their base with overseas connections. Eldor would be operating in the middle ground, of a generation that was fast becoming international in its outlook. It hadn't been difficult to get Eldor a job in Boston. His ancestry and his mastery of English assured it. He was energetic, confident, and had even won a bank incentive award of a five-dollar gift certificate. It amused him how the Americans were so incentive-conscious. He was sure they had copied it from the Germans. He purchased a pipe (a plastic meerschaum) with the certificate; but it still amused him. Until he was served with his draft notice. Then he protested diplomatic immunity and wrote his father that he was coming home. "I'm subject to the alien laws," he wrote. "They want to take me into the American Army. What irony, for the son of a Luftwaffe colonel. I can never serve with them, Father. Their lives are mockeries of falsehood and bravado. What must their peacetime armed forces be like? This is impossible." He packed and prepared to return to Munich, when he received his father's reply.

ELDOR:

When I was two years old I remember *my* father putting a stick on my shoulder and telling me to march with him. He paraded me around the lawns for two hours until he was satisfied. I kept up the step. You realize, of course, that I didn't want to keep up the step. I didn't even want to march. But, there are things we don't want to do that, mostly because we are men, we must. If you want to come home at this point I won't blame you. Army service is, from your viewpoint, unnecessary. But there is so little room for manhood in the world that is now. Remember what I have wanted my sons to become when they *are* men. Remember and decide; I shall applaud your choice. But we need the business.

> Your devoted father,
> KURT VON LIEBERT

Eldor knew that he must endure it for his family. They had suffered enough already. His mother had been killed in an air raid at the end of 1944. He was told that the British had done it. Eldor was six and didn't feel too badly about it until later. He and his companions would play free in the hills above the communal nursery where they had been installed, all sons of officers. They played soldier most of the time and he would cry if he was captured by the Americans. He had been told that they were all cowboys and carried ropes and six-shooters. They would rope him and tie him to the backs of their cow ponies and shoot at him as he went bumpety-bump, bumpety-bump, along the Bavarian countryside.

So as a dutiful son he enlisted in the Army Medical Corps

21

Reserve for six months' active duty and an obligation for five and one half years of ready status—as an alternative to the draft. He knew that the American soldiers were aware of his nationality, and he had his hair cropped to the scalp to accentuate the sharp lines of his face and jaw. It was a bother sometimes to keep his shoulders thrust back so that the scapulae touched, but he endured it. His father would have been proud.

Starting off with the attitude that it was a complete waste of his time, he would complain to his barracks mates: "You call this a democracy? You have alien laws that stipulate that a foreigner in the United States for the purpose of learning a trade, going to school or marrying a citizen is subject to the draft laws as any American is subject to the draft laws. Ridiculous!" He wanted to show them he could take the roughest they could hand out, and desperately wished to be in the infantry.

But the Army in its infinite wisdom, guided by the achievement tests taken during Eldor's first week in basic training, indicated that he could be best utilized as a clerk typist. It was a blow to everything Teutonic in him, and he responded by punishing himself. He would outrage his fellows in clerk typist school at Fort Dix by doing twenty push-ups before every meal outside the chow hall. He would also run back to the barracks after finishing; not, as most people did, to get to the latrine first, but merely for the sake of running. "That fanatic Kraut," they called him, and resented the fact that he refused to take the easy way out. "The gung-ho bastard," they said, irritated with anyone who was trying to keep his stomach flat. He finished his six months' training with a diploma from clerk typing school and extremely well-developed deltoid muscles. Returning to the bank in Boston he discovered he still walked erect with his scapulae touching. He had never learned it in Germany, but, to the bank employees, as to the soldiers he served with, he remained an auslander.

The night before leaving for summer camp his roommates (both American employees of the bank) tried to get Eldor to go out drinking in Boston, even though they objected to his closely cropped military haircut. He declined, feeling too apprehensive about the next morning. He stripped to his shorts when they left and began touching his toes, raising his arms over his head, touching his toes again. Then he went down onto the carpet and did push-ups and sit-ups. Then he

22

checked his gear once more. The uniform was freshly starched. The boots were spit-shined so that he could see his face in the light on the toes. He was satisfied. Eldor von Liebert didn't have to set the alarm for the morning. He would automatically awaken at five o'clock. He wondered briefly what his roommates thought when he refused to go out with them. But only briefly. "It doesn't matter," he decided and went to bed. It didn't matter because *he* knew what was really important. His roommates were only going out to drink. Eldor von Liebert was going to war.

Von Liebert and Eros Winter returned to the bus together, pleased to be allied against the foreign sea of Reservists, pleased that neither had ordered a hamburger to go. Or even so much as a coffee, regular.

The troops spilled into the morning, while traffic began to whiz by along the New York Thruway. A man got out of a green Ford—the kind of Ford that government employees or fire chiefs use. The man walked up to Eldor and Winter as they moved through the parking lot toward the bus.

"You guys with the National Guard?" he asked. He picked his nose surreptitiously. "Off for your summer camp, huh? Pretty soft. I was in for the real thing. Duration plus six months." He picked his nose again. It was apparent that it was a nervous habit. The kind of twitch a race track tout might have if he were signaling someone into a corner to deliver a winner.

"Actually, buddy," Eros replied, "we're agents of a foreign power. Infiltrating Camp Cannon." He was in no mood for a helpful, friendly civilian chat.

"Very commendable," the man replied, ignoring the comment. "Just don't give out any information to anyone. Zip a lip and save a ship." He picked his nose again. It was very disconcerting.

The stranger wore a sport jacket and gray slacks with a checkered shirt and one of those Texas-style string ties with a monogrammed silver holder. He had crepe soles on his sensible brown shoes and his feet were terribly big, possibly size thirteen. Eros never really could believe big feet, his own being 9C and just perfect, he thought. There was something so paddling about guys with big feet. He didn't care much for string ties, either. He had never met a squash player who wore a string tie. Eldor really paid no attention. He considered it a conversation between Winter and the stranger. He rarely

23

talked to people he didn't know. Panhandlers on the street offended him particularly. He also disliked being stopped by deaf people with little cards asking for money. He avoided infirmity whenever possible. But he waited for Eros to finish.

"I'm going up to the Canadian border," said the stranger, who acted as if it would matter to the Reservists. "On my vacation. Hear there's wonderful game fishing around the Thousand Islands."

"Oh, yes," said Eros, "the biggest whitefish in the East. Nice talking with you." He moved, with Eldor, toward the bus.

"I like to see our servicemen so alert and looking so fit," the man said, picking his nose and proceeding toward the restaurant.

"What a strange man," Eldor commented.

"He must be queer for the Medical Corps," was Eros's answer. Eldor laughed and they went back onto the Trailways together.

No one on the bus spoke very much from that point on. Camp Cannon was within striking distance and there was a collective sinking feeling among the members of the 229th General Hospital. "Why, isn't it two weeks from now," someone said, "instead of now?"

"And why aren't you a beautiful broad instead of a fat-assed cook's helper?" someone else answered. They were good questions, but no one pretended that they helped the morale.

THREE

As they sped through Utica everyone looked wistfully out of the windows. "Utica," someone noted out loud, "used to be the whorehouse capital of upper New York." Everyone strained their necks looking for storefronts that one day might have housed whores. They were all disappointed and the bus drivers strained their feet on the accelerators knowing that their objecting load would soon be dumped on the United States Military Reservation of Camp Cannon. It was only forty-five minutes away from Utica, twenty thousand acres of barracks and brush.

The base was used primarily for summer training, and closed from October to the beginning of May when a company of misfits, usually from Fort Dix, would be detailed to paint, repair, rake, build and bring to life the lonely ghost-like installation, forty miles from the Thousand Islands and the Canadian border, it was a flat base, with little vegetation other than pine trees and scrub. The land was hard-packed and dusty, with clay deposits that made for impossible mud conditions whenever it rained, and dull, unyielding sameness when the sun burned the earth dry. The men of the 229th didn't have mixed reactions when they flashed by the guard posts at the gate. They all unreservedly hated it.

Every man, regardless of his civilian occupation, looked upon the long yellow-and-green buildings with the barracks numbers painted on the sides as his own private Buchenwald. "Shit, we're really back in," someone managed to say aloud in each one of the three buses. It approximately echoed the thoughts of everyone. None of them could look at the clusters of barracks and the impersonal, regimented larger structures with names like Bowling Alley Number 2 or Theater Number 3 and not worry about the real worry: rice paddies and black-pajamaed Victor Charlies. It caused an immediate general depression.

Even the driver of Colonel Beauregard's big black Buick, Sergeant Lennie Baer, slowing down to the more military fifteen miles per hour, could not help feeling his mouth go dry, as if the dust from the hard-packed soil had crept into his lips. But Sergeant Baer still knew exactly where to go; he and the Colonel led the buses around deserted compaany areas, down by an airstrip and heliport, by a rifle range, through a narrow street known as Commander Bullock Road, lined with laundries and small beer halls, then off into the boondocks where there was nothing but pine and yellowed crabgrass.

"It's going to be important this week to work on morale, Sergeant," said Colonel Beauregard. "If we can keep the men busy enough the first few days we'll be able to slide into the routine and it won't be too bad for them. This field training can't be helped. But we've got some sort of clinker this year. There's someone from Washington coming up to observe us. I haven't been fully briefed yet, but he's expected up here sometime today. But I'm not concerned, Sergeant. Fine unit; fine workers; good people with us. Right?" He didn't wait for an answer, merely using the driver as a sounding board. "I personally had hoped for parallel training this year. Damn shame to be in the field. Supporting this National Guard Division on maneuvers the way we're doing is always so political. Lot of brass around. Lot of brass. And they're so careless, these Guard people. Tanks forever running over the personnel; grenades not primed correctly. Too many accidents when these men are only infantry or artillery for two weeks in the year.

"That's what they signed up for, sir," ventured the sergeant. "Be good for 'em. Too soft in the winter. Only chance to give 'em some discipline. As a matter of fact, I'm in favor of gettin' 'em up a bit early this year and giving them some PT before breakfast. Since we're in the field away from the main base, it's easy to play things as we feel like it. Right, sir?"

"I don't care what you do with the troops, Sergeant Baer. Just get me a Superior efficiency rating when the Inspector General comes around. And keep that Washington joker off my back. I want a tight ship this summer."

"That's what you'll get, sir. If it's up to me. I know you're busy, but I like to know that you're behind me. In the managing of the men, I mean."

The Colonel was thinking about Major Marjorie Stavropolis, the Greek nurse, and whether it would be propitious to try to take her into his tent that afternoon. Perhaps it would be a little premature. It was driving along Bullock Road that made him think of her. "She makes me feel like a damn bullock." He felt himself getting excited against the pants leg of his dress khakis, which was uncomfortable. He forced himself not to think about her. At the same time, in *her* bus, Marjorie Stavropolis was thinking about the Col-

26

onel. "Little shrunk-up bastard," she thought, "wonder if it'll help my promotion along any if I make a brief trip to his tent this afternoon. All it ever takes is a brief trip."

Major Marjorie Stavropolis was a nurse in civilian life; she worked in one of Boston's largest veterans hospitals. She was thirty-six years old and earned sixty-five hundred dollars a year. Making the rank of major the previous summer with the Reserves meant an additional twenty-four hundred. This included longevity pay, since she had been in the Army Nurse Corps since Korea. But she had made major the hard way. It was not easy to be the Colonel's lady, especially for five years. Especially in view of the fact that she considered him such a little shrunk-up bastard. "Barely makes it up to my cervix," she would say, smiling to herself.

She lived alone at home in Boston and had had her own apartment for only a very short time. It was lousy to be thirty-five before you could afford your own apartment, she thought. Privacy was always one of her desires, ever since she had been little, and it was one of the things usually denied her most. Greek families were notoriously large. Hers had been large and close and they all lived together, grudgingly letting an occasional stray move out with his wife on his own, then finally bringing baklava over to the deserters for a peace offering. She had really black hair, no fooling around about it at all. She was tall, about five seven, and her figure wasn't the best, even for age thirty-six. "I'm a nurse," she'd say. "There's nothing new you can show me, buster." She was tough, the kind that gives lousy backrubs. Stingy on the alcohol. She recognized this and took steps, through the military, to insure her old age against loneliness. She wanted to be a full colonel in the worst way and her ambition put her square in the path of the lust of Colonel Gayle Beauregard. Her rise through the ranks from first lieutenant to major in five years was astounding to all but herself. Her Greek ancestry gave her instinctive knowledge in the ways of pleasing men, inherited from the sunlit days of the golden past along the Aegean.

Being a small-town political dentist and therefore relatively unsophisticated in these matters, Colonel Beauregard was, by stages, shocked, surprised, curious and delighted by the glories that were Greek. He would have made her a general had it been possible for a nurse in the ANC to rise higher than colonel. She was in charge of all the wards of the 229th and she considered it not just an assignment, but a moral obligation.

Of course, she wanted to have babies. Every woman she knew wanted to have babies, despite what they may have pretended. She was, because of this dilemma, ambitious yet coy, bitchy yet generous, masculine yet extremely soft. But where the military was concerned she could very well have been a wheat commissar in the Ukraine. The fatigue uniform that nurses wore in the field covered her chunky legs utterly, but it made her breasts look larger than they really were. Compared with the other women in the unit she had *the* cute face, no hair on the upper lip, no distinguishing moles. In fact, she had rather a pleasing complexion and soft olive skin—especially soft on the shoulders where the Colonel loved to nuzzle. She may have been just another hard-bitten, efficient nurse in the veterans hospital, but she was the undisputed queen of the 229th. Every man from Colonel Harden, the executive officer, right down to PFC Waldo Reed, the Chaplain's assistant, wanted to have a crack at her. The fact that some of the wiser men would make lewd comments when she wiggled by didn't bother her at all. That was just sour grapes.

Major Marjorie Stavropolis was taking fourteen pairs of silk panties to summer training. This put her psychologically a few jumps ahead of her fellow nurses right from the start. They usually took G.I. underwear issued to incoming female personnel, which were cotton with elasticized tops that always snapped with the slightest bit of use, consequently riding down instead of up. They were uniformly white, as well. Major Stavropolis had all the pastel shades; in secret, she always put a few drops of Arpège into the crotch before she donned them. This she considered very wicked, but effective. Along with her duffel of uniforms, she packed a small leather suitcase with toilet articles, writing paper, thirteen of the fourteen pairs of pants (the fourteenth she would wear up on the bus), and right on top a small jewel box from Shreve, Crump and Low, containing a diaphragm and her Patient's Instruction Manual. (The Pill gave her side effects: bloating and the itch.) Originally the jewel box had contained a set of cuff links she had given her brother for graduation from college. After he removed the cuff links he saw no further use for the box. But his sister was both resourceful and Greek.

Colonel Beauregard forced the image of his summertime woman out of his mind. "First of all, we've got to get all those tents up. And I want them laid out exactly as I directed back at the Army Base. Officers will be toward the west with two latrines of their own, one for male and one for female, plus a small one-holer for myself and Colonel Fruitman. On second thought, just for me. Three large personnel tents should be enough for the men, on the north side. Hospital tents in the east, forming a corner with the mess tent next to our administrative sections, which complete the square on the south side. I want lister bags in each corner. Men have to have access to a lot of water and it's got to be available. I also want a supply of fluoride pills given to every soldier. That's of extreme importance. I don't want creeping decay while they're away from home."

The sky was gray. The wind blew across the flatness of the base, bending the scruffy pines. Only the outline of the black Buick and the three Trailways buses broke the monotony. The procession turned off the hardtop and onto a dirt road that was guarded by two white-helmeted and putteed MPs, who motioned with their black sticks to proceed, saluted as the Colonel rode by, and returned to the position of parade rest, their feet spread apart, hands behind their backs. The men looked out the windows at them as the buses passed. Soon they were out of sight and the buses turned left at a fork in the dirt road. There were about a dozen civilian vehicles parked in a dug-out area reserved for the purpose. They were the automobiles of the advance party sent forward a day earlier than the rest of the unit. These were the patriots, devoted to the 229th enough to leave before anyone else to find the camp site, arrange for messing, set up an initial command tent, and provide enough liaison with the base's permanent people to facilitate the arrival of the Reserve. Parked alongside the civilian autos were the unit vehicles: three deuce-and-a-halfs, four ambulances, two jeeps. There was also one khaki staff car that happened to be a Ford. No drivers for the vehicles, or any human, for that matter, was visible in any direction. Advance party people were always ordered to meet incoming troops.

"Where do you think that idiot is, Sergeant?" asked Colonel Beauregard. The idiot he was referring to was the officer in charge of the advance party, Warrant Officer Kenneth Keohane, a claims adjustor in civilian life. He became a warrant officer because he worked so hard at handling the supply duties in the unit when he was an enlisted man. The supply room was kept efficient and orderly by Keohane. Everything from canteen cups to toilet paper was schematically arranged, usually alphabetically. Kenny Keohane made sure that his men were neat and orderly, just like his supplies. No officer ever had to wait for an item ordered from Kenny. After sixteen years of service in the Reserve, they rewarded him with promotion to warrant officer. That particular rank in the Reserve is especially for people who like to work in an efficient manner, and most of the warrant officers continued to work even harder to justify their promotions. Kenny Keohane just sat down and quit. The administration didn't demote him for this obvious shirking of duty, simply because of his good nature and because of all the paper work that would have been involved for everyone else. So he just sat down and quit; they couldn't do a damn thing about it. As a result, the canteen cups got hidden between mess kits and fatigue shirts. Toilet paper was no longer found on the T shelf, but more likely on the S or the A. Kenny became more elaborate in his filing of material, developing secret codes that he would think clever at the time, like filing combat boots under S for Dr. Scholl, then forgetting his idea completely when it came to find the items again. "When you've got rank," he would say at those moments, in utter resignation, "you're supposed to be able to delegate authority. O.K., Wasserman," he would yell to one of his flunkeys, "find the lootenant a pair of boots, size 10D."

"Wasserman's a bright boy, Ben," he would tell his visitor, flicking a cigar ash into a butt can on his supply desk. "Knows where everything is, all the time. Too busy to bother with it, myself."

At home in Lynn, Massachusetts (a shoe city and not even very historic), Kenny could be had by any claimant willing to donate a pittance in the form of a stereo set, golf clubs, or just plain cash. Warrant officers were supposed to be flexible like that. As a claims adjustor he cost Workingman's Mutual a good deal of money. But he usually covered his tracks well. Parties that contributed nothing to his well-being found their claims pared to cost.

All three of the buses pulled into the cleared-out parking area, directly behind the black Buick. "No one is to disembark until I find Keohane and the advance party. Understand?" the Colonel ordered. Sergeant Baer understood.

"Get me my bullhorn," said the Colonel. The sergeant found the bullhorn on the floor of the back seat and handed it to Colonel Beauregard. The Colonel pushed the button activating the battery-operated instrument. He blew into it a few times to see if it was functional, and pointed it toward the woods, about two hundred yards beyond the empty military vehicles.

"Keohane. Warrant Officer Keohane," he yelled into the voice magnifier. "Where the Christ are you?" The scrubby pine forest caught the words and threw them back into the wind that ripped unstopped over the flatness of the ground. "Christ are you . . ." came back the echo.

"Warrant Officer Keohane," he tried in the opposite direction.

It wasn't really an answer, but "Toooooooot" came back to them, the sound of an ambulance horn, more in defiance than anything else. The "Toooot" got larger, until the ambulance came into sight around the dirt road. It was entirely covered with white sheets, except for the windshield. The sheets were held onto the vehicle with string tied under the body. The words "Mobile Plasma Station" were lettered in red across both sheeted sides of the ambulance. Kenny Keohane was at the wheel, a long cigar in his mouth, medic's whites as his uniform. He had two men beside him in the cab, dressed identically, but minus the cigar. Anyone could tell who was boss of the Mobile Plasma Station. When Keohane spied the black Buick he slammed on the brakes and spun the ambulance around as if to move away in the opposite direction. Then he thought better of it, slowed to a halt, killed the motor and got out of the cab.

"O.K., you guys in the back, easy with the patients and tentage. The unit's arrived and we've got a lot of work to do." He said this at the top of his voice, then ran to the rear of the vehicle. He opened the twin doors, jumped in and disappeared.

The Colonel and his sergeant walked over to the white-robed conveyance. The sergeant opened the doors. There was Warrant Officer Keohane, frantically attempting to pour the contents of six kegs of beer through a hole in the floorboards of the ambulance. There were four other men in the rear, also dressed in white, with stenciled lettering on the backs of their uniforms: Type O Positive. Two of them were rubbing their bottoms around and around on top of four gigantic cakes of ice situated in the middle of the floor. They were trying to melt down the ice as swiftly as possible.

"What is the meaning of this, Keohane?" the Colonel was relieved that none of the base brass was around to witness the scene. Sergeant Lennie Baer was outraged at the bootleg operation. It was so unmilitary.

"Colonel," Keohane said, lapsing into a heartwarming brogue, "I guess it's red-handed you've nabbed me." Then he leaped to the offensive. "But there's no one else knows where everything is in supply. We're both stuck."

"Are you trying to make a deal with me, Keohane?"

"Ohh, not a deal, Colonel . . ." Keohane knew that Colonel Beauregard was a politician. He never would have ever submitted to the dentist's sodium pentothal. You couldn't give a political dentist leverage like that. Keohane hedged his bets. "It's just, sir, that we had nothing to do really, after we supervised the choosing of the campsite. You can see what a happy choice it is. Pine grove. Inaccessible. And you can see any brass coming from all directions. Post lookouts. When anyone brings patients in, they'll have trouble finding us. Idyllic spot." (He had never used words like idyllic until they made him an officer, even though he had known the words before. His commission, had set him free intellectually. His imagination roamed now, unencumbered by the onus of being "enlisted." He would never have had the guts for the mobile plasma station when he was a sergeant.)

"All right, Keohane," said Beauregard. "Assign your men to start erecting the supply tent. My adjutant will tell you where it's to be located. Bring your ambulance around to where my tent is going to be and we'll save what's left of the beer for the officers tonight. And you men can get your rear ends off of those ice cakes." They were glad to do it.

FOUR

At first, Master Sergeant Lennie Baer was bewildered by the Colonel's leniency. Lennie Baer was a stickler for good form. In civilian life he was a salesman of coats; a very meticulous salesman was he. The equipment in his duffel bag was folded neatly and arranged just so. He was the same way about his coat samples and his swatches. Every coat was folded neatly into his sample cases, the lining on the outside to protect the material. The swatches—Harris tweed, Shetland, cashmere, vicuña—would follow on top.

Lennie Baer was extremely hairy. The hair grew black and matted, from high on his neck all the way down through the pubic area and continuing down his legs. One continuous forest that he was alternately ashamed or proud of, depending upon who was viewing his chest. It was too much trouble to cut, or even to trim. It really did grow back faster. If he didn't wear a T-shirt in the Army, the open collar of his fatigue jacket might look as if it sported a black ascot. Lennie wasn't the ascot type. As a matter of fact, Lennie was a son of a bitch. This was generally conceded to be the case among the men of the 229th General Hospital, of which Lennie was the first sergeant.

But at home he had a special way of endearing himself to the receptionist or the secretary at the retail outlets that he visited in his territory. He would give her Tootsie Rolls. Not a lot of Tootsie Rolls; just a few. But she would always remember Lennie Baer and occasionally, while nibbling on the fat earlobe of her boss, she would say: "Why don't we do some reorders with Lennie, the Tootsie Roll man?" And the boss would say, "Who?"

And the receptionist would tell him about Lennie. The boss was usually amused enough to grant the reorders. Lennie's prices weren't too much out of line. His coats and materials were cut well enough for a medium-priced line of men's coats. And he became moderately successful as the Tootsie Roll Man. Successful enough to leave the place he had been living and move with his wife Doris and daughter Regina out to Malton, Massachusetts, where some of his old friends lived. They thought that he was a good, conscientious salesman of men's coats. They didn't know that he was a son of a bitch, because none of them ever served under him when he was a

33

sergeant. He stayed in the Reserve because he felt that the Army was a little more important than his life as a salesman. People in the military snapped when he hollered, "Snap to!" There was something fine in the order of it all—through channels. The right way; the wrong way; the Army way. The Lennie way *was* the Army way. There was nothing to sidetrack him. No insecurity. They even gave his family Quarters Allowance when he was away at camp.

The night before the 229th moved out, however, Lennie had been nervous and touchy. His wife had mistaken his desire for fish to mean salmon. He meant halibut; the salmon only increased his irritability. He watched his daughter iron her hair and got more irritable. He couldn't wait for the morning. The only redeeming factor was that his wife Doris knew that she was expected to Do It the night before her husband left for camp. He let her be the intellectual in the marriage, even let her have a trial subscription to *Réalités,* which she displayed prominently in the "parlor," as she called it. Being the intellectual, she knew that she was expected to Do It. Especially since she had made the salmon-halibut error. It made up for a lot of things.

She had made it easy for Lennie by getting into his side of the twin maple beds they maintained for sleeping. Lennie was in the bathroom, brushing his teeth and spraying some deodorant under his arms (but surreptitiously, with the sink running. He usually perspired terribly when he went to bed with her. But Doris, the intellectual, knew that he used the deodorant. She could always smell it. From the old days when he used the smear-on kind, to the middle or roll-on period, up to the current spray mist which was much more delicate, though perhaps not so effective.)

Lennie had indifferent sexual relations with his wife. For the past five years or so, he had felt the urge only intermittently. Doris, willy-nilly, felt the same way. She knew that Lennie was conscious of his inability to be "too frequent" with her; he gave her presents instead. But she never let on that it didn't matter to her, because she liked presents. But the night before summer camp was different. Lennie didn't have any trouble at all "doing it." His imagination forced him to think of his Tootsie Rolls and the very idea helped him over the rough spots. He never had trouble the night before camp.

Doris touched him in bed and he was frighteningly large. The thought of its size filling her was exciting and she was ready for him faster than even she wouldd have imagined.

34

"Doris, Doris, Doris, Doris," he intoned in rhythm and the ridiculousness of the name in his mouth almost spoiled it for him. He was thinking about whether or not the Colonel would let him take his duffel up in the Colonel's black Buick, instead of storing it in one of the buses, and he felt ashamed of the thought because it really did feel good filling Doris up. Doris meanwhile, pulled at the hair on his chest and almost forgot herself for a minute. But Lennie, the Tootsie Roll man, didn't waste any time and she could taste all too soon a piece of pecan stuck in her teeth from a sundae she had eaten earlier. She wished it had been walnuts. They were easier to get at. But, it was the ritual. Another year, and the last time in two weeks for Lennie; a sad time for Doris, for she thought it really could have been special. The effective salesman of men's coats, moderately priced, could offer a neck caress after he had finished. The First Sergeant of the 229th General Hospital could fall asleep almost instantly, still concerned about the details of summer camp. Lennie Baer dreamed of channels . . . channels.

At Camp Cannon, Sergeant Baer found it difficult to understand why Keohane had any leverage over the Colonel. But he kept his mouth shut. The Tootsie Roll role was all but forgotten with the softness of his well-worn fatigues. There was something about the faded insignia on his arm. Six stripes, three pointing downward, three rocking upward, meeting just right.

The Colonel answered the sloppy salute of his supply officer with a brisk snap of his forearm across his own brow, turned on his heel, and, with his master sergeant a discreet one-and-one-half paces behind, returned to the buses where all but the three bus drivers remained in their seats, some men still asleep from the long ride, and most of them apprehensive about living in tents on the open ground. They were hooked on six-year contracts; but all longed during hot, sunshiny summers for their work back home in their air-conditioned offices in the hot, sunshiny cities.

"Open the doors and fall the men in, Baer," said the Colonel. Out of the first bus stepped Colonels Fruitman and Harden, the adjutant and the Executive officer of the 229th. At home they were both doctors: Harden a general practitioner who believed in prescribing birth control pills to college girls as standard procedure, and Fruitman a low-pressure gynecologist in the North Shore area of Boston. Fish and scallop country. Iodine country. Which made for a high incidence of uterine problems, at least on the North Shore of Boston. Doctors Fruitman and Harden indulged in a fair amount of good-natured fee splitting. "Logrolling, the government folks would call it," Fruitman said. (He was very affable. He put his patients at ease.) "You scratch my back, I'll scratch yours." Dr. Harden always countered, "It's the American Way."

The colonels were followed, more or less according to rank, by the other twenty-five officers of the 229th, among whom were eleven nurses who also had commissions in the Army Nurse Corps (all registered nurses were officers). Then there were five enlisted WACs, all with the rank of sergeant. These were fatter and less desirable than the nurses and did most of the secretarial work. One of them, great, heaving Sonya Faust, arranged stencils as she walked, and was as absorbed in her work and as dedicated as a St. Bernard. They rode with the enlisted men in the rear two buses and didn't even mind when they had a steady diet of linguistic "fucks" passing over and around them in the conversation of the men. But the WACs said it themselves at camp and didn't seem to mind at all. They said it with rather a lilt to their voices; it made them feel like one of the boys.

The 229th fell into three platoons, one composed of officers, the other two of enlisted personnel, with separation done by assignment. When not in formation the officers joined the men, forming two complements, the professional complement being headed by Major Fugue, a Veterans Administration surgeon with a strong sense of duty. This complement consisted of all the doctors, dentists, nurses and enlisted personnel who staffed the various wards of the hospital. It also included X-ray technicians and laboratory assistants.

The administrative complement was commanded by Major "Sonny" Beanstock, who owned a slaughterhouse in Needham, Massachusetts. He always carried hog crop forecasts in his back pockets and speculated a great deal in hog bellies, the number of slaughterings in various months, tallow contracts and pork bottoms. He had once come very close to cornering the market in pork bottoms, September delivery; but the Exchange had stepped in at the last minute to stabilize the market. Beanstock never could quite forgive the government and took his meager revenge by being an ineffective complement commander. He was due for retirement at the end of camp and was bitter, since all requests and maneuverings for promotion had been denied him. The fate of a United States Army officer, as is the fate of all officers, is to be either promoted or retired.

Everyone referred to Sonny Beanstock as "The Butcher," but never to his face. He had carried too many sides of beef around the Faneuil Hall markets when he was a young man not to have developed massive shoulders, chest, and back. He no longer carried sides of beef, but he did work out daily with weights at a suburban country and health club. Hot steam, wet steam, rubdown and reaming out with soapy oak leaves attached to a duster, dip in pool, lift weights, row, bicycle, weigh, shower, weigh. He fell into the routine in order to preserve his pectorals, which bulged from their covering of thermal undershirt.

All the troops were assembled and silent. "HOSPITAL, ATTEN-HOOT," called the adjutant, Colonel Fruitman. One hundred and fifty-five heels clicked into place beside one hundred and fifty-five left feet. More or less together. Three hundred and nine arms whipped down to the sides of the bodies. The arm of one of the cooks was in a cast. It was his left, or non-carrot-chopping, arm. He, too, could serve. It was all right.

"REEPORT," screeched the Colonel.

"First platoon present and accounted for," immediately echoed the officer standing in front of the officers' platoon.

"Second platoon all present, accounted fo', sir . . ."

"Third platoon present and accounted for." They went through the motions of soldier-playing, following the predetermined forms. A photographer was on hand to send pictures of the first formation back to the hometown newspapers, for everyone at home would be thankful that *they* were not holding live grenades or coping with gas masks.

"Section commanders—take charge," came the final order prior to dismissal.

"The delegation of authority," thought Specialist Fourth Class Eros Winter, "goes down the chain of command until it hits me. All I ever do is stand here with a thumb up my ass waiting for an order to remove it." He was still hungover.

FIVE

Colonel John Fruitman found it a strain to have to carry his wooden mallet with its head down. So he decided to carry it at port arms, like an M-1 rifle. He had never really carried an M-1 rifle, having been stationed during the Second World War solely at Fort Riley, Kansas, caring for cases of trench foot shipped in to him from the Pacific. He stayed in the Reserve partly to be assured at least one two-week vacation from his wife each year; partly for the camaraderie of his fellow officers; and partly for the respect everyone was forced to show him as adjutant of the unit. His duty was to coordinate the movements of the 229th General Hospital, and he had very little opportunity to practice his medical vocation. He said about himself, "To this day, and I've been in practice for almost twenty-five years, I've always maintained a decidedly nonprofessional interest in the pussy. I mean, when it winks, I know goddam well it's winking right at me." There was rumor of a law suit filed by one of his patients on the North Shore, early in the 'fifties, which was squashed by his lawyers out of court. Fruitman never talked about it himself. It was only rumored, around the campfire as it were.

He was leading a contingent of men from the bus area over to the west side of the bivouac site. There the hospital tents were to be erected: large, heavy, khaki-colored, tents of which the three biggest, that were to be for hospital wards, weighed close to three hundred pounds apiece. Dry. In the rain, the wet canvas would make it practically impossible to erect them, and would increase the weight to something just over six hundred pounds. The tentage was folded end over end over end, and tied with a slip knot like a big khaki present. The tents' own ropes were used for this job, the pegs being secured in the midst of the folds. When stretched out on the ground, the ward tents were thirty feet long by eighteen feet wide and when erected could hold between twenty to twenty-five men each.

Field training was a necessary exercise for the 229th General Hospital. ("Flexibility is the key to our Reserve," said General Roderick Grosbeck, the Commanding General of the National Guard, Minuteman Division, from Massachusetts.) The 229th was supposed to support the division in its war games during the two weeks of camp, operating its field hospital and acting as a clearing station to evacuate casualties, both simulated and actual. The wards of the 229th could handle only about sixty patients efficiently.

"We'll fake the rest of the beds, if need be," said Colonel Beauregard. "It's no different than gerrymandering one of my districts." It really wasn't gerrymandering at all. Not even like it. But the Colonel was fond of interspersing his conversation with bits and snatches of political jargon. It was to remind his associates that he was a leader in Real Life also. Three smaller tents were laid out next to the wards. One for surgery, one for X ray, one a combination Dental and A&D Section (which was Admissions and Dispositions).

"All right, men," commanded Colonel Fruitman. "We'll put up the ward tents in the middle and work the others in around them. First we gotta plant them pegs; here's the mallet. I've got the beginning of a hernia, I think." He chuckled to himself at the joke. A few of the men laughed also. Not at the joke, but at the bother he took to excuse his handing the job on to someone else. There was an unwritten directive pertaining to the 229th's camp erection: everyone was to pitch in and help, including officers, nurses, and WACs. And they did, making it a contest to see how fast the job could be done and the baggage moved in. No patients could be expected until the next afternoon, anyway. Casualties to the National Guard division on maneuvers would be evacuated to the Waterville Memorial Hospital in the town outside the gates of Camp Cannon.

Groups of male and female personnel moved to other sections of the area, dragging tentage and mallets with them. They were split up into three different groups, other than the group with Colonel Fruitman. "Butcher" Beanstock took his boys over to erect the mess tent and the two administrative tents. Colonel Harden supervised the raising of the officers' tents, one for male, one for female, and one for Colonel Beauregard. Sergeants Baer and Skippy Dennis were in charge of the planting of all tentage housing the troops. There would be three of those. Colonel Beauregard stood in the midst of the encampment area and unstrapped a .45 caliber revolver which he carried strapped in a hip holster. It was not issued by the Medical Corps. Nor was it standard for this type of unit, which even in wartime was not issued firearms (except, of course, if a recalcitrant medic were suddenly shipped out to a line company and handed an M-1. Then it would be assumed that his mission was to be cannon fodder). Beauregard placed a blank cartridge in the chamber and spun the cylinder a few times. It amused him to fire upon an empty chamber untill the blank went off. It was the closest thing to Russian roulette he would allow himself. It had never exploded upon the initial attempt. Never. He put the .45 into the air and pulled the trigger. The roar surprised him and he jumped a little jump of surprise. It was the signal to commence erection. "COMMENCE ERECTION," commanded Colonel Beauregard.

A fantastic image crossed Marjorie Stavropolis's mind. The men only laughed. Then "Whump . . ." four mallets came down almost simultaneously upon four stakes in the four sectors of the hospital area.

The work proceeded with enthusiasm for the first ten minutes or so. Until it became not enthusiasm but drudgery. Then the doctors and other officers wearied of their pose and passed on the chores to the enlisteds, who proceeded to jam fingers, bang toes, split pegs, curse, and/or stand around pretending to be busy. The canvas of the various tents was all stretched out upon the ground and pegs inserted into the loops of rope connected to the material. They were hammered into the ground diagonally, so as to catch the loop of the ropes directly in the niche cut into each peg. The job took longer than usual—because the mallets weighed so much and there were only four of them to go around, an oversight on the part of Kenny Keohane and the supply section which everyone cheerfully accepted.

There was much of this camaraderie in the 229th General Hospital.

It took an hour and a half to get all the tent pegs banged into the turf of Camp Cannon. Then Colonel Beauregard again poised himself with the blank .45 pistol for what was called: "the simultaneous raising of the tentage." He felt this must be an impressive sight, if viewed from a distance. "I wish the damn General was here to see it," thought Beauregard. All the pegs were in, all the ropes attached; all the long tent poles were under the canvas, where stout lads manned them, ready to lift on the signal. The idea was to see the flat plain all of a sudden burst with life: the birth of a city. The Colonel was nothing if not theatrical in his approach. He readied his index finger and held his breath, slowly squeezing the trigger as he had been taught. . . .

"Boy, you ain't never going to relieve whatever you got in your insides, unless you get them latrines dug," said

Cameroons Jackson, platoon sergeant of the professional complement. He was talking to Eros Winter, who was leaning on his shovel, resting. Eldor von Liebert was digging away, mechanically, spading the dirt, lifting up a good shovelful, throwing it to the rear. "Frankly, Sarge, I don't give much of a damn whether or not it gets dug or it doesn't get dug." Eros was being frank with the sergeant. He liked him, in fact. Eros had learned from past military experience that the lazier he was about details assigned him, the sooner he would be reassigned and other, more willing hands called into the task. The sergeant tried reasoning with him. "Look at old von Leeber," he argued. "He don't complain about no deetail. He just do it. Ain't no way for a man to get along in this Army. Ain't no way for a man to get along in this life. Where you think you'd be, or I'd be, if I had a job and 'stead of doin' that job I just stands around and jaws. I'm surprised you ever made spec four."

"Nothing surprising about it," Winter asserted. "I worked in Personnel in another unit and put my name on the promotion list. The C.O. was too busy to notice when he signed the order; I didn't want the responsibility, or I'd have boosted myself to sergeant." He took a perfunctory shovelful. Von Liebert was already up to his waist in the hole he had been digging. The sergeant made no distinction between the two men. He viewed them only as soldiers. He had belonged to an all-Negro outfit in World War II, and was forty-seven years old. He looked thirty: big-muscled, big-headed, very dark; no lines at all marked his face or gave his actual age away. He could easily have been a professional soldier of the sort that still makes one remember active service, because Chesley Jackson never looked for the way around anything. He believed in duty, the chain of command, and his own dignity, which would brook no compromise.

Thus, Eros Winter was nothing more than a gnat to him. Jackson didn't understand how anyone could disobey orders in the Army. Winter was of the breed who didn't learn their lessons, and died in the surf at Omaha Beach or Anzio or Guadalcanal. Winter was a wise guy, and worse, a bad soldier.

Von Liebert was almost finished with his hole. (The idea was that both holes would be six feet deep. Ready-made wooden boxes with spring lids would be placed over the pits and canvas strips strung around the arrangement. Eventually four more pits were to be dug. The latrine, when built up to full capacity was to be a six-holer. The only anticipated con-

41

gestion would be around breakfast time—or directly afterwards, to be more explicit.) Sergeant Jackson pulled over one of the boxes, raised the lid, dropped his pants and sat down. "If you made a good latrine, von Leeber," he drawled, "I'll just inaugurate it for you. When a man's gotta shit, soldier, he's gotta shit."

"BANG," came the blank report from the Colonel's pistol, and the three men could see shapes rising in the distance as the tent city sprang to life, simultaneously after all.

"SHEE-IT MAN," Jackson yelled in excitement, "we got ourselves a mother lovin' home."

Everyone felt a little better when the ridgepoles were secured and the ropes tightened with clamps. The hospital was almost an actuality. Homes and wives and children were as distant as if the men were overseas. They were removed from the real world by only a day and four hundred miles, yet the masquerade of two weeks' khaki and discipline was complete; they hadn't forgotten civilian life, but already it was tough to believe in. It wouldn't have been the same had they merely been transported into already existing yellow-and-green barracks. There would have been the depressing changeover to (almost) refugee-like living: waiting to be processed, waiting for chow, waiting for the weekend to finish, with nothing to do, since the actual business of training offically commenced at eight hundred hours, Monday morning. Now an air of jubilation wafted over the encampment.

Sergeant First Class Marlon Pinto, the mess steward of the 229th, had coffee steaming in a huge steel pot, and Lipton's chicken noodle soup in another one. Anyone could have their choice, or both, if they bolted their soup, emptied their canteen cup and filled it again with the coffee, a most interesting combination. The lunch had been assembled and packed the previous night at the Boston Army Base; it consisted of two sandwiches apiece (the theory of a hot meal in the field for the troops having been exploded long since): one bologna with mustard on the bread, one slice of ham with nothing on the bread, and one chocolate bar apiece for dessert. For fast energy.

The men split up into the inevitable small groups to squat or sit on the ground and eat. There was time to smoke. The lucky ones found trees to lean against. The officers tended to move in the general direction of the administrative tents. They laughed easily and felt superior in their access to the female personnel. The men were sullen and tired and envied the officers who had women that would talk to them. Winter and von Liebert had returned to the camp, drawn their sandwiches, and found a vaguely grassy spot.

"What a lovely picnic," said Winter. "No mustard on the goddam ham." He pulled the bologna from the other sandwich and threw it into the bushes. "I hate cold cuts," he added, and shifted the ham to the bread with the mustard on it.

"You might have asked me if I wanted it," said von Liebert.

"Are you kidding? I never could figure out what people ever saw in bologna and salami," Winter countered. "Maybe salami, if it's fried up and put in with scrambled eggs; but in the raw . . . forget it. Tastes like old balloons."

"You eat anything, if you're hungry," was all that von Liebert would say.

"Christ," said Winter, "I'll even have trouble with the chocolate coconut bar. Can you see the candy people fighting with their low bids to see who gets to sell this shitty stuff to the troops? I think they stopped manufacturing this brand fifteen years ago. Millions of them must have been sitting in the Army Base, ready to be shipped to millions of starving Europeans—the good old Marshall Plan."

"How generous of our conquerors," Eldor said, chewing thoughtfully on his bologna and deciding that it was basically a Teutonic meat. He felt himself wandering in his thoughts, the luncheon meat starting to catch in his throat, when he was interrupted. . . .

"O.K., von Lipshit." The voice sprang at his unconscious thoughts. "On your feet." Sergeant Baer was standing next to the tree. He had changed into his fatigue uniform, whose yellow sergeant's stripes made a brilliant contrast against the dark green of the uniform. Eldor stared at the insignia, unable to get up.

"On your feet—Kraut," the order was repeated. "I ain't got all day. I want you to empty these barrels into the dumpster." No matter where the area, there was always a gray metal monster with a cavernous opening for the deposit of waste, garbage, and refuse.

Eldor felt his stomach knot, felt his face darken with heat. The adrenalin pumped quickly throughout his body. The idea of being a foreigner was ever present in his consciousness. He was quick to take affront; he knew from the beginning that he was an auslander. He suffered the little indignities at the bank, the friendly jibes at his nationality, that at home he wouldn't have tolerated. Only slowly had he learned that the

43

American national character exhibited this bantering, this ir-reverence, as a matter of course; it meant little or nothing. He suffered many bloody noses as a child for small causes. He would have suffered many more as a man, had he not been so relentlessly analytical. "The American takes everything as a joke," he finally decided. "I shall do my job and learn to con-trol myself." And of course, he respected the order of things, natural or not. Eldor and his friends at home, some of whom had been members of the Hitler Jungend, often discussed the Jewish "problem" and the "final solution." They secretly believed that any country, given the same circumstances, would have acted the same, It became easy after a while. El-dor's older brother, Kurt, had been killed after the Bulge, when even women had been pressed into service in a last-ditch attempt to prevent total disaster. Kurt had been Sturmbann-fuehrer; leader of his Wolf Pack. Eldor's pals, too, had lost relatives and friends during the war. War was the reality, El-dor still maintained. "It is never too late to start winning," his father added. "Press your advantage from the start."

But von Liebert had never encountered malice. Enemies; but never malice. He had had no previous dealings with Sergeant Baer. Why was the man singling him out? He got to his feet, fists clenched, said nothing, and stalked toward the barrels that the sergeant indicated. Winter didn't move. He still leaned against the tree.

"These Krauts think they got a right to sit on their ass," said Baer to the air; then to Winter, "What's the matter, you a Nazi sympathizer? Can't you find any better friends around here?"

"I'd love to, Sarge," Winter countered, "but you and the Colonel wouldn't take me up in the Buick. I like class."

"Always gotta be a smart guy, Winter. Smart guys end up head down in the grease trap. I can fix it for you to have KP a few times in the next two weeks."

Winter rolled with the punch and got to his feet. "That's enough, Sarge. I take it all back." He made a strategic retreat. He didn't care whether von Liebert carried barrels for the whole camp or dug latrines or washed pots and pans or cleaned out field stoves. The mere threat of KP was enough to make him reevaluate his new acquaintance.

Eros was furious as he pulled his duffel bag into the tent, to see that most of the choice spots were taken. He screamed at the men who dared to preempt him: "Un-ass them barracks, men . . . drop your cocks and grab your socks . . . fall out and fall in on yo' equipment." He yelled as many obscenities as he could conjure up from his six months' military experience. People looked at him and he kept yelling into the tent, searching among the dim light afforded by rents in the canvas for some decent spot, some level spot, his own little piece of dirt to bunk down on.

At last Eros found a relatively even few feet of ground, picked a folded cot out of the pile inside the tent flap and snapped it rigid. Kenny Keohane's boys from supply were already stringing wires and electric fixtures from the roof, and Eros made sure one of the bulb outlets would be over his bunk.

"It ain't so bad," said the electrician. "Better than bein' in pup tents with only one other guy. Least we got cots 'stead of sleeping bags and ponchos."

"The jerks measure everything in relative terms," thought Eros, looking around the tent to see if anyone had the foresight to bring along an air mattress or a pillow. But he didn't believe anyone in the 229th would have the brains to plan for such a contingency. He liked to reinforce his theories empirically. Otherwise he wouldn't even have bothered to look around.

Von Liebert came into the tent shortly thereafter and switched with someone to get the cot next to Eros. It was not a choice location. The ground where the German set up his bunk sloped toward the right. He would have to build up his position with newspapers and magazines. The only light inside the tent came from four plastic windows, opaque rather than transparent (the generator for the bulbs had not been connected yet); although the sun shone brightly outside, the canvas smell and the dampness of the ground, coupled with the fact that very little light came through the plastic, made the atmosphere chokingly close.

Eros lay on his back, holding his squash racket up straight on his belly, switching the grip from right hand to left hand.

"What are you doing?" Eldor asked him, placing his full duffel bag at the foot of his cot.

"I'm figuring out a method of changing hands quickly, so that I never have to use a backhand. I can't hit those soft drop shots very well with my backhand. They just won't drop close to the tin. Ever play squash?"

"Just some tennis, actually; but not since school. No time for games. I keep in shape, but no time for games."

Winter twirled his racket, still looking at the roof of the tent. "That prick of a sergeant bothers you." he said.

"I know he's Jewish and, I suppose, bitter. Everyone who's Jewish is bitter," was Eldor's immediate reaction.

"And I suppose *you* didn't know and your family didn't know. You all did merely what you were ordered. Hitler betrayed you," Winter mused, checking the strings of his racket for slack.

"Can't we just change the subject?" asked von Liebert. Winter was willing. He had problems of his own.

Eros was plainspoken. He did not conceal what he felt. This was good, Eldor decided. Sometimes stupid, but good. He is a lot like me. He felt compelled to say something. "My father was a soldier, my family a military family, and tradition in my country says that you obey your commander. The discipline brings victory." He knew the American would understand.

"No speeches, Red Eagle," Eros mocked. "I'm a simple con man . . . ER11341082. Don't give me Löwenbräu, I ordered Black Label. Hardly fodder for a Putsch. I don't give a damn anyway. Let me tell you about the Philadelphia Boast. It's a corner shot. Just drops dead!"

The personnel tent was full now. The men had no sheets or mattresses, merely two blankets, with either a laundry bag or a folded towel for a pillow. Sergeant Skippy Dennis was disappointed that the cots were so crowded together. It would be tough to masturbate at night without being caught. Being one of the senior NCOs, he usually had his own room and masturbating was no problem. He needed constant pressure relief, as he called it.

"*Chacun à son goût,* darling," he would say; meaning, he would take what was available. He was commander of the tent and strode up and down, looking for the most advantageous spot. He decided finally to bunk nearest the tent flap and proceeded to pull from his duffel his air mattress, sheets, foam rubber pillow, pillow case and his own blue blankets, one hundred per cent lamb's wool. "Teal blue, darlings," he said to no one, flinging the blankets helter-skelter upon the cot. Then he stood back and watched the way they fell. Dennis was a decorator, awash in a sea of non-believers.

What made it so difficult was, Boston socialites were not supposed to be queer. Skip Dennis had fought it a very long time, almost until his twenty-seventh birthday. But the pressures of his occupation, the desire to be successful and liked, could not be denied when added to his *basic* desire. He let himself by seduced by Monk Lassick, of Lassick Interiors, on a magnificent Récamier sofa, in Lassick's Beacon Hill apartment. Skippy wanted a job with Lassick very much. He had been working and hating it in the showroom of a fabric and wallpaper distributor. He knew he had the charm and talent to be a success in the decorating business; but it was tough to get hired by any of the existing practitioners in Boston, unless one happened to be a particularly great and good friend.

The Army had triggered his discoveries about himself. After his graduation from Cornell, with an A.B. degree in English literature which prepared him for nothing (he had written his thesis on George Eliot, with emphasis on the premise that Effie was the precursor of Lolita), he vegetated. At a coming-out party in the spring, one of his classmates had told him about the six-month program in the Army. "You're going to have to do *something* about it, unless you're 4F or a student. And it's only six months. Then it's easy to miss meetings. Just go to summer camp, two weeks a year. If you change your addresses at all, they'll take at least a year to catch up with you. A snap."

Skippy didn't think he was 4F. He had rowed light-weight crew for two years in college and skied a lot during the winters. He was well built, full-lipped and dark-haired. He spoke with a rather affected accent that no one he associated with ever noticed. Because plenty of them also spoke with affected accents. He was best friends with a lot of girls. They confided in him. He always had the latest gossip about who had gotten whom pregnant; who was smoking pot; who was seeing a psychiatrist; whose mother in the crowd had the worst drinking problem; and other stories his friends loved to hear. Skip had the word on everyone. And he had the same feeling about homosexuals that all his friends had—they never touched his world. They never touched his coming out parties, or his 210 races off Marblehead, or his duck hunting in the fall in the marshes along Narragansett Bay. He never noticed fairies, any more than he noticed panhandlers along Newbury Street, any more than he had ever noticed public high school boys in college, or Jews or Negroes or Irishmen or Italians—the pure strains, that is.

Skippy had found himself surrounded by the enemy in the Army. Every element that he had refused to recognize he was now forced to live with, eat with, defecate next to, and so forth. He didn't move his bowels for the first five days of basic training, an ordeal that rewarded him with terrific cramps and a chewing-out from the NCOs, who rode him without any mercy. Finally he blurted out in formation, "I haven't moved my bowels for almost a week and I can hardly stand up straight . . ." His sergeant personally took him on sick call the next day, explaining to the medic: "Doc, this man ain't shit in a week, fix him up with something good and proper." An enema and hourly administrations of Feenamint loosed the dam, and Skippy lost his self-consciousness about functioning under the eyes of a dozen or more men waiting to use his particular pot. It got so that he even felt like one of the troops because of it. It was a victory over the squeamishness he had exhibited about any bodily function.

It was his platoon sergeant who had first planted doubt in Skippy's mind. He found himself fascinated by the looks of the tall blond young man from Boone, Iowa, who had served with valor in Korea and later in the stockade at Fort Knox, where he had been sent for attacking a second lieutenant. Subsequently (the young sergeant had been too mortified to tell the whole story), it came out that the second lieutenant had propositioned the young blond sergeant. He had often been told that he was prime "queer bait," being fair and smooth-skinned. But he was a farm boy, raised hogs, and was even offered a basketball scholarship to Grinnell College, which his pa had turned down. He would, in his own words before the Military Tribunal, ". . . have truck with a few of the hogs down on the farm, if me and my brother Sam coulda held 'em down, and o' course we'd have our share o' gals—but another guy! Sir, that'd shock the damn overalls right offen pa—I don't care if it was a direct order from a sooperior officer—" The blond sergeant was acquitted.

Skippy Dennis couldn't keep his eyes off the skin and body of his platoon leader. It got so that he would plan to be in the shower at the same time with the sergeant. He couldn't help himself, he got excited looking at him. During those times he would quickly switch the water to cold and let it drain the excitement with its shock therapy, saying, "Nothing quite like a cold, brisk shower, Sarge." The Sarge would grunt and blow his nose. (Combat veterans, even under thirty, don't do much talking to recruits.) Still, nothing happened.

After that, Skippy would never take a chance, never declare himself to anyone that he wasn't positive would reciprocate. The frustration took him pretty far out. He would go into New York City on weekends to buy muscle building photo magazines for men and thumb through them, looking for studies of two or more men together. He would compare the bulges in the various briefs and be pleased with a matching bulge in his own uniform. Finally, he let himself be picked up in Times Square one night on leave, just to see what it would be like.

It was better than he had expected, and Skippy was launched. But he found that his passion was a problem, once he resumed his civilian status. It would never do for him to be a Boston banker or financial advisor. He had majored in English, which gave him a certain cultural head start and an awareness of such subjects as art and music. So he gravitated toward the decorating business, starting out at sixty-five dollars a week, selling fabrics for a Boston representative of a New York wholesaler. He did have a flair. He knew how to find old steamer trunks in the junk shops and Salvation Army stores, buy them for two or three dollars, polish them up and have decorators sell them for one hundred and fifty dollars, as front hall depositories for galoshes and rubbers. *Très chic!* He knew what walls to break through, and where original beams and brick should be exposed. He knew he could go with the decorators to their special bars and drink Rum Cassis, the drink of the year in the trade, and giggle about the chokehold they had over the women of the suburbs. And what he didn't know, he soon learned.

Yet something in his New England background kept Skippy in the Army Reserve, even after his six-year enlistment was up. "There's a lot to be said for power," Monk Lassick told him. "I'm fascinated by the idea of submission to an authority you *must* obey, or be punished by. But of course, there is again an authority over you. If you came to work for me, *I* would have to be that civilian authority." Lassick peered at him over the top of his brandy snifter and arched his eyebrows. Skippy shivered a little, knowing that it would amuse Lassick to draw him into that kind of relationship. But he was there in the apartment for that very purpose. He had left his classmates who still played touch football on Sundays, with special dispensation from their wives. He had moved to the fringes of the cuffless league. But Skippy clung to the Reserve as an escape from what possessed him on the outside. He reenlisted when his term was up and was promoted to platoon sergeant in charge of the Administrative Complement of the 229th. It was enough to prove to himself, for two weeks every summer, that he could leave the effete circle of muslin and toiles and play soldier with men. It was always a relief to return home, bursting from the strain of denial, lonely for the companionship and the conversation late into the nights at the well-done Beacon Hill salons of his friends. Summer camp was like going cold turkey for Skippy Dennis. Wheeling into the fifth floor decorators' showroom to riffle through the fabrics on Monday morning was like taking it into the main line.

"I think damask would be lovely inside these tent flaps," Dennis thought to himself. "That would be a true test of my ability, making this a showplace of the modern United States Army. Everyone could have spreads for their cots—in a variety of colors, a veritable riot. The more diversified the colors, the better to camouflage the true purpose of our mission. But I suppose I'd have to go through the chain of command to get it approved. The Colonel would never go for it. He's such a stickler."

Dennis noticed von Liebert and Winter talking together on the same bunk. He was attracted to the contrasts in their looks. Winter, dark and patrician, with a sensuous mouth that smiled often; von Liebert, with his strong, hard look about him, red hair cropped almost to the skin. They were a good looking couple, he thought.

Then he thought, "Forget it," and forced his hands to open up his duffel and take out his mess kit, field pack and helmet liner. "Bitch," said Skippy Dennis out loud.

It was about that time that a green Ford pulled in behind one of the ambulances of the 229th General Hospital and stopped. A man with a string tie got out and asked one of the doctors attached to the unit where he could find Colonel Beauregard. The doctor pointed out the Colonel's tent.

The afternoon was very gray as the man walked toward the tent. The wind had begun to blow big tumbleweeds across the flatness of Camp Cannon. Here and there, scatterings of men were securing their tents. Pegs were being hammered into the ground deeper than before; ropes were being drawn taut; lister bags full of fresh water were being strung at strategic intervals from small saplings and birch trees. Clouds covered the afternoon sky: not rain clouds, but stratus and cumulus which meant that August was there and the lush part of the summer gone. Monotony and the Army had replaced the frivolity of the bus ride and the camp-pitching. The stranger noticed that the men were all in fatigues, replacing the Class A suntan uniform which they would wear only at Saturday's inspection and again upon the bus ride home, in two weeks. The man placed a finger in his nose thoughtfully and walked into the Colonel's tent. He greeted Beauregard.

50

"I'm Rufus Soule, Colonel," he said, taking his finger from his nose and extending his hand. The colonel was reluctant to shake, seeing where the man's hand had so recently been.

"What the hell, we're in the field," Beauregard quickly decided, and grabbed the outstretched hand, pumped it once, then let it drop.

"I'm from the Washington Agency," Rufus Soule continued, "come to observe you. And I'm afraid that observation is only part of this special assignment. There's a lot more to war and peace than just merely training. Your 229th General Hospital could play a bigger role in this cold-hot war world of ours than you ever thought possible. Why don't we have a go at it?" The man smiled and moved a finger into his nose.

The Colonel found the habit difficult to ignore, but he tried to play the game. "We've been waiting for something special, Mr. Soule," he said. "The men and women of my unit you will find cooperative and willing. Come to my headquarters. Perhaps you'd like something cool, or something hot. We have both." They walked away together, with Rufus Soule wiping his finger on his decidedly civilian pants.

SIX

"Gentlemen," the Colonel greeted his officers and NCOs at the special staff meeting he had called. "Let me introduce Mr. Rufus Soule of the Central Agency."

Soule wore a pepper and salt jacket, with dark slacks and black pointy shoes. His string tie was black and cinched in the middle with a silver clasp. He was short, possibly five eight or nine, and gave the impression of being fat, though he wasn't, really. It was just the poor fit of his clothes, as if he had gone by mistake to the Fat Man's Shop and picked out the first items he saw. Soule acted as if he didn't care how he looked. And he didn't.

"You gentlemen will notice that I am dressed in civilian clothes," he began. "This is not because I am without service in our Armed Forces. As a matter of fact," (again the right index finger inched toward his nostril), ". . . I have been decorated in wartime by—not only our nation—but the recovering nations of Europe. This is nothing new to the Soule family. My father, Rufus Soule, Senior, was even commended by Montenegro in the First World War. Little Montenegro, down on the Adriatic Sea . . ." He paused, a patriotic pause; then continued, allowing the creeping index finger to finally enter his nose, probing. The audience was mostly officers. A few of them reached for handkerchiefs, reminded of their own needs.

"When you are young," Soule continued, nodding to the junior officers in the tent, "there is little to do for your country other than an occasional solicitation for the United Fund or purchase of a Savings Bond. In my day, we were glad for a chance to steep ourselves in glory. I'm sure the prospects of this possibility made you join and remain active in the United States Army Reserve program. I'm here as the official representative of your government to allow *you* to steep yourselves in this glory." He paused and looked around him at the faces of the officers. Colonel Fruitman sucked in his gut when the Central Agency man's gaze swept over him. He wanted to look in shape, in case anything should be demanded of him.

". . . There was a time when my trousers were bloused and I wore the screaming eagle of the 80th Airborne Division on my sleeve. Some of you older men must have been in Sicily,

Italy, Normandy, where I was—" All of a sudden he let out a shriek—"AIRBORNE!" Yelling at the top of his voice, his head jerked toward the right, string tie bobbing in the same direction. He seemed satisfied with the response that he saw.

Skippy Dennis moved a few chairs back toward the entrance. Chesley Jackson nudged Sergeant Baer, winked at him, and whispered, "This cat is somethin' else, ain't he?" Baer just gave Jackson a dirty look. Baer knew his place, and the civilian was from Washington.

Baer had never really been south of Baltimore, where he once went as a substitute for Bernie Slosberg, who had the New Jersey, Maryland, Pennsylvania territory, but was sick. He remembered meeting a congressman in one of the strip joints on East Baltimore Street. He met him in the men's room, where the congressman was having his shoes shined. The congressman was very jovial and drunk and told Baer that he had to see Washington: the Capitol, Arlington Cemetery, and especially the Smithsonian.

"They've got John Dillinger's cock there on display. In a big goddam test tube—pickled, it is. Bis as your forearm . . ."

The congressman promised Baer a ride on the underground railroad if he looked him up. Baer promised to send him some cashmere swatches so he could have a custom coat made. (Both promptly forgot their promises, but Baer never forgot about John Dillinger.)

"I get carried away occasionally by the old war cries," the Central Agency man continued. "I realize all of you people are medical, and, in effect, actually civilians." A few voices tried to protest that, no, they were all soldiers; but Rufus Soule would not be denied. "Now I know your intentions are good. This is why I have been delegated by powers not present . . ." He paused and looked over the expectant faces in front of him. "Colonel Beauregard has been *most kind to offer his full cooperation.*" He became funereal: "The 229th General Hospital has had a fine record. They have been present in effective form for two World Wars and the Korean Conflict. They bear unit citations for bravery and victory in the European Theater and with our United Nations forces. You all are aware of this."

Soule was not boring his audience, because they had absolutely no idea why he was there. None of the officers or noncoms had ever seen an Agency man before. He continued, "Now in view of your record, I'm going to level with you. The 229th is not a Priority One outfit. Despite the fact that your Colonel and his staff have repeatedly attempted to assume this

53

status, you have been unsuccessful. This means that in case of full national emergency, or the continuation of the present Vietnam affair, you men would be in no immediate danger of being reactivated. Yet we must prepare for just such emergencies in the future. You know how serious this is, gentlemen. Hence, our Reserve system and your summer sessions. This year your training will consist of something very special; so special that it must not be whispered, or rumored, to any of the enlisted men." Soule continued to pick his nose with regularity. Beauregard wondered whether Washington approved. *He* certainly didn't.

"I don't have to tell you, gentlemen," Soule went on, "that my mission here is classified Top Secret." Everyone was deadly serious; Colonel Fruitman was biting his nails; Butcher Beanstock was leaning back on his camp chair, staring at a spot on the ceiling, trying hard not to concentrate on anything but his slaughterhouse back home. Everyone dreaded something horrible, and the continual nose explorations of Rufus Soule had made everyone a little jerky.

Sergeant Chesley Jackson longed for a Kleenex. He had been well brought up and it was unthinkable that he would pick his nose in public. He even felt guilty about it when he was alone. His palms were sweating, and he watched the droplets run over the pink of his hands into the darker areas leading to his wrists and forearms. He liked doing things the Army way. It gave him an extra twelve hundred dollars a year, to supplement his hundred and ten a week salary as wardmaster in the Chelsea Naval Hospital.

He had five children. His wife worked in private homes, doing laundry and cleaning. She even worked for some of the officers' wives in the unit. Hard work was his only release from thoughts that would otherwise have depressed him. Seeing a civilian in the midst of the uniformed officers and noncoms seemed strangely out of place. Jackson liked everything orderly. His world was predicated on playing by the rules established by anyone who had been there before. The pepper and salt jacket confused him. Jackson, when he distrusted a man, made sure he walked way around him. He was a big man, but he wanted no trouble. Just to be let alone.

"I want you gentlemen," Soule continued, "to come together under an oath. I want you to believe, as I believe, that the United States is threatened constantly from her enemies, both on the outside," he swept his hand grandly around him, "and from *within this country* itself." Soule fingered his tie cinch. A new habit. A generator had been hooked up and its hum formed a continual background for his speech, like an electric guitar stuck on a D-minor chord, accompanying a coffeehouse poet. Two naked electric bulbs were the result of the generator's actions; they shone dimly upon the scene.

Chaplain Papps thought the man was getting carried away. He disliked hearing anyone else speak. He used to shut off Roosevelt on the radio, and never could finish reading anything by Winston Churchill. *Sinners in the Hands of an Angry God* he tolerated, but only for its emotional content. He was his own favorite preacher, patriot, and politician.

"I want you gentlemen to reaffirm your faith in our Bill of Rights . . ." Soule went on, his finger on the alert for nasal congestion. Colonel Harden was making mental notes to consult his Osler's *Practice of Medicine* for any accurate diagnosis of the problem. Unless, of course, the man was using it as an identity cover-up. So that all anyone would remember about Soule would be that he had his finger in his nose.

". . . and our Reserve system. You are the commanders of the 229th General Hospital and we see talent in your ranks. How would you men like to volunteer for a secret mission for your country? It is my job to train you and inform you of the nature of this mission. This will necessitate reactivating your unit. Probably for a period of one year, or until such time as we actually utilize your particular training. How do you feel about *that,* gentlemen?"

Colonel Beauregard instinctively leaped to his feet and saluted smartly. The generator seemed to increase its hum and the bulbs burned a little brighter for a moment. Everyone else reacted slowly and remained rigid in their chairs. The officers and senior noncoms of the 229th, with the exception of their commander, suddenly felt very much like civilians. Except for Sergeant Chesley Jackson and Sergeant Lennie Baer.

Baer was excited and eager. He loved the Reserve and he loved the Army. He would lead his men. He would throw away his vicuña swatches and trade them for some cotton patches that he could ram down the barrel of an M-16 rifle. He sat in his camp chair and pushed the fist of one hand as hard as he could into the open palm of the other. Then he switched hands and repeated the process. Isometrics. He had to start getting fit. Becoming too soft around the gut. He sucked in his breath as hard as he could and held it for ten seconds; then he pushed it out and held it for the same amount of time. Isometrics. Take two inches off his waist in a month.

He'd be ready. The hell with the Tootsie Roll man.

Sergeant Jackson took sober reconnaissance of the situation, mostly from a financial point of view, and came up with an advantage to himself: "I take home barely $5150 per annum, not countin' the twelve hunnerd from the Reserve. But I takes food, rent, liquor, entertainments, and every which thing from all o' that. I never got nothin' left. Five kids gotta go to work soon's they is old enough. In the Army I'll be pullin' down $370 a month basic pay, and $22.50 maybe, if this job takes us overseas, plus a extra hunnerd almost per month for quarters allowance. That's just $492.50 per, an' a damn sight betta than I do shaving veterans' balls at the VA. Man, this cat jus' solved a lot o' problems for ol' Cameroons Jackson." He was content; his biggest problems would be solved. Jackson stopped sweating and started to relax.

One of the junior ROTC lieutenants was shaking over in a corner, leaning against one of the tent poles. Silent sobs racked his body and his face was in his hands. Major Fugue, ex-combat surgeon, terror of the Veterans Administration Hospital in Jamaica Plain, went over and slapped his face. "Have you lost your mind, son?" he barked. "This is war!" He kept slapping, but the lieutenant kept shaking his shoulders, the way women laugh, and silently was scared.

Skippy Dennis was the first to verbalize his reaction. "I can't go on active duty, sir," he said. "I've got the old Williston manse to do, Empire, drawing room all in blue, my first commission. Three thousand dollars in drapes alone; bathroom fixtures in Italian marble. I've already torn down two walls . . ."

"Dennis!" yelled Colonel Beauregard, still at attention. "You are a soldier."

"I'm a decorator," Skippy shrieked. "I don't know what kind of game this is, but I've got my career to think about." His voice would not have been out of place in an art nouveau boutique. But he had golden sergeant's stripes on his sleeves, his brass buckle had been polished with a blitz cloth until it shone, and there was not a Tiffany lamp in sight.

Colonels Fruitman and Harden conferred over their respective clipboards, with their schedules written in triplicate. "Jesus," said Fruitman, the gynecologist, "this'll wreak merry hell with my practice. There's that young Ramsden in Peabody that somehow got hold of my patient list. Probably through that receptionist I fired last year—you know, the nosy, prudish one with the big knockers. Ramsden's been

56

sending my patients cards on Easter, Purim, their birthdays, you name it. With his photograph on the inside, always in various medical poses: like ready to remove an ovary, or poised for a D and C. A real hard seller. I'll lose business to him, I know it."

"*You'll* lose business, Fruitman," said Colonel Harden, the executive officer, "My practice is twice the size of yours, not to mention my wife is twice as hard to keep quiet as yours. What am I going to do with her when she hears? She'll never believe me. Who's my congressman? I'm in an essential industry."

Rufus Soule was still speaking, above the confusion of words and thought.

". . . we Agency men are taught to be able to think clearly, despite contradictory action. I know in my heart that you, in your hearts, are all with me. Stand and salute the flag!"

Bullied and cowed, the commanders of the 229th General Hospital got to their feet. "Where is your flag, Colonel?"

The unit insignia guidon and the American flag were outside the two tent flaps in front of the command tent. Sergeant Baer ran outside and returned with the flag, still stuck in its stand.

"God, man, you're dragging it along the ground," said Soule, running himself to rip the standard from the eager sergeant's grasp. Soule righted it and kissed it upon the fifty star section, first checking his finger to see if it was clean. "Repeat after me, Reservists . . ." They all stood dumbly while Soule raised his right hand and incanted:

> Auto safety very soon—
> Put a Yankee on the moon,
> Jersey of a Green Bay Packer,
> Button of a Willkie backer,
> Our Reservists give 'em heck,
> Bring back Madame Chiang Kai-shek.
> Down the left and up the right,
> Central Agency, FIGHT, FIGHT, FIGHT!

"Forget it. Don't repeat it," he commanded. "It was just to get you fired up. Seats everyone. I haven't told you your mission yet." He ripped back his suit jacket to reveal a leather shoulder holster, the flap buckled and fastened. He unsnapped the flap, and with his right hand reached into the holster for a quick draw. Several of the spectators ducked. Colonel

57

Beauregard was frightened, but he kept his chair and sat a little taller. He had to be an example to his troops. From the holster Soule pulled a Hershey bar and started to peel off the brown outer wrapper. Then the white inner paper. Then he broke off a healthy section and put it into his mouth, sucking on the chocolate. He put the rest of the bar, carefully closed off on the end with the extra paper, back into the shoulder holster and buckled it. Then he took a quick opportunity to pick before continuing. "I always believe that energy in my profession, at the right moment, can be more important than weapons. My only weapons are my hands, and, if necessary, this huge cord." (He displayed his Thuggee cord.) "Hershey bars pack incredible energy into their product. But you must suck, not chew on them for the most effective reaction. To maintain self-control in this pursuit, I buy the kind with almonds: protein is the key to health. Think about it, gentlemen."

Most of the men were thinking about home when Major Marjorie Stavropolis walked into the command tent with a pitcher of coffee on a cafeteria tray. "Coffee, fellas," she bubbled. "Marlon thought it might be a help." (Marlon Pinto, the mess steward of the 229th, loved his job and drank a lot of beer.)

Major Stavropolis felt herself center stage. As the undisputed queen of the 229th, all the enlisted men secretly hungered after her luscious Aegean breasts. And she had hips to match. She was so sure of her preeminence that she flaunted her rear end, now covered in regulation olive-drab fatigue pants, and said the hell with it. "In the valley of the blind, the one-eyed man is king, n'est-ce pas?" Chaplain Papps used to say about her. But she knew that something was wrong as soon as she looked at the Colonel.

He was as rigid in his chair as a West Point plebe eating a square meal, staring right at Rufus Soule and not even recognizing her entrance. Usually he devoured her with his little close-together eyes, his moustache twitching at the ends. She distrusted men with eyes set close together. "No man for you," her mother used to tell her, "ever will have the eyes of a pig, close together in his head." But her mother never understood ambition. "If pig eyes make me a colonel, it's pig eyes for me," she had decided. She set the tray down on the table and turned to leave.

"Don't go, Major," said the Agency man. "You are the ranking lady present and part of this operation depends on the effective control of your women." She stopped by the tent flap, surprised; but sat down next to one of the junior lieutenants, who motioned her over to an empty chair. Soule poured himself a cup of coffee, shook the Pet milk can into it for a moment, and continued: "Upon reactivation, you will be reassigned to an area somewhat south of here, awaiting deployment for a military operation in the Caribbean area.

"The unit will proceed as normal for most of the first week of camp, supporting the Minuteman Division and operating as a clearing station for any sick or casualties on their infantry maneuvers. Toward the end of the week, you will start preparing the unit for reactivation—psychologically. It will be a shock, I know, to the enlisted personnel; but naturally, you as officers and senior noncoms are prepared intellectually and emotionally for such a happenstance." He took a bite out of his Hershey bar and a slug of coffee. "No one outside the tent is to be informed of the nature of this mission. IT MUST NOT LEAK. There will be no tolerance of security lapses. We will conduct an exercise that will determine positively that *you* are the medical unit to be activated. In this exercise, we shall support an infantry assault upon an island in the Thousand Island Group, uninhabited, naturally. Resistance will be from some of your own people in foreign uniforms, designated as the Aggressor. How well you support the infantry will determine just how great a role you will play in the proposed activation. I am assuming that the 229th General Hospital will have no trouble in performing this rehearsal successfully. You have been chosen over every other general hospital in the country's reserves. I know you gentlemen, *and* lady—" he leered at Stavropolis, "—are up for this ball game."

Somehow Soule knew he mustn't pick his nose at the climax of the speech. This was crucial; so in desperation he reached for another piece of his Hershey bar, which evidently was a tranquilizer for him. He popped a very large section into his mouth. It contained three almonds, which were distributed every half inch. It was a *very* large section. His glands produced no saliva; he began to turn quite blue, gasping for breath and trying to spit out the candy which had become lodged in his throat. His head and then his shoulders and arms began to shake. The chocolate popped out on the table, but Soule could not control himself. His mouth foamed, spittle dripping out of the corners; his eyes, wild and rolling, showing nothing but the whites. He clutched his head with flailing hands, trying to stop its jerking. He rolled to the floor now, in full paroxysms, uncontrollable, his string tie becoming knotted around his neck. "Joanne, Joanne," he sputtered,

59

choking. They were the last words he spoke.

Colonel Harden was the first to move. The others were all too stunned.

Colonel Fruitman yelled, "Stuck NUT," and ran from the tent in pursuit of his medical kit. Harden leaped to the man's side. Sergeant Jackson joined him and they held the agent down, trying to calm him.

"Get me some needle and thread," Harden yelled.

"Not here, sir," someone yelled back.

"Dammit, I've got to get that tongue."

Colonel Harden grabbed for the wagging tongue, missed, grabbed again, caught the end; with Sergeants Jackson and Baer holding the limbs quiet, he held the red protuberance against the man's cheek.

"Where is some god damned needle and thread; doesn't anyone have some pins?" The tongue was threatening to get away. Marjorie Stavropolis leaped forward and removed two safety pins holding her fatigue shirt to her pants. She handed them to the Colonel.

"Flame these, nurse," he said to her.

"Yes, Doctor." She put the points of the safety pins under the flame of a match. The Colonel held out his free hand, palm up. "PIN," he ordered. "PIN," she answered and slapped the open device into the hand. He placed the tip through the tongue of Rufus Soule and again through the cheek wall. Then he closed the clasp and let go. Soule lost consciousness and a little speck of almond popped onto the ground. Nurse Stavropolis stood up and began to lose her fatigue pants.

Colonel Fruitman returned at the gallop with his black emergency bag and was relieved to find that he had been too late.

Colonel Beauregard now stared thoughtfully out of the tent flap into the twilight. It was after six and the sun was barely filtering through the bivouac area, which was ringed heavily by pines and dark spruces. The Board of Selectmen of Brookwood would miss him. Margaret and the children could get along fine for the duration. He rubbed his hand across his crew-cut scalp and thought about other leaders and other destinies. Something inexplicable, some dark brooding inevitability, had brought him to this moment. "Imagine," he thought. "Gayle Beauregard chosen from all the other medical unit commanders in the country."

"Worried, Beau?" Marjorie Stavropolis, one hand supporting her fatigue pants, rubbed his arm with her free one.

60

He looked up at her; they were outside now, alone together for a moment.

"I've been chosen, Marjorie," he said, looking very tender, his gaze passing through her and beyond to the Thousand Islands—one of which dumbly awaited his assault force. A few of the enlisted men were having a game of catch, waiting for evening chow, which was delayed because of the arrival and the erection.

"These boys are young," he said. "Innocent. They know nothing of the hours ahead. Stay with me, Marjorie. Help me do my duty as I must." She reached for him, there in Waterville, New York, hard by the Canadian border, forgetting for a moment her sagging pants. "These are times," she thought, "when a man can be conned."

Major Fugue came out of the tent. "Patient resting comfortably, sir . . . he'll pull through this fine. We've loosened his clothing and removed his shoes. Quieted down, but I think we should maintain the safety pin for a while."

"Do whatever is necessary, Major. Then dismiss the officers. Warn them that secrecy is essential. Put Soule in Ward B and separate him from anyone else brought in tonight. He's told me that an aide will join him tomorrow. I'll see you at dinner. Move the men out to chow." Major Fugue saluted smartly. It was returned, and Fugue moved to obey an order.

SEVEN

Within five minutes of the staff meeting breakup, news of the briefing was out. Warrant Officer Kenny Keohane learned from a terrified junior lieutenant, who was into Keohane for seventy-five dollars from the floating crap game Keohane ran behind the motor pool.

"Jesus, Mary, and Joseph!" Keohane gasped in disbelief. He had the 229th figured to be the last unit available for any sort of active duty. Something must have been mixed up in the messages and orders. It couldn't be the 229th. They were just a fuck-up unit from Massachusetts.

"Geographical distribution," he reasoned, finally. "Politics. Or cannon fodder. They want to sacrifice *me*, Kenny Keohane!"

He was irrational at the thought of himself, wading ashore while tracers lit the night assault. While jet fighters sent rockets in ahead to clear the beaches. While bodies floated by him in the soft warmth of the Gulf Stream waters. Death among the Trade Winds. He pictured himself, the wild minstrel boy far from Washington Street in South Boston, far from Downey's Cafe, spending St. Pat's Day or even de Valera's birthday—face down in some Caribbean sand, while his blood mixed with conch shells and tropical algae.

"It ain't my way o' doin' it," he decided, and clutched at an imaginary wound in his belly, bloated now from the beer he had been drinking in the mess tent that afternoon. He was considering shooting off a toe. "We've got to make everyone homesick," he mused aloud. "We've got to screw up the maneuver. Pinto," he yelled, "another six-pack."

The mess steward came through the rear of the mess tent, wiping his hands on his apron, which was covered with flour. He had been making cherry pie for the troops' supper. He tried to do something special when cooking in the field, and pastry he considered a speciality. His heart was in the right place. The troops dearly loved pastry. So he turned out chocolate cakes and éclairs, all manner of pies—cherry, apple, banana cream, blueberry, mince—as well as turnovers, tarts, many-tiered iced orange cakes. Alas, all inedible because Marlon Pinto was the worst pastry chef in the Army. At home he worked the late shifts in various cafeterias around Boston: Hayes Bickford's, Waldorf's, Sharaf's; anywhere he could be a combination counterman and short-order cook. He loved to be around food and loved to eat it. He personally consumed much of the leftover pastry returned each night from his mess operations. Naturally, he always over-made, in the hope that leftovers would be plentiful. He was never disappointed.

There was much noise in the mess tent and Pinto, who had promised to bring beer to Kenny Keohane, was nervous about leaving his post. He brought no beer out with him, despite his promise; so Keohane and the lieutenant walked him back into the mess area where they moved into the officers' line, their mess gear in their hands. The lieutenant kept close behind the warrant officer, as if a moment's separation would leave the young officer unprotected, liable to be snatched away and placed in reactivation status on permanent duty. Keohane was confident. Moving through the line, whenever the young man would nervously question him about some aspect of his apprehension, Keohane would smile and whisper: "Screw everything up. That's all . . . screw up." It seemed to soothe the lieutenant's nerves.

Sergeant Skippy Dennis had leaked the news almost immediately to the Colonel's regular driver, who didn't shave yet. Dennis liked the driver's smooth skin. The Colonel's driver went directly to Eros Winter, to whom he owed a favor. He thought that it might rouse him to some sort of action. Winter and von Liebert were just dipping their mess kits into the barrel of boiling water placed outside the tent for sterilization. The water in the barrel was never boiling, usually lukewarm, and filthy. No one ever wanted to dip their kits; but a sergeant was stationed next to the barrel to make sure that everyone did.

Major Butcher Beanstock was in charge of sanitation. The barrels were part of his job. "Trichinosis, dysentery, and just simple runs are the dread of the sanitation officer. Officers and nurses will dip once before meals. Enlisted personnel will dip twice, or until the officiating noncom deems the mess gear ready for loading."

The Colonel's driver grabbed Winter by the sleeve, forcing his hand into the hot water.

"Ow, you stupid bastard," Winter yelled, pulling his hand out of the barrel, still holding the handle of his mess kit—to which was attached his canteen cup, field knife, fork and spoon.

"Did you hear that we're being activated, at the end of camp?" the driver blurted out.

"We're what?" Winter answered calmly, disbelieving.

"What did you say?" von Liebert asked, not quite understanding.

"We're being put onto active duty. Dennis told me. He just came from a staff meeting. We're going on some sort of maneuvers, then the orders are going to be cut and we'll be in the Army for real."

The line shuffled slowly forward as each man positioned the aluminum sections of his mess kit, connected by a metal loop on the handle, side by side, ready to have the food spooned onto them. Everyone was pleased to be eating at last. The driver pushed into line next to Winter and continued to tell him of the rumored reactivation.

"Dennis would kill me if he knew I told you."

The cooks, cook's helpers and KPs manned the hot steam tables, ladling out the food. The two senior cooks gave out the meat portion of the meal, making sure that no one got more than one fatty pork chop. Winter and von Liebert held out their gear and moved down the line, taking mashed potatoes, gravy, peas, canned peaches and white cake—all balanced precariously on the narrow aluminumed mess kits. However, the brown pork chop gravy refused to mix properly with the peach juice and the two remained separate but equal.

"You can't be serious," Winter said, numbed at the thought of being on active duty. He had planned things so well—getting assigned to a ridiculously simple unit. He could miss meetings with the 229th and not get picked up for it. He could come and go as he pleased at camp. He was all set to apply to the Colonel for a Control Group in the fall, which would allow him to miss regular meetings altogether.

"You can't be serious," Winter repeated. "Me, get a bullet up my ass from a citizen soldier cleaning his rifle behind me? Not in *this* unit. Not on your maiden aunt's dildo, you can bet on that! I'd go queer first. I'd take a Section Eight. I'd even go in the Marines. But not with this unit, baby. Not me—no war with the weekend warriors!"

Von Liebert tried to be controlled. "What kind of man are you?" he said to Winter. He knew that his father would want him to accept authority.

"Are you crazy?" Winter countered. "Is this some kind of suicide pact? Do I look like the goddamned Charge of the Light Brigade? We're obsolete. We're leftovers, like these pork chops. Middle-aged men all around us playing soldier and trying to be serious about it! Just so some governor can watch *his* boys parade on Memorial Day or so we can get called out

64

on New Year's Eve to patrol the highways or get called to pile sandbags around some old lady's toilet that's overflowed. Politics." Winter's reasoning worked him up to an act. The mess tent was full of khaki bodies and the noise of bitching and eating filled the small space. Winter got up on to the bench and banged his spoon against the side of his canteen cup. It immediately got attention.

"Boys," he started, "we have been had. The men of the 229th have been betrayed. We're fat and civilian . . ." he stuck out his belly for emphasis, "but we are being called into active duty. You think this is going to be another two weeks of dust and beer? You aren't going home in two weeks; you're being kept in, courtesy of Uncle Sam. As my sergeant in basic training used to say, 'Your hearts may be home with your sweethearts, but yo' ass is mine.' "

Sergeant Baer stood up at the end of the tent. "Sit down, Winter," he yelled.

"The hell I'll sit down! I want some explanation of this. Is it true or not? Where are we going? What's the story?"

"The story is that you're a soldier and you take orders from your superiors," Baer said. "This isn't playacting. You're being paid to come here. You signed up. You raised your hand for a six-year obligation. That's a contract, and you are contracted. Now sit down before I come over there and sit you down."

Winter scaled his pork chop bone at the sergeant and hit him right in the name tag over his right breast. Von Liebert tried to drag him down from the bench and he banged his canteen cup on top of the German's head. A few officers had come into the tent, hearing the commotion. All the men were grabbing at the uniform lapels of the sergeants, trying to find out if what Winter was saying was true.

"Are we going to war?" a young law school student wanted to know. "I've got to get to the telephone center; mother's going to be worried."

"Ahhh, Winter's just bullshitting," said another.

Baer half walked, half ran across the mess tent, going after Winter. The latter leaped off the bench and caught the sargeant full in the face with a peach section he held in his hand. "You're going to the Colonel," Baer grunted, grabbing for the young man, trying to tackle him.

The law student was yelling futilely, "Are we at war, are we at war?"

Von Liebert felt strangely detached, not at all nervous about the rumors. He watched while Winter went down under

65

the tackle and lay on the ground, yelling: "Up the Republic, Down the Reserve!" They thrashed around, rolling from one side of the dirt floor to the other, until Winter felt the center tent pole up against his combat boots. He began kicking at the pole until he felt it give. It crashed upon one of the steam tables, scattering mashed potatoes and gravy over everyone. The heavy canvas floated down on top of officer, noncom, combatant and cook, pinning them down like so many netted butterflies.

The canvas writhed and wriggled against the outline of the pine grove, until, one by one, the men found ways to crawl out from under the tent. Winter was carried off to the Colonel by Sergeants Jackson and Baer. The rest of the men, after re-erecting Pinto's mess tent, were given close order drill with broom handles by Skippy Dennis, for discipline. There was nothing like close order drill to let the soldiers know who was boss. There was no talking in the ranks. They were ordered to concentrate on: "Double to the rear to the right flank, HARCH." Eldor von Liebert loved to drill and his right oblique movements were precise and military.

EIGHT

There was no stockade, as such, at Camp Cannon. It was assumed that in the Reserve there would be no need for one. So Eros Winter was incarcerated in the back of an ambulance, under the guard of a very nervous PFC with fixed bayonet.

Colonel Harden had had a busy day. He had not only pinned Rufus Soule's tongue to his cheek, but also had given Winter a shot of nembutal: one grain to calm him down. Winter was sullen and hunched into the back of the vehicle, staring at the nervous PFC with eyelids purposefully drawn. It made him look menacing.

"Have you got any rounds in that rifle, soldier?" Winter asked him.

"The p-p-prisoner is supposed to remain silent, orders of the Colonel," the PFC stammered, raising the bayonet off the ground and pointing it.

"Don't you realize, son, that you are about to have your freedom taken away from you? Don't you want to be promoted to spec four? Ever?" Eros paused. "Because unless you start thinking for a change, you'll never find yourself out of the Reserve."

"You mean this active duty thing?" the PFC said. "I'm a hardship case. I'll be sprung on a hardship. Tom O'Neil's our representative. He brings around a basket at Christmas, with nuts and candy and fruitcake. Sometimes even a ham. I don't like ham; but mother sticks a lot of pineapple on it. I try and have a little bite of pineapple with every bite of ham. It's like medicine."

"Funny," said Winter. "I feel the same way about ham, and I hate cloves."

"What're cloves?"

"Oh, little black things that help to take away the taste of the ham. But pineapple definitely turns the trick for me, too. Now, Turnkey, how about pointing that bayonet in another direction? I'm not really dangerous. Just playful."

"Think I want to be busted?" the PFC said, continuing to point the bayonet.

Winter shrugged. "Suddenly you're an old trooper, huh?" he said disgustedly. "What it really means is, that there'll always be war because you love to play soldier. Everyone loves to play soldier. You played with cap pistols, water pistols, plastic tommy guns with hidden compartments for your gum, and everyone on the block gets turns at being Ho Chi Minh or one of the baddies. Then you and everyone else grows up and does everything to avoid it: bad backs, trick knees, conscientious objections; you're asthmatic or rheumatic or queer or great with child or anything to get out of the Army. But after you've been caught, something happens and you're kids again. One day and look at you, you're a goddam joke. A soldier. A poor asshole PFC with a bayonet on his M-1 and no rounds in the chamber. And they lock *me* up in an ambulance. I bring a squash racket to camp and I keep my sanity, for Christ's sake."

"Who are you calling a-a an a-a-asshole, Winter?"

"You, you jerk. Sitting here keeping me from doing what? Just keeping me from making some sense. We'd be about as much help in combat as a company of Brownies."

"There, Winter, is where you're wrong." It was Colonel Beauregard, who had opened the rear doors of the ambulance and pulled himself in, holding his hand on the open holster containing his forty-five revolver. "We react most successfully to stress, more often than not," he said. "You should read Thucydides sometimes. . . . You gave us a bad time there awhile ago. As a matter of fact, you've been giving us trouble ever since camp started. Why? You're in the Reserve through your own choice, and in this unit presumably through your own choice. You're no conscientious objector. What do you do in civilian life? I went through your 201 file and found no record of occupation. I assume you do something."

"I went to medical school . . . briefly, sir," Winter said. "And I plan to go on for some degree. Maybe law. Maybe business. I'll try anything. Until then, I hustle squash."

"Why didn't that go into your 201 file?"

"Squash is a game, sir. Played with raquets. On a small, well-lighted, whitewashed, enclosed wooden court. I make enough money at this to indulge myself until it's time for graduate school to start. When I finally get out of graduate school, there'll be time enough to think about a job."

"You're obviously intelligent," the Colonel reasoned. "There's no excuse for someone like yourself not to take an active and productive role in the Reserve. Instead of fighting us. Are you looking for a commission, Winter? Sometimes you college-bred men resent taking orders from officers. You could have gone ROTC; why didn't you? It's not too late you know, my boy. There are correspondence courses you can take, special Army schools you may attend, and, if you achieve some special skill—assuming there is a slot for this skill—who knows, you're old enough to qualify, perhaps within six months, as a first lieutenant."

"I'd rather you bust me back to private, sir," Eros said calmly. "I don't want to be reactivated. That's fairly clear. For you people that are mad to get to the front, I have news. I want to get back to the rear. Let me do my five and a half years and take my seat. You can have everything back that I took from the Army, including that case of the clap I got down in San Antonio."

The Colonel didn't smile. "What kind of an imposition is this on you, Winter? I don't see that it's much of anything at all. This is your country. In an emergency, you are the vehicle of its defense. You act like you're the only soldier here. Remember this, mister, Specialist Winter runs around the Army, the United States Army doesn't run around Specialist Winter. I'm beginning to understand what you specialize *in*. Are you chicken, mister, or just plain difficult?" The Colonel was pleased with himself. He thought he sounded a good deal like Cagney. It was as easy as telling a patient he would have to remove a certain number of teeth and order a full front plate.

"I said I'll try anything; but I didn't say malaria or typhoid or splinters shoved up my nails. The hell with limited war. Drop a bomb and we're obsolete—infantry, artillery, Medical Corps, the whole bureaucratic mess." Eros rambled on. "Where are we going to put the tourniquets when the fallout doesn't break any legs or cut any arteries? We're a medical unit with no one to treat. All the doctors are just up here to get away from their hospitals and practices and collect money in both places. The men bitch and moan and drink enough beer every night to buy Gussie Busch eight more circus wagons and horses. All the politicians support the National Guard and the Reserve, since they all get gravy out of it and an honor guard for holidays. I suppose we'd have no one left to parade except for fat old American Legion leftovers. Christ, I should've joined the Shriners. At least they sponsor charity football games." He continued, "Assuming these two weeks are a necessity, I put up with them because I can't get out of them. But reactivate this unit? I mean, really . . ."

The Colonel did not intend to compromise his unit's reputation. He couldn't stand an Article Fifteen on the record of the 229th. Both Rufus Soule and the evaluator from Corps level would be quick to pounce on any detail that could foul up activation plans. Beauregard had already decided to curtail the free time of the men, place a strict censorship upon all outgoing mail, and place the unit almost incommunicado, to maintain secrecy and military discipline. Soule was just recovering and wouldn't know about Winter's performance. Beauregard had tried reasoning and only infuriated Winter; now he would try bribery. "You know, son," his voice was calm and in control, the voice of a man inching his way toward a star on his shoulder, "there's a T O and E slot open for a physical culture sergeant in the Professional Services Section. Specialist Balter was slated for it, but I'm sure the staff could reconsider their choice if you decided to play ball on the management's team. It would mean no KP, no details, no guard mount, no inspections. You could even carry a clipboard during the Saturday review of the troops: your own clipboard with a ballpoint pen attached with blue gimp." Blue gimp; the robin's egg blue of the infantry. Everyone dreaded the infantry, but liked their decorations. Robin's egg blue was such a flattering color for most infantrymen.

The officer did flatter Winter, but he was much too lazy to accept it. Only if he were really certain that the Colonel's punishment would be to restrict him to the company area would be knuckle under at all. Beauregard took Winter's silence as a demonstration of his own persuasiveness. He pressed on. "We'll give you your own platoon. You can give them PT in the mornings, if you want. You can march them to details and to chow if you wish, even make them sing cadences: *hi de, hi de, hi de ho, let's go down and count some mo,*" Beauregard rattled at him.

Winter smiled. "Sorry, sir," he said, pressing his luck. "But how about letting me go to town tonight?"

This exasperated Beauregard. "Winter, you try my patience. You don't seem to realize that what we have been chosen for is a mission for men. If you're not patriotic, at least try and act like you got a pair. You know I could have you court-martialed for this."

"Oho, fine," Winter leaped at the idea. "Get me court-martialed. Much better than making me a sergeant. No Leavenworth in the Reserve. No stockade. Sorry, Colonel, I really don't give a damn about the other guys. If I can get out on a Section Eight, fine. Wonderful. Only don't preach. Give me a nice, quiet discharge and I won't mess up your unit. Put me on active duty with the rest of the boys, for *your* promotion, and I'll do everything I can to influence the boys in the trenches to fuck up. And I *mean* fuck up."

The Colonel showed red up to the roots of his white crew

cut. Red to the tips of his ears. He didn't know how to handle a man who didn't care. But there was no more he could say. He stood up too fast and bumped his head on an attachment hanging down from the ceiling, to which ambulance litters could be connected. He dropped to his knees and grabbed his scalp, rubbing vigorously. He belonged to the school that twists an ankle or stubs a toe and must force the injured member into immediate action. "Walk it off, walk it off," he would tell himself. Not being able to exercise his head, he felt that the circular, round-and-round movement of his hand would relieve the pressure on his scalp; make the offended area forget the pain in a frenzy of activity.

"Cool your goddam heels in the ambulance tonight, Winter, and we'll see how you respond in the morning. It's been a trying day; perhaps sunlight will bring some reason. Goddam ambulance," he muttered, still rubbing the injured spot.

"What about me, Colonel, sir?" asked the PFC guarding the prisoner. "I've been here for three hours. When do I get a relief? I'm kind of cramped, sir."

"Cramped, son? On the job, boy! You're a soldier now, not home doing whatever you do. Duty first. *Espérance!* You understand me, son?"

"I think so, sir. Only I've been on guard duty for three hours. I'm kind of tired. Don't you think . . ." he trailed off plaintively, batting his big, long-suffering PFC eyes.

"Good night, soldier. I'll see you get commended in the morning report. Winter, we'll consult further tomorrow. I'll make sure your toothbrush and toilet articles are sent over tonight. Wouldn't want any of my men to go without brushing. No fluoride in the reservoirs up here. Brushing is, for that reason, all the more important. You may be a prisoner, but you're still a soldier and hygiene must be observed."

Noting that the interview seemed to be over, the PFC, in the prescribed manner of military courtesy, yelled: "ATTEN-SHUT," and leaped to his feet in a half-crouch, bringing his rifle up to the present arms position. Winter, partly in conditioned reflex, but also mindful of the low ceiling and its hanging knobs, came to semi-attention and saluted smartly. Colonel Beauregard was so surprised at the sound of the command which bounced off the steel sides of the vehicle that he jumped to attention and began to fling his right hand to his temple to return the salute. In a precise brace of posture, in the proud Beauregard tradition, he flung his head once more against the metal litter attachment. Then he crumpled to the

71

floor. Both the PFC and Winter rushed to their prostrate commander and now four circling hands began to rub. Winter, as he rubbed around and around, incanted:

"Fillet of a fenny snake, In the cauldron boil and bake; Eye of newt, and toe of frog, Wool of bat and tongue of dog; Odor from a noncom's rear, Colonel's bump, please disappear!"

"What are you doing to my head?" The Colonel looked up at the two ministering to him.

"You seem to have a bump, Colonel. It's swelling," Winter said very seriously.

"That's where I hit my head, you idiot." The PFC kept trying to rub the Colonel's head. "Stop!" he was commanded, and the Colonel got up, putting on his hard garrison cap with the big golden eagle and the scrambled eggs signifying his rank. He opened the rear door of the ambulance and stalked out, slamming it shut behind him and bringing down the bolt installed especially to keep the prisoner in his mobile cell.

Major Marjorie Stavropolis was waiting in the khaki staff car for Colonel Beauregard, in the parking lot behind the officer's latrine. Unlike Winter, she was pleased to be going on active duty. It meant a much quicker route to promotion and a way to branch out her activities. In the Reserve, she really had no access to a General. If the unit went on active duty, however, there were bound to be officers' clubs where she could ingratiate her mammarian personality with the existing brass. Her peripheral vision had always been excellent. She would make out. Gayle had been good to her; but she felt no guilt. Her rise from lieutenant to major in seven years had been meteoric and not without its compensations on a personal level. She was free during the year to carry on in the various Veterans Hospital circles she frequented without having word of her affairs seep back to the Colonel. He sent her presents on Christmas and on her birthday and paid her dentist's bills, such as they were (although he made her visit a competitor, so as not to arouse suspicion. She did have some annoying root canal work done the previous February, so that now she couldn't bring her lips way back for a full smile without betraying too much gold. But the sum of money involved was not insignificant, and she felt pleasure in the taking of it.

So the summertime affair drifted into receptive coolness during the bulk of the year. She had no aspirations to marriage. She made no allusions to this to Colonel Beauregard. She took their relationship for what it was: a convenient relief

72

from the pressures of citizen-soldiery. It was a relief to the Colonel as well. Marjorie Stavropolis figured that by retirement, she would have laid away enough capital, plus her assured pensions from the Army and veterans' nursing, to travel back to Greece. She had always wanted to see Medea performed in the original. Even though she barely understood a word of Greek. A simple σὲ 'αγαπω learned from a waiter in Boston, would suffice under ordinary circumstances. It meant: "I love you!"

She saw her warrior then, staggering across the parking lot, pausing to rest against the fender of Colonel Harden's Cadillac, which had been driven up for him. "Goddam general practitioners," he muttered. "Licensed to steal. They all drive Cadillacs or Continentals. Hope he blows out where the rubber meets the road." He rubbed his shoe bottom along the surface of the front whitewall, smudging it. Satisfied, he walked a little more steadily toward his staff car. Colonel Harden would like to be company commander. That much Beauregard knew. He also knew that his executive officer had made disparaging remarks about the dental profession to Major Stavropolis. "It's lonely here on top, Marjorie," the Colonel said to her, when she repeated the conversation. She only giggled wickedly at the time.

She reached over and opened up the driver's side for him. He gratefully slid in behind the wheel of the Ford, sinking back into the comfort of the cushions. "Christ, what a day. Do I need a drink! That Winter. I'm going to have to do something about him. I wish I knew what."

It was hard to relax. He sat, pushing his hands against the wheel, flexing and loosening his muscles, talking into the windshield and not really at her. She sensed his difficulty and slid over toward him, putting her arms around his neck. She took off his cap with the gold braid on the brim, and removed her own summer gabardine officer's hat. She shook her head, letting the blackness of her hair sweep over her shoulders, and pulled her Colonel to her mouth. He let out a little gasp of air, going under as if he were being given oxygen for the first time after a mild coronary. It was a surprise to be enveloped by those big lips. Kissing the Major always tasted like olives. He could picture an olive grove, with the Parthenon in the background and maybe a few goats, when he kissed her. She put everything into it, working on his top lip (not very pleasurable, since the bristles of his moustache were rubbing the wrong way); then the bottom lip, chewing until she felt the urgency of his tongue. It was wild to French kiss a dentist.

73

With a smack, the suction was broken and they both breathed heavily. "Let's get that drink," said the Colonel, sure of himself again. He started the engine and moved out of the parking lot, keeping a self-imposed blackout until he hit the hardtop. For discretion's sake.

"Do you think, that if we're reactivated, there's a chance for my promotion, as soon as it's official?" she urged. The Colonel said nothing, but looked straight ahead. The military signs were posted along the road for twenty miles an hour.

"Gayle, I said, do you think my promotion will go through faster if we're activated? I mean, you want me with you, don't you? I *could* transfer out. The 452nd needs another nurse. There's a slot for me."

"There's a slot for me, too, my little Venus, and it's right in there—" The Colonel jammed his right hand up the gabardine skirt until his outstretched fingers met the resistance of the Major's black girdle.

"Gayle," she shrieked, pulling at his fist with both her hands. The Colonel momentarily took his eyes off the road.

"Amazing that a man of my age can get so excited," he thought. "I don't usually lose control like this. Ahh, the human body can only stand so much. The warrior, home from battle, taking his woman. Rightfully his . . ." he thought again, and again jammed his hand up the Major's leg. This time he hooked the first two fingers to arrive under the elastic material. He held on, lobster-like, while she struggled to free herself. She wasn't used to his taking so active a role.

The khaki staff car careened down the road heading out of the boondock area toward the main post and the safety of the officers' club. "Look out, Gayle," she screamed, having the presence of mind to jam her military high heel onto the brake. In front of them, in the middle of the left lane where they were driving, was a tank.

They came to a halt as the Colonel regained the wheel. Major Stavropolis regained the two inches of the girdle that she had lost during their skirmish and smoothed down her skirt. The Colonel flicked his high beams up toward the turret of the tank and saw that the hatch was open. He got out of the car. Lying on the road in various poses of drunken irritability was the crew of the tank. They wore fatigues and the patch of the Minuteman Division on their sleeves. They were a sergeant and three specialists. They saw the Colonel and one of them made a motion to get up and salute.

"Ahhh, sit down, Sal, he can't be RA. Must be from that

74

Reserve Hospital down the road. Want a beer, sir?" asked one of the reclining specialists. "Shut up, you idiot, and on your feet," said the sergeant, not daring to invite an officer to cocktails.

Colonel Beauregard had to brake himself down from excitement to anger; but the transition was rapid. He couldn't believe such insubordination. "You men, on your feet," he began slowly, coldly. "I want you to report in a military manner, and I want it now. I want an explanation from the senior person present as to the reasons for your tank being across a military thoroughfare. I want the reasons why you dare offer an officer an alcoholic beverage." His voice was slowly rising in pitch and intensity. "In short, soldiers, I want to know why the HELL you are lying drunk in the road."

By this time, the men had risen to their feet and were holding salutes, waiting for a returning one from the Colonel. He saluted smartly and snapped his hand to his side. They lazily dropped their right arms and grinned at each other. All except the sergeant, who was scared. "I'm terribly sorry, sir," he stammered, "but we had ignition trouble in the tank. We're on maneuvers with the Minutemen—"

"I gathered that, Sergeant," the Colonel noted sarcastically. He was beginning to enjoy himself. He hoped Marjorie was watching from the car. A hero.

"Well, sir," the sergeant started again, "we stalled across the road and we were waiting on the unit to come down and repair it. We ain't had dinner yet, and we had this case from the beer hall that we bought during mail call. Anyway, one of the boys thought, why waste? I mean, we ordinarily are off by now and already drinking; so, since the tank might have to be towed home—"

"Why didn't you place signal flares around your tank? I might have been injured by your irresponsibility."

"We did, sir, on our side of the road. We never figured anyone'd be driving on the left. We only had two flares. You can look at 'em. They're on the other side of the tank facing the oncoming vehicles. Did you get out of control or something?"

The sergeant was not being at all flippant, being one of those men who equate officers with God. The Colonel decided he would bend with the circumstances.

"Well, Sergeant, I advise you to open and empty all of your remaining beer cans and remain inside your tank until the repair crew arrives. Extremely dangerous, what you were doing. There could have been a serious accident. I won't report it this time; but I'll warn you. If you want to be a non-commissioned officer and a leader you can not allow discipline to break down. Get these men squared away and acting like soldiers."

"YES, SIR!" The sergeant snapped to attention, as did the other men. They cared a little more now, relieved at being let off. If an MP patrol had caught them . . .

Beauregard did a precise about-face and walked back to the car. He drove away slowly, staying well within the twenty mile an hour limit. It would be a good example for the men he had just left.

As soon as he was out of sight, the men began emptying—but sipped as they emptied. Pour, sip, pour, sip. Then they held the cans to their mouths, ripping imaginary grenade pins out. They lobbed the cans toward the open hatch of the tank, yelling, "BOOM" and pretending there were Viet Cong inside.

"Boom, little slope-eyed bastards; how do ya like them apples?" they continued to yell, feeling like heroes.

Marjorie could tell that the Colonel was mad at her for resisting his fingers before the tank incident. She wanted to make it up to him. He was looking straight ahead, intent on the road, speeding up toward the small airport maintained in the summer for visiting dignitaries inspecting the various National Guard divisions at their two-week encampments.

"I'm sorry, Gayle. It's just that you were so rough." He said nothing. "I'm really sorry . . . dear." That was the strongest term of affection she would allow herself. But it was special for that reason, reserved for real moments of tenderness.

She slid over in the seat once again. It was made easy for her, as the Army had not yet gotten around to providing bucket seats in their staff cars She placed a hand on his uniformed thigh. She opened her hand and laid it, palm down, rubbing up from his knee almost to where the seams were joined on the two pants legs. But not quite. He looked straight ahead. But not quite. He felt the fingers and he opened his legs, just a bit, in case the fingers might be seeking a freer access. Marjorie was wise enough to realize that when you came right down to it, the most successful way to triumph over the Colonel was on the tactile level. A few essentials usually turned the trick.

The Colonel had slowed the car again in the event that Marjorie wasn't just teasing. He'd rather have it as a surprise,

76

and if he were going to be surprised, he wanted to be ready. She *wasn't* just teasing.

Being of the old school—at least militarily—the Colonel wore his trousers equipped with buttons. Modern Army green did not include a zipper for Colonel Beauregard. He was for colonialism, and had a globe at home in his library of the British Empire under Victoria.

Fumble, fumble, snap! Fumble, fumble, snap! Fumble, fumble, snap, the Major groped in the dark. As each button came undone, Beauregard jammed his foot down on the accelerator as though through its actions her actions, too, would be accelerated. The automobile lurched forward, slowed down, lurched forward and slowed again, until at last the hand of Greece met the risen pride of the Medical Corps. At the final lurch of the Ford, a siren sounded in back of them; the Colonel's eyes flashed up to the rearview mirror in time to catch the blinking red beam of the military police. They pulled alongside and signaled him to the side of the road. Two six-footers in immaculately pressed uniforms, with spotless white puttees and helmets, walked from their vehicle. The Colonel frantically stuffed. "Bull Run," he exclaimed, a soldier to the end. Outflanked, but thinking swiftly, he pulled his khaki blouse out of his pants, covering the pelvic area. Stavropolis shimmied her rear end, just as swiftly, over to the far right-hand side of the front seat. The Colonel rolled down his front window and stuck his head out at the MPs, making sure that the golden eagle was most apparent to them. The hat was pulled down low over his eyes and they caught it full in the beams of their flashlights.

"Somethin' the matta, sir?" one of them drawled. "Seen you comin' down the road kinda jerky." He stuck the flash into the window, and saw it, sneaking from behind the folds of the Colonel's shirt.

"Outside," the MP ordered immediately, "with IDs swingin'. You too, ma'am," he indicated Stavropolis. "Outside."

Colonel Beauregard had no choice. Reservists were under the jurisdiction of the permanent base personnel, the Regular Army. The long-necked hillbilly MP withdrew his head and himself from the window of the staff car and stood a little apart, hand on his holster. He was the type that believed all the training films about counter-insurgency. You could tell when someone was a Chinese communist. Or a Viet Cong. Chinese were the most dangerous. At least the guy dressed as the Colonel was not Oriental. The second MP went around

77

to the passenger's side to open the door for Major Stavropolis. She swung her legs around and disembarked like a real lady. She fumbled in her standard-equipment black leatherette handbag, careful not to let the corporal peek in and see her Shreve, Crump and Low cuff-link box that contained her folded-up diaphragm. She produced her Reserve Forces ID card with her picture done some years before, showing her hair shoulder-length. The corporal looked at her, looked at the picture very hard, and again back to her. The IDs checked out. The MPs were disappointed. They thought they really had something.

" 'Kay," one of them said. "You clean, Major. Sorry for the commotion." He smiled, leering slightly, and threw her an MP salute with all the corners squared.

The Colonel appealed to the manhood of the MPs to forget the incident.

"Shee-it, sir," said the hillbilly, "We all of us gets hot pants now and then. Don't reckon officers is any different from us in that partic'lar respect. My pardner, here," he waved a hand at his companion, "he got him a continual hard on, like to burst. Don't stop him from bein' a sharp trooper though. Sorry to bother you, sir . . ."

The door slammed and Bearuregard drove off. The MPs laughed and laughed. "Highway handjobs. What's this ol' Army comin' to?" They laughed some more and couldn't wait to tell the boys.

"It's been a helluva day, Marjorie," was the only thing Beauregard said as they drove past the airport, past the long rows of yellow-and-green barracks, past the service club and the chapel and the enlisted men's beer hall.

Guitar-twanging, drum-beating sounds of rock and roll from the jukebox drifted out into the summer night, into the window of their car. Beebe and the Pacemakers pounded out, "I got a woman, 'way over town, she good to me. Ohhh, yeah!" And the Colonel smiled.

"What are you smiling at, Gayle?" Marjorie asked.

"I'm smiling because of the Army that never changes. The rock and roll in the jukeboxes and the beer halls. The kids drunk on a few cans and chewing on hot pencil-sausages. I love the Army, Marjorie. It's clean and honest and everyone knows what to expect. I love my family, but somehow, here it doesn't mean much to me. Not because of you, either—and don't take that wrong. It's a compliment. I love dentistry. God knows I give up plenty to stay with the Reserve. Not because of politics, either. Where can a man have real glory today?

Nowhere. Except maybe professional football. Where can a man my age have power and command men? Nowhere, in my particular situation. I'm too old for Vietnam. I'm excited, Marjorie. So help me. I'd like to go back there and whip Winter's ass personally. Or make love for four hours. Which is it? Make it three hours."

Discretion was the better part of this particular valor as they pulled into the parking area for the Camp Cannon Officers' Club.

"Let's have a little Happy Hour," Marjorie said. "Then we'll settle that special problem of yours." She smiled a promise, thinking, "Fat chance." He smiled back, having no doubts at all that she would settle it.

NINE

The lounge of the officers' club had red imitation leatherette chairs. Only permanent bases had the real thing. Camp Cannon had been used as a World War Two training center for the thousands of spillovers from Fort Dix and other eastern distribution points. With the enactment of the Armed Forces Reserve Acts of 1952 and 1955, Cannon was reopened to accommodate many of the National Guard and Reserve units on their two-week summer training period. There was pressure brought to bear on the Pentagon to outfit the officers' club properly with a large mahogany bar and dance area. But nothing ever happened.

Rufus Soule, recovered from his attack, was sitting at the largest of the low tables, wrapped in an afghan like an Indian, sipping from a frosted martini glass. Little nibbling sips, with barely a few drops entering his lips at one time: slurp, slurp. Slurp, slurp; he listened to the conversation around him. He seemed to have no more interest in picking his nose. The martini had taken up the slack. Seated around him were the Colonels Harden and Fruitman, arguing with each other, each eager to ingratiate himself with the Agency man.

Major Fugue, the chief surgeon, was sitting to Soule's left, but seemed unaware and uninterested in the conversation. In fact, his only interest since childhood was cutting. He had a knife and fork in his large, powerful hands (one of the nurses in the 229th manicured them every day that the unit was in the field). He was dissecting a bratwurst. He had cut the sausage lengthwise, then diagonally, then into quarters. Then he observed the results and ate it. "The consummate surgeon," was how he described himself. Humans posed a different problem than bratwurst, and Fugue's history proved it.

Bitterly disappointed with his residency at one of the least-favored hospitals in greater Springfield, Massachusetts, he enlisted in the Army. It was two months before Pearl Harbor, and his seniority had assured him a majority early in the war. He had remained a major through the Pacific campaign, where he gained experience. Luzon, the Philippines, Bataan, and the road back: Iwo Jima, Guadalcanal, the Philippines again, Hawaii . . . Major Fugue touched all of them. He was free from malaria, tall, sunburned, handsome in a strong, reassuring way. Men were cheered by the presence of this doctor. Wounded limbs relaxed; fevers were eased; battle fatigue cases ceased their ravings. His appearance inspired confidence. He was so calm, so unruffled. Yet he would remove normal appendixes; cut arteries; puncture spleens and livers; cause innumerable cases of peritonitis; nick the spinal cord in performing lumbodorsal sympathectomies; remove tourniquets too soon and apply others too loosely to prevent shock. He was transferred from island to island, most times with the general staff wishing a Jap sniper would pick him off.

Ironically, the only positions he could get upon discharge were in Veterans Administration Hospitals; he drifted from Navy bases to various Army installations, ending up outside of Boston. He maintained his commission and remained in the Reserve, hoping to be able to cut on the National Guardsmen in the summertime. He only dealt in an advisory capacity in the VA hospital at home, and, of course, only with old campaigners. He longed to cut a civilian, a real white-collar worker or stockbroker or advertising executive. So he practiced on his bratwurst in the officers' club, waiting for maneuvers to start.

"Butcher" Beanstock, who completed the table, was studying a chart on the price fluctuation of tallow contracts for the previous year. "I really think this price structure is going to become permanent," he was saying. "The big soap manufacturers—Lever Brothers, Colgate-Palmolive, Armour—are all going with tallow as the major ingredient. Used to be, eight per cent of a bar of soap, ordinary hand soap, was tallow. Now, appears like thirty-five to fifty per cent is the normal amount. If I had known that six months ago—well, hindsight, hindsight . . " he trailed off wistfully. His fat knuckles showed white around the rim of his glass of beer. He gripped it tightly, as if afraid it might get away from him. He, too, had a plate of bratwurst, with sauerkraut, set before him, and was eyeing it critically. He spent no wasted effort in the dissection of the bratwurst. He just kept it in his mouth longer, chewing slowly, examining it with his tongue, until he could announce to the gathering: "Seventy per cent chopped pork shoulder, inferior Government Inspected Grade Three; thirty per cent beef waste, probably Florida cattle; plus dashes of pepper, both black and red, plus sodium nitrate." Then came the swallow and the satisfied look, as if he had just beaten the panel of *What's My Line?*

Colonels Harden and Fruitman were getting drunk. Both were very concerned with their respective practices, in view of the recent developments. They pumped Soule: "What exactly is the operation to be?" they asked. "Will we be activated for more than a year? Will there be any danger to the men—or us? Will we be sent out of the continental United States? Will the Minuteman Division as a whole be involved—or just the 229th? Does this precede a general mobilization of the country? Will it carry campaign ribbons with it?"

"Now, gentlemen—" Soule laughed, "all in good time. The Colonel will be here shortly and we'll commence then."

Pleased at being the prime mover in the operation, Soule hugged the afghan tighter around himself. He had changed his string tie to a more formal black one for nighttime wear; it hung down outside the blanket. All the doctors of the 229th had agreed that it was important for Soule to keep warm after his ordeal.

As for the afghan, one of the nurses crocheted, tatted, and knitted all during camp. One summer she had made argyle socks for all the officers, and plain green for all the enlisted men—one hundred and fifty pairs of green. She had started the afghan the previous weekend; then, fingers flying on the Trailways bus up to Camp Cannon from Boston, she had almost completed it. When the fit hit Soule, she moved into high gear; hooking, braiding, cross-stitching, and biting off loose ends. She presented the afghan with a card: "To Mr. Rufus Soule from the Nurses of the 229th General Hospital—get well real quick." She figured that it was important he stay warm. It was such a pretty afghan, all purple and nubby with little balls of wool all over the place, that Soule decided to wear it to the officers' club, along with his black string tie.

"Basic black goes well with any color," he reasoned, picking balls of wool off his afghan for a change.

"Well, all the troops are assembled, I see," Colonel Beauregard roared in greeting. He was entirely calmed down, with Stavropolis at his side prepared for the worst. Everyone hastily stood up to greet them. Soule's martini looked awfully good to the Colonel; he ordered a round for himself and Stavropolis. He was asserting himself and she allowed him to do so, smoothing her skirt down primly, almost covering her knees. It wouldn't do at that particular juncture to have skirts riding up. That was for offices, not for staff meetings. The drinks came, plus another round for everyone else, and the Colonel removed a small loose-leaf notebook from his jacket pocket. With pen poised, ball point at the ready, he told Soule to commence the briefing on the operation.

Soule spread his hands on the table, raising and lowering his fingers like a spider doing push-ups, and paused for effect.

"The first week of summer camp, the unit will function normally, supporting the Minuteman Division as a field hospital. You will be arousing no suspicions and doing nothing out of the ordinary. I have an assistant arriving tomorrow who will act as my secretary and liaison officer with Washington and the local townspeople, to assure the absence of leaks. The men and women will have off-duty hours, assuming they can maintain security. This includes any weekend pass they would normally be entitled to. On Monday, 18 August, security will commence; in short, your mission begins 18 August . . ."

Across the room, someone had put a quarter in the jukebox for three songs. Officers' clubs were not allowed rock and roll, unlike the service clubs of the enlisted men. The Confederacy had left its mark on the Army of the United States: in its rhythms, its bluegrass country music, and the easy drawl of its speech. At the grass roots were farmers from Mississippi, itinerants from the dust bowls of the Southwest, red-necks from Georgia, sodbusters from Alabama, drifters from Tennessee. The music in the enlisted men's jukeboxes—from Fort Knox to Hamburg, from Korea to Fort Benning, from Fort Leonard Wood to the Mekong Delta—echoed of guitars and blues. For if the memories of home had been good, none of them ever would have left. The music was the good part, and they carried it with them.

In the officers' clubs it was old Dinah Shore and McMullen blouses: Enoch Light and the Light Brigade, Troy Donahue singing "Summer Place"; rather than The Mamas and The Papas, or any of their cousins. Here were men who found themselves in the Army mostly by accident or from lack of any other reason save expediency. They touched, lingered briefly, drank the officers' club Scotch or bourbon, and returned to wherever they had come from without ever learning most of the slang which made the Army for everyone else.

The first song of the set had just finished; the automatic arm of the Seeburg Special began to swing down upon Kay Starr and her echo chamber.

Warrant Officer Kenny Keohane, seated nearby, could stand it no longer. He had been raised in the rock and roll tradition. He insisted on the beat to accompany his drinking. It was impossible to control himself—his Celtic sentimentality was too overpowering. He felt he carried great peat bogs in his soul; the leprechauns clawed at his shoulders; Shaw and

83

Lady Gregory corresponded in his dreams. But Black Label, not Guinness's Stout, had coursed through his system since three that afternoon, and it was then ten-thirty. So he carried his plea to the colonel. Not for Mother Machree, but for the Barrack Room Ballads and the songs of his enlisted past. The malt had dulled his good sense.

"Colonel, sir," Keohane reported to the next table, "do you think it's at all possible that we get a new selection of songs for the jukebox while we're here at Cannon?"

His query had been forceful. It was obvious that he was treading on dangerous ground, interrupting the Colonel's briefing. Spittle had already formed in the corners of Soule's mouth; but it dried quickly at Keohane's intervention. He wrapped his afghan around him like a sulking child told to retire in the middle of his favorite TV program. He made his irritation plain to the Colonel by his silence. Keohane waited for an answer, oblivious.

"Do you think we can get a different selection of songs for the jukebox?" he asked again.

"Can't you see we're discussing something rather important, Keohane?" the Colonel said.

"Well, I know, sir; you discuss something important every time you meet with the staff. But you realize, sir, I don't want to sound presumptive, sir, but morale is important to the officers also. We remain much more effective with an evening of pleasure behind us. I don't mean unwarranted pleasure either, sir." He was respectful. "Just the simplicity of relating to music that touches us."

Soule was sinking down into the afghan, pulling his head lower and lower into the enveloping folds of the purple wool. He knew when he was being upstaged. He made his right hand in the folds of the blanket very stiff, fingers outstretched, and banged the edge of his hand into the palm of the left, keeping up the callus which he had worked so diligently to grow in the first place.

"Growing the callus on your effective karate hand," he had been told in training school outside Washington, "is like growing flowers. It takes care and constant work, love, and attention. It is an effort of the will as well as the flesh. If done correctly, your callus, like a rare and beautiful flower, will take root and bear fruit." This was a literal translation taken from the Chinese instructor, recorded on tape and transcribed onto mimeographed sheets, then passed around, one to a trainee; although the English was never quite so effective as watching the slight, polite instructor, black belt around his waist, singsong the ritual to his students.

Soule worked at putting himself into a killer trance: "Will yourself into a little ball, like a porcupine; will yourself into a little compact ball, like a porcupine; will yourself into a little dynamic compact ball, like a porcupine," he muttered to the various portions of his body, shrinking down farther and farther into the afghan, his head almost disappearing. He brought his knees up against his chest and bundled his head right down next to them, still muttering—"Then, then," building up a crescendo of noise—"THEN—" He leaped out of his seat, upsetting bratwurst and sauerkraut, beer and frosted martini, and whistled his right hand right by the head of Keohane. The blow, if it had landed, would have broken the soft bone across the bridge of Keohane's nose, sending the splinters, jagged and sharp, into the softer material of the brain. As it was, the right hand continued down onto Butcher Beanstock's dinner plate, severing his sausage into two separate parts. It was one of the neatest cleaving jobs Beanstock had ever seen. He admired the fact that there were no split ends on the severed sections of the sausage.

Soule returned to his afghan, calm as hell. Keohane got the hint and did a hurried about-face. Strategic retreats he knew about. Back with his boys, he sipped a Black Label—a long, thirsty, disaster-avoiding sip—and brooded about being reactivated. "I kind of like Kay Starr anyway," he grudgingly agreed.

"But we'll travel along, singin' a song, side byyy si-ide," the stereo sounded, and a pair of nurses from the unit got up to dance with each other. Slowly and formally they encircled each other's waists and did a box step around and around on the small dance area. No one thought it strange. The male officers were only about twenty-four hours from their wives and the nurses hadn't started to look as good as they would in a few days. Or even after a few excise-tax-free drinks. Time was on their side. The nurses could afford to wait. They circled slowly around and around, waiting for their chances.

Keohane switched to boilermakers and sang along with the record, now playing a second time. "Don't know what's comin' tomorrow, maybe it's trouble and sorroww, but we'll travel the road, sharin' our load, side by si-ide—"

He was joined by two young lieutenants, both interns at home; one of them married, the other engaged. They were at the stage where wives meant more to them than their country; activation terrified them. They told themselves it was their medical career that would be jeopardized at this time. They

85

had to return to their hospitals. They couldn't take a chance on missing favored residencies. Actually, it was because they were horny. They wouldn't look at the nurses who danced with each other.

At Colonel Beauregard's table, Rufus Soule was outlining the duties of the 229th General Hospital. "First, gentlemen, and lady," he said, "our purpose: the government is planning a punitive and definitive action against a hostile Caribbean nation. This will be accomplished mainly through landings and air assault by self-exiled natives of the island. It will be supported by units from our Armed Forces—naval, air, and army. As proposed, this is to be effected around the first of next year, just when the island is lulled into relaxation by the political holidays enforced by their leaders. Even though in extreme poverty, they are forced to take days off from their farming to celebrate. The rank and file want to be liberated. They want to export their cigars. And it is painful for us to coexist with an offending gnat like this island in our own hemisphere. Not only painful, but embarrassing. We've chosen now to begin doing something about it. The Pentagon thinks it is a good idea to show our overall preparedness by utilizing some of our finer Reserve units to support this operation."

Colonel Beauregard interrupted, "But generally we function as a rear echelon hospital. Our major experience is not in the field."

"Ahhh," answered Soule, "this is also the Pentagon's idea. Show our versatility, our patriotism. This is part of the reason you train as a field hospital this summer and not in cantonment." He continued, ignoring the questioning looks around him. "As I said, this first week you will conduct normal operations, assisting the Minuteman Division. They won't be involved in your maneuvers the following week, except to provide covering fire for you and enough authenticity so that I may observe the performance of the 229th. It would be unfair to say that you are the only hospital under consideration for this honor. And may I underscore the word *honor*. Think of the publicity inherent in successful military operations of this nature. Magazine coverage. News media. Television and the newsreels. There you'll be, with your boys—perhaps a national parade in Washington after the victory. Local parades once you reach home. Testimonial dinners, tributes, certain promotions for you officers. I would be proud also. Somewhere in the background; for you wouldn't see me again. My duties take me where they must. You understand. I can't linger over memories. Anonymous. We prefer it."

Colonel Harden couldn't wait any longer. He nervously interrupted: "The men already are spreading rumors about activation. What do we do to control them and still keep up some kind of morale? We don't want parents and wives on our necks if this comes off."

Soule had the answer. "Low pressure. Soft sell. This is the key. Push patriotism and the rewards of a successful operation. Mostly, they will be kept in the dark about the real purpose. All they need to know is that they *may* be activated if the necessity arises. I say, emphasize *may*. Don't let them know this is conditional upon their performance next week. They can have normal off-duty hours for themselves and normal fifty per cent on, fifty per cent off, for the weekend. After activation the clamps will go on. Not yet. We want a good, solid demonstration of Reserve effectiveness. Pentagon wants it impromptu, not rehearsed. Show the men reacting to stress as in actual conflict; the way they do in Vietnam. Proves what the brass is thinking about American preparedness anyway, even for the citizen soldier. Eventually, the 229th will prove the validity of maintaining an active Reserve."

"What will the procedures be?" Harden interrupted again. "Most of us are doctors and dentists, not tacticians."

"I've got the plans with me," Soule said, allowing himself a tight smile. "Wednesday, 18 August, which is a week from this coming Wednesday, 11 August, we shall break camp under blackout conditions at night. We'll load the hospital onto trucks, and your vehicles that were brought up from Boston. By prescribed route, we'll travel to rendezvous X, on the shore of the St. Lawrence. From there, the next morning at 0630 hours, one hundred and fifty men, thirty-five officers, eleven nurses, and the five WACs of your outfit—minus fifteen men who will act as Aggressors—will take pontoon rafts with half-tentage and row to one of the islands in the Thousand Island group. They will establish a hospital, complete with fifty beds, dental emergency operative, X-ray and neuropsychiatric facilities. This will be effected within a perimeter already presumably established by native troops, with assistance from special advisors of the Army. Naturally, full battle conditions will prevail. The small force of aggressors will attempt to disrupt, to the best of their ability, the landing and the hospital establishment. This, in brief, is your assignment. Questions, now?"

Keohane and the young lieutenants watched Beauregard's

table with suspicion. But all they saw were expressions and moving lips. No sound reached them over Kay Starr.

Colonel Beauregard had been thrilled with the prospects after the job was finished. He was confident that the maneuver was a simple and readily accomplished fact. Colonels Harden and Fruitman were both doctors and opportunists. They didn't like the deal they had gotten themselves into, but were both determined to make the best of a bad situation. They both, in their own minds, weighed the fiscal possibilities of postwar heroics. Dr. Fruitman envisioned photos of himself in battle gear in frames of black wood on the walls of the waiting room of his office. His women patients could mull over the virility of their gynecologist. ("Nothing like a manly gynecologist. Make their little dinguses relax. Make them have confidence in me. Be good for my practice eventually. Write off the year as a net loss.")

Stavropolis felt her shoulders shaking silently, as from some sudden chill. She couldn't control it. Her arms and upper body were growing gooseflesh. She projected herself into the staff car of the Joint Chiefs, leading the parade in Washington, the silver eagles of her rank shining proudly on her shoulders. Colonel Stavropolis! She could take on a General for sure, then. Her man would always have to outrank her. But what if Gayle were made a General? Maybe their destinies *were* linked! That thought calmed her down.

Major Fugue exercised the tips of his fingers, making sure they were flexible. He checked his nails and cuticles for dirt. His handsome lips drew back over even white teeth in his most charming smile. With victory, perhaps an appointment to a major civilian hospital, perhaps—oh, it was too exciting to conjure—prefrontal leucotomies, cholecystectomies, thyroidectomies, gastrectomies. His hands were independent of his body now, moving without control, slicing, cutting, probing. His right hand had to grab the left to stop its gyrations.

Butcher Beanstock was thinking of meat, scarce meat, tough-to-obtain meat. Ever since Vietnam prices had soared. Now they would go higher! Top of the round, chuck, brisket. Choice—that he could mark prime. His influence would allow him to allocate all the meat he wanted from his slaughterhouse to the butcher shops of the Boston area. Coupon books like the good old days. He didn't even want to think the words "Black Market." Someone might notice him licking his lips. Someone might notice his thought-bubble. He sweated greasily, until dark patches showed under his armpits and his forehead shone as if it had been rubbed with neatsfoot oil. "The wife can run the slaughterhouse; I'll direct as an absentee. Bring back the good old days," he thought. "There's no wind that doesn't blow some good . . . let it blow on Beanstock, O Lord, let it blow on Beanstock."

Colonel Beauregard felt himself coldly efficient. He kept his mind on business, asking Soule, "How soon after the operation will we be on orders to activate?" It was important to pass on the reins at home smoothly, especially the fluoride in the Brookwood Reservoir.

"There is an extremely good chance," Soule said smugly, "that after camp you will be temporarily assigned to your homes, yet on alert. I would suggest getting your respective affairs in order. You may be called at any time after that . . . if you are chosen." He nodded, to signal that he had finished, and pulled the afghan tighter around his shoulders. There was a slight chill. "Call me Rufus," he added as an afterthought. "Let's have another round, take the chill off. And please *do* call me Rufus. It's an old family name."

Colonel Beauregard called for another round. He had had enough; but everyone else seemed more than willing to stay on. He looked over at Marjorie Stavropolis and tried to catch her eye. She was staring at Soule. "Marjorie always did like afghans," thought Beauregard, wanting desperately to take her out of the officers' club and back to the Ford.

The two nurses who had been dancing with each other got tired and returned to their seats. "I'd swear you've led before," said one of them.

"Let's have two more rye and gingers," said the other, flushing slightly.

TEN

"Open up the doors." The banging woke up Eros Winter, who, resigned to being imprisoned in a company ambulance, had curled up with two blankets on one of the long seats and fallen asleep. The young PFC guarding him had removed his boots and leaped up to pull them on, knowing he must appear in full uniform for the brass he suspected was knocking.

"Open up these doors." The banging continued and Winter stared hard into the darkness at the rear of the ambulance. He was thinking quickly, "What could the Colonel want now?" Then he yelled, "Knock, knock, here's a knocking indeed! If a men were porter of hell-gate, he should have old turning the key."

Winter felt lucky being the prisoner; *he* could remain covered and warm. The PFC unbolted the doors and Eldor von Liebert burst into the ambulance, brushing aside the surprised guard, who had left his weapon underneath the bench where he had been sleeping.

"You can't come in here," the guard floundered; but Winter had already leaped from his warmth and together they pinned the young man's arms behind him. Von Liebert placed his hand over the guard's mouth. He tried to bite, but von Liebert increased the pressure and the mouth couldn't open against the German's hard hand.

"If you keep your tongue quiet, you can drink with us. I shall cause no trouble; merely, I want to talk to my friend. Shake your head if you agree and we let you go."

The guard shook his head in agreement and they let him go. Eldor unzipped his field jacket and removed two bottles that he had stuck into his pants top. "See, Liebfraumilch. Cheap in the United States, only one dollar twenty-five cents a bottle. Cheaper still in Germany. Not cold, but good. I have had one already myself tonight and I decided to come and talk with you about what you are doing." He pulled one of the corks and passed the bottle to Winter, who took a long swallow and passed it back. A little of the wine dribbled down his chin and neck onto his T-shirt.

"You're right; not cold, but good," Eros said. "Where the hell did you get these?"

"Do you think I go into battle without a bit of courage? You believe the myth about the invincible Germans, I take it.

90

Well, it's true. But I bring up five bottles Liebfraumilch in my duffel, each surrounded by five pair of stockings, winter issue, and separated so they do not bounce together and make all my uniforms smell of wine."

Winter smiled. It was a pleasant surprise. He was sure the German was coming around to his opinion of the maneuvers. Eldor poured the guard a canteen cup full of wine and handed it to him. The guard was too intimidated at this point to do anything but take the cup, retire to his bench, and drink it. He was thinking about his congressman and whom he could borrow some stationery from to write Washington.

"Well, Eldor," Winter started, "I'm not quite sure how we're going to pull this thing off, but I'm glad you're in it with me. Of course, you're lucky. All you have to do is say you're going back to Germany and you're out of it. I've got to prove to them that I'm an utter misfit, or so detrimental that it's not worth their while to keep me in the unit. Not good for the ego. But it's smart. I've got to save the kid for better things. Another swallow." Winter reached for the wine.

"But you're wrong, Eros. It's not just yourself that counts. There is the importance of your country. Can you turn them down if they need you? Would you fight to defend your freedoms?"

"No, *my* freedom," Winter replied. "Singular."

"This is not the spirit that built America," Eldor said.

"Just the spirit that built up my family," said Eros. "I'm sure the Pentagon wishes we didn't exist. But now that we're here, no one can get rid of us," he added. "Now, Washington is harassing us, probably to prove that the Reserve may be more than just a dust and beer operation, and that it's worth the millions of dollars the government spends on us every year. The truth is, that it *is* nothing more than an excuse to sop up two weeks of dust and beer. A little training and a big joke, just to promote a few paunchy dentists and lawyers who don't know that World War Two is over. Peacetime irrationalism, that's what it is. Bread and circuses, so we can remember the goddam Minutemen."

"You are, I think, a cynic," Eldor said. "An opportunist."

"*Realismo,* I believe," Eros countered. "I can afford to believe in it. They just want us for prestige, a showcase for the system. Only under duress am I a part of it, and I want out."

They talked and drank; the guard listened, thinking them both mad. Winter held his wine well and was glad he didn't have to spend the night in one of the personnel tents, for it had started to rain outside. The tents leaked. They were cold. The sunbaked dirt, hard and dry during the day, would turn to mud. The ambulance was warm and the wine felt good in his belly. The rain came down heavily now and beat a bongo on the roof of the ambulance. There was thunder in the distance, moving closer, down from Canada. Nights were never really summery up at Camp Cannon. Winters saw snowfalls drifting in places to twenty and thirty feet. Spring was probably the most pleasant time; even then, the flowers lived briefly, starting late, finishing early. July was usually hot. By August, what the Canadians called the *sang-froid* season had set in. Unpredictably hot days with sudden rain. Blankets at night were a rule then. August seemed like mid-September to the troops used to the more clearly defined weather of Boston.

Eldor von Liebert, in the middle of the second battle, began to talk of home. It had been a long time since he felt relaxed enough to say anything about his family. He went on about his father justifying in his mind the long periods of absence, the distance between them, and the longing that he felt. Winter was a good listener. He understood the effect of wine, or liquor, or loneliness, and he preferred to remain aloof, a sounding board for anyone else's weakness. When von Liebert had talked himself out and slurred his words to the point of incoherence, mingling German with English, Eros told him it was time to sleep.

"Back to the rack," he said, and smiled at his own sobriety. It was rare, under military conditions.

Eldor was drunk. This was rare, also. He grew sullen, defiant. He lurched to his feet and slammed out of the ambulance, slipping in the muddy ground of the parking lot, The rain was falling very hard and he stood in it, bare-headed, his fatigue cap in his hand. He threw his head back at the rain, letting it catch him full in the face. Suddenly, he straightened up. His hands went to his neck and he began to unbutton his jacket. He took it off. Then he took off his T-shirt, sucked in his chest and felt the cold water on his shoulders and back. In the distance he could see the tents, outlined large and darker than the night they were superimposed upon. It was long past lights-out. From the headquarters tent a recording of "Taps" had spent itself, the trumpet sound dented from repetition. No one outside of headquarters had heard it. The sergeants had confiscated flashlights and enforced a no-reading ban after lights-out.

Eldor braced and started to march toward the tent where his cot waited. "Auslanders, auslanders," he muttered to himself, feeling like a discovered spy who preferred to put on his own uniform so as not to be shot in a disguise. He marched, naked to the waist, feeling like the master of the rain and the wind. Alcohol had made him bold; he thought of the bank vice-president's daughter in Boston, with whom he had been so polite. "She would like to see me now," he boasted to himself. "I would show her who the timid teller would be."

He sang as he marched toward his tent in a strong baritone, which he supplemented by saying "BOOM," very loud, on the ends of the lines.

> Die Fahne hoch, die Reihen fest Geschlossen, BOOM,
> S.A. marschiert in ruhig festen Schritt—BOOM,
> Kameraden die Rotfront und Reaktion erschossen—
>   BOOM—
> Marschieren mit uns in ihrem Geiste mit . . .

"BOOM," he yelled, the final drum roll sounding from his chest. He came to an abrupt halt and clicked his heels together. How strange, he thought, to have remembered the forbidden Horst Wessel song. How strange the memory was, for he barely remembered ever hearing it. The thought sobered him and he almost softened But the shock of the rain straightened him up quickly, his dog tags bouncing metallically on his naked chest.

He made his decision and put his head inside the entrance flap of the nearest tent, where he knew Sergeant Baer was sleeping. "Jew," he screamed. "Swine of a Jew." Then he turned and ran, ran toward his own tent, thinking he was surely being hunted, running for his life, certain the big sergeant would be after him. His heart flip-flopped and he went sprawling into the mud, covered with the wetness and filth of the clay ground. He had run over a support rope and thought that Baer would find him and kill him. When nothing touched him on the ground, he leaped to his feet, gasping for breath, hearing whistling sounds in his ears. Adrenalin coursed through his arms and legs; he raced into his own tent and found his cot in the darkness.

He felt elated. No one had caught him; he had defied the American military authority. He was too excited to sleep. At last he had done a brave thing and spoken out. He threw his soaking jacket and T-shirt to the foot of his cot, removed his boots and pants, and threw the two khaki blankets over his wet, cold body. The tent roof spun around when he tried to shut his eyes; it was only after concentrating on one particular spot, staring at it very hard until his eyes hurt, that he was able to pass out triumphantly.

Only Skippy Dennis had seen him come in. Dennis had always been frightened of rain, and thunder made sleep out of the question. Only the presence of so many people around had made it bearable; so he got up and bed-checked all the men in his charge with his flashlight. The usual procedure would merely reassure him that there was a lump approximating a human under the blankets (even a well-placed pillow would do).

Dennis liked to look in silence on the faces of his men. "His boys," he called them. If someone had particularly regular features, nose a bit aquiline, chin a bit unbearded, nostrils a bit dilated, breathing a bit unsteady, he would stop and examine him. "Everyone looks so peaceful, when they're asleep," he pondered, musing particularly over one Italian boy who, during the day, was the biggest wise-ass in the unit. The full mouth, usually stretched in a grin or a leer, was closed and serious, the brow relaxed. The contrast of the dark, slick hair against the whiteness of his laundry bag, which he used for a pillow, made Dennis almost want to put out his hand and caress the head of the sleeping boy. "I understand your violence by day, *caro*," he whispered to himself, continuing on his rounds.

Von Liebert had made no attempt to conceal his absence. Dennis decided that it was not worth the effort to get himself dressed and go out into the rain. No one was worth going out into the rain for. He could report him in the morning. People who made trouble made him nervous.

So he lay awake, thinking and listening, and jerked out of his musing involuntarily when von Liebert came racing in. Dennis could tell that he was drunk; he had heard the fall and the curses outside the tent, and could hear the rapid breathing. He wondered about the German. Did he have something going with Winter? Monk Lassick had told him that all homosexuals suspect every other man of being the same way. "It's only natural, my boy," Lassick had told him. So naturally he suspected Winter and von Liebert, wishing he could suspect himself and someone in the 229th. Then he hated himself for his weakness and tried to think about sailing.

He thought very hard about how to tie clove hitches: the imaginary moves of the rope, slowly crossing over and looping through and pulling taut. The process would lull him to sleep. Everyone has their own gimmicks for insomnia. Clove

94

hitches were better than being forced into thinking about his particular frustrations.

"Fuck the German and Winter, anyway," he finally said to himself, and smiled at his use of the Army vernacular. He would never have said it at home.

But Sergeant Sonya Faust never heard the storm, paid no attention to the rain, wasted no thoughts about life. Her stubby fingers moved rapidly over the keyboard of her Royal, typing out special orders, menus, daily bulletins, and rosters. Type, carriage release, type, keep the margins. Never make a mistake; for mistakes are never tolerated on military documents. She typed by candlelight in the headquarters tent, grinding out the material like a great fat, soft, amorphous machine. The flesh of her great arms jangled from the fingers' pressure on the keys, clickety click, clickety click, oiling the wheels of the 229th General Hospital.

It was six-thirty on Sunday morning, the next day. The men had eaten breakfast and were in formation. "Publish the orders," commanded Colonel Beauregard, doing a smart about-face.

The rain of the night before had given way to intermittent sunshine. But it was a painful morning. The shock of a five o'clock rising was apparent on everyone's face—except the ones who felt their impending mission was serious. They were a hard core of fanatics. They had shaved with cold water from the lister bags, so that their faces shone with the scrapings. They cared about appearances. Military and sharp. It was a holy undertaking for the Colonel and for Major Fugue, his set of Swedish steel scalpels hooked onto his pistol belt alongside his canteen. He was looking forward to battle-field promotion to colonel and hadn't shaved a narrow ridge along his upper lip. Colonels were distinguished. Moustaches were distinguished bits of hair.

Sergeant Lennie Baer stood in front of his company, facing the staff officers, proudly sucking in his belly, proud in the starched fatigues that his wife had grumbled about preparing. "But you won't get it there anymore," he thought, remembering the old Irving Berlin song, "This Is the Army, Mr. Jones"—not smiling, but feeling tough and independent. The military laundry on post would do his stiff-starching without complaining. Stiffer than a wife could do.

Chaplain Papps, with his assistant, Specialist-Fourth Class Waldo Reed, stood apart on a little knoll overlooking the

95

scene. Papps had carefully chosen that little knoll as the spot from which to survey his flock. He was pleased with the prospect of administering last rites and treating battle fatigue cases with words quoted from John Wesley and his own impromptu interpretations.

Cameroons Jackson, looking too big for his faded fatigues, stood in front of his platoon and listened for orders. He believed explicitly in chain of command. "I'm salutin' the Natural Order. If I had a bar on my shoulder, I'd expect a salute, too," was what he would say, when questioned about his loyalty. He hated chaos and could cope with it only through the violence which he abhorred—which passed him by mostly because of his bulk. When he had order, he could lie back, let the world parade, and nothing could bother him. His daddy had told him and his six brothers and sisters to pay attention and keep their noses clean and worry about doing a good job on their own. Cameroons like to sing, and his favorite song was "John Henry," sung to the beat of the hammer, with a grunt on the ends of phrases. His wife would readjust to Army life, he was sure. She was a good woman. Understanding. Patient with him whenever he came home drunk (which was seldom); patient with his lusting after other women (which was seldom, since he never got too many opportunities); and best of all she was a good mother. That was most important for a woman to be—a good mother. She'd readjust to Army life, and he was already prepared.

The men, officers and enlisted, split into their two complements, were given the "at ease" command and came to parade rest, feet spread apart, arms folded across their backs. They were unusually sharp that morning, but apprehensive. A little scared, they were forced to think of themselves more in terms of soldiery than they ever had done before. No one made wisecracks in ranks, or farted, or belched. They all knew and all saw Soule behind the Colonel. He had traded his crepe-soled shoes for a pair of 13D combat boots, making that much of a concession to camp protocol. Over his shirt and black string tie, which was still visible, he wore a field jacket with all insignia removed. He wanted to make it clear that there was no overlapping on the part of government agencies. He listened wearily to the rehearsed procedures of military tradition. Once more the 229th was ordered to attention.

"COMPANEE," yelled Colonel Harden, the executive officer.

"COMPANEE," echoed all the subordinate staff officers.

"PLATOOON," immediately yelled the platoon leaders, in

96

case no one had heard the previous order.

"SQUAD," yelled the respective squad leaders, jealous of their prerogatives and wanting to get into the act.

"ATTEN-HUT," commanded Harden and again the unit sucked in bellies, threw out chests, held a few breaths, and waited. When Harden was satisfied with the time it took everyone to cover down and straighten up, he yelled, "AT EASE"—and again the unit relaxed.

"What foolishness," thought Soule, the omniscient observer, feeling coldly efficient and superior. He was the elite of the cold war. He and his fellows moved behind the scenes where the battles were really fought. "This is all just window dressing; poor slobs, to have to be picked as our pawns in this deal. But a good show for my benefit."

Colonel Beauregard stepped in front of his troops to give them the word for posterity. At his elbow hovered Sonya Faust, breathing in short jerky breaths as the pleasure of taking dictation from the Colonel quickened her metabolic processes. Her ball-point Piggy-Back refills nestled in her breast pocket, warm and full of ink, ready to enter the lists in the event of a failure in her regular pen.

"Men and women of the 229th General Hospital," Beauregard began. "There have been a lot of ugly rumors about some secret mission, during the past twenty-four hours. I want to clear up these rumors, for they are nothing more than that. We intend to carry out the conventional activities of ANACDUTRA, i.e., we expect to support the Massachusetts Minuteman Division in their war maneuvers, supplying hospital beds and facilities and evacuation maintenance. Now,"—and here he paused, kicking the dirt, as though he was experiencing difficulty in finding the right words. It was merely for effect—"We are going to have a rather special exercise the second week, that I want to tell you all about. Mr. Soule of Washington's Central Agency will be passing among you—"

"With an offering plate—" came a voice from the obscurity of the administrative complement. There was immediate silence as the Colonel glared at the impassive ranks and the sergeants in charge scurried into the rear to find the offender, who had used a falsetto voice. After a while they found no one and the Colonel was forced to continue.

He pawed the dirt a little longer, sheepishly, and then, with renewed determination, pressed on: "We shall conduct a joint exercise with the infantry and artillery of the Minuteman Division concerning Civil Defense in the upper part of the

97

New York State region. I am not at liberty to reveal our official destination, but it will involve land and water operations. We are to be the medical support unit. There will be organized resistance from an Aggressor force recruited from our own ranks. Some of you men will be designated Aggressors; you will train separately, in the confusion and diversionary tactics we could expect if we were in actual conflict. Do you read me so far?" He didn't expect an answer; he just needed a place to stop for breath and make sure no one was giving him the finger. This often happened in unit formations. They still resisted khaki. His eyes rested on Eros Winter for any sign of insolence. But the specialist stared straight ahead, giving no clue to his thoughts.

Winter had been released in a sort of general amnesty brought on by morning and the Colonel's satisfaction. For Beauregard, who was getting into the swing of summer training, had been administered what he liked to call "an exceptionally good boff" before breakfast by the unpredictable Stavropolis. In this burst of post-coital generosity, the Colonel figured that one night under guard would be enough to force Winter to give way to reason. But Winter had no warmth of post-coital tenderness. He had been released just in time to miss breakfast, and felt mean and stiff.

He mistrusted the move, naturally, and kept glancing around, expecting to be snapped up by the post MPs and kept incommunicado for the duration. But all seemed to be forgiven and the Colonel ignored him. Eros was still confused; he stayed quiet, looking for some clue to the Colonel's plans for him. He was much too complicated in his approach to people. He distrusted their motives—either attributing too little intelligence to the characters he encountered, or accusing them of such subtleties of nature in his own mind that *they* would have been shocked.

Eldor stood next to him in formation, very hungover and not remembering much about the previous night. But he kept a weather eye out for Sergeant Baer, who suddenly seemed to take no notice of him. He, too, was suspicious, or felt twangs of conscience. He hated to admit to himself that he had lost control. But his military haircut made him feel better. It made him stand tall, as a trooper should.

The minds of the men in the ranks were on their large intestines. The typical eight-course Army breakfast was quite different from grabbing a glass of instant energy, or a cup of black coffee back home, while their wives lay in bed. It was a difficult transition and their bodies cried out in need. The only positive aspect about Army eating was that it broke up the monotony. So did trips to the latrine.

So they began to fidget, shifting weight from one leg to another, as the Colonel explained the training: "Your complement commanders have the roster lists for your various assignments. We will spend the morning going over these assignments and making sure everyone understands, understand? All right, any questions?" He didn't expect or want any; but someone raised a hand. The sergeant in charge naturally tried to discourage this by grimacing at the soldier; but the soldier, undaunted, said, "Sir, I have a question." The Colonel, waiting to dismiss the formation and retire to his own personal latrine, stopped.

"Will we," the soldier began, "be free to go down to the quartermaster supply this summer and pick up four extra pairs of low-quarter shoes?" It was the inevitable question, the unnecessary question, the question that puckers the sphincter and makes it wait. The men in the ranks groaned.

"Soldier, we'll talk about time off some other time. Take down that man's name, Sergeant," Beauregard said to no sergeant in particular. Naturally, all the sergeants rushed to get his name, brandishing clipboards and attached pencils, their special sign of rank. The young man had no name tag on his fatigue shirt. Unthinkable. Hadn't everyone been warned to take appropriate action with respect to name tags?

"Unforgivable," said Skippy Dennis. "What name, please?"

"What's your name, trooper?" said Lennie Baer menacingly. The soldier cowered.

"Unfor-fucking-thinkable," said Cameroons Jackson, unforgiving and towering over the private. "Sound off your name and sound it off like you got a pair."

Before he had a chance to answer, Baer was yelling at the Colonel: "He ain't got a name tag, sir; he ain't got no name tag." The field first sergeant had to be colloquially correct. So the Colonel was forced, despite his urgency and the urgency of all, to deliver a lecture on the use of name tags. It was in the Army Regulations and Beauregard commanded by the book.

"You *will*," he said, "repeat, WILL, wear name tags at all times in order that your superiors may identify you. We want the 229th to be uniform and SHARP, get me? No one unit is sharp with some men in name tags and others not. Army AR 114-10 states that all personnel will at all times be adorned with name tags. You will henceforth be so adorned!"

Sergeant Jackson led the whimpering boy off by the arm.

He had also forgotten his mandatory sewing kit.

By the time the Colonel dismissed the formation, there was an extraordinary scramble toward the latrines that Winter and von Liebert had dug the night before. Men crowded around the movable wooden shack that was dragged into place over the six holes, waiting in line like so many applicants for unemployment compensation. They only had fifteen minutes before inspection and the beginning of the hospital day.

The Colonel ambled back to his one-holer, secure in the knowledge that his area was inviolate, a bit of solitude due the preeminence of his rank. His staff waited discreetly in front of his small, one-personnel tent while he went in back with a late copy of the *National Geographic*—one that featured a cruise of the *Yankee* around the Greek Islands. Now that he was involved with Stavropolis once again, he wanted to be culturally aware of her antecedents. "I'm interested in the whole person," he reasoned to himself. "It's probably why I'm a successful lover." He felt so good that he allowed himself a whistle. Just a few notes. He very seldom did anything that he didn't consider he could do well. It pleased him to whistle tunelessly; the noise came lilting out over his moustache.

However, the noise coming out of his personal latrine had no lilt to it. At first he was shocked that anyone would usurp his prerogative. Then he was angry. He dropped the magazine where he stood and burst around the canvas cover to his privy. There on the Commander's seat sat Major Sonny Beanstock, concentrating on his dual purpose of relieving himself and studying hog receipts at the twelve major midwest terminals since April, in a monthly publication from Chicago.

"Beanstock!" the Colonel yelled. "What in hell are you doing in my latrine?"

Beanstock was surprised. Red-faced, he apologized: "I'm terribly sorry, Gayle—but I never could have made it to the officers' latrine. That formation lasted too damn long. I was running after it was over, but—that damn bratwurst last night must have had much too much entrail waste in it; much too much."

"And you had much too much bratwurst. But there's no excuse I'm going to accept. Get up and get out of here." Beauregard was furious. This was one of the pleasures of camp. Along with his mania for fluoridation. No animal except man excreted in the same place continually, followed by other animals of the same species, continually, for periods of years. It was impractical, illogical and unsanitary. He objected to using the same toilet at home with his wife and children, and always powdered his behind with talcum before he would unlock the door. His wife thought he carried things a little too far; but after all, he was the commander, and he must have had a good reason for doing anything he did.

"There are things I shall not tolerate, Beanstock. Am I allowed no privileges at all, or would you like to sleep in my tent as well?" Beanstock knew the Colonel was being sarcastic, because the Colonel was screaming; he scrambled to finish his task and get out of the way. The Colonel strained again to whistle, as he watched the sweep second hand of his watch, timing his subordinate.

It took Beanstock forty-seven seconds; then he went shuffling out, wearing an apologetic grin. "I'm sorry sir," he said, hoping the use of the "sir" would excuse his mistake.

Beauregard said nothing, but went straight to his task, the continuity of his morning doubly ruined. After ten minutes of nothing happening, he got up in disgust, throwing the *National Geographic* against the side of the tent. "Shit," he said to himself. Which was ironic, for he left his private latrine feeling constipated and miserable.

ELEVEN

"Confidentially, Gayle," Soule was telling Beauregard, "I've got this thing. I'm sure it had a lot to do with my, ah, problem the other day."

They were walking together around the encampment. In the distance they could hear the staccato burst of machine gun fire. The Minuteman Division was going through simulated attack under simulated fire of blank cartridges, which sounded real, nevertheless. Colonel Beauregard walked as tall as he was able, throwing out his little chest and springing forward on his toes as he walked.

"Compensate, compensate," he told himself, and made sure tha his uniform was extra sharp, that his boot tips glinted with the polish from a deodorant pad. In time the boot tips would crack from the deodorant, but he could requisition innumerable pairs from quartermaster supply. It made him wonder if the stuff did that to boot tips, what did it do to armpits? That's why he used the spray type, although his scientific background made him constantly suspicious of new products in cans, bottles, squeeze packages and plastic wrappers. Even if the Pure Food and Drug Administration had approved them.

"Everyone is fraught with graft these days," he'd tell his wife. "Can't trust anything but your own research, Margaret; don't give the children anything I don't guarantee first."

Soule was thoughtful as they walked, so thoughtful that his index finger crept up to his nose. It relaxed him, knowing that he could breathe easily. "My life has been a transient one," he said. "I almost committed suicide once. Really. I couldn't find anything I was happy at. The Agency must have followed me for years, perhaps since college. For a while, I edited *Lint,* a magazine of the middle-right, very close to the ground swell of Grange thought. Kept my body sharp, also. Important to have healthy mind in strong body. It was the motto of *Lint,* as a matter of fact. Then Vietnam came, and I leaped into it as a chance to redeem a sense of something I had lost. In Saigon I discovered this 'thing' about myself. I became a mystic, lost in study, took books out on patrol in the paddies. Understood *Das Zeitalter des Sonnengottes* the minute I picked it up. You know, I was special.

"But I needed the companionship of a woman to set me
102

free. Had this girl in Saigon, Gam Sun was her name, means hor d'oeuvres in Indochinese. She had gone to Hanoi University, strangely enough. Taught me her kind of mysticism. I took her up to the front, smuggled in my footlocker. She was very small and had the power to make herself even smaller. An act of will. Put her in under my rolled-up khaki socks and my toilet kit, very comfortable. Drilled a few holes in the sides so she could breathe. Needed no food, put herself in a trance. Camouflaged herself and came out and joined me at my command post, looking out over the Mekong Delta. Very quiet; knew the V.C. were out there all around. Chinese were in it then. They made very little noise. They're all issued plimsolls to go with their quilted uniforms; very quiet.

"She talked to me. Old Vietnamese tales of childhood, fairy tales, and I felt all sort of, 'A neater, sweeter maiden in a greener, cleaner land.' Then we heard the trumpets and the fireworks, and the attack started, thousands of them yelling and screaming and the night becoming day in the flares going off. Gam Sun was very calm. Accepted it. Made me not afraid. Put herself into a trance there on the lines, and I couldn't fire my rifle for looking at her, so peaceful and assured, like when she was covered by my socks and toilet kit. Then we were overrun and they cut her down and continued toward the rear, still yelling and screaming, but very silent on their feet in their tennis shoes. By an act of God or Buddha, I was spared.

"Was contacted as soon as I was discharged from the hospital in Tokyo, lost and not knowing what to do. Couldn't face the magazine again. 'We want you, you can help us,' the Agency said; no one had said that before, so I joined them. Found me another woman, which I told them was necessary. That's what I wanted to tell you. She's coming up from Washington this morning. I kind of blank out without her. My secretary as well as inspiration. Does as well as a man in any situation, that's why Washington lets her stay around. Not just expense account, either. She's got the calling. On the payroll, too. Just want to warn you that I hope none of the men get any ideas. She's special. Dangerous."

"I know. She's your girl," said the colonel, understanding. He would never tolerate anyone bothering Stavropolis, either. It was a sore spot. He had been forced to bust a young captain once for dancing close to her at the officers' club. He had caught the officer trying to force a knee between her legs while they were listening to the "Blue Tango." "Tango, my ass," he had said at the time. "He's jamming his leg in her crotch and I'm going to bust him for it." He did, too, all the way back to second lieutenant.

"Not just that she's my girl. Actually that's a misnomer. She's dangerous because she has visions. She hears voices. She has even had communication with Gam Sun—"

"You mean—"

"—exactly. Spiritual dictation, she claims she takes. Been very useful to the Agency. Been in touch with most of history's intelligence operatives. Claims to hear voices all the time—*her* voices, she calls them. Fantastic woman."

"Do you—I mean, have you slept with her? You spoke of this need. I've got the same problem, if you want to call it a problem. You see, this Major Stavropolis—"

Soule had grabbed him by the throat and was choking him. The grip was very strong and Colonel Beauregard was flailing his arms around helplessly. He could feel his tongue about to go lolling out of the side of his mouth. Flecks formed on the top of his lips. Soule relaxed his grip suddenly, but still held the throat loosely with both hands.

"Don't ever say that to me again. No one has touched her. She is inviolate, a mystic." He fingered his silver tie holder reverently. "Why, my chief even issued a directive at one point not allowing any of the personnel to date her, or even take her to eat at any place that serves luncheons for over ninety-nine cents. Safer that way. No danger of martinis."

"Well," said Beauregard, "I certainly didn't mean anything by what I said." He rubbed his neck gingerly and swallowed a few times to prove to himself that he still could. He was hurt that he didn't have a chance to brag to Soule about his Greek major. "I'm looking forward to meeting her," he managed. "She sounds fascinating." The Colonel, like the struggling politician he was, could see the strange light leap into Soule's eyes and recognized the arrival of this woman as having to do with worlds he didn't understand. He felt a shiver of fear at the incomprehensible forces that worked on higher planes than even he, the commander of the unit, was privy to. It made him feel smaller than his five foot five. He felt like slouching lower; the spring left his step. They walked on in silence while the sun struggled to break into midmorning behind some clouds. Then it had the pine grove to contend with, which kept anything but occasional filtered rays from getting through the closely grown trees.

Men who had been leaning on shovels or picks or mallets, securing the tents and digging small drainage ditches around them, began to look busy as the Colonel and Soule approached. Most of them had nine-hour work days ahead, with only two hours of work to perform. Featherbedding was always a problem. Most of the men who saw them approach would straighten up, salute, and say, "Good morning, sir." Beauregard got tired of this; they strolled toward the parking lot where he knew that there would be no damned saluting. The parking lot was off limits during working hours to all personnel.

It was 1000 hours and the trucks and tanks of the Minuteman Division were rumbling by on the hardtop. Dozens of heavy and medium trucks lumbered in low gear, not able to get above second because of the pace of the tanks in the lead of the convoy. Officers in jeeps scurried up and down the sides of the columns shouting directions, grinding their motors, spinning their wheels in the mud which was left over from the night's rain.

The commander of the Minuteman, General Roderick Grosbeck, was in the lead, standing up in the back of his jeep, scanning the scene with binoculars. The fact that he could only see the face of the driver of the truck directly behind him didn't matter. He was scanning the scene with binoculars, his steel pot on his head.

Suddenly, Beauregard and Soule saw him pitch backward onto the head of his driver, the binoculars flying also and banging him in the nose. The General's jeep, flying the flag with the one gold star from its antenna, had suddenly jammed to a halt to avoid an oncoming Lambretta which swerved out of the jeep's path and continued to career at full speed around one side of the jeep, around the other side of the truck next in line, around the left side of the tank after that, around the right side of the jeep following the tank. Hunched over the handles of the scooter was a figure dressed in khaki fatigues, combat boots, field jacket and the green beret of the U.S. Special Forces. Goggles hid the eyes of the driver, who seemed intent on slaloming the entire column. All the vehicles braked and halted; only the General seemed worse for the damage. He disentangled himself from the steering mechanism and ordered his driver into pursuit. The driver swung the vehicle around abruptly and took off up the side of the road in the ditch, mud flying out behind. The entire column, confused, began to turn also on the narrow road, intent on doing the most natural thing—following directly anything in front of it. Within minutes the convoy was hopelessly snarled in submerged vehicles, gears grinding noisily. Some were backing up, others trying to maneuver forward or around. The General yelled to the rear, the wind whipping his robin's egg blue scarf out behind him: "Not you, you idiots, just me, just me."

"You want to drive the jeep, General?" his driver asked incredulously.

"You fool, I want *you* to drive the jeep and *them* to continue out to the firing ranges!" Now in a complete frenzy, he yelled back at the column, "HEADS WILL ROLL FOR THIS, HEADS WILL ROLL! Catch me that scooter, boy; catch me that fucking putting scooter. I'll clap that soldier in irons, I'll throw him in the hole."

In pursuit of his dignity, the General left the column to muddle for itself. Most of the men of the Minuteman Division were used to sudden and drastic changes in their commander's decisions. They passed it off to a new and exciting training exercise.

But the quarry was undaunted—indeed, was unaware of the chase. The fatigue-clad figure did not slacken until the column was totally and successfully passed. The Lambretta turned only when the opening in the pines showed the way to the encampment of the 229th, where the driver released the accelerator handle, quickly shifted down one gear, sending gravel spinning into the mud of the road, and accelerated once again, on toward the parking lot.

"That's Joanne," said Soule, holding his hands together reverently. The tone of his voice was hushed.

"That's *who?*" said Colonel Beauregard in deisbelief.

"That's my assistant. She must have come all the way from Washington on her scooter. Don't offer her a bath, though," he cautioned hurriedly. "She'll take it as a slur on her ability as a warrior."

"Her what?"

"Ohh, don't you worry, and don't you think it's so funny. She believes that she's destined to lead an army."

"You mean on a Bonus March—like Coxey?" The Colonel didn't mean to joke. He seldom did. But he couldn't resist. Immediately he was sorry, remembering the threat in Soule's eyes, and the bruises on his own throat. But the intelligence man didn't seem to notice. He walked toward the Lambretta, grinning, big feet splaying out in either direction. The scooter came to a halt, rearing back like a horse. Beauregard expected to hear the "neigh" as the front wheels came crashing down onto the ground. The driver cut the motor. Off came the green beret. Off came the plastic goggles. Zip, and off came the field jacket.

"Joanne," said Soule, with unbelievable tenderness, "this is

106

Colonel Gayle Beauregard. Colonel, this is Joanne Moxie, of our staff."

There was a sudden roar in the near distance: grinding axles, stripping gears, burning rubber, curses of men, shouts of commands.

"Honored, Miss Moxie," said the Colonel, not knowing whether to extend his hand or not. She reached out her arm and grasped the Colonel's hesitant hand, shaking it twice, firmly, up and down, then releasing.

"Your palm sweats, Colonel. Are you nervous or just naturally sweaty? No great leader of history ever had sweaty palms. I've researched it fully. But, no matter, you can be taught self-control." She shook her head to clear her hair of any foreign matter, mostly the dust accumulated on her trip. It was cut short like a poodle's, easy to arrange, and light brown. In anyone less determined it might be called cute. As it was, her haircut was proper for her military costume and framed a face that was cleanly defined, yet somehow soft. It was the kind of face one longed to cradle between two hands. The cheeks invited touching. Her eyes were set wide apart and were very big and brown, the lashes dark and curling upward. The upper lip was dry, no sign of sweat, no sign of hair. The mouth pouted ever so slightly and there was just the hint of a lisp somewhere in her speech. If anything, the mouth was too full to be perfect; the lips were puffed out, rather than drawn thin. No lipstick colored the mouth, no black lines defined the eyes. The nose was straight and rather on the thin side. It was impossible to see into the nostrils. She stood erect; the combat boots, despite the dust covering parts of them, were highly polished six-and-a-half triple A's. The fatigues were tailored tightly across the smallish chest and the hips.

Colonel Beauregard was struck by her attitude. "You certainly are a no-nonsense girl, Miss Moxie," he said. "The moisture on my hands is most likely dew . . ." He felt obligated to say something.

"Dew, at 1100 hours, Colonel? I think not. But don't be disturbed. I know the pressures of command. This is why Rufus and I are here to assist you."

The roaring in the distance became louder, until the group was engulfed in vehicles of all types milling around them. General Grosbeck was in the lead. He stood up in the back of his jeep, sputtering with rage, not only at the girl in front of him, but at his entire Minuteman Division, which was attempting to populate the 229th's parking lot. Weapons were at the ready: the tankers had lowered their hatches, blank cartridges had been loaded into BARs, light machine guns manned on top of the two-and-a-half ton trucks. National Guard colonels flitted about the General's jeep like so many gnats.

Everyone screamed at once for an explanation until the General grabbed his bullhorn and switched it to loud. "AT EASE," he yelled, blowing two or three of the lighter colonels back a few yards. "I WANT ALL OF THESE VEHICLES OUT OF THIS AREA IN TWO MINUTES!" He checked his watch. "PROCEED AS DIRECTED TO THE RANGE AREA AND COMMENCE TRAIN FIRING, DO YOU READ ME? I REPEAT, PROCEED WITH SCHEDULED TRAINING OF THE DAY, DO YOU READ ME?"

Soldiers from the hospital tent area began arriving to watch the proceedings. A few of the medics cheered the arrival of the infantry. "We're saved," someone yelled, and immediately disappeared into the throng to escape detection. The column reorganized under the command of various colonels, majors, and captains. A few of the injured were placed in ambulances and taken to the admitting tent of the 229th. The General motioned to a squad of troops, in full field pack with fixed bayonets, to surround the Lambretta and its rider. They were the elite squad of the Minuteman Division, mostly former Boston College hockey players gone a little soft now, but with the unquenchable willingness to punch out civilians. They were designated by the General, with approval from the Governor of Massachusetts, to protect the commander from any threats to his person. They were very loyal and were allowed to be bullies. They ate at special training tables and wore orange scarfs tucked into their T-shirts like ascots. Most of them didn't even wear T-shirts. That's how tough *they* were.

Joanne Moxie looked very confidently at them. She turned to wheel her scooter over next to a civilian Mercury. The ex-B.C. hockey players poke-checked her, back to the middle of the circle.

"What the hell is the meaning of this, Beauregard?" sputtered the General. He had forgotten in his rage to snap off the bullhorn and his voice covered the area. The elite guard stood their ground. Everyone else was stunned.

"This is Miss Moxie, sir," said Beauregard apologetically. "From Washington—you know, with that special assignment." He lowered his voice and lowered one eyelid slightly at the same time. "She's with Mr. Soule. She's here to assist him."

General Grosbeck put down the bullhorn. He saw Joanne as the possible pinup of the Pentagon, her picture adorning the desks of the Joint Chiefs, her phone number in the red phone books of leaders of SAC and NATO. He had made a tactical error and wiped his brow with a big blue polka dot handkerchief.

"Oh," he said. "I was just routinely curious as to why anyone would want to entirely disrupt our convoy on the way to the ranges. I suppose there was some perfectly understandable reason. Else, I assume it would never have been done. If I had known beforehand—"

He noticed his squad still with bayonets on the ready. "At ease, for God's sake, men. Can't you see this is only a lady?" He grinned at Beauregard and the two Agency people. "Squad, atten-hut. Right shoulder, h'arms! About-face! Fowaaad, h'arch!" They moved off toward their waiting special truck that followed the General's jeep. As they marched they sang the Boston College fight song: "For Boston, for Boston, we shout her praises high . . ." They were precise in their steps and very military, hair cut close to the scalp. They were always very much in evidence after B.C. football games at Alumni Hall, wearing maroon corduroy jackets. They stuck together; yes, indeed.

The General was anxious to leave. "Gayle," he said to Beauregard, "get those fools that fell off the trucks by their own carelessness back on their feet and back to duty, as soon as possibly feasible. You're doing a fine job, son; fine job. No army can move unless its hospitals function at the optimum. Yes, sir, fine job." He clambered back into the jeep, this time taking the passenger's seat. The bridge of his nose was bleeding, where he had been struck by the binoculars. He rubbed his hand over it, trying to wipe it all away.

"Sorry if I caused you any surprise, ma'am," he said to Joanne. "Nice meeting you, sir. By the way, if you know by any chance General Gozen down in the Pentagon, well, he's an old battle companion of mine—the Bulge, oh, lots of campaigns in the last one—say hello to him for me. Old friend. Well, good luck," and he was off after his departed column. He was wiping his bloody hand on the back of the driver's shirt as his jeep turned onto the blacktop.

"General Gozen is a slob," Joanne remembered out loud. "A Desk General. Psoriasis on elbows and knees."

Colonel Beauregard marvedled at the way they treated rank. He had worked and plotted and maneuvered for years to make Colonel and be given a command. Where was the order that directed him to knuckle under to civilians? He felt his moustache begin to bristle as it did when he was angry. He had always thought of General Grosbeck as an unreachable man. He himself was a politician. But Grosbeck had brought politics to the highest plane. Commanding General of the Minuteman Division! It was a title to conjure with. And he had backed down from these two! When the anger wore off, he was wary and not a little frightened. Mystery frightened him. He liked everything out in the open where he could read it loud and clear.

Joanne looked around and stretched, her arms thrown wide to the scene. "Ahhh, the animus mundi. Smell it, Rufus. What it must have been like. All the way up from Utica I thought about the Indians."

"Which Indians?" Soule asked her.

"The Hurons, the Mohicans, the tribes along the St. Lawrence. Now just scraggly pines. No animals. No natural savage. Just displaced persons. But smell the air, it's wonderful: hams smoking in the cookhouse, bacon curing and turkeys hanging down from the rafters. We can give direction to these displaced persons, Rufus. Make their palms all dry, make their nostrils smell what *we* smell."

"Yes," said the agent, wiping his dirty fingers along the sides of his pepper and salt jacket.

The Colonel sniffed suspiciously. He smelled only burnt rubber and gas fumes from the recently departed vehicles. Camp Cannon looked to him like a scruffy piece of neglected merchandise after a sale: wrinkled, drab, handled and passed over.

"Come, I'll show you the rest of the paradise," he said craftily to Joanne, "and I'll tell you both about progress toward our operation. Glad to have another hand aboard." She strode along in front of them, breathing deeply and audibly in and out, in and out. She took long strides, slapping her green beret against her left thigh, using it as a swagger stick.

Colonel Beauregard strutted alongside Joanne Moxie like a peacock. After all, it was *his* command. "Damn women that think they're growing pricks," he thought to himself. It cheered him up.

Kenny Keohane found Eros Winter spitting into the Inedible Garbage pail and reading Lawrence Durrell. He was supposed to be loading the pails onto a truck.

"You want details every day, Winter?" Keohane asked him. "It's easy to arrange, so long as you're uncooperative."

Winter spat again, trying to make the saliva go "snickkk" in a long line between his two front teeth. "I used to be able to do that," he said, "but braces killed me. For two years I never smiled."

Keohane was irritated. "We can make it tough for you, Winter. We can break you if we want."

"Why don't you go back to your motor pool, Keohane, and swim a few laps? What's so special that you take time off from the crap game to check me out on KP?"

"No need to get wise with me, son. I'm on your side," answered Keohane.

"You took a commission and you're on my side? That supposed to be funny?" Winter said. "I know I'm hooked for six years."

"What about war?" said Keohane.

"O.K.," said Winter. "What about war? Too much has changed since Korea. A diplomatic mistake to keep the pump primed is no excuse for a war. One week on, one week off, with R and R in Hong Kong and Christmas with Phyllis Diller. If that's a war, I'm Mother Courage."

"Who?"

"Forget it, sir," said Winter, turning to shoulder an Inedible Garbage pail onto the rear of the open truck. He had stuck the paperback Lawrence Durrell into his back pants pocket.

"Wait, Winter, I need you."

Winter turned at the plea and waited. The truck driver wouldn't care; he had plenty of time.

"Baer doesn't like you," Keohane began. "You're on the Colonel's shit list . . ."

"Tell me something new," Winter smiled. "I don't give a damn for the others. I'm just not going on active duty for some half-assed political gambit that's been hatched in Washington by some ex-Admissions Dean at Harvard, or wherever. I'm not going to be fed into the Univac."

"That's just it," Keohane interrupted, "you can help all of us out of it."

"You're an officer. You won't mind active duty," Winter said suspiciously. "You've stayed in for some reason. Whatever's at home is bad enough to let you stay in the Reserve by your own choice."

"I'm an American," Keohane said angrily.

Winter laughed. "In peacetime you're an Irishman. That's

111

number one. Only in war are you an American—or when you're a tourist. What do you need me for?" he repeated.

"They'll notice you. Soule will. Beauregard will. You'll take the brunt off of us. We've got an organization, and a plan. I'll get you off details, off the shit list, if you join us." He saw Winter hesitate and went on: "We want out as much as you. It's madness for this outfit to be activated. We'd all die. Even if we were stationed on Governor's Island. The Reserve is fine for me: contacts for insurance, paid vacations, officers clubs. But I ain't a soldier and no one is seriously telling me I am. No civilian in crepe soles, that's for sure."

Winter smelled the garbage and the steam from the field stoves and was halfway there . . .

"I'm with you, if you take Eldor, too," he said. "Only if you take Eldor."

"You mean the Kraut? The Red Eagle?" Keohane was amazed.

Winter laughed out loud. "Yes, the Red Eagle. He's got a hard on for Baer. Deep-rooted, like the Nuremberg Trials. They can't ease him out of the unit. He'll be helpful. Better he's loyal to us than to Beauregard."

"You're a prick, Winter," said Keohane admiringly.

"Well," Winter answered. "Dad always said I'd be a great surgeon someday." He tipped over a can of garbage with his boot and left it, coffee grounds steaming on top of twenty dozen eggshells. They both looked at the spilled garbage and walked to the mess tent together, where Keohane would spring Eros Winter from KP.

"It was more than a fair exchange," Winter thought. Then he saw the Colonel approaching. He was with Soule and Joanne Moxie. The Colonel was engaged in conversation with himself, waving his hands grandly about, indicating his private preserve, his efficient field hospital. Eros Winter stared at Joanne and found her wildly attractive. Eros Winter never expected this in the Army. It was a most pleasant surprise. Winter always felt the challenge of squash . . . and women. He took off his fatigue cap and moistened the tips of his fingers with spittle. Then he smoothed his hair down over his forehead. Keohane saw the trio approach and stiffened to salute. Winter straightened up also.

The Colonel wished that he could have Winter lodged for two weeks in the rear of that ambulance. He'd feed him chicken soup, Pinto's apple turnovers, and coffee with condensed milk for two weeks. Shape him up . . .

Winter smiled the smile he took from Mike Hammer: the one with all the teeth.

Joanne Moxie smiled. Eros noticed she used the one with all the teeth also. Orthodonture, he thought. They don't make natural mouths like that anymore. She's beautiful. Probably wore a night brace for eight months or so until the teeth set right. Then a turtle for a year, with little rubber bands that kept breaking and snapping against her inner cheeks. Poor little inner cheeks.

"I like to see enlisted men who honor a lady in this manner, son," she said to Eros. "But, as you can see, I come uniformed and equipped to be treated exactly as any soldier in the field. Please put your cap back on." Her eyes stared blankly at him. She didn't really notice his hair smoothed over his forehead; she didn't really notice what he considered his best pose of attractive indifference. That irritated Eros. He placed his cap back on, low over his eyes, so he could peer out darkly at her. He stared at her until she was forced to acknowledge it by focusing her attention on him, and not on something behind the back of his head. He had already begun to condition himself to being deprived of women, at least until the weekend. Even then, there was no certainty. Maybe all the young women in upper New York State had moved away to Buffalo or Erie, Pennsylvania, to seek their fortunes. He couldn't count on meeting anyone, and his luck certainly hadn't been good lately.

Concentrating on getting himself out of activation, he was not above double-crossing Keohane. One plan was to admit he was a member of some subversive group, like the Society for Preservation of the Memories of Sacco and Vanzetti. That would raise hell with the brass. He could demand to sign a DD Form 98, stating that he advocated overthrow of the U.S. Government. That would spring him for sure. He could probably get Eldor out also by claiming that he belonged to the Association of German Nationals or *Reichsdeutsche Vereinigung* and that he favored the extension of the statute of limitations, or that he subscribed to the association to help Dr. Mengele buy his own orchid plantation in Argentina. That would spring them both. What was he thinking of? Why spring the German? He could even get himself discharged as "unfit for military service," as an incorrigible. But going in with Keohane would release the whole unit from activation. What did he give a damn about the whole unit? He didn't. But it was a chance to strike a blow against the Establish-

113

ment. He couldn't do that himself. They'd just dismiss him as a nut or a coward. He was a coward, true, but he'd be damned if anyone else could say it or know the truth. Better to throw in with Keohane and bring the whole 229th General Hospital around his ears.

"That woman has changed all this: Joanne Moxie," he thought to himself. The woman had changed all that because there was no doubt now that he'd throw in with Keohane. It was convenient. Operating by himself, the Colonel would probably lock him up again; or, at the very least, he'd be given details continually and kept on post. Couldn't get to her without freedom. "So join Guy Fawkes," he told himself, still looking at her and smiling.

The Colonel, Soule, and Joanne Moxie moved away in the direction of the ward tents. Beauregard was anxious to stay as far from Winter on every occasion as possible. Soule had noticed his discomfort. "Isn't he the young man who made the disturbance yesterday in the mess hall?"

"How did you hear about . . . yes, he was." The Colonel was resigned to dealing with the intelligence man. "Causes us occasional worry. But he's on company punishment now. Confined to the area. Intelligent, but a disturbed young man. That's obvious. Manic, I think. Probably a frustrated officer."

"Might make a good candidate for the Aggressor force," commented Soule. "Perhaps too disruptive to be with the regular unit on the assault maneuver. Channel his aggression in a harmless direction. Keep him segregated, but busy. Out of the way. See the way he looked at you, Joanne?" Soule had noticed, jealously, and couldn't resist mentioning it. It wasn't quite love that he felt for Joanne. He could adore her from a distance. Soule knew what he would have to give up when he joined the service. It was often lonely, yet he was dedicated. Since the Chinese took Gam Sun away from him, he could not be unfaithful to her memory. He'd cry when he thought of her specialty, Bird's Nest Soup, and of the sweet way she'd make him take off his combat boots before she would let him into her parents' house. She worshipped the size of his feet. They were what first attracted her to him, seeing him in a bar with other G.I.'s, walking toward the men's room, the big feet splaying out in all directions, never quite sure where they would lead him. She thought Rufus Soule's feet had minds of their own. She tabbed him for a potential mystic. He was a pushover after that. He loved Gam Sun to walk on his back with her ninety-two pounds to ease his tired muscles. Then she would make love to his feet and recite poetry by Lac

114

Tikao, Tang Li, and Bashe. Everything was reduced to utmost simplicity. Even making love to the feet. Soule, at first horrified, began to look upon this with good grace and tenderness, out of respect for Gam Sun's needs. He didn't think it was unnatural; more than that, after a time it became a need for *him*. He had transferred all his erogenous zones into his feet, for the pleasure of the one who gave him pleasure. He didn't dare suggest his need to Joanne Moxie. He just wriggled his toes inside their woolen socks and crepe-soled coverings, and kept his desires to himself. "They also serve who only stand and wait," he thought about his toes, and smiled grimly through the longing.

Not that Joanne reminded him of Gam Sun at all; just that she also was mystical, aloof, and dedicated. She worked with him, for him, and had known the Chief (though not so well as he, certainly), and she believed in her ability, in her own destiny.

"I was born to greatness, not from a family sense, but to achieve it," she told him. "We are confronted by enemies all around, who would sap our strengths, destroy our freedoms. My voices tell me that I shall lead men in preserving these freedoms, even sometimes against their own wills. Men don't know their own minds; they're not detached enough from their desires. *My* only desire is to serve and to let the ignorant know what is best for them. I lift my hope beside the golden door of preserving liberty; I lift my lamp of belief." She told that to Soule shortly after she came to Washington to seek enlistment with the Agency. They were at The Shadows, a nightclub near the Washington monument.

It was a historic night for Soule. Joanne had been dressed in a man-tailored suit, blue and chic. Her hair had been long then, down in back practically to her waist. She refused to put it up. She liked juxtapositions, contrasts. A comedian had been commenting on the news, riffling through a paper and jabbing satirically. Joanne had gotten indignant because he criticized J. Edgar Hoover and the Senate Subcommittee on Stream Pollution. "My voices tell me that this man is dangerous," she told Soule and she threw a tumbler of bourbon at the entertainer. The glass missed him. The bourbon caught him in the throat and even sprayed his newspaper. The comedian went after her at their ringside table, which was a mistake. Soule, the gallant Soule, demolished the comedian. It took a week for the Agency to fix it. Threats to the management finally did the trick.

Joanne was hired for her spunk, although the adminis-

115

tration thought her perhaps a bit too zealous. She was originally hired as a cipher clerk. She could speak fluent French, Italian, knew the Hebrew alphabet and the hand signals for The American Stock Exchange. She was for the capitalistic system and was one hundred per cent American. They also admired brains in the Agency, and she had been Radcliffe, Class of 1958. Her visions, which she had been experiencing since childhood in White Plains, New York, kept her untouched and practically dateless through high school. No one wanted to bother putting up with her nonsense; she was an object of ridicule. Besides, she got better marks than most of the boys. "Stuck-up bitch," the girls would say about her and jam mean notes through the grill in her hall locker. "Flat-breasted Indian," the boys would say, not wasting more than a few words on her. She hadn't exactly given herself up to God, but she had given herself up to her idea of herself, and remained true to that idea until such time as her voices said that destiny had arrived.

She thought that destiny had arrived during her junior year in college when, dressed all in white and standing up in the rumble seat of a companion's De Soto, she exhorted a number of undergraduates in Harvard Square to picket Woolworth's for refusing to serve Negroes at the lunch counters in the South. Most of her companions came from places like Lake Forest, Illinois, and had never even seen a Negro. But they cared desperately and they carried signs around Woolworth's that said things like: "This may be a five and ten, but we deserve to eat like MEN," and "Stick your hamburg and your roll, look beneath the skin at SOUL!" It was an impressive demonstration and Joanne was carried away by her role as organizer. She went out that night and got very drunk with one of her companions, a young Negro who had gone to Exeter and dressed Savile Row. She let him get her naked in his dormitory while a Martin Denny record screeched jungle noises at them from a stereo set. When he started to pant at her: "I want to miscegenate you; I want to miscegenate the ass off you," it spoiled the whole idea somehow and she fled, leaving behind her white shoes and some daisies she had bought for him. She knew that her time was yet to come.

Soule became devoted to her, finding a Platonic substitute for his lost Oriental love. He read a lot and threw himself violently into his work. Only secretly, at night, would he betray any longings and be forced to soak his feet in corn starch and Epsom salts for an hour at a time. It was some relief, but not much. He resented Winter's paying attention to her, as he resented anyone "not of the Agency" aspiring to something beyond his reach. In Soule's opinion it was much like social climbing, and, in view of his callused hand edges, it was in fact quite a bit more dangerous.

Eros Winter watched her walk away toward the hospital wards. "MMMmmm," he said to Keohane. "I am very definitely joining you. Look at that twitching little rump. Under fatigue pants yet. Tell me it's a possibility, Keohane. No, don't bother. *You* know, man, that *anything* is a possibility. I practically promise to keep my nose clean, all for the common cause; here's me hand on it, as they say in your country."

"I'm very pleased, Winter," said Keohane. "Let von Liebert down gently, but give him the word."

"Do I show him the secret grip?"

"Just leave the poetry and symbols to me, Winter. I'm the Irishman. You just keep your friend in line . . . and forget about that woman, if you're smart."

"HER?" said Eros. "Are you kidding? That's my Summer Romance."

TWELVE

The first week lapsed into the usual routine of summer camp. There were the poker games continually running, every time there was a five-minute break or a lunch break or a coffee or latrine break, or after dinner waiting for the trucks to take them to the showers. Very few men had been given TPA, Travel Pay Allowance, and permission to bring up their civilian automobiles. Roughly five per cent of the enlisted men and ten per cent of the officers had cars at Camp Cannon, making them the subjects of extreme social pressure. Only the worst people received TPA. Permission was very political, usually involving overtime work at the Army Base during the year, and special carting jobs like promising to bring up officers' golf clubs or taking someone's wife shopping. You had to swallow your pride to ask these terrible people for rides to town. But the only other way was the sporadic bus service provided only seasonally for the soldiers and operated at a loss by the town of Waterville.

Summer camp was only halfhearted in the field. It was just too dirty and uncomfortable and home was too close to everyone's mind. This year it was worse than usual, with most of the enlisted personnel worrying about being recalled to active duty. That was the major topic of conversation—along with the weather, which had been rotten.

The sky brooded and the men bitched. The only constants were the sound of typewriters and mimeograph machines from the administration tent. Sonya Faust hovered over her machines like some prehistoric beast protecting her breed from extinction. She had a stenographic pool of four other WACs and assorted enlisted men to do her bidding; the weather was forever the same inside her tent—musty. It was like the lining of an old trunk before it is aired for the packing away of children's camp clothes and tennis balls. Sonya's life was dedicated to the 229th General Hospital, which had lured her away from overtime at the Prudential Life Insurance Company to overtime with the Army Reserve. The 229th had given her status and master sergeant's stripes. Thus she was unquestioning in her loyalty. She drooled over morning reports; she chuckled over stencils; she put special orders to bed and breast-fed KP rosters. Her life was an orgy of paper work and she rooted around in it like a Guernsey on Spanish

118

fly. She had no need of ink erasers or liquid eradicators. She was mistakeless: the highest achievement of her art. She wore G.I. issue T-shirts and her breasts flopped to her waist. Anyone could see her that first week, covered with ink by noontime, her grey hair streaked with it, her forearms blue. She used carbon instead of mascara and she ate her food with number two pencils.

Everyone loathed her, except for Butcher Beanstock, who was in charge of the administrative complement. He would sit next to her at mealtime, firing dictation, while she spilled chili on her Gregg pad; pork and beans on her Gregg pad; Bella Pizzarettes on her Gregg pad; and say to her—"Marvelous, Sonya; so efficient, Sonya. Can you write to the Dressed Beef Futures Market for me, Sonya? Ahhh, that's the good girl, another bite. Oops, not on your pad again, more liver paste? Too bad. 'Dear Sir: Due to my assignment to the United States Army Reserve . . .' Not too fast, am I? Ahh, I love to watch you eat, Sonya. All work and no play, my dear . . . Where was I?"

She was half in love with Major Beanstock and longed to brush the cigar ashes off his fatigue front, to make him neat and presentable. She loved him for being "natural" as she called it. Never pulled rank; always called on her for special assistance; never made her salute him; always called by her first name, not Sergeant Faust as everyone else did. Sonya liked to think of herself as Sonya. After all, she was a woman and demanded a little respect. Even if she was an enlisted woman, not like some snobby nurses she could mention. She could paint her lips up pink, too, if she had the time away from the typewriter. Could be good and pink and proper; get the blue off her lips and show a lot of those smarty-pants that she had what it takes, too. And knew what to do with it. Then she would get mad and turn the crank on the mimeograph like crazy, sometimes running off as many as two hundred extra copies of the daily camp bulletin. "Waste not, want not," Butcher Beanstock would caution her—but softly, allowing her that small indiscretion.

Meanwhile, Major Fugue could hardly contain himself for joy when a series of unfortunate accidents struck down a dozen members of the Minuteman Division. That afternoon he encountered two simple fractures of the femur, one compound fracture of the tibia, and one greenstick fracture of the pinky, which he artistically splinted with a Q-Tip until a permanent splint could be applied.

One young man was carried in on a litter, complaining that

his steel pot had given him a headache in the very top of his head. Fugue hummed to himself as he felt all around the head, chanting: "Oh, Oh, Oh, To, Touch, and, Feel, A, Girl's, Vagina, Ah, Heaven," which was his medical school *aide-mémoire* for the twelve cranial nerves—Occipital, Optic, and so forth. He could never touch a skull without remembering the simple formula. It made him happy to recall medical school, before he was forced into internship and residency. The chief surgeon had said: "Gentlemen, this is where we separate the men from the boys; the wheat from the chaff, as it were; the *doctors*, gentlemen, from the mere apprenti—good luck, gentlemen."

Major Fugue had such very bad luck. First, that botched tracheotomy, where he had forgotten to remove the ball-point cartridge from his pen and the ink went down the esophagus. And it wasn't his fault that none of the natives *or* aides on New Guinea ever washed their hands.

Fugue checked the emergency medical tags of his patients with glee when they came out of A and D Tent. "A banker, nurse; a real banker. Well, a teller—but he works in a bank on State Street," he cried out with glee, his handsome face spread in a handsome grin. "I've never touched a banker before. I bet they're not like ordinary men, nurse," he told his assisting lieutenant, a nurse in civilian life with a complexion like a pizza. "Ahh, they feel different, these professional men. Wonderfully substantial. Feel him here. Doesn't it feel like handling money?"

"Not unless he's keeping quarters in his nose."

"All business, the frustrated old bitch," he thought. Her ill humor didn't deter him or dampen his enthusiasm. He hummed and sang all afternoon as he went from banker to male-stenographer (crushed sternum), from busboy (suspected appendix) to a real-life stockbroker (hernia from carrying air-cooled machine gun), with whom he established an immediate rapport. He felt his bedside manner was developing very nicely; he was becoming fairly confident about operating on civilians. It was wonderful therapy for him. He sidled up to the broker's cot where the young man lay, left leg elevated to relieve the pain. "Understand you're a stockbroker, son," he said perceptively, checking his clipboard with the man's medical record. "Heard anything on the Street about the Pennsy and Central merger? ICC going to go along with it, you think?" So smooth. He knew all the terms. His hands were steady.

"Can't you do anything about my ball, Doc?" the broker asked him. "My ball is killing me."

"You're a professional man, son. Highly trained in civilian life. I'm surprised at your language." Major Fugue was shocked indeed.

"Evidently, Doctor, I'm cursed with a highly unprofessional ball. Uh, it's the other one, Doc. The left one. You know, the one that's normally lower than the other."

"I'm aware of the position of the testicles, my boy. Ahh, you seem to be sold short here somewhat. Heh, heh," said Fugue, knowing he was touching all the right bases. Know your patient. Rule one. Have some familiarity with his outside problems. Modern medical people have to be virtual Renaissance men. His good looks exuded confidence and he couldn't remember when he had felt so completely happy.

"He's turning blue," said the nurse.

"Prep him for surgery!" Fugue exclaimed. "And make sure some of the younger doctors are present to observe. I want to shape up this professional service section. They might as well get used to emergency field surgery. Just like real war, eh, son?" he asked the broker, who was moaning on his stretcher. "Nurse, get one of the ward attendants to shave the affected area. We don't do those jobs, you know." And he walked away to the surgery tent.

Tony Gurruzi did all the prepping in the 229th General Hospital because he was a barber in civilian life. He talked to the patient about politics, baseball, women, and told him one joke he had heard recently about Moses and Jesus in a celestial golf match. That was mechanical conversation, to prepare the patient emotionally for Fugue's knife. As Tony Gurruzi's finely honed razor stroked off the terrified broker's pubic hair, he hummed a little rhyme to himself that always amused him: "Ahhh, when we shave-a the face, we sometimes botch; but-a never a slip when it comes to the crotch." It was a busman's holiday for him. He even brought up some back issues of *Esquire* for his patients to read before he was ready for them. Why take a chance and bring up *Ring Magazine* or *Silver Screen?* You knew what to expect from patients who were not at all like his regular customers back home. He always knew what *they* liked to read.

Chaplain Papps had no official tent. So he wandered around looking for business. He was the type of man who hated to accept his cash payment at the end of the two weeks' training unless he felt he merited the pay. One summer he was desperate and found no one to help. His conscience forced him to donate half of his pay to the Methodist African Missions. It made him feel especially good, what with all the current news about civil rights and emerging nations.

Chaplain Papps wore his silver bars proudly. His uniforms were all tailored, befitting his station in civilian life. "Anywhere within twenty-five miles of Cambridge, we Methodists are forced to put elbow patches on our tweed jackets. Don't much mind them; matter of fact, they're rather comfortable. My wife even puts them on my *new* tweed jackets. She tends to go to extremes, my wife." He strode in and among the various departments of the hospital, nodding here and there to those who might be traditionally sympathetic; going out of his way to cock a friendly eyebrow at the Jewish personnel. He had a maddening habit of whistling, "What a Friend We Have in Jesus" whenever he was feeling good, and "Nearer my God to Thee" whenever he was in what he referred to as his *Titanic* mood.

He had been doing mental gymnastics, which he pursued whenever he felt a particular problem pressing. He wanted to confront Eros Winter, but he didn't dare try until he felt in particularly good shape. "Would a pack of schoolboys take on the Dallas Cowboys without training?" he asked himself. "Certainly not." He had favored the professional football analogy ever since the difficult times of the early 'sixties, when no one lingered over his sermons or stayed for coffee on Sundays save Miss Ginch, the organist. He regarded the Dallas Cowboys as his own and God's personal enemy. He would do exercises in his mind: questions and the answers to confront someone like Eros Winter, such as, "Did you ever consider Christ as a buddy? I mean, someone you could take down to the squash courts and steam bath afterwards? Well, consider it, Winter." "Do I believe *He* has the answers for everyone? What do you mean, Mario Savio? Well, think of the Sermon on the Mount. You have? No matter, I can refute anything you have to question. Ask me, you son of a bitch."

The conversations that Chaplain Papps had with himself inevitably ended driving him crazy, and he would find himself in Marlon Pinto's mess tent begging a wafer of Canadian bacon to chew on. He always ate when he was bored or frustrated. Since he had no specific assignment, he hoped that one of the National Guard soldiers would request spiritual attention. He specialized in field work dealing with sexual frustration, and prided himself on his sermon: "That foolish moment—let me help you over it," which always seemed to work; although it relieved no particular frustration save Chaplain Papps's own.

While he chewed on an uncooked piece of bacon and watched Pinto prepare pie crust from an Army menu book, one of the ambulance drivers from the motor pool came in looking for him.

"Chaplain, sir, excuse me, but you're wanted over at the X-ray tent."

Answering the call of God, he grabbed two more pieces of bacon and hurried off to X ray, which occupied the rear half of Major Fugue's surgery tent.

A very fat master sergeant ran the X-ray lab. He was an IBM programmer for Liberty Mutual Insurance Company and was very self-possessed. Time and again he had exposed himself to the radioactive rays of his machines without bothering to protect himself behind the specially constructed lead shield.

"I'm a gambler," he would explain. "Look at it this way. I'm fat. Yes, don't argue with me—fat. My wife is even fatter. We've got mechanical problems. I, she—we. I'm not embarrassed about it; it's a fact. It's fairly obvious that we're bound to have fat kids. What can solve that? It's heredity; all our ancestors have been fat. For generations. These X rays could do something to my genes, get at my gonads and put some skinny genes in them. It's a chance; but like I said, I'm a gambler, *capish?* Be good if kids of mine didn't have those mechanical difficulties."

Chaplain Papps strode into the tent, determined. "You have something for me, Sergeant?" he asked.

"Yes, sir," the sergeant said. "Soldier complaining about pains in his chest. Says they only happen when he thinks about his mother. Here's the casette I shot of him. Shows nothing in the chest. Good picture, too. See that delineation—"

"Where's the soldier, Sergeant?"

"Over there in the corner, sir—the one with his head in his hands."

Chaplain-Captain Papps walked slowly over to the soldier in the corner, who sat on a camp stool thoughtfully provided by Camp Cannon supply. Papps smoothed his hands down the sides of his face, composing it, reassuring himself that it was smooth. It *was* smooth; he ran an inquisitive fingertip along the bridge of his nose to make certain that the eyebrow was intact. He feared that one morning he would awake and find that he had two eyebrows, like other men.

Not that he suffered from pride. Ah, the unpardonable sin. It wasn't quite that at all. But he believed that a man of his faith should somehow be set apart, not merely by his faith, but by some outward sign of his election. He was sure the eyebrow had grown as such a sign.

"It can't be that bad, son," he used for openers. "X-ray sergeant says you've got nothing visible in your chest that should cause you any serious trouble. You've got some other kind of problem. I'm Chaplain Papps, Methodist; but father to all, I like to think." He stood above the soldier benevolently, knowing he'd get a respectful, positive response. The soldier kept his face in his hands and didn't look up at all. The Chaplain laid a hand on the boy's shoulder. "Wouldn't it be better if you told me about it; told someone about it? Could there be something the matter home? You've never been away at summer camp before, perhaps?" Papps found over the years that often this struck a respondent note. Boy, homesick, doesn't like the Army; develops sympathetic pains in various portions of the body. A little spiritual guidance and it fixes them right up. Cinch. He was feeling confident about it already.

The boy looked up. He had been crying and his hands where his face had rested were wet with the tears. "I can't go home, sir," he said finally, his voice sounding very sorrowful and far away. "I can't ever go home again. It's too terrible."

Papps was warming to the boy immediately. "What a fine boy," he thought. "What concern for something I'm sure I can straighten out in a moment. Oh, I'm earning my pay this week; I'm putting in overtime outside the unit scope."

"There's never anything so terrible, son, that doesn't look somehow a little more bearable by telling it. As the good Lord puts the sun in the sky every morning, so also should we start every day determined to do a little better job; be it in the military, or home in your civilian occupation." He said it very well. The boy seemed to be nodding, agreeing, ready to speak.

"I'm sure I've knocked up my first cousin, Chaplain. She's thirteen. I can't marry my first cousin. I can't have my uncle for my father-in-law; not *my* uncle."

Papps's face froze. He could feel the ponderous eyebrow twitching uncontrollably up and down, violating his forehead. He backed away from the soldier almost in horror.

"I didn't rape her or anything, Chaplain. She wanted it, honest. But now *I* don't want it. I'm really sorry now—"

Once the boy started, he wouldn't stop talking and Papps continued to retreat, backing by the Kodak X-ray machines, by the lead shields, by the developers, by the fat sergeant whispering to him, and on out into the cloudy day where he found he still had one piece of Canadian bacon left. He ate it hungrily, the whole piece at one bite.

"Looked like an Anglican, anyway," he mused. "The bishop would never approve."

Cameroons Jackson didn't bother messing around the company area at the end of the day. As a professional among amateurs, he sought the companionship of permanent party sergeants at the NCO club. Unlike others of the 229th, who rushed to get into civvies as soon as evening formation was over, Jackson maintained the quiet dignity of his Class A suntans.

"Man, you in the Army now," he would say to the men in his charge. "What you want to go gettin' it confused with bein' a civilian? You all a bunch of dumb fuckers. Don't know where you at. Suppose in civilian life you all the time puttin' on your fatigues?"

"Don't believe it for a minute, Sarge," they'd tell him, hurrying into their chinos and blue button-downs and unshined brown loafers and their windbreaker jackets that usually had the college crest on the breast pocket, or their name written across the back.

"Shee-it," Cameroons would snort, pulling up his black tie tightly against his Adam's apple; "you guys is nothing but ambig-u-ous; how you 'spect to produce anything if you all the time am-big-u-ous? When we go active, see how quick them chinos is stashed back with your wives and kids. Chinos and blue shirts—she-it."

Cameroons could absorb a king-size can of beer. He didn't drink it exactly, just tipped it up to his mouth and sucked in. Long ago he had learned the trick of opening the trap door in his throat and with one quick swallow taking down the entire contents of the can. The trick had kept him in beer all through France and Germany and all through countless summer camps in the Reserve.

Tonight he was holding forth on sex. "Broads made me know—man, I'm tellin' you—*know* how much they hunger after this stick. Not just this stick of mine; but yours, his, all of ours. Americans they just hypocrites, frightened to admit it. Everybody so conscious and scared, man, I been so close to re-uppin' just to get my ass away from all that FEAR. It just crawl the corridors in the hospital where I work, in an' amongst the canned goods where I shop, and around all the stools at the bar down on the corner. What we got to be scared of here in the NCO club? We bitch and drink and fight if we got a mind in that direction. But the big thing is that we ain't scared and our wives ain't scared and there is some motha-fuckin' order to the whole thing. Don't matter if we like it or not. Man don't have to like everything. Just gotta get himself along in this world."

Jackson sloshed some beer around in his mouth and tried to clean between his teeth, where some particles of a Slim Jim hot sausage had lodged. He had a big capacity, but he was getting drunk. "Gettin' drunk in summer camp is like goin' to prayer meetin',," he said. "You're not sure you want to; but after the tie gets loosened up a bit, you don't mind it a-tall. Fact is, you like it."

At the NCO club they didn't talk about the Man or voter registration or Martin Luther King. They drank and boasted about exploits in Berlin and Tokyo and Fort Sill, Oklahoma; of fights in Paris and Panama and whores on the Reeperbahn and where their daddies had grown up and why they joined The Profession—until Cameroons Jackson wondered why the hell he was on the outside. The two permanent party sergeants bitched and loved it; swore they'd get out after the next hitch and loved it; laughed at Jackson for being a civilian and loved it. When he looked like he might be getting mean they paid up and left, secure within their military pay voucher limits, knowing a lot about the next meal and the next payday. Knowing a hell of a lot more than Cameroons Jackson.

"It's just too fucking easy," he told himself, the voice hammering away inside his head, way down deep where he couldn't shut it off. He was very steady when he walked out of the NCO club. No cabs were in sight and it was about a mile and a half across the airport to the bivouac area. The small control tower blipped its light alternately red and yellow; Jackson played a game with himself, trying to blink alternate eyes along with it. When he got good at it, he stopped and just talked to himself. "Man, is this cat co-or-dinated; my eyes quicker than most men's feet."

He was sore at the sergeants he had met and sore at himself for drifting into memories with them. "It ain't the realistic attitude," he told himself. "I could've picked to stay in. Probably be Master Sergeant Jackson now, E fucking 8. Oh Lord, why did you pick this black man to be such a fool?" He shook his fist at the control tower; but it didn't do anything but blink back at him mindlessly, red and yellow, blippety blip, yellow and red.

"Blink *black,* you fucker," he yelled at the tower, *"blink black."* And maybe it did as he walked back to tent city; but if it did, the night covered it pretty well.

The adjutant and the executive officer of any military unit are not unlike Broadway producers. They are the guiding spirits, the organizers, the liaison people between the highest echelons and the enlisted drones. Their clipboards are the fullest; their regulation Army brass whistles aare the loudest. Men jump when they command, and fear the repercussions if they move a little too slowly to please the adjutant and the executive officer.

"O.K.," said Doctor-Colonel John Fruitman, "she's all yours, old buddy. A bit reamed out, but still nicely intact."

"The fortunes of war, Colonel," responded the executive officer, Colonel Harden. "We take what we can get. Such as it is."

He walked from the room, leaving Fruitman with a free game still remaining from the fifteen free games he had won on the pinball machine. They were at the Quito Bar and Grill, ten minutes down the post road from Camp Cannon. It was two-thirty in the afternoon and they had arranged to take one of the nurses from the 229th out for a few beers after lunch. The nurse knew what it meant to be taken for a few beers in the afternoon.

Ten summers previously, they had arranged with Johnny Sure-Shot, the half-Indian, half-French Canadian who owned the Quito, to borrow his room over the bar for midsummer rendezvous. Six out of the ten summers they had been successful. They could promise promotion to anyone ambitious enough to be interested. But they insisted on joint ownership. It kept both of them from ever getting sloppy or sentimental about it. They believed in the American system of checks and balances.

All would be clear to the girl before they made the trip. The pattern remained familiar—a quiet ride to the Quito, leaving camp in the afternoon (ostensibly to go to the PX), a beer apiece, and then the pinball game to see who would go first. Dr. Fruitman invariably won, since he would professionally maneuver the side flippers.

"It's all in the thumbs," he would laugh at Harden. "We specialists have that manipulative dexterity that you old house visitors lack."

The lights on the machine would flash and the sounds of it would hum and ring and clatter as the score rose throughout the five-ball cycle. Then it would be Harden's turn, and in the midst of his excitement, suddenly—"Shit, tilt." He always, in his anxiety, would slap the side of the delicate machine and lose his nickel, along with any chance at firsties.

"You are greedy, Colonel Harden; all your balls have rolled over to one side . . . Come, my dear Lieutenant, we'll leave the good colonel to mull over his mistakes for a while."

She would laugh nervously and move toward the stairs with Doctor-Colonel Fruitman. Most of the time she, who-ever-she-might-be, would take a beer with her. Beer can be an aphrodisiac. Afterwards she would remain, wise in the ways of men and their needs, while Fruitman retired to the machine and Harden would enter the room. Her uniform, blue gabardine with blue gabardine cap, would be laid neatly on the chair. There was no need to rush. The sheet would be pulled demurely up to her chin, although there was no need to be coy, either. She answered a need in them; they answered a need for her. Strictly an arrangement. When they were all done once (there was time, but not *that* much time) they would return to the car.

"A few free games left," Johnny Sure-Shot would call after them, positive that if they knew they would not leave so soon.

"Got to make formation, Johnny, use them yourself with our compliments."

They drove off in silence. Sometimes she would say to Colonel Harden, who was second most of the time, "I think you did it inside of me on purpose. You promised not to do it inside of me."

"That's silly," he would respond. "Who ever heard of a pregnant captain?" The thought of the promotion usually assuaged her; if there did turn out to be complications, a transfer out of the unit was easily arranged by the adjutant and the executive officer. After all, they had power.

Skippy Dennis was good at putting things out of his mind. If he wanted to think he had never queered anyone, he damn well never had. On the same level, he could be absolutely convinced that a story, a lie he would tell, if told enough times, was truth. He operated on the fringes of things, barely toeing the line of reality. But he was having trouble avoiding the thought of active duty. He couldn't sleep at night for thinking of outs. The extreme, of telling the chaplain or one of the doctors, that he was homosexual, was too much for him to bear. He didn't think of himself as homosexual. "I've just sampled a variety of experiences, that's all," he told himself.

"The complexities of modern society demand a variety of experiences. How does one cope if one does not taste them all—well, perhaps not *all*—but how can one understand prejudice, for example, unless one understands the nature of differences in people?"

He ran a continual dialectic with himself and emerged the hero in each dialogue. But at summer camp he felt cheated beyond belief. Just when his decorating career was moving in some positive direction. Just when the important contacts had been made. Just when he had been given his first commissions—then to be plucked out and put back into uniform for some indeterminate period for some indeterminate reason.

"Is there, then, no free will?" he asked a faceless God, sitting somewhere at the top of his tent. "Are You that perverse, not to like me *or* my plans for the old Williston manse? Is that it, God: You don't care for rep curtains in the downstairs john? You don't like the throw pillows on the upstairs window seats? Do You realize that the job will be given to that bitch, Wickes?" (Wickes was a co-decorator at Lassick Interiors; but already considered old hat. He had made a lunch-hour pass at a customer, something considered absolutely bad form.)

"Always keep them guessing," was Mr. Lassick's continual advice. "Makes for a neater presentation, cleaner lines—business during business hours, Mr. Dennis." Mr. Lassick was very stern and had learned to control himself. "If you don't learn control in the first two years in this business," he elaborated, "then move to Detroit or Los Angeles. *If* you are going to remain in Boston—*with status,* mind you—control is the touchstone of success. Control, my boy!"

As a result of remembering his employer's advice, the whole first week of camp Sergeant Skippy Dennis practiced control. First he sent a postcard to Lassick saying: "Human beings wonderfully adaptable, am using shantung swatches to poke down the barrel of my rifle. Have made sharp-shooter, with oak leaf clusters. Best to Mrs. Williston, et al. Love—Audie Murphy."

"Subtle yet ambiguous," he thought; he made sure that the picture on the front of the card was the one with all the uniformed soldiers practicing grenade tossing. He practiced self-control next by denying himself green vegetables; then by doing twenty-five sit-ups, daily, in the morning; but especially by trying to imagine no other life but that of a sergeant in the Army.

It wasn't easy, for Dennis was young. The longer the week

lasted, the less imaginative his cravings. He felt like an alcoholic in a bar full of empty bottles. Every soldier he saw, every man he ordered on detail, became a love object, as the idea of being separated from his job at home became intolerable. So he began secret decorating projects; such as attaching yellow and green dye markers to tent ropes, and telling officers, "a splash of color here, a splash of color there, transforms living in the field into something more bearable." The officers would wonder about him and have someone else remove the dye markers. He began wearing turtleneck jerseys in various colors under his fatigues, until the Colonel noticed it and demanded he revert to the plain white T-shirt. He brooded over a further artistic approach to the Army and became a tyrant during morning police call, demanding that his men pick up every bit of paper minutiae off the ground: "We start with sterility, men, sterility; and then, we clutter."

They would waken to find crepe paper, red and gold and orange, strung from the ropes of the tents, inside and out. "Like the motions of the dance," he would tell himself admiringly. "Symmetrical and planned—crepe paper, cheap yet effective, strung like a college prom. Lower the ceiling, Skippy Dennis, violate space with new forms that give meaning—"

Until one of the boys awoke one night to find his nose being tickled by something. He grabbed out instinctively and pulled. Crepe paper has a way of stretching and finally giving with a jerk. (It was a difficult medium for a decorator to work, but Dennis felt himself up to the task.) The soldier rose with a start. "What the hell?"

"Now look what you've done," said Dennis from above him, standing on two piled-up footlockers. "I've got to start this section all over." He was dressed in host pajamas, red, the Japanese type, with the collar turned up and buttoned against the night chill. He had his hands on his hips and was staring angrily down. "I try to introduce a little un-monotony into your dull, uncomprehending lives and you strike out blindly to destroy it. Anarchist!"

"Huh?" said the soldier, still half asleep and not quite believing what he was seeing. "What you doing on top o' my footlocker?"

"I'm beautifying your home," Dennis answered. "Go back to sleep."

"You're the creep that we've been cleaning up after every day. What kind of nutty thing is this to be doing? What time is it, anyway?"

Other men were beginning to wake up around them. "What the Christ is going on?"

"Cool the noise!"

"I'm gonna haul a little ass if there's not quiet—"

"Shut up!"

"MORONS," Dennis yelled at the top of his voice. "HUNS, VISIGOTHS, I'm doing this for you. Some beauty in your lives to replace the beige sameness," he appealed. "You don't deserve it, none of you deserve it."

He began tearing at his crepe decorations; snatching at the Chinese lanterns that he had planned to string; pulling down the few travel posters of the Costa del Sol that he had planned as the *pièce de résistance*. Then he came tumbling down off the footlockers, hard upon the dirt floor, a mass of colorful crepe and spindly lanterns. Dennis bounced right up and dashed off to his bunk area which, within his privilege as a sergeant, he had screened off from the others by Army-issue mosquito netting.

Eros Winter emerged from a dream about Joanne Moxie, astride her Lambretta, in time to fling after the retreating artist: "Oh, fudge, Sergeant, oh FUDGE," because he felt that some comment was necessary. He wasn't sorry at all.

THIRTEEN

At eleven hundred hours the 229th bitch box snapped on with a hollow breathing noise. Colonel Beauregard had had Keohane and some of his electicians install the two-way intercom system, run by the already overtaxed generator, in order to make announcements from his headquarters without calling a special formation.

"This is an announcement from the Colonel," the bitch box said. Someone hissed back into the two-way complex, making it audible to the entire hospital.

"We don't have return noises like hisses pin-pointed yet," the Colonel's adjutant said in a fury, ". . . as to location, that is; but you officers in charge of the various tents be on the lookout for this form of insubordination."

It was obvious from the chattering in the background that the Colonel was anxious to get on; once again the adjutant introduced him.

"In order to show the Governor and the Archbishop," the Colonel began, sounding very tinny over the intercom, "who are reviewing the Minuteman Division and the members of the 229th General Hospital this Saturday morning, the state of physical preparedness that the Reserve is in," he paused as there was a great inhalation of breath among his unseen audience, ". . . we are introducing a graduated series of physical training exercises for the entire unit. Today we shall exercise at eleven to ease your undoubted shock. Tomorrow morning we try it directly after reveille, before chow, at 0630 hours."

There was a general hissing now, an isolated cry of "Sic Semper Tyrannis," and a chorus of "No PT" from the third estate. The Colonel paid no attention, smiled grimly to himself, and continued thinking that leadership was not the most beloved of roles.

"Sergeants Dennis and Jackson will be in charge of the physical training. All those personnel not on strategic duties dealing with care of patients will fall out in the company area in front of your sleeping tents."

He was gone, replaced by Colonel Fruitman, who screamed an authoritative "FALL OUT ON THE DOUBLE," into the box, mostly for the benefit of Rufus Soule, who was watching the proceedings with detached interest.

"IF YOU MEN PERFORM CREDITABLY ON THE

PARADE GROUND, THERE IS ADDITIONAL NEWS," he added, sweetening his tones a bit. "Mind you, I said if you perform so as to do honor to yourselves and the Army. There will be an enlisted personnel dance at Service Club Number One on Wednesday evening, chaperoned by the officers. The ladies attending will not be strictly from the unit," he paused; "although our WACs and nurses will be there, if they choose. There will be a contingent of nurses in training and Red Cross volunteers from the civilian hospital in Waterville. Carry on." He clicked off the intercom, not wanting to have Soule hear the comments sure to follow the dual bomb.

Pinto fell his KPs, including Winter and von Liebert, out of the mess tent and marched them personally to the assembly area. He believed in PT, along with foods that provided the basic amino acids. Most of the other unit personnel scrambled for their section leaders to get permission to man the wards. Nearly everyone found some excuse not to fall out for PT.

When Colonel Beauregard emerged with Fruitman, Soule, and Joanne Moxie (who was wearing a khaki jump suit and combat boots) they saw only a dozen men, including Marlon Pinto in his flour-covered apron with his six KPs. The other five had no stripes on their sleeves and were designated as mongoloid by their fellows. Sergeants Dennis and Jackson had split the group into two groups of six, when Sonya Faust came lumbering out of the administration tent wearing high blue sneakers untied and flopping along the ground. She ran breathlessly up to Dennis.

"Ohh, Skip," she panted, her mammoth chest heaving up and down like a jellied casaba melon, "I'm about to launch an absolute diet. I'd love to get some exercise. May I join the boys? Just on every other beat—please?"

Dennis shrugged and pointed to the end of the line. Women bored him. Ugly women disgusted him. "Suit yourself, Sonya darling."

Sergeant Dennis wanted less than anyone else to go through PT, let alone conduct it. He looked at Cameroons Jackson for a clue. Jackson had professionally laid aside his fatigue jacket and stood flexing in his white T-shirt.

"Not a very big turnout, considering you have one hundred and fifty enlisted men," Soule commented to the Colonel.

Beauregard needed no other hint. "Where are the rest of the men?"

"Sir," Jackson drawled, "I just lead this PT. You need someone who knows how to indulge in these physical exercises, you call on ol' Jackson. I ain't my brother's keeper in the

133

particular respect of keeping track of the whole en-tire unit. Just too big a job for me. They's other sergeants, sir, for counting heads."

Jackson's apology made sense to the Colonel, who screamed for Baer, his first sergeant. Baer came on the trot, his whistle banging him on the chest at every step.

"Why are there only twelve men on PT, Sergeant Baer?" the Colonel wanted to know.

"Evidently, sir," Baer answered, "they're all on permanent or strategic duty and can't be spared. Funny time to have PT, at 1100 hours, isn't it, sir?"

The Colonel showed red right up to his white-haired roots. He tried to hiss at Baer out of the side of his mouth, so that Soule and Joanne Moxie would not see. Moxie was taking notes on her gunmetal clipboard. The Colonel was frantic at what he felt was nothing but inefficiency around him.

Eros Winter was busy trying to zap Joanne Moxie with his eyes. "She refuses to look my way," he thought to himself; "afraid to let these big brown ones look her straight in the face." He kept staring at her, hoping the power of wishful thinking would let him zap her from a distance.

Colonel Beauregard stiffened his body, trying to bring himself under control. With tight-lipped authority he said to Baer, "Sergeant, carry on the PT with the personnel present. Tomorrow morning we shall fall out a half hour early—I mean everyone—and do not only the daily dozen exercises, *including* the squat bender, but shall run a mile as well, *before chow*. Am I understood?"

"Yes, SIR," snapped Baer, looking his commander straight on, yet betraying no emotion, as he had been taught early in his Army training. He saluted.

"Then carry on, Sergeant," Beauregard said, returned a sloppy salute, and about-faced, with Soule following him.

Joanne Moxie stayed on. "I'd rather like to join with the unit in the exercise, if you don't mind," she said to the departing Colonel. It sounded more like a statement than a request.

He didn't like her a bit. "Of course, ma'am," he said graciously, adding to himself, "Hope you sprain your groin on the squat benders."

She put her gunmetal clipboard down and moved next to Eros, who was in Jackson's half dozen. Jackson didn't want his assignees to witness the cadences of the others. "I never liked any of them other boys looking on my arithmetic answers back in grammar school neither. They knew who to copy. Don't want Skippy Dennis copyin' off my cadences

134

neither," he reasoned to himself, and snappily ordered, "DE-TAIL, 'TEN-HOOT. A-BAWOOT FACE." He made it mean and guttural and they obeyed him with precision. He marched them along in his own deep-throated fashion, well-suited to his long strides, arms swinging easy and naturally: "HUP," pause, "HUP," pause, HUP, HOPE, THARIP, HO." He went way down low in the throat with the "HO."

Joanne Moxie had no trouble understanding. She marched along in perfect cadence and wondered at the back of Eros Winter's neck. He had soft little hairs there and they were all standing on end. The summer sun had bleached them blond; somehow they had eluded the barber's straight razor when Eros had gone for his pre-summer-camp haircut. Thre was no accounting for it, but she felt a tingling, answering what she felt must be going on under the surface of *his* neck. The insides of her thighs began to get strangely warm; so much so that it was almost painful to march. Her rational mind beat the idea away. "It must be these damn jump suits. Look good," she thought, "but don't breathe very well. Give me a good karate kimono any day. These Occidental uniforms. Unfunctional!" And she swung along with the "hup pause, hup pause, hup, hope, tharip, ho," until the insides of her thighs tingled with more of the strange ache. She found she couldn't take her eyes off Eros Winter's neck.

When Cameroons Jackson commanded, "DE-TAIL HALT," she didn't pay any attention, and marched right into the neck she had been staring at. Eros turned around and winked at her, bringing the corners of his mouth up in a conspiratorial grin, as if she had planned the accident.

"The idea is to wait until I'm facing the other way, baby," he told her. She reacted immediately as if slapped, bringing her knee up hard and fast toward Eros's privates. He brushed it away neatly with the side of his upper leg and ran toward Sergeant Jackson in mock terror.

"Now, you troopers," Jackson bellowed; "you going to settle down and physical train, or screw around with each other? I got all day and I just as soon spend it monkeying around with you candy-behinds, as in doing something more productive."

The seven bodies fell into line with Joanne whispering menacingly at Winter, "I am here both to observe, and to discipline my body so it may better serve my principles. You better see to it that you don't muddy the waters of our nation's progress, young man."

"Young man!" Eros laughed. "You've never seen joints
135

bend until you've seen mine." He leered at her and she noticed.

"We are now ready to commence the first exercise," called Jackson to his troop, who waited at attention. "Exercise number one: the side straddle!" he yelled. "Eight counts, read-y . . . huh!" he grunted, jumping with both feet apart and clapping his hands over his head. Nobody followed him except Joanne Moxie, who jumped easily and lithely.

"What you think I'm doing this for, my health?" yelled Cameroons to the others. "I ain't giving no demonstrations; I'm leading you. Ready? Huh, he, huh, he, jump, two three fo,' eight two, thrip, fo', seven, six, thrip, ho," he counted. Everyone maintained his own pace and the clapping hands sounded a discord. Except for Joanne Moxie. Eros joined her. They kept in perfect cadence with one another, keeping track, each of the other, with the corners of their eyes. Her close-cropped brown hair flopped up and down in back, the bangs banging against her forehead, even and smooth. Eros moved through his motions just as easily; when Cameroons Jackson signaled a halt with a "Finish, two, thrip, four, halt!" it had been so much like a coordinated dance that he was sorry to see it end.

Von Liebert didn't quit with Jackson. His pace was double time. He jumped to his own beat, which he felt should be twice as rapid as that of the colonial Americans by historical precedent.

Eros and Joanne Moxie calmly awaited the next exercise. Winter didn't puff because he'd be damned if he'd give her the satisfaction. After they had gone through running in place, push-ups, touch-your-toes, they came to the squat benders.

Joanne Moxie was very conscious of people's auras. She smelled the essences of people to whom she was attracted and catalogued them in a file in her mind. When she came upon something that reminded her of the past, she could instantly isolate the smell of that long-gone person.

"I like the smell of this enlisted man," she thought about Eros Winter, and she liked it better as they got deeper into the PT. The squat bender consisted—again in eight counts—of leaping to your feet and coming crashing down upon one leg. Then alternating upon the other leg, bending at the knee. By three counts everyone was hamstrung. But they kept going, each at his own peculiar pace: Jackson and four nondescripts doing one full jump every thirty seconds, then resting; von Liebert keeping strictly to the eight counts; Joanne and Winter maintaining their little sweaty *pas de deux* in mutual satisfaction.

She was candid. Between leaps she said to him, "I don't know where you get your aura, which I sense, but I am intrigued. Are you by any chance a Leo person?"

Between leaps he answered, "July the thirtieth."

Without missing a beat she told him, "I am going to recommend that the dance be held, on the basis of the performances of you and your comrades. I shall attend the dance myself and perhaps talk with you about being a Leo person. I do like the aura of Leo people. They smell different from other folk."

Eros was ecstatic. "What a piece of good fortune," he thought, "to be the first spec four on my block to get laid at summer camp."

"I am an enlisted man by choice," he told Joanne, "having turned down many offers of commission in order to observe better what makes the common man tick. I am a student of life."

"Oh, I'm getting through to her," he thought, "nicely, nicely; by using the rhythms of her own affected speech. She's the type that has either given herself to every under-privileged group, or she's a virgin. Never been in love. Summer romances are my favorite."

"My first name is Eros," he said to her simply.

She caught the message. "How very lovely. Are your parents Greek?" Her eyes shone as she inhaled his essence, slightly changed now that he was no longer unsure of her response. She appreciated subtle change.

But Jackson interrupted them: "Fall in, troopers," he roared. "Column of twos and move out. Route step, HARCH!"

Joanne and Eros walked side by side and he thought about being in the Israeli army and getting to do something like that every day with women. "They've really got the right approach to the military," he thought. "Provide all the essentials to your troops. Recognize the needs and satisfy 'em. They have the roots of an advanced civilization. Good thinkers." They marched side by side keeping step with each other. "Like the Haganah," he whispered in her ear.

She felt proud to have discovered such a diamond in the rough at Camp Cannon. "We can do some PR releases on him, if the unit is activated," she thought. "Rufus will love the idea. Sensitive soldier on maneuvers. Sensitive, sensual, smelly soldier," she thought, and again felt the strange warmth seep inside her thighs. This time she didn't wonder at it, but watched the clean line of his face, skin tanned with the dark hair falling over his eyes under his fatigue cap. She became excited at the idea of being interested in someone on KP.

Since Skippy Dennis couldn't observe the commands that Jackson gave his men in their exercises, he decided to let his own group play games. "Games that will tax the imagination, yet allow free play for the body," he thought, day-dreaming of Greece. "Games with beautiful boys on the shores of the Hellespont."

"Sergeant Faust," he called to the ubiquitous Sonya, her sneakers high and blue and unlaced, "you may take three giant steps forward." She moved her mammoth body and leaped, one, two, three giant steps closer to Dennis.

"Go all the way back," he demanded. "You forgot to say, 'May I?' "

She lumbered back to the starting point, visibly disappointed, her head drooping down on her chest. Later in the game, when she was allowed two umbrella steps, she remembered to say, "May I?" and twirled around and around, almost losing her balance and slipping to the turf. Dennis gave her a combination of giant steps and umbrella steps that let her reach him first, before any of the others, who were mostly given baby steps. But then, the others weren't as wild about the game as Sonya Faust was. They wanted as little exercise as possible.

"I like people who care about winning to share in the spoils," Dennis said to himself. He felt awfully good about letting Sonya win. "Let's not give traumas where traumas aren't due," he said most beneficently. "You have won this PT game in record time, Sergeant," he said to her, "and as a prize, you may choose the exercise to follow."

Sonya almost leaped up and down, she was so happy. At last she was out with the men on actual training and not being just a behind-the-lines administrative person. She didn't hesitate a moment, but yelled out, loud and clear—"Red Light; let's play Red Light. You be the teacher, one, two, three," she chirped.

"Oh, Christ, not Red Light," one of the nondescripts from KP muttered. But he was only a private first class and didn't matter. Dennis silenced him with a raised eyebrow. The PFC muttered more to himself and scuffed the dust with his combat boot. Dennis let Sonya Faust win the Red Light game also. She charged lickety-split at the sergeant when his back was turned and came panting to a halt, her sneaker laces still quivering from the shaking they were taking, when he turned slowly to see if he could catch anyone in movement. He pretended not to see her and repeatedly sent the others back to the starting line, allowing Sonya to advance. She was generous in triumph in the second game, turning to the others and asking if there were any requests.

"Yeah," said the KP refugee. "How's about some Red Rover, Red Rover?"

Sonya didn't care much for Red Rover. It meant holding hands with the lower-ranking enlisted men; but she was as good as her word and divided the group up, three and three. She was just beginning to call out the first name when Cameroons Jackson and his little party route-stepped by, Eros and Joanne Moxie swinging along in their own newly learned cadence, oblivious to the others.

"What you think you doin', Dennis?" Jackson roared at him in amazement. "This PT, or you runnin' a picnic?"

"Well," answered the decorator, "I thought perhaps a bit of free expression would help the morale. They've performed very well, actually."

"Man, are you shitting me? For if you are, shit me not. This here's the Aah-my, it ain't no playground. Get these troopers in line. Fall 'em in behind me on the double. And what that typing sergeant doin' out of uniform?" he indicated Sonya and her nonregulation blue sneakers. "This ain't no basketball court. Man, I tell you again, this here's the Aahmy. Nobody wants to listen to ol' Cameroons Jackson. You all gonna drive me bananas."

Jackson was hot, and he was not looking forward to the upcoming dance. Almost everyone else in the unit was. He realized that and spat again, feeling his mouth start to go a little dry from the effort.

"The bitter and the sweet, Marjorie. The bitter and the sweet," Colonel Beauregard was telling Major Stavropolis in his tent after noontime chow. "Give soldiers a taste of home, a bit of bread and circus, and then—lead them off to war, refreshed, replete. *Voilà*—you have fighting men with a memory of things to get home for. They'll fight harder, believe me. Ahh, this dance was a brilliant stroke. Then a long briefing the next day on the Operation. Then the weekend off. Then, the plan goes into effect, with rested and happy troops. You've got to out-think these civilian soldiers, Marjorie. They haven't been in long enough to be brainwashed.

They're still thinking in terms of nine to five and then home. Got to be one jump ahead. That's it, a little lower, near the lumbar; ahhh, good girl."

She was rubbing Nivea skin lotion into his back, a duty she performed every day in the field. "Got to keep the skin of my back toned for your hands, right, girl?" he asked her, not really expecting an answer. He had no doubt that she was the most privileged major in the Army Nurse Corps.

She worked her thumbs into the flesh, kneading the muscles of his back, moving slowly below the level of his white Army skivvies covering the gluteus maximus. She could feel him stiffen. "Not there, Marjorie You know how it puckers me." She moved higher and he relaxed; the pink skin began to acquire the feel of a rubber doll.

When the Colonel was good and relaxed she spoke softly into his ear: "What about that promotion if we're activated, Gayle? Should go through without much problem, don't you think?"

Colonel Beauregard lay on his stomach on his cot. "Hmmmmm," he answered, drooling onto his pillow. He was almost asleep.

"I wonder if every mistress has always hated her protector?" she wondered to herself, hating the Colonel. "He thinks he's so safe. Little son of a bitch; just wait until I'm a colonel, too. Thinks he can lay one finger on me then, he's got another something coming. Let him find a new agreeable lieutenant to promote. He'll be small peanuts to me then." She squeezed a huge glob of Nivea onto his back, for spite, and watched the liquid spread and run. "Greasy slob," she said aloud.

"Hmmmm," said the Colonel again, oblivious to the hate and the Nivea. A trickle of his drool ran down the pillowcase.

After showers and shaves the following evening, the men were trucked and ambulanced to Service Club Number One for their promised dance. Everyone, by order of the Colonel, was dressed in khaki suntans with ties, spit-shined low-quarter shoes, and polished brass. The Colonel had allowed no one but a small crew of fire guards and detail men to remain behind; those were generally the hardest core of recently married personnel, who resisted temptation like early Christian martyrs.

The Colonel feared a lapse of morale if the men were allowed time to think about their predicament. He wanted to leave nothing to chance. "Only leave the simpletons behind," he ordered his staff. The functioning hospital had disposed of

140

all except some flu cases, the more difficult patients having been transferred to the permanent base hospital or the civilian facility in the town of Waterville. The 229th was supposed to handle only emergency treatment, then ship the patients to the rear for more permanent care.

Nurse Jane, a first lieutenant with an incredibly pitted face, was left behind on the wards, with a few harmless privates to serve guard duty and one of the minor nonmedical officers who could function as combination telephone operator and OD. Nurse Jane had not believed the doctor who told her when she was a little girl not to scratch her chicken pox. This accounted for her pocked face and her willingness to stay behind from the dance. She liked to flip sheets off male patients and see them all shriveled up and small in the groin. Nurses were not supposed to pay any attention to that kind of thing, seeing it so frequently. But Nurse Jane paid attention. As soon as the trucks and ambulances pulled out of the parking lot she hummed to herself and headed for the first sheet with a patient under it.

Kenny Keohane was humming to himself also, having been delegated to supply the beer and soft drinks for the dance. He still had fifteen cases stashed out near Route 30 on the way into Waterville, hidden near a clump of birch trees. He could sell them at a profit. He used orange and root beer and even a raspberry-flavored dietetic beverage as loss leaders, and discouraged among his followers the use of beverages in flasks to supplement the carbonated drinks. He was interested in pushing the beer.

"Don't you know that beer is the official drink every major armed force in the world?" he told one of his boys, who had brought up a fifth of bourbon from home. "What drink do you think of in terms of 'having a few with the boys?' Beer, naturally! Then play it like a soldier. Button those buttons; square those corners; drink that beer!"

The soldier left his bourbon back in his duffel bag reluctantly. But he left it.

Kenny's motor pool boys were hesitant to go to the dance. They weren't at all sure that it was a reward. "What kind of broads they gonna be, Kenny?" they asked.

"Oh," said Keohane, in the midst of counting church keys, "we'll just have to see when they get here. The Colonel promises a surprise. By the way, I had a little talk with him this afternoon; he has another surprise for us." Keohane barely looked at his men; but flickers of a grin appeared around the corners of his mouth. The jaws of his men dropped slack and

Keohane turned serious. "We have been chosen to act as the Aggressor Force during the assault exercise next week, along with two officers and a few other enlisted men. This is a great honor the Colonel has bestowed upon the motor pool, and I want you to know I intend living up to it." He beamed at them. They were confused, but fiercely loyal.

Upon Kenny's orders they carried the cases into the service club, up the stairs, through the alcove with its bulletin board of coming events. ("Mondays: Whist with prizes; Tuesdays: Bingo with prizes; Wednesdays: Talent Night—bring your instruments; Thursdays: Watch Corporal Lester Loomis perform his Magic; Sunday afternoons, after Religious Services of your choice: Ping-Pong and Shuffleboard.—Ethyl Annise, USO Advisor.") They placed the beer and soda in a large cooler directly under the small stage of the main Auditorium.

The band was already there, blowing air into their instruments, making discordant tuning noises. There was a piano (a Baldwin upright, donated—as it said on a brass plaque above the keyboard—*for our servicemen from the estate of Harry Lee, beloved father, uncle, husband, and provider, 1943*). There was a trumpet, a saxophone and a bass to go with the piano. These instruments were brought by the band who looked as if they, too, were bequests from the mysterious estate of Harry Lee.

The band had been recruited by the resourceful Miss Ethyl Annise, who had long since exhausted the rest of the upper New York State territory of volunteers among local musicians. She longed for the days when Camp Cannon had been a jumping-off place for troops going overseas. She remained after the war because she liked the town and the proximity of the Thousand Islands and Canada and the memories of the big USO Center she used to run—where the only man who had loved her, Staff Sergeant Myron Zimmerman, had sipped his last cup of coffee, bitten the last bite of the powdered-sugar doughnuts he liked so well, and shipped out for North Africa. She never heard from him again; but she lingered on, working in the town library in the winters when Cannon was closed, returning to do good works with the Reserve and National Guard units in the summer, hoping against some strange hope that Myron Zimmerman would reappear and take a fresh bite out of her powdered-sugar doughnuts.

These band members actually enjoyed playing for charity. They were curious about people from outside of Waterville; their only major difficulty during dances of this nature was

142

paying attention to the music when they really wanted to gawk at the soldiers and their carryings-on.

There was a father and son team in the band: "The Musical Musicofs." The father was the local piano teacher; the son had rebelled musically and played a saxophone. This son, Bruce, especially liked to gawk. His friends—not knowing enough to call him a voyeur—called him "The Gawker" because of his habit and his large collection of pornography.

The trumpet and bass were friends of Bruce's father, but not fond of each other. The bass prided himself on having played in a chamber music society when he lived in New York City. In his mind this set him apart from all the local musicians. The trumpet refused to play without a mute. He loved the "waaa waaa" sound. It reminded him of speakeasies he had played when Utica was a wide open town in the twenties and thirties. So he played everything from marches to ballads to "Taps" with a muted horn; as he said, "The devil take the hindmost."

While the motor pool boys were stashing the beer in the cooler and arranging the potato chips in china bowls around the hall, two small school buses pulled up in front of the service club. In the front bus was the contingent of older women: librarians, Red Cross volunteers, teachers and the like. As Miss Ethyl Annise put it. "Anyone with maturity and grace who wishes to take a few turns on the floor and make someone away from home a little bit less homesick." That bus was half full. The driver had waited for fifteen extra minutes in front of the local hotel, Twombley's ("soon to be the new Waterville Astoria"), which was the pickup place; but still the bus was only half full.

The second bus was jammed with "all those young ladies of education and proper manners who would also like to take a few turns on the floor and make someone away from home a little less homesick." A fair amount of boy friends were irritated that their girls were going. But most of the girls were curious, or bored with home, or patriotic (since there *is* such a thing as patriotism in upper New York State), or ugly and dateless on a Wednesday evening in the middle of the week. The occupants of this bus were noisy and apprehensive. They came up to the white and yellow service club singing, "You Are My Sunshine," which was the right song to sing under the circumstances, because all the girls were sure of the lyrics and they didn't have to hold back. Not even a little bit.

They came out of the bus and scrambled up the stairs of

143

the club, crowded through the door, and headed for the ladies' room. They pushed in front of the older women, who got most annoyed and muttered to themselves.

One youngster with a platinum streak in her hair, the only one in her group of friends allowed to bleach, and therefore somewhat of a leader, snorted: "Crusty old maids. Think you're gonna do yourself any good in the ladies' room anyway? All you could do in here is tinkle." She swept past triumphantly, her friends all broken up by her comment. She would unbutton another button at the throat of her pink angora sweater, the button her mother always checked to see if it was closed.

The WACs and nurses were driven to the dance by the officers, who were ostensibly coming to chaperone—actually, to participate. The nurses felt self-conscious in their uniforms, and were at a distinct disadvantage vis-a-vis the women in civilian dress.

"Remember, girls," Major Marjorie Stavropolis had told them while they were dressing, "There's a very good chance some of the girls there tonight may be considering careers in the WACs or the Army Nurse Corps. Let's keep our chins up and walk tall. Make the Colonel proud of you."

The other nurses and WACS winked at each other. They saw Stavropolis, with her especially fine figure, all set for the dance. They peeked into her tent to see her putting on her laciest Merry Widow, that the Colonel had probably given her. But nevertheless, they did try to set some sort of example, walking two by two into the service club, ignoring temptation to hide in the powder room, and moving directly into the hall.

Sonya Faust felt in terrific condition after her Red Light triumph of the previous afternoon. She was wearing her Army-issue high heels; but they were sensible heels, not higher than two inches. "I feel reckless tonight," she confided. "My calves feel all tight, good shape for dancing. I might even ask that Sergeant Pinto to dance the polka with me. Don't you just love his artistry with the chow?" She had taken special pains to get all the carbon stains off her fingers. That's how serious *she* was about the dance.

Colonel Beauregard, Rufus Soule, and Joanne Moxie arrived together in the staff car. Soule was wearing a blue nine-month suit. All of his suits could be worn in most climates for nine months.

"I believe in functional dress," he told the Colonel. "This is dacron and wool, really quite substantial. If headquarters sends me anywhere in the world, I don't have to be obviously wash-and-wear. My nine-month suits can mark me as a native anywhere. You see, functional!" He had changed his string tie in the silver clasp to match the suit, but his crepe-soled shoes remained the same.

Joanne was dressed in a suit of white leather. She affected white. "I first heard my voices at my coming-out party," she told Soule when they first met. "I was walking down the stairs of the ballroom. My father was on my left arm. I had my long white gown and long white gloves and my bouquet was marigolds and lilies; I heard them speaking to me then." Ever since, she believed that white was her *color*. For the military dance she had selected the specially fitted leather suit, pleated skirt, short bolero jacket over a white blouse with puffy sleeves.

"It's not a fetish, Colonel," she explained to Beauregard, who looked quizzically at her. "It's just that I like the feel of leather."

"Oh," was all the Colonel said, trying to understand.

Motors began to roar closer and closer as the trucks and ambulances of the 229th moved at their military twenty miles per hour to the dance. One of the enlisted men had brought a guitar from home. As they bumped along he chorded and sang, "Just listen to the jungle and the rumble and the roar, as she glides along the woodland to the hills and by the shore—" Everyone was quiet, listening to him playing his guitar. His music was the only sound they would pay any attention to in the Reserve; that, and the transistor radios which blared all day and night in the tents, until somebody tired enough or big enough ordered them shut off.

Eldor von Liebert got a strange lump in his throat, although the music was foreign and unfamiliar. His shoulder blades hurt where the scapulae had rubbed together as he stood up so tall during PT that morning, and during the rest of the day. He was still exhausted from his sixteen hours of kitchen police the day before. Sergeant Baer had kept after him until the field stoves were spotless. He was beginning to think in American: "I have had it with that bastard," he thought, listening to the fading chords of "Wabash Cannonball" and bouncing along the road. He imagined himself a prisoner of war, riding with all the men who were enemy soldiers; he wished for the first time that he didn't have to put up with the pride of his father and his family, when it only marked him a fool. He pretended that none of his guards were watching him, and that he had lunged for the rear door of the ambulance when it slowed to round a corner. There would

145

be shots, but with luck he could make it to the border by the time it was dark. Then he would be safe. Farmers would hide him; they would have heard of his father. They would be loyal to one of their own. The fantasy obliterated the fact that he was totally uninterested in the dance.

Then the vehicle halted and Master Sergeant Lennie Baer threw wide the doors to the ambulance from the outside, allowing the summer air and noises of the peepers in the trees to float in upon the soldiers.

"All right, you guys—don't look so anxious," he said gruffly. "C'mon out of the ve-hicle. Hit the dirt."

"This ain't combat, Baer," someone yelled from the rear.

"No one ever explained the difference to me, wise guy," he answered. "Outside!"

Von Liebert was slow to move, his reverie still a fact of the journey.

"What's the matter, Kraut?" Baer said to him. "Afraid your goose step will be hard on their toes?"

No one laughed, as they might have. It wasn't meant good-naturedly and was not taken that way. Eldor tensed until his Adam's apple pushed hard against the knot of his military tie. Then he brushed past Baer without a word; the sergeant stood practically in his path, daring him to do something. "Self-control is the key to mastery of the world," his father had told him when he was a child. He remembered. "You don't mess with a noncom when you're nothing but a piece of shit," he also remembered from basic training in the American Army.

Eros Winter joined Eldor, going up the steps. He was anxious to avoid any kind of violence, he played percentages and knew that if Eldor and Baer came to blows he himself would have to be involved. He didn't like being involved where someone else was concerned.

"No sweat, buddy." He slapped von Liebert on the rump. Eldor hesitated, then set his lips and let himself be led up the steps by Winter.

FOURTEEN

The dance was beginning and Eros felt good. He had been first in the community shower back at camp, a psychological advantage for any Army social event. His suntans were tapered and pressed. He had had a Puerto Rican draftee polish his brass and his low-quarter shoes until they stood tall, and his mouth tingled from a squeeze of Lavoris, which he had administered himself.

Yet Winter admitted to a twinge of nervousness as he scanned the dance for some sign of Joanne. He brushed back the dark hair falling over his eyes and rehearsed what he would say to her.

The men of the 229th milled about inside the service club like eighth graders at a cellar party. The band struck a chord as Colonel Beauregard walked to the stand and raised his hands in greeting. He wore his dress uniform, with campaign ribbons, and had on his white gloves. The chord was a G-major with muted trumpet, which fit right in.

"I'm sure the boys of Massachusetts," the Colonel began, "are most pleased to see such charming products of the state of New York. I'll be brief." His moustaches bristled with pleasure. He believed he had suckered the unit into complacency. "We officers aren't here to supervise, only to make sure you all have a fine time. I don't want to delay any longer. Make sure you ladies go easy on the root beer. Maestro—if you please." And the muted horn of the uncompromising trumpet player broke into the opening set with "Stars Fell on Alabama."

A scattering of the brave broke ranks and moved in a small khaki wave toward the girls. Miss Ethyl Annise felt herself on the threshold of tears. "We played our little drama," she sing-songed to herself; "we kissed in a field of white . . ." She couldn't imagine where she could find a field of white in Waterville, New York, but she thought it sounded so nice she let the tears come unashamedly. The band was accompanied also by a chorus of hundreds of beer can tab-openers being torn off their moorings. Even the hesitant and the chaste felt the need for the first swift can—the one to loosen the tongue, prop the courage, redden the eyeballs.

Eros Winter noticed Joanne as soon as she came into the room. He was wild for white and, for the first time in his memory, ashamed of being an enlisted man. He had always worn his specialist's insignia as a sign of his private rebellion against the inequities of the military. Now he wished for the privilege of rank. He couldn't very well butt into the Colonel's conversation with her and the other officers.

"I believed in a hierarchy of the intellect," he told himself, "or at least the superiority of the *idiot-savant*. But it doesn't cut any ice all of a sudden. Right here where I want it. Right here where I live," he said to himself, looking down at the starched fly of his trousers. "Scratch a specialist and you get cannon fodder, Winter," he said to himself. "If I didn't dig her so much, I'd shrug it off." He pretended to shrug it off and to studiously ignore her. She'd be kooky enough to come looking for him. "These liberal broads are for the downtrodden. She'll be around."

He sought the solace of a pop-top can and found Miss Pink Angora Sweater struggling with one of her own. "Why rip, rip, rip when one zip does it," he told her, lifting the can gently from her grasp. It opened easily for him and he flipped the tab away into a corner.

She wondered at his touch. None of the boys in Waterville were so careless as to flip a tab top like that. Mostly they put them in their jeans pockets. For a moment she was confused, but swiftly caught herself. After all, she was the most advanced of her girl friends. Hadn't she four hooks on her bra when she was only fourteen? The other girls still wore undershirts (the cold wind blowing down from the Canadian border tended to inhibit breast growth until a later age). She thrust her chest out at Eros and tilted back her chin to take a large swallow from her can. Lightning fast, he reached forward and undid another button on the angora sweater. She never noticed. He was on it, successfully, and back before the beer passed the trachea. She smiled at him.

"See, I didn't even get a drop on my chin. Your Boston girls aren't the only women who are sophisticated."

"You are so right," he said. "As a matter of fact, they haven't even got around to discovering angora yet; a delicious piece of sophistication."

"You talk funny—but I suppose it's meant as a compliment. My mother got it in Syracuse. She goes there to Republican meetings. She's very active."

"How about you? I mean, you know the legend of the Angora rabbit?"

She was suddenly aware of the unbuttoned button and that the upper lace of her four-hooker was showing. But she was, by now, afraid that it would be unsophisticated to attempt to do anything about it. She was flustered at having to play it straight. She didn't know that angora came from a rabbit; so she tried the defense used by generations of upper New York State girls.

"What are you, queer or something?" she said.

Eros Winter just smiled enigmatically and offered his arm, aware that Joanne had noticed from across the room. Eros led her, unresisting, onto the floor; she came into his arms like a lobster, clutching and clawing and wanting immediately to demonstrate the Waterville dancing syndrome: arms of girl around neck of boy, arms of boy around waist of girl.

"Uh-uh," Eros told her, removing her arms from his neck. "We're being patrolled." He saw assorted officers glaring at him from positions they had taken up around the dance floor. He felt again the inequities of rank.

"It's not as good this way," she said to him with a pout she had practiced.

"It'll get better," said Eros, rubbing his upper body sideways, back and forth, across the angora. "Doesn't the sweater get all bally in front when it's rubbed?"

"No one ever rubs it much." She breathed into his ear, not wanting to miss her chance to get a little culture via Boston.

"Tell it to the Marines," he said, and proceeded to try to make it bally in back, sliding his right hand lower until the fingers rested at the top of her bottom.

"Tell me about the Angora rabbit legend," she said.

Eros was warming to his task. "The wool of the Angora can only be taken during lovemaking. The rabbit's, that is. At that time it retains its special soft quality, that makes it so valuable for sweater sets, babies' tippets, mittens. It ruins the lovemaking, but they make millions of people happy. What's one session more or less for a rabbit?" And he zeroed in on her neck, despite the ever-closing circle of officers, who frowned and were ready to deprive him.

Angora Sweater gasped. She had been on the fourth leg of an intricate box step and was concentrating. "You know," she said, "I don't even know your name."

"It's Combat Kelly," said Eros, and whirled her away toward the beer cooler, where Kenny Keohane was holding court with his boys. He winked at Winter and approved. The beer was loosening up Keohane's thought processes. He was trying to find some way to get von Liebert into the Aggressor act without upsetting anyone.

"Not all the men are dancing," reported Colonel Harden,

149

who had done a swift reconnaissance of the hall.

"Well, light a fire under their tails," retorted Gayle Beauregard, insistent. "We're the hosts for this show and I want every female dancing. I don't mean the unit females. I don't give a good goddam whether they roll bandages or polka with each other. I mean our guests. Get the men on the floor. Married or not. Pretend it's wartime in the USO. They'll forget fast enough. Have special dances; pair everyone off. And sell a little more of that tonic. I don't want it all left tomorrow. I don't like to leave rough edges. Smooth everything off. Button all buttons and roll a tight bed. That's the way the Army should be run."

Colonel Harden didn't argue. "Yes, sir," he snapped, and strode to the bandstand to carry out a direct order.

The band was playing variations on a theme of "Moonglow," a special arrangement by Musicof *père* at the piano. He would use it as his theme song and intersperse it somewhere in each set, never subtly, almost like passing out handbills advertising his band. They came to a halt at Harden's intercession, all trailing off at different times.

"We haven't rehearsed breaks very much," Mr. Musicof apologized. Harden waved him off, but he *did* get a chord from the players to get everyone's attention. This time it was a G-seventh.

"Uhhh," Harden started, still waiting for everyone to quiet down. "The dance seems a little hesitant. I must apologize for the men, in some cases. They're still battle-fatigued. To get the ball rolling, I think we should have a fun dance for everyone. Officers included." He relished that touch. He knew that Colonel Beauregard hated to dance. He didn't like everyone to notice that Stavropolis was two inches taller than he. Three, in high heels. "We're going to do the Mexican Hat Dance and I want two lines facing each other. Boys on one side, girls on the other. Let's move now." He didn't want to sound stern. He wanted to sound jolly and MC-ish.

The over-forty women were quick to move. The younger girls, especially the ones that already had been dancing, uttered audible "awwwws," and "what is this anyway, a lonely hearts club?"

Eros was irritated. He knew that everyone hated people that make out.

"Does that mean you can't dance with me anymore?" Angora Sweater asked Eros.

"It means I'd like to ball the entire surface of your oh-so-ballable sweater. Let's take a stroll around the campus," he

150

said, moving toward the door of the club and squeezing her hand. She moved her thumb along the top of his fingers. It was the caressing finger, the thumb. She had used it to advantage at dozens of Saturday afternoon matinees when she was younger; and afterwards, when she began getting permission to go out at night.

Instantly they were hemmed in by the ever-alert circle of officers, directed by Colonel Fruitman. He was checking bulges.

"It's a great business, this gynecological business," he used to tell his medical colleagues at home. "Every woman in the world a potential client. No other business in the world like it. No overhead; no inventory; everything clean. Cash where I can take it in. Mason jars full of quarters in my cellar. Every woman I meet, I can picture in the stirrups. Clink, clink, little smear, and ten dollars in the bank. Ring, ring, cash in the Mason jar."

He and some of the junior officers moved in on Winter. Fruitman took one arm of Angora Sweater. Winter took the other.

"Now, my dear," the Colonel began, "I'm Colonel—Doctor, actually—John Fruitman, a ladies' doctor. You understand. Being a ladies' doctor, I'm sure you'll realize the sense of my suggestion to stay in the club for the Mexican Hat Dance. Specialist Winter tells me he wouldn't want to deprive you of a chance to meet any of our young men."

"Sorry, sir," Winter replied, pulling gently in the opposite direction, and sneaking a peek at Joanne Moxie, who was watching. She looked away. The pleats on her skirt swirled around her legs as she abruptly turned. Tan, he noticed. Then she does take off her fatigues occasionally. Ankles aren't thick, he mused. Her knees don't make faces. Can't tell about the thighs. Thighs pretty much of a mystery.

Colonel Fruitman interrupted him. "Winter, I'm sure the lady would like to meet some of our unmarried personnel tonight. Why monopolize one of the most attractive guests? Have you shown her pictures of the children?" It was a stroke of genius on Fruitman's part. Even Winter had to laugh. His denial would be ridiculous. Angora Sweater was blown.

She looked shocked. He could only play along, amused to be outwitted by something so simple. "You touched the top of my bottom!" She was outraged. "That's practically adultery." She grabbed for the button of her sweater and, her reason restored, stalked off with a toss of her platinum curls. "I should have known anyone with a name like Combat Kelly

151

would be married," she muttered, moving toward the beer cooler.

She joined the end of the Hat Dance line, opposite Waldo Reed, the Chaplain's assistant, who leered wickedly, waiting for her to start bouncing. "How would you like to come over for choir practice this Sunday?" he asked her, flashing his special brass that indicated his military role with the clergy: diagonal crosses over a tablet which simulated the Ten Commandments. Nondenominational as hell.

The circle of officers forced Eros to the male line. The entire hall was taken up with females holding hands, and men yelling "Dah-ress right, dah-ress!" giving way to their left and extending their right arms aat right angles to their bodies. "Ready—front!" ordered Colonel Harden, and the men's arms snapped to their sides. They stood ready. "Loosen up gentlemen," smiled Harden. "This is a dance. Get acquainted."

The two Musicofs, father and son, loved the lilt of the Mexican Hat Dance. They didn't await the signal, but nudged each other; Bruce the Gawker, on his saxophone, broke into the first bars: "Ooo wah, oo wah, oo wah, oo wah, oo wah, wah, wah, oowah," he wailed, and was soon followed by the bass, the muted trumpet and the tinkly Baldwin upright. Officers and men all joined in the spirit, along with widow, nurse, WAC, and teen-age camp follower. In pairs the line came apart and scattered the couples all over the hall.

Kenny Keohane ended up with Marjorie Stavropolis, and wasn't the least bit pleased about it. He didn't like opportunists. "No room for two of us in this unit," he confided to her, leaping first on one foot, then the other, then on both feet.

"O.K. Why don't you transfer out, Keohane?" she panted at him, when they whirled around in the whirly-around part.

He hated the fact that she took the advantage of calling him by his last name. It made her less of a woman and more of a threat. He knew that she wanted to be activated. Keohane missed a beat on purpose and kicked Stavropolis in the shin.

"You bastard, Keohane. I'll get you for that," she hissed. But they couldn't skip another beat. She knew that Colonel Beauregard had his eye on her and that he would want her to be an example for civilian girls, who were also leaping about, breaking the ice with their enthusiasm.

Cameroons Jackson had drawn Joanne Moxie. This was

quite all right with Joanne. She welcomed the big hands in her own.

"He should be so naturally graceful," she told herself, and was surprised by his lack of coordination. "It's easy, Jackson," she said to him. "Just throw out one foot, then the other, then quickly, one, two, three . . . then we join hands and go around for a bit." She had stopped while everyone else jumped around them. Cameroons had almost never danced with a white woman before. Taken them out plenty in Europe, yes; danced with one he was reasonably sure he wasn't going to bed with . . . no.

"Time for old Cameroons to quit, I think, miss," he said to her with much dignity. "Getting too old for this kind of foolishness."

"Then would you like to talk or something?" she asked him. She specialized in understanding and thought she had the key to—as she called it—"interpersonal relationships."

Immediately Jackson responded in his own mind to the invitation. "Amazin,' " he thought. "They still lusting over my stick. Always knew my theory not completely bullshit. Educate one of these women and they know—oh, how they know—that you have suffered at the hands of the privileged for centuries. You gonna lose three thousand years of suffering in their willing arms. I is one clued-in cat to these interpersonal relationships."

"Let's get some air," he said. "Just a few steps of modern-type dances makes a man dry. Let's take a few beers with us."

"Oh, I don't drink beer," she said, not wanting to go outside with him, but not wanting to offend him either.

"That's all right, miss; they both for me," he chuckled, feeling confident. And he grabbed two cans and opened them, while the others danced the Mexican Hat Dance and Joanne desperately looked around for Rufus Soule to protect her.

Cameroons Jackson led her out of the service club into the quarter moonlight of August. He threw down one of the beers in one long thirsty swallow, hoping to impress her with the feat. Then he slowly crushed the can in his big left hand. "Can even do it lefty, an' that's the one most men weak with," he told her proudly.

"What do you do in civilian life, Jackson?" she began to ask him, backing up against the railing of the porch and making sure that the buttons of her bolero jacket stayed buttoned. He moved closer. The act looked like the preparation for something and Joanne was frightened. She romanticized

153

the scene, seeing Jackson stripped to the waist, the plantation columns burning behind him, and red splotches on his white pants, his eyes shining against the flames and lust spreckling his lips as he came after her in her fifteen crinolines, her parasol poised to jab at his vitals.

The beer had made him bold and he was ready to dispense with the preliminaries. "Why is it," he asked, "do you and your sisters prefer us blacks when we are available and you can't get caught? I had a minister once, used to talk about forbidden fruit—how we mustn't be tempted. How come *you* are the ones always tempted enough to make the first move?" If Jackson was right, it was no time to be philosophical; but for once, he had to know. He sipped on the second beer, tasting it instead of throwing it down.

Joanne Moxie began to get a headache. She knew she was going to hear her voices. Her stomach felt queasy and her forehead felt as if it were going to break out. She scratched it, but there was nothing there. Her brown bangs reasssured her.

"Jackson, I look on you as just another human being. No other feeling. I'm interested in all of God's children; there are no differences for me. I thought you might be uncomfortable dancing that ridiculous dance, so I suggested a little talk. No human being is so basic as to suggest that a talk means anything more serious. Let me explain it to you in terms of—"

Jackson interrupted her. "You is shit out of luck, miss, 'cause here's one cat that's *that* basic," and he lunged at the bolero jacket, ripping it open and grabbing for the pleated leather skirt. "I love women in pleats, baby." He figured the endearment would make it easier. She was just messing with him anyway, he figured.

And that was when the hard rubber squash ball hit him square between the eyes and he suddenly didn't see the pleated skirt or the moon anymore.

"Hi, Sarge," said Specialist Eros Winter, sauntering onto the porch. "Did you see my squash ball?"

Cameroons Jackson was the natural man; he didn't question the interruption any more than he questioned the reason that Joanne Moxie had come out on the porch with him. If the game was up, it was up. He couldn't make it with a witness. If something was there, he could wait. He was good at waiting. He understood, although it hurt, that Winter had done him a favor. Drunkenly, he reminded himself to go easy on the kid in drill for the rest of the week.

"Suppose you saved my ass, trooper," was all he said to

154

Winter, before he left them alone and returned inside to the music.

"You see . . ." Winter said to her softly, wild for her white outfit. She was softened up for him. "You see," he said, "you can't forever be sure of yourself. This is the Army and there *is* a chain of command. But glands don't respect rank. There isn't a man in the world that can't be pushed *too* far." Joanne shivered a little, although the night was warm.

"There is no such thing as lust," she insisted, "when you try to relate to someone, when you try to understand someone else's point of view. I have a clinical approach to people; they don't touch me as anything other than different human beings. That's why the government finds me effective." But perspiration beaded her forehead. She still felt queasy, and a little foolish in her white outfit against the contrasting khaki and green of the military post that surrounded her. She didn't feel like a civilian and she didn't feel like a soldier. She wasn't quite sure what she felt like, except that she felt like a woman. She put her fingers to her temples and pressed very hard. She could see Eros grinning at her; he looked very intimate and close and she even considered being wrong. It was something she hadn't considered for years.

Eros didn't have the softest serve in the world for nothing. Timing was the essence of his squash—and of his success with women. He could turn his racket slightly and cut the ball dead into the corner; he could lob it back within a millimeter of the wall; he could blast it by an opponent's outstretched arm—all by knowing instinctively what they would least expect. With women, he applied the same principles: if they expected a gentleman, he was crude until the time for a decision had to be made, then . . . all softness. They would say, "Eros, I don't understand how you can be so different one minute to the next—ooh, not there, that's a dangerous place."

"Contrast, kitten, contrast—it's the genie of the lamp," is all he would say.

He didn't advance on Joanne; he floated to her with great tenderness. He didn't even appear to be moving. All she knew was that he was suddenly holding her very softly; then harder, until she couldn't keep pressing her fingers to her temples but had to put her arms around him. He raised her chin on a level with his mouth and said, "I've never kissed a secret agent before; what is it like, I wonder?"

She was amazed at her response *and* her ability. "I've never kissed an enlisted man before, so we're even," she said. And they both realized at the same time that they had done nothing. So they rectified the mistake.

Her lips were, as he expected, fiercely compressed.

"Ahhh, these untouchables have to be taught so very much," he thought. "I wonder if it's worth the bother." He was as clinical as Joanne Moxie pretended to be; he never intended to fall in love. He just liked being taken care of from time to time.

"The biggest thing they fall for," he said, "is themselves. Find their essence, from probing their childhood, and fix yourself on the same azimuth. Nothing works like self-reflection. They can't believe anyone has as good taste as they. Terrific! By the time they realize that you've actually got *worse* taste than they, you *want* them to know that. Fun and finis! My family coat of arms: a Harlequin with a yellow streak. But we're long-lived; always die of natural causes. Never even an ulcer. The whole family would die of ulcers, anyway: we tend to vomit from dairy products."

He tried again, but Joanne resisted this time and worked herself out of his grasp. He let her go.

"What you're taking advantage of is not me," she said. "It's merely my relief at being taken out of a touchy situation."

"What you need, yourself, is a good healthy beef injection," he told her. "You and your 'essences' and 'atmospheric quality' and your 'causes.' It's all a lot of crap. You're no different from millions of other American young women with an overabundance of education and a decided lack of common sense. You don't even know how to kiss. You and your fatigues and your voices. I'm not the Dauphin, for Christ's sake. I'm just Specialist Fourth Class Eros Winter, trying to do my time and get out. Why are you trying to confuse the issue?"

He actually got wound up in his Philippic and she, being nothing more than a fool, was interested in the fact that he could get serious. She wanted to try again. The music reached them through open windows; it sang, "In time the Rockies will tumble, Gibraltar may crumble—they're only made of clay—" and they tried again and it was still no good.

"Like this, government girl," he said, and reached up with his hand and softly caressed her mouth with his fingers. Her lips were red and full and she instinctively moistened them with her tongue. They separated slightly and he took the bottom lip between his teeth and bit a tiny bite. Then he did the tongue, slowly at first because she pulled away slightly at the

156

contact; then with greater insistence, until something told her to answer, and she did.

"Well, *hello*, woman," he said to her after some time, and he felt the glow right down to his polished low-quarter shoes, spit-shine agleam from the reflected light inside the service club.

"Don't tell me it's never been like this before," Eros told her. "There's plenty more to come. And you might as well learn it from an enlisted man. In another week, this boy's getting out. Maneuver or no maneuver, peacetime patriotism is not for me. I put my flag away in the attic with my plastic Tommy gun when Korea ended. Let the green berets fight the brushfires. Keeps them off the streets. Leave me to do, or not do, at home, as I choose. That's my interpretation of the American way."

She felt him espousing a cause and she was proud. She came back for more of the wonderful discovery. He was ready. He was willing to modify any of his causes for what he felt to be the greater good. She was learning. Her brown bangs were wet with the emotion generated by their kissing.

"You look like a little sheep dog; a toy poodle," he told her.

She smiled at him and saw the happy light in the corners of his brown eyes. "My father told me not to trust people whose eyes were too close to the sides of their noses. He'd say that you had close-together eyes," she told him. "But somehow it fits the symmetry of your face." She liked his grin when she said that.

"That's a great rationalization," he said, "brought on solely by the fact that you feel you have to justify kissing with your tongue. By the way, what *did* you call what you were doing before? You were no bargain."

"Maybe I knew everything you did already. But I wanted to wait."

Eros felt discomfort then. "You can never be sure about a woman," he thought. "That's what makes it all a fraud; makes it a bitch. I'm not big enough to get above anyone's past."

The beer had blurred his vision and he thought he saw two Joannes. He reached for one of them and she eluded his grasp.

"Did I say something wrong? You know, this is funny for me. I'm not my own boss," said the voice of the other Joanne that stood beside him.

Suddenly, he wanted Angora Sweater: professional, soft, stupid, uncomplicated. "The moth for the flame, you idiot," he said out loud to himself as the band inside switched to the

157

communal beat of the Bunny Hop. "Dah ya, dah ya, dah ya, dah ya dah, plink a plunk a plink a, chord, chord, chord," as the bass piano and muted trumpet swung into the familiar parlor dance.

Joanne wondered at him and felt the complications of touching another human being. She had tried to avoid it for a long time. She realized further, to her horror, that her voices had issued a *real* presentiment. Probably a punishment for dressing in civilian clothes, instead of her comfortable familiar battle gear. The chills and queasy feeling she had felt earlier were not due to any emotional apprehension. She had just gotten her period. She left Eros on the porch.

He wished he had something as simple as moon madness; that he could develop a hairy face and fangs, sink his teeth into the jugular of Colonel Beauregard and make off to some secret cave with Major Stavropolis, there to promote her to colonel through his own private ritual.

"While you're messing around, the wheels are turning, Winter," Kenny Keohane said to him from the half-light.

"I'm not interested in your Irish romanticizing of an intolerable military situation," Winter replied. "Just tell me what you want me to do and let me go home. I'm a simple city lad. I carry out instructions well. Lay it on me, Keohane, it's a buyer's market."

Sonny Beanstock was bouncing his breasts up and down to the Bunny Hop, holding onto a Red Cross woman from the town of Waterville. He was trying to explain to her how frozen pork bellies were traded. It threw off his rhythm and he managed to jump smack into her heels. But it was worth it if he could gain a convert to the commodity market from the boring routine of common stocks. The Red Cross woman had confessed to owning a few Mutual Funds, and she became his prisoner for the evening.

"You can become wealthy overnight," he told her, as he bounced to the uneven music. "One cent fluctuation means thirty-five dollars per contract. You've been wasting your time with those slow movers."

Out to the side he went with his left foot, twice; out to the right he went with his right foot, twice; jump up one; jump back one beat; jump forward three, and wiggle all tails. Beanstock heard the loose change in his pocket jungle, jangle; he heard his keys to the meat lockers in his abattoir (which he always carried on a big thick ring) go clink-a-clinka; but he kept bouncing and clutched the Red Cross girl tightly. She in turn held onto Major Fugue, who had managed to find a secretary to a law firm. He squeezed her girdled thighs as if, by pressure of his hands, he could squeeze the secrets of civilian anatomy into his surgeon's fingers. Then they could move with assurance along the rib cages of people other than gas victims of Château-Thierry and battle fatigues from Bataan. The secretary held Colonel Beauregard, who excitedly jumped and caressed the ample waist of Marjorie Stavropolis, as she twitched and told him that he tickled.

The beer had moved well. Keohane's boys had gone for many more cases and, in order to push the soft drinks (which had been neglected by all except the older women), they began mixing carbonated beverages with the beer in big white paper containers. No one noticed the difference and they were able to sell a great deal of orange beer, raspberry beer, root beer beer, and an occasional ginger ale beer. It was a magnificent success.

Even Miss Ethyl Annise indulged herself in a root beer beer that made her eyes smart and her tummy say howdy; she allowed herself a dance with Marlon Pinto and whirled him by the orchestra to request, just one more time, "Stars Fell on Alabama."

"You gotta taste my cheesecake," he told her earnestly. "The only cherry cheese made with Gouda—"

She just said, "Mmmmm," and dreamed she was in the arms of her Sergeant Myron Zimmerman, long ago before anything had happened and there were no weekend warriors. Only young men who were real and not playing with plowshares. She held her skirts away from her with her left hand and turned around and around.

But the mad conformity of the beery Bunny Hop got them all into the circle, snaking around the floor. Skippy Dennis had dredged up some crepe paper and draped brown and white strands from one end of the hall to the other. It wasn't quite what he haad in mind, but it did lower the ceiling. He was mad to lower ceilings. He sat on the sidelines until the Bunny Hop, when he saw his opportunity to join the end of the line and grab hold of Angel Lapidus, a honey-colored PFC who worked as a ward attendant. He had seen the boy do a variety of South American dances no one else even took the floor to perform; he was fascinated by the movement of the hips. "Fluid," thought Skippy, "like that rose and ebony staircase I'd love to do, winding round and round. Seemingly non-connected. Let me get my hands on those hips; I'll learn a secret; I'll become a more fluid decorator; motion will be the key to my art." And he slipped into the line, feeling the PFC's hips grind with the music, excited by the hip bones which slipped in and out of their sockets like a disjointed camel's gait. "I feel so pagan," he whispered to the neck of the PFC; but the boy was intent on the rolling of his own hips. Skippy held on tighter and forward, back, one, two, three up, felt pagan to himself.

Beads of sweat oozed on the foreheads and dripped down the noses and into the mouths of the band players as they beat out the hop; the snaking line had affected them also. They increased the tempo and whistled, plunked, tooted, and boomed their instruments while the jumping feet of the dancers slapped the hardwood planks on the ends of phrases. Red and blue gels in the four spotlights connected to the ceiling beams moved slowly over the line, illuminating for brief instants faces intent on getting the proper feet out of the way at the proper time.

"I'm set free, I'm really set free," thought Sergeant Lennie Baer as he pushed his forearms toward each other and against the massive hips of Sonya Faust. He knew she wouldn't mind his practicing isometrics during the Bunny Hop; she would understand, if anyone would, what readiness meant to the 229th General Hospital. Lennie Baer and Sonya were two of a kind. Dedicated to the Code of Conduct; dedicated to their ten General Orders; dedicated to Colonel Beauregard. He liked the solidity of an ally, even during Rest and Relaxation periods. He thought of the lost Tootsie Roll man and his wife Doris and daughter Regina. They would never understand his dedication. A woman like Sonya Faust would warm her man's feet on her back on a cold night. His wife wouldn't even get him an extra blanket. He watched his Colonel and the other officers and felt good following them in the endless jump of the dance. "We're all pulling together," he thought, "toward the common end. I have a leader." He felt safe and pushed all the harder, making his muscles bulge with the exertion, feeling it doing some good. Sonya understood and hopped all the faster, trying to bring him to some sort of psychic climax; understanding his need and feeling close to love . . . close to love.

Only von Liebert stood off from the dancers, standing alone near the beer cooler, not even wishing for dark beer but for a different time and a different place.

"The stupid faces," he said to himself, feeling bold from the effect of the alcohol on his stomach. "There's nothing beneath the surface of these faces. They understand nothing. They are up here for entertainment. They care not at all about training; nothing about discipline; nothing about learning. I think I can go home now with honor; they have nothing to teach me except by their miserable example. To be the Reserve is less than a joke. Winter is a dreamer and a fool. Also an American—he can go along with the foolishness. It is no longer anything but a waste of my time. I *will* be an Aggressor with Keohane. He needn't worry about me any longer. These men do not deserve a full-time military. They all deserve their piggish civilian lives, like my roommates: women and liquor, pleasure and avoiding work. If the enemies of America knew of her weaknesses, she would have been mastered long ago. Would they even fight for their homes? Hah, they cannot even do ten push-ups in the morning."

He strutted, making noises with his heels on the floor, purposely off tempo with the beats of the dance. The red light of one of the spots caught Butcher Beanstock going by, making him appear even more jowly and fat than he really was; making him appear bloodied by the drippings of his own slaughterhouse, as he hopped up and down, talking of beef futures and pork bellies. Eldor von Liebert didn't care any longer. He had the only rank that counted: natural preeminence by virtue of his intellect. He could conquer his emotions. He didn't give in like the pigs who bounced around him; he yelled at Beanstock as he went by, "Guns will make us powerful. Butter will only make us fat. Guns will make us POWERFUL," he yelled. "BUTTER WILL ONLY MAKE US FAT!" He was heard above the thumping, and Butcher Beanstock pulled from the line to look curiously at the German private first class. Von Liebert saw the red spotlight cross the major's fat face once more and braced himself. "Ich bin von Himmill Gefallen, schweinhundt!" he said briskly. "You will stuff yourself on suet and leave us nothing but sausage to pick from your bones. And we shall pick, make no mistake about that!"

"Get yourself into the truck, soldier," Beanstock commanded him, the Red Cross woman coming to his side, brushing strands of stringy hair from her damp forehead. The line continued by them, picking up the slack in the empty space left by Beanstock, closing up the ranks as they had been taught to do and paying no attention to the fallen comrade. "You're drunk, soldier," Beanstock said once more. "Get outside into the truck. I'm not going to tell you again."

Von Liebert drew himself up to full height and sneered at the fat officer—"Better you put yourself into the truck. It is high time that rank made some sense around here." Beanstock involuntarily felt a twinge of fear. Von Liebert made no effort to order his sentences; he sounded foreign, a conscript alien under American command. The young man stepped toward him and Beanstock gave a little gasp, reaching for the arm of the Red Cross woman. But again the slack appeared in the line and Sergeant Baer ducked out of the Bunny Hop, letting Sonya Faust attach herself elsewhere while he walked slowly toward von Liebert.

"Outside," he snapped to the soldier. Then, to the retreating Major Beanstock, Baer said, "Excuse me, sir, this one's a special problem. From the beginning. He resents anyone telling him what to do." Baer saw his order threatened; saw the breaking down of the chain of command. He was enraged, no longer caring whether the offending soldier was a German or a Turk. He saw a hole in the bottom of the sea.

Von Liebert saw only idiocy compounded, and strode quickly to the sergeant. He slapped him across the cheek with his open palm. Bodies piled up against bodies, as those who had witnessed the slap stopped in the midst of their leaping. Baer forgot suddenly that he was a soldier; forgot that he had to maintain the dignity of a noncommissioned officer, and remembered only that he was a salesman of gentlemen's overcoats. He kicked for the groin and caught Eldor von Liebert on the upper thigh. Von Liebert felt like pulling his Luger sidearm from his polished holster, shooting the man through the head, and leaving him to be disposed of by subordinates. Slapping his thigh to grab for the pistol, he felt only American Army khaki and the broad stitching contracted out to hundreds of local uniform companies throughout the United States.

Baer had been brought up in Roxbury Crossing, a melting pot of nationalities, where, if the first kick missed, you didn't wait for rebuttal. He pounded a short right to the square jaw of the German, and followed with a roundhouse swing which bounced off von Liebert's chest.

Eldor suddenly couldn't believe that he was enduring that kind of insubordination. He was above such indignity. "Shoot the dog," he yelled. "Shoot him and drag him away," he screamed, while the blows rained off his mouth and ear and stomach and he began to cry, rackingly and horribly, so that even the enraged sergeant was forced to stop his punishment.

Winter grabbed for Baer's arms, but the sergeant was so enraged he swung an elbow into the plexus of the intruder and turned to take on countless enemies who might have been

162

lying in wait. The snaking line of the Bunny Hop had turned into a shambles.

It was what Kenny Keohane had been waiting for. He ordered his men into action and they reluctantly left their partners and began pushing aimlessly through the crowd, trying to incite anyone incitable. Someone poured a Metri-Cola down the back of one of the nurse's necks. Metri-Cola was felt to be expendable. He didn't excuse himself, but hurried on to spill some more somewhere else, while the nurse followed after with pen and notepad to get his name.

Colonel Beauregard had been planning to slip out, assured that the dance was a success, to drop a few fluoride pills into the Waterville reservoir. He hurried back to the scene, only to find his way blocked by one of Keohane's boys, who had wrestled a large local lady to the hardwood floor.

The Musicofs, nothing loath, broke the band into "Roll Out the Barrel," just to let everyone know that they were patriotic and backed Uncle Sam's boys to the hilt, the whole way. Musicof *père* winked at his son between notes. "We've got the blues on the run—" he played, and yelled over the yelling; "That's the spirit got us out of them trenches and into Flanders fields, son. Man for man we can handle any army in the world. See that spirit—" and his enthusiasm seeped into the others and they played as they had never played for the Elks or at the Odd Fellows Hall.

"It's that boy's fault," thought Joanne Moxie. "He's a catalyst for these other types. Gets their juices running, their sap rising. I must warn Rufus before he gets all our juices running."

She wiped furiously at her lips. The bottom one still smarted from where Eros had bitten her. She cursed her white outfit and longed for the fatigues and combat boots that fitted her so well for the command of men.

"Dresses put us at their mercy; nothing between the legs. No wonder most of us are neurotic. Give me a good pair of fatigues, any day."

She strode with long, purposeful strides toward the major melee, giving the military "double time" signal to Rufus Soule by jamming down her clenched fist, like a signal bell rope.

"It's anarchy," yelled an ex-law student, grabbing at her pleats as she hurried by. "The world is run by law, not confusion. I can cite you examples: see *Wilson v. U.S. Circuit Court of Appeals*—riot at dance hall in Bayonne, New Jersey . . ."

He was frothing, unused to such confusion, and grabbed

again at Joanne's pleats, needing a civilian straw to grasp. Rufus Soule misunderstood his panic, and clubbed him across the back of the neck. He fell to the floor, sputtering of precedents, his mind loaded with facts.

"Now's the time to roll the barrel—for the gang's all here." The band came crashing to the climax, and began all over again.

Kenny Keohane madly signaled one of his boys, who raced onto the porch and returned with a large cardboard box. Keohane ripped the top off, and in the confusion, with Colonel Beauregard directing his staff in the blowing of their whistles, lobbed a tear gas shell into the midst of the crowd. It rolled under the sensible shoes of Sonya Faust, by the spike heels of Angora Sweater, round and round through the legs of the Colonel and his staff, past the bloody mess of von Liebert, who still stood at attention commanding his nonexistent subordinates, and spread its foggy atmosphere into the nostrils and brains of the men and women of the 229th and their guests.

Women shrieked, eyes ran with tears. The weak vomited from the smoke in their lungs; the strong blundered toward the exits, all enthusiasm for the fight sapped from their systems. Cameroons Jackson carried two bodies out, one under each of his massive arms. He just sniffled slightly. Since Colonel Beauregard was shorter than most, he reacted worse than most, and had to be led outside by Marjorie Stavropolis who, in her loyalty, gave him first aid as he lay on his back with legs elevated against the porch railing.

It was left to Colonels Harden and Fruitman, wheezing and coughing, to summon up enough incentive from the silver leaves on their shoulders to direct the evacuation. The civilian Red Cross women actually stayed the calmest and led the guests and the soldiers out into the night air to be walked around until the coolness calmed their eyes.

Miss Ethyl Annise knew that she was going to have a nervous breakdown. She swallowed two Nembutal dry, without water, her body racked with sobs of mortification. Keohane's men had broken all the windows of the service club in their enthusiasm to disrupt the dance and dissipate the tear gas; now only brief clouds of the irritant floated in patches around the beams and the brown and white crepe paper. The band was stunned and kept their seats. Gas licked at their feet and wafted from the trumpet's aperture when the player blew to clear it.

Rufus Soule and Joanne moved among the wreckage, while

commands and coughing echoed into the hall from outside as the ambulances and buses were being loaded with the departing dancers. She and Soule wore portable gas masks, which he had produced from a sling bag that was never very far from his person. It said, "Compliments of Charlestown Travel Agency" on it; but it actually contained the necessary tools of his profession. He was taking notes on the damage and the evening.

"Not a very smoothly run event," he made a muffled comment to Joanne, who kept irritatedly brushing at her skirt while tear gas kept appearing from under its folds. "It's beginning to appear as if Beauregard is not in very good control of this unit. Perhaps we made a mistake in their selection." Joanne just grunted, thinking about Eros Winter and her own weakness of the early evening. They passed on out of the club, still in their strange masks, conversing like two recently landed astronauts slightly afraid to breathe the air of a new world.

The noises of departing buses and vehicles filled the night with new fumes, new sounds; the cries of apologies from the official party dimmed in the distance as Beauregard and his staff yelled, "Goodnight, sorry. Goodnight, so sorry," at the retreating taillights of the guests from Waterville.

"Tough to mix the military and the civilian. Tough break tonight, sir, going so well; tough break, sir," said his staff to the Colonel. But there was no consoling him that night, and Stavropolis drove him off in the staff car toward their tent home, while he sulked in the passenger's seat. He hadn't even had time to salt the reservoir with fluoride.

Eros Winter stayed behind in the darkened service club, laughing and crying and thinking it all very grand. He was alone, save for the two Musicofs, who stayed because no one had dismissed them, and Miss Ethyl Annise, who stayed behind as a ship's captain stays behind.

"It was magnificent," Eros roared at them. "The last of the big Prussian spenders—the Ring of the Nibelung reenacted for you in upper New York State, with ogres and beautiful maidens and serving wenches to goose." Tears streamed down his cheeks and his nose ran; he laughed and choked, seated on a folding camp chair, with the red and blue spotlights still crazily spinning their slow dance above him. Then he got serious and stood up, weaving strangely from the effects of gas and beer, and went to the cooler where he opened four cans. He brought one to each of the Musicofs on the bandstand; then bowed, handing one to Miss Ethyl Annise.

"Play a waltz," he said. "Any good, old, standard three-four waltz. On the second thought, I'll sing one, and you join me."

He had them hypnotized by his teary hospitality, and they poised over their instruments. He bowed to Miss Annise and asked her, "May I have this waltz; it's very special. May ah have this dance, Magnolia, honeh?"

She blushed a little and rose to come into his arms. They swung to the middle of the ballroom and he moved with her gracefully. She followed just as well, and they went around and around as he sang softly, soon joined by the musicians:

> All the madness and the gladness
> Of the Gold Star Mothers' schmaltz,
> As they rubbed their eyes with sadness
> To the Activation Waltz!

Musicians and dancers kept the proper decorum and formality; when they had finished, they all agreed that it had been a lovely dance, a lovely waltz.

FIFTEEN

It was Saturday morning. Instead of the traditional inspection before pass, the 229th was to march in review along with the entire Minuteman Division. The Governor of Massachusetts and the Archbishop of the Fall River Diocese were flown up for the ceremonies, which annually marked the return of the division from the field to garrison. The 229th General Hospital (due to the peculiar nature of their second week duties), did not return to barracks. Since their facilities served the division, however, General Grosbeck felt that Colonel Beauregard's unit deserved the distinction of marching with the National Guard. They deserved the honor of hearing the praise of the Governor; they deserved the honor of receiving the blessing of the Archbishop.

Colonel Beauregard was furious. It took more than the ministrations of Marjorie Stavropolis to calm him down. She used two squeeze tubes of Nivea on him, and even, for appeasement's sake, gave in to a few of his special requests. It only helped a little. He was still frightened that the unit's performance at the dance had irrevocably colored Soule's attitude toward the 229th.

His fears were well grounded. Soule took Joanne Moxie for a walk around the encampment the next morning and made her take shorthand notes while he dictated a letter to his superiors in Washington. While he dictated, he pounded the edge of his right hand against a pine board. Then he changed hands. He watched her out of the corner of his eye. She had been acting strangely since she came to Camp Cannon. He didn't like seeing her in a dress at the dance. It made her like all other women. She belonged in uniform, leading her troops. He scuffed his big feet as he walked, feeling the goodness in them, feeling sensual about his crepe soles, feeling nice and alive as he dictated and scuffed.

"To the Chief: Medical Unit ill-advised and ill-organized. Personnel sloppy and not overly patriotic. Tend to believe that if activated, would underachieve. Can't tell how would respond in actual combat situation." ("Strike that last bit, Joanne," he noted. "Never can tell how anyone will act in combat situation. Continue letter.") "First week's training of hospital operation average but adequate; physical condition, average; enthusiasm, average; anticipation of possible activation, on the whole, poor. Details later."

"Sign it for me. Use blue code and wire it." They continued to walk in silence, Soule still regarding Joanne as somewhat changed. Perhaps it was her hair. She had swept the bangs off her forehead and combed her brown hair, parted, to the side. She caught him looking and interrupted her own thoughts.

"Bangs are so little girlish," she said, almost apologetically. "I'm thinking of letting it grow long, in a pageboy."

"It won't fit under your helmet, your steel pot," Soule said, pouting.

"Well, this work only takes another week and then we'll be back in Washington. Perhaps I'll take a more social role for the service. Infiltrate embassy parties, or something. I can't be so obviously . . . it's almost butch, you know."

"What if the 229th *is* activated? We'll be assigned along with them. You'll need your helmet then."

"Not much chance of that after your report, is there?" Joanne said.

"True," answered Soule, and they walked on in silence. He wished that she would keep her bangs. Gam Sun had had little black bangs. He wished that he could remove his crepe-soled shoes and wiggle his toes in the crabby burnt grass. Pleasure and pain in the crabby burnt grass. Soule wished a lot of things, and decided that he was opposed to change. In frustration he smacked the side of his hand very hard against the board, hoping that Joanne would tell him, "Stop, you might hurt yourself."

But she said nothing. She only kept smoothing her soft brown hair to the side, preserving the part.

"It's an ill wind that doesn't blow Kenny Keohane some good," Keohane told his boys jubilantly. His men grinned at him. Eros Winter and Eldor von Liebert were there, Winter grinning with the rest of the men at the success of the dance. He knew, through the unit gossip, that Rufus Soule was displeased with the 229th. He could also tell that he had broken through Joanne's reserve and that, with a little more initiative, he could bring it off. He had written and sent her a note. Titled *Mystical Maid,* it began:

> *Mille regrets for my attack*
> *Beg forgiveness on my back*
> *Pack a lunch and bring your sweater*
> *Picnic with me and Lambretta*

> *To the country, no reprisal*
> *Watch my true apologis-al*

And he signed it—*Rasputin, the monk that wasn't a monk.*

Von Liebert grinned wolfishly. His outlook had changed since his beating at the hands of Sergeant Baer. With the next morning and a hangover, he was no longer irrational; he just want to get Baer. He wanted to get out of the United States Army Reserve and no longer felt dedicated to doing a duty inimical to his feelings. The pettiness and politics and waste of time had decided him. It had also decided him on a course of retaliation before he got out. Not in the open; but where no one could blame him . . . during the assault operation, where he was one of the designated Aggressors and where he could play the same dumb game as the rest of the Reservists. He practiced his grin, as he was sure Winter practiced his, and was pleased when it came out sadistically. It was good to be decisive. He liked paths of action and all his paths were paths of war.

Baer had been officially reprimanded, but was too valuable to the unit to bust. Von Liebert *was* expendable, the Colonel decided, and he had no congressman to write to.

"He'll be leaving the country soon, Sergeant," Beauregard told Lennie Baer. "This incident will force him out of the unit. I don't like them any more than you do . . . and I understand why you did what you did. The bastards never learn, do they? That's why we're here, Baer, isn't it? To keep your children and my children from fighting the same fight that our generation and our fathers' generation fought. Who do they think they're fooling? They come over here; learn our technical skills; go to our schools; bed our women . . . then go home and straighten out their own countries. With *them* in the saddle, pissing on the United States. All the time with the same mask of friendship. Well, they don't fool you and me, Baer; not old campaigners like you and me. Eh?"

"They sure don't, sir," said Baer, proud of his Colonel's talking to him man to man.

"Officially, you are reprimanded," continued the Colonel, shuffling papers on his desk. "Off the record now, you're a patriot. Your people would be proud of you." Colonel Beauregard welcomed the chance to be a liberal.

"All of us wouldn't walk calmly to the boxcars, Colonel," Baer said proudly. "All of us don't take things sitting down. We have vivid memories."

"Good work," the Colonel said. "Good work, Lennie." He

had used Baer's first name; there was no greater praise. Each thought he understood the other; Baer smiled at his commander, saluted and walked from the headquarters tent. He thought of calling his wife and telling her what he had done. "No," he decided, "why take a chance on having a woman ruin a beautiful moment? Enough for me to know what this has meant." Fulfilled, he strode toward the hospital tents, looking for soldiers to harass; looking for swastikas to stomp and enemies to punish.

Kenny Keohane continued his self-praise, taking complete credit for getting the unit one hundred per cent passes for the weekend. The Colonel was still hoping that the men would be sufficiently appreciative of the good treatment to perform well in their attack mission.

"I'm willing to give away little things for the greater good," he told Stavropolis, when she questioned the wisdom of the generosity. "I'm putting it on the basis of one man's agreement with another man, even though all those people are children. They bitch collectively and get happy or sad together, just like youngsters. What are soldiers but sheep, anyway; chessmen made for commanders to move on any board we choose? Commanders give, or they take away. I've planned too long for a star on my shoulder to have it fouled up on these sheep. They'll do what I say; I know what I'm doing."

Marjorie Stavropolis said a silent "Baaaaaaa" and hoped that he was right. She also had planned too long for an eagle on her shoulder to have it fouled up, on either those sheep or her particular mustachioed ewe.

Eldor and Eros Winter left the motor pool area and moved toward formation in front of their tents. Keohane had briefed them on their assignments as Aggressors, saying, "Our duty is to blunder about ineffectually and render the unit impotent. Remember Bunker Hill . . . it means home." Winter had snorted.

Everyone had shaved and had their mandatory haircuts for the Governor and the Archbishop. "You men want to have hair growing out of your ears for His Excellency? The soldiers of God can't fight without looking sharp," Colonel Harden had told them. "A proud army wins battles and wars. No hairy warriors ever won a battle." He wasn't too sure of the truth of the statement, but it fitted so nicely into his sanitation lecture that he couldn't resist. It was mandatory in the Medical Corps for the sanitation lecture to be given before the men went on pass. It would make them aware of the pitfalls of leave in strange places. Doctor-Colonel Harden liked to give the annual speech. He did it with éclat. The men were lined up, as usual, with officer complement, professional section, and administrative section, at attention and awaiting orders to move out to the parade grounds.

"Just a few cautions this summer, men *and* ladies," Harden began. "I include you all, because we're all big people, adults. Anything can happen during annual summer training. Recognize these dangers as adults—and no sniggering in ranks.

"The Minuteman Division, whether you're aware of it or not, has been afflicted by a number of paternity suits over the last decade. I would like to keep the fatherhood slate of the 229th clean. Let the National Guard suffer, but let the hands of the Reserve be unbloodied. You may draw, if you so desire, protective devices from the dispensary before leaving, along with mimeographed directions that should be self-explanatory—I ran them off myself last night. For those of you not so inclined, I recommend a trip to the scenic Thousand Islands and/or abstention." Here Colonel Harden looked directly at Chaplain Papps, who strenuously objected to the tone of the annual lecture. Only through his insistence and threats was the word "abstention" included. The female personnel chafed at the presentation; especially the nurses, who thought it most unnecessary. Most of them possessed literature from the Planned Parenthood League.

"Why must he insist on underlining the lust of men," thought Sonya Faust, all the while looking hungrily around for any likely candidates for her own weekend.

Harden continued. "Rather than dwell on this aspect of sanitation, since the mimeographed sheets should suffice, I might mention the prevalence of fungus infections, especially from the use of—ahhh—latrines, shall we say, to be military about it. I realize the ultraviolet-treated seats, such as those specially prepared at Howard Johnson's, are not always convenient to your plans and needs. Take this in the form of an order: this weekend, effectively place toilet tissue around the plastic rims. Men and women, believe me! You'll be doing yourself a favor in nine out of ten cases. Other than these few precautions, remember that you are soldiers of the United States Army and representatives of the 229th General Hospital. You have reputations to uphold and tradition to maintain. Avoid Bermuda shorts wherever possible and, medically speaking, stay with wine or beer, if you *must* drink. Drinkers of gin will be considered on report. Bed check at

2400 hours Sunday night. I expect all of you—singly and not in pairs—in your beds by that time. I do not expect pillows or rolled-up blankets stuffed into the bedclothes, but real bodies, with real dog-tags around the necks. You've got a busy time next week, so get some rest. HOSPITAL," he commanded, and they all readied themselves; "ATTEN-HOOT; ABAOUT—HACE; FOWOOD—HARCH!"

The dress-uniformed General Hospital moved out toward the parade grounds, and even Colonel Harden, flushed with the pleasure of delivering his favorite lecture, had to admit that they were swinging together.

"Starting to look like soldiers, eh, Soule?" said Colonel Beauregard, smiling at their precision. Soule had to admit that their training seemed to be progressing. Morning PT and marching had at least taught them to stay in step. Joanne Moxie felt the corners of Winter's note scrape at her bosom where she had hidden it. She tried to pick him out of the marchers, but he was obscured by the mass of khaki.

The Camp Cannon parade ground was impressive that sunny Saturday morning, with the bandstand decked in American flags and the state flags of Massachusetts next to the reviewing stand, peopled with National Guard brass, the Governor's staff, and cassocked attendants to the Archbishop. General Grosbeck had assembled his division, fresh from a week's field training, scrubbed and brushed them and made them feel proud that they had come through it; proud to be finishing up the toughest week. There was little trace of the recent civilian in the crowd. The Division's seventeen tanks, M-48 Pattons, were washed and greased, and the tankers' helmets were painted in various colors, a concession to their being elite. Their heads poked out of the hatches as the machines rumbled onto the parade grounds, the sun reflecting off their goggles and flashing at the spectators. The tanks were followed by the teams on the mortars, recoilless rifle and artillery units, the wheels of the weapons bouncing along the hard, grassless turf, kicking up the dust into the eyes of the marching squads. The rifles of the infantry had been disassembled and cleaned, gauze patches repeatedly rammed down the barrels until no trace of oil remained. Everyone was in full field pack, clean fatigues, and steel pots as if marching off to battle. Even the local citizenry was invited to the show, a payoff for allowing the intrusion of Reservists each year into its territory. Folk had come from as far away as Syracuse to witness the display of Massachusetts military might.

General Grosbeck was pleased as he stood beside the

Governor, who sweated in his vest with the American Legion watchfob, and the Archbishop, who fingered his most expensive beads as he tried to figure the odds on seventy-five per cent of the division being Catholic. "Else why am I up here?" he reasoned, and not without cause.

Grosbeck answered a question from one of the assistants to the Archbishop, a promising young man who had been quite a football player and had chosen the cloth to fulfill a promise to his mother. He had asked why one small segment of the division was dress in suntans and not fatigues. "That's our support hospital," answered the General. "We have them marching at the rear in case they have to pick up stragglers or stroke victims. They're Reserve, not National Guard, and only marching as a favor. Commanded by a dentist, nice chap, Colonel Gayle Beauregard." The young man nodded and looked solemn. He couldn't remember any Beauregard who ever played football.

The tanks moved out across the field leading the procession, the treads clattering staccato to accompany the division band, which brassily began with "Stars and Stripes Forever." The artillery and weapons followed, with the boys from eastern Massachusetts infused with march music. They didn't have time to feel foolish or unmilitary or unpatriotic because they had plenty of company. It was something to be marching on a sunny summer morning, feeling fresh and clean, with steel butt plates secure in their right palms and their right forearms parallel to the ground, left arms swinging free in time with the beat of the drums. Helicopters hovered overhead, manned by Army crews, moving over the column, their rotors whirring a counterpoint to the tanks' bass. The band switched to "Seventy-six Trombones" as the infantry followed the heavy weapons onto the parade ground, moving parallel to the reviewing stand on the far side. Then a left column and another left column, so that when the command came—"EYES RIGHT," the heads could snap to the right and view the Governor and the Archbishop for an instant. As they passed, and were ordered—"R'DDY FRONT," they could resume singing the lyrics to themselves of the popular march and feel good about the whole parade.

The 229th were conspicuous not only by being last, but by the fact that they were not carrying weapons. Colonel Beauregard marched at the head of his company with his staff directly to his rear. Then came the officer detachment with Major Fugue, the chief surgeon, looking handsome and confident. Major Marjorie Stavropolis led her nurses, swinging

173

crisply by, dressed in their blue gabardine summer uniforms, their high heels covered with dust raised by the earlier marchers, their nylon-covered thighs going "swish, swish" as they rubbed against each other smartly, never missing a beat. Then the men of the 229th, the clerks and drivers and corpsmen and lab technicians and cooks and social workers and power generator operators and wiremen and pharmacy specialists, all with their garrison caps at the proper angle cocked over the right eye. Again their brass and shoes were polished and their clean uniforms fitted snugly over their expanded figures. They knew very well their right from their left. Master Sergeant Lennie Baer walked at their side and called out the cadence in a loud, bullhorn voice, professionally, not at all like a medical corps sergeant but like a tough old infantry veteran. The band responded by briskly switching marches and blasting the brass section into the calypso beat of "Mama No Want No Peas, No Rice, No Coconut Oil."

Eros Winter's imagination was thrilled by the sight. "At last," he thought, "a breakthrough. General Foch at the Marne. Santa Anna at the Alamo." The sun hit him full in the face and it felt good to be in the middle of the ranks and hearing the music. He loved parades. In an outburst of generosity, he began to sing along with the band as the 229th executed a smart column left toward the reviewing stand. "Mama no want no peas, no rice, no coconut oil," he began in perfect rhythm to the stepped cadence of left, right, left. "Mama no want no peas, no rice, no coconut oil," he continued. "Mama no want no peas, no rice, mama no want no coconut oil, all she want is brandy handy all the while." Then he whistled the repeated tune and his peripheral vision could take in the smiles of his comrades. Naturally, Sergeant Baer viewed it as an interruption, but as they were passing in review he could do nothing but glare, and bellow "EYES RIGHT," and shudder as all but Winter snapped their heads toward the reviewing stand. Winter was much too carried away with the lyrics of the song to pay any attention to commands. "That young man shows spirit," said the Archbishop to no one in particular, although everyone within hearing nodded. He was wearing his dark traveling suit of fifty per cent Dacron and fifty per cent wool with the light red collar and light red cap. "I'll bet he's from west of Boston," said the Governor, who had grown up west of Boston himself. "I can always tell by the throaty voice—industrial fumes in the air, you know. Good working people." He never lost an opportunity to remind himself of his humble origins.

"I used to call the cadence myself, before I was commissioned in the Pacific," said General Grosbeck, not to be outdone. "Spunky of Beauregard to have his medical unit so spit and polish, good show of him," he added. By then the last of the 229th Hospital had marched by and they began to swing around behind the already assembled Minuteman Division. They all would then bare their heads, with steel helmets or garrison caps over their hearts and hear "The Star-Spangled Banner," followed by speeches from the Archbishop and the Governor.

When the last tank motor had stilled, cannons raised in salute toward the regiewing stand, when the last "AT EASE" command had echoed across the parade ground, General Grosbeck rose. The flags whipping in the strong August wind were the only sound. Eight thousand men awaited their commander's orders. General Grosbeck waited silently until even the flags lay limp on their poles. "DIVISION," he yelled as eight thousand breaths sucked in and readied themselves, "ATTEN—" and eight thousand right legs prepared for action—"HUT" came the order, and the Massachusetts National Guard, accompanied by their Reserve Hospital, snapped to rigid attention.

The General paused and looked them over. They had begun to harden in the last week; they were beginning to take things seriously. There was no cynicism in their intent look at the dignitaries in the stand. They knew what was expected of them; for, after all, were they not soldiers? The elemental simplicity of the Army was subtly spreading itself like an extra blanket over the Reservists. It gathered them up equally, fed them, clothed them, and gave them for a time the peace of mind that comes with not having to make a decision.

Winter wished he was sitting in the stands and had a balloon to hold.

The Archbishop, timing himself beautifully, rose and looked over his audience. He had a microphone with amplifiers set up strategically around the field. It was one of those moments where he believed Christ would provide him with a self-amplifying larynx. "These young men," he thought, "rich with the gift of youth." He, too, filled with joy at the sight and he was proud that he could bless them.

He was a handsome man, not too vain, but aware that his looks made an impression. His brothers had kidded him when he announced years ago that he was going into the seminary. "You just think you look good in black. Don't forget the unpardonable sin!" But the Archbishop used it to good advantage. An attractive priest often got invited into homes of wealthy and social parishioners. He knew which of his flock were secretly in love with him, and he accepted invitations to cotillions and dinner parties at the Ritz and luncheons at Locke-Ober's; he did partake of libations . . . if properly prepared. ("A man of good taste," his wise bishop had told him, during his novitiate, "is doubly blessed—and may serve God by his example to others.") And the Archbishop remembered his own education, reading secular literature; subscribing to *Ramparts* and *Commonweal*; studying bridge, and being noted for having the best sand wedge in the Fall River archdiocese. He was number one in America in fund raising among all his fellows; and especially admired the Borgia Popes.

But God did not see fit to amplify his larynx and the steady voice sounded emotional and shaky as it filtered through the artificial sound system. "In nomine patris et filii et spiritus sancti," he intoned and then caught himself as he suddenly realized the nondenominational quality of his audience. The audience was confused. The Catholic personnel had expected it; the others didn't understand . . .

"The warrior home from the fields of battle," he began again, "finally able to lay his weapons and shield aside and return to his loved ones for whom he fought. Is this not the purpose of the warrior? The hope of the soldier?" "Hope of the soldier . . . hope of the soldier," echoed and re-echoed across the parade ground. The wind started again and the Archbishop's hair, white as the pages of an unprinted Bible, blew over his eyes as he continued. He took the sudden wind as a sign that his greetings were going well. He could see in his mind's eye everything he wanted to say.

" 'Well done,' are the commander's words of praise. I add a 'Well done' to this, knowing that helping to keep freedom strong, and America free, is doing God's blessed work here on earth. I see a lot of familiar faces in the ranks, a lot of young men I have known from childhood. A great many of you are strangers, also. But make no mistake. No one is exempt from the work of the Lord, regardless of what type of building you enter to worship him, be it a Gothic cathedral, grand and buttressed to the sky, with stained glass—a process handed down from generation to generation, glorifying the works of Our Lord—or a simple white country church, or a flagstone modern with a six-pointed star in the window. The point is, you give thanks somewhere. Yes, thanks for being privileged to defend these freedoms and these families; thanks even for

176

the voice of dissent and demonstration . . . but not to the point of foolhardiness."

Chaplain Papps fidgeted in his position of attention. He hated to be spiritually guided by anyone else. "Damn Papist," he muttered, feeling his eyebrow twitch with displeasure; he held his breath for fear that, through some Divine error, perhaps the Archbishop *was* actually in coommunication with God. The second passed and he was still intact. "Damn Papist," he muttered again, more sure of himself this time. He was surrounded by the amplified rasping, but he held himself erect and felt Christlike, suffering the position for so long.

"Try and carry the principles of manhood you have learned in the Army back with you to civilian life. At least *you* go back after two weeks. Honor, justice, charity. Remember, men, the song is ended, but the melody lingers on. God bless you all. Please be good enough to join me in the Lord's Prayer and a moment of silent meditation for all those killed in battle or drowned in the depths of the sea." He felt compelled not to ignore any of the services. He had always favored the Navy and had his own Herreshoff 12, which he raced occasionally in Narragansett Sound, when it wasn't too choppy. The muffled repetition of the Lord's Prayer hummed in the quiet monotone over the filed. Eight thousand heads bent; all save about fifty whispered the words. During the minute of meditation everyone either blessed their families or prayed not to be called to active duty. There were only two atheists among the 229th General Hospital. One thought about the shined tips of his shoes, and the other thought about Jean Genet.

The Governor waited about two minutes, figuring that a Governor's prayers would be more weighty than the ordinary man's, and walked to the microphone, nodding to the Archbishop as he passed. The governor belonged to the Ancient and Honorable Artillery Company, which paraded each year on the Boston Common and had drumhead elections. He belonged also to three separate veteran's groups. Thus he was no stranger to uniform, and always enjoyed the annual ceremony of reviewing *his* National Guard. He had toyed with the idea, a number of times, of calling out the Guard in the middle of the night just to see if they were really on the ready. He had been dissuaded by his aides, who figured that the soldiers might forgive him; but that the soldiers as civilians *and* voters might not. The Governor was noted for his sudden changes of staff.

"I'm honored to see *my* boys marching so well and staying

in step," he began, hoping to win them over immediately by being a good guy. They all laughed to ease the tension of standing at attention. All they needed was a signal.

"What an asshole," someone said, inaudible to all but his own squad. They laughed the loudest and the Governor smiled down in their direction.

"Now you know that one of your major functions is to assist in periods of civil unrest; or in time of nature's unrest. Thank the lord that we have no levees to overflow, and that we in Massachusetts, regardless of religion, color, or background, have learned to live in a harmony that is a model throughout the land."

Cameroons Jackson had in his mind: "What about de facto segregation?" but he kept it to himself. With Jackson the question was purely rhetorical. "Don't want my kids bussed to some other damn town every day," he thought. "Kids gotta be schooled where they grow up. Bad enough them white hippies come to clean up our playgrounds, now they tell us to take the kids away from home. Why don't they move our *houses* to the neighborhoods they sending our kids to? Oh, no, sir! That's different. De facto segregation is O.K. at night, when you're minglin' on a social basis. It's really de fucto segregation, with you know who on the receivin' end." He hadn't voted for the Governor. He hadn't even voted for the Mayor. "An' if they was runnin' the Archbishop, I'm certainly not votin' for that cat; somethin' about a man denying his own gonads, I never trusted."

The Governor spoke from three-by-five cards prepared by one of his assistants. He had been forced to turn down a ballet opening, a speech honoring the retiring Sheriff of Suffolk County, and a breakfast engagement with the Temple Brotherhood of Jewis Masons in Braintree. He was partial to the breakfast, since he loved bagels and whitefish and found it sticky to order them at home. Being of Italian descent and particularly aware of the poverty of his childhood, he paid special attention to minority groups. "I love 'em all, I tell you—because I appreciate what it's like. Those bastards on Beacon Hill and State Street—they got water in their goddam veins. Passion, that's the answer to politics! Those bankers and lawyers have inbred themselves right out of power. In the next generation, if the trust funds depreciate enough, *my* sons, out of Harvard College and the Law School, will be running this state while their kids'll be drinking themselves to death at the Somerset Club."

It made him all the more confident to see his troops massed

178

and attentive. It made him feel more and more like Fiorello La Guardia. He even wanted to read the funnies over the radio to the kids of Boston on Sunday mornings. But no one listened to the radio anymore.

His three-by-five cards followed along in logical sequence. The key words were typed in capitals and offered enough memory jog to complete the greeting. He liked patriotic speeches; they were easy to write and easy to deliver. He could make them sound sincere because he believed what he was saying.

"I'll do anything necessary to win an election," he told his aides in private. "I'll fib and I'll be tough and I'll toy with the borders of dishonesty; this is life. But no compromise on my country or my country's flag." This is what the Governor constantly saw: a vision of the United States as it was immediately after the First and Second World Wars, with parades and flags and everyone thrilled to be American. Seeing his troops reminded him of that time and, since he was touched, he expected the same of his audience. He trembled with emotion when he finished, calling upon the Guard to carry on the fight for freedom begun in earlier generations.

"It may be necessary today to call you out to patrol highways on New Year's Eve. That is the price you pay for our way of life. Tomorrow you may be on the highways, or shall we say the roads, leading to Hanoi or Moscow or Shanghai. Be proud to serve these two weeks; they are small time to give for a lifetime of America. Carry on, Citizen Soldiers; the ghosts of the Concord Minutemen, whose name you proudly bear, look down upon you and smile their approval." Exhausted, but pleased with his delivery of the major address, the Governor fell silent.

The band, on prearranged signal, burst into a Sousa medley; the Color Guard of the Division, answering the police whistle of their sergeant, stepped out to the drumbeat, swinging again by the reviewing stand, leading the tanks and the weapons, the infantry and the 229th General Hospital, which tailed on like a caboose, away from the parade grounds and off to be issued their passes for the weekend.

The sun was still high, but the shadows of the marchers stepped out like so many daddy longlegs by their sides, always staying three paces away.

Rufus Soule, Joanne Moxie, and Colonel Beauregard rode in a jeep. The Colonel was pleased. "I honestly didn't see a man out of step. They looked fit and ready. I told you that it takes a few days to get the civilian out of them."

Soule had to admit that it had been impressive. He enjoyed parades himself, but hated to march. It would take hours of Epsom salt treatments to bring his feet back to the soft normality he enjoyed.

"It was a good show, Colonel," Soule admitted. "The unit, with the exception of the outburst of that Winter, performed well. Perhaps my superiors knew what—" But he caught himself and stopped in midsentence. He knew better than to question the Agency that employed him. He looked at Joanne, but she made no sign that she had noticed his use of the forbidden word "perhaps".

"She's too well trained to betray anything. Smart. Efficient," he thought. Actually, she was thinking of what to bring on the picnic with Eros Winter. She felt herself being nudged by Soule.

"How about going over to view the assault scene with me this weekend? The Colonel and I and a few of the staff are driving over to the Thousand Islands to take the excursion boat. We'll do business and pleasure. I'm anxious to see firsthand how difficult the course looks. I've only seen it on maps."

"Oh, Rufus," Joanne said, "I'm terribly sorry, but I planned to do a little communing this weekend. My mind is terribly dusty. I just want to get on the Lambretta and have it take me, kind of automatic pilotish. There are things on my mind and I'd like to have a change from official duties. Get off by myself."

The Colonel was present and Soule couldn't argue with her. Neither could he give her a direct order. That would be too tacky on a beautiful Saturday. So he said nothing. He let it pass, as the Colonel prattled on to him about his plans for the unit once they were activated.

"Whatever Washington has in mind for us, we're ready. A few more personnel and we'll be up to full strength. 'Course, confidentially, if we're activated, I think it would serve a stronger position, both for the unit and the total effort, if there were a star on my shoulder. Make *you* look good also, advising the chosen unit. You'd have a good friend then in the military. Believe me!" Beauregard picked an informal moment when he felt good fellowship could stand a test.

Soule just looked inscrutable, one of the tricks Gam Sun had taught him. It consisted of slitting his eyes and thinking about Buddha. But Beauregard noticed it and his little nostrils dilated with fear of unknown powers.

"Not egg salad sandwiches," Joanne said aloud, thinking of picnic treats.

Soule said nothing. He was still looking inscrutable and it usually took three or four minutes to wear off. Colonel Beauregard, thinking it was a code between them, became more frightened and concentrated very hard on the dust kicked up by the jeep that was getting into the eyes, ears, noses and throats of his marching General Hospital.

SIXTEEN

Eros Winter didn't like riding on the back seat of the Lambretta. He mistrusted all machines. When he invited Joanne for a picnic he had no doubt she would accept. He also had absolutely no idea where to go. The confines of Camp Cannon were out of the question and patrolled at all hours by regular Army MPs, embittered by the fate that had stuck them in the boondocks for the summer.

Joanne was anticipating Eros. "I know you came by bus, and I did some scouting on my own while I was on the road. There's a delightful dam, part of the town hydroelectric project, right down Route Three from the base. Concrete and shining. Trout and rock bass in the river. We'll buy supplies and I'll take us there."

"You're sounding like you're in command of this expedition. Did I invite you or am I wrong?" He still felt the tension in her, her will to dominate.

She wore white shorts and a blue and white McMullen blouse which she hadn't realized she still owned. It was in the bottom of her rucksack, which had "Ditty Bag" stenciled on it. So amused was she by the prospect of playing schoolgirl that she put it on. She even checked the cute collar to see if it still had pin holes from her old circle pin. It did and she felt nostalgic. Then she snorted, but put the blouse on. She threw a blue cardigan sweater over her shoulders, stepped into brown thong sandals and she was almost ready. She had showered and washed her hair. It was short enough still to dry quickly in the sun and she had no need of a set. It was lustrous and soft. She brushed it very hard until she felt her scalp glowing. She used no perfume or toilet water, liking the smell of soap on her body and wanting nothing so nice as that to make her feel beautiful.

Joanne Moxie seldom thought of herself as beautiful. She was usually too busy planning, or doing, or worrying. And she hated to be told that she was beautiful. She would much rather be told that she was superior. That was the important thing. She never was quite sure how to approach herself and, because of this, no one else had learned to approach her. Eros Winter's casual assurance and his breach of her normal scheme of things threw her off stride. She suddenly realized that she had breasts that rose and fell and a strange feeling in her loins, which she had previously written off as a kind of depressed area. She was fully prepared to go through life a virgin, dedicated not as a nun approaching her vows, but rather as Hershey Chocolate, never advertising because they never felt the need to.

Eros was waiting for her in the parking area, also dressed in civilian shorts with a short-sleeved red turtleneck jersey. He wore blue sneakers on his feet and grinned at her as she advanced purposefully toward him, seated on her Lambretta.

"How'd you like the parade?" he asked her.

"I like parades," she answered. "I liked your note and it's a nice day for a picnic; all necessary questions answered."

"It's not even a starter," Eros said. "I'm lucky I'm here at all. The first sergeant wasn't going to give me my pass. But then the Colonel got a call from the post HQ. General Grosbeck liked my singing the cadence. Can you imagine anything more ridiculous?" He laughed happily.

Joanne liked the way he laughed so quickly. She had never seen him irritated. Did he take anything seriously? She kicked the starter and it caught immediately. She didn't like to ride without wearing a protective helmet and reached for hers, which was attached to the rear grill.

"No. Pas de protective devices," he said, removing her hand and placing it back on the handle bar, over the clutch. "We're doing it au naturel all the way. I want to whisper in your ear while we're riding. Maybe even nibble. No bugs are going to squash against your goggles. We're not going *that* far, I hope."

She didn't protest and they moved away from the scrubby boondocks of the field hospital and down the road to the gate, the Lambretta putt-putting well within the twenty mile an hour limit and Eros holding onto her waist from behind, laughing to himself that he should be shielding him from the wind. The MP at the gate looked them over and then stiff-arm signaled them on their way. Eros gave him a thumbs-up salute as they drove past. He squeezed her waist a little, relieved that their progress had not been questioned at the sentry box. Joanne would have hated to phone in her problem to Soule for clearance. She was irritated, realizing for the first time Soule's belief that he had a demand upon her that went beyond the Agency. It had never dawned on her before and she angrily down-shifted to second gear, making the change harsh as she wheeled the scooter off the highway onto a narrow road. She pulled into a Red and White variety store that sold gas. "Get everything you need here. One stop for it all," the sign said in the window.

She killed the motor and jumped purposefully to the ground. Then she remembered and waited for Eros. *He* would make the choice. He felt like saying, "Good dog, now sit up and beg"; but he just smiled and took her arm, quietly leading her in, up cracked wooden stairs and through the screen door.

"Shut that door quick, son," said the old woman behind the counter. "Flies love our goods." Shelves were piled high with dusty cans and bottles. One entire wall was covered with packages of Junket, all flavors, that looked as if they had been there for years.

"You have any beer here?" Eros asked, sure that in some cellar nearby they had laid in a supply of dusty beer cans filled with near-brew from Prohibition when the trucks of Legs Diamond and Dutch Schultz rumbled down from the Canadian border past Waterville and on to New York City.

"Beer we got," the proprietress said. "Wine, too. Real imported wine. We don't get much call for it, though."

"We'll take two bottles of white and one six-pack of beer; make it Utica Club. May as well support local industry."

She cackled and wrote in a big yellow notepad. "Win!" she called out to the darkened rear of the store. "Bring me up some of that wine we got stored away, and some of that Utica Club from the cooler."

"What you want to go drinkin' wine fer in the afternoon?" came a voice.

"Don't," she yelled back. "It's for a customer and his wife." Any couple that patronized her she assumed was married; for wasn't every couple married?

Eros picked out a whole baby Gouda cheese, half a dozen tomatoes, which he squeezed professionally, some slices of ham in gelatin, and a long loaf of French bread.

"Usually we have to throw this stuff out, or Win and I cut it up for toast. Get two loaves a day, because a French Canadian couple from Montreal once bought one and Win keeps hopin' they'll come back. Never any call for it though. You two French Canadian?" she questioned with immediate mistrust, as if they, too, would disappear, never to return for any more French bread.

"No," Eros answered. "We're leaving."

They left, with their packages stuffed in a large brown paper bag, and got onto the scooter again, with Eros balancing the goodies while Joanne drove to her secret spot. Before they rounded a curve they could hear the roar of water. The scooter putted a *cantabile* over the water's bass. They rounded the curve and drove onto a wooden bridge, bumping over the

184

surface and watching the white water flow from the dam about half a mile upstream, churning into white foam as it fell and racing over rocks and logs before it continued as a river. They stopped on top of the bridge and watched, Joanne excitedly following the swiftness. "Wouldn't you just love to be in a canoe down there?"

"Stern or bow?" Eros asked her, and was sorry. She had been relaxing. It was no time to put her on edge. He laughed and put his arm around her, making it all right. "I'd like to make a portage with you, kitten. Who knows what mission the Army will send us on? Have they got a Canoe Corps?"

"Forget the Army for a while," she said and her face clouded. She was fearful for him, apprehensive that he was to be activated. But he knew there was only a week of training left. He and Kenny Keohane would see to that.

They parked the Lambretta in the bushes, walked up to the large concrete dam, and, carrying the paper bag, climbed the steps to the top, where every few yards giant black wheels were placed which controlled the gears and the sluice gates. About thirty feet below then was a pool of water sheltered from the roaring wet and formed by residues seeping into the riverbank. Eros climbed down again and forced the wine bottles into the mud of the pool, underneath the cold water. Then he returned to Joanne, who sat leaning against a concrete support, her face uplifted to the sun. He handed her a beer. He sat down next to her and tapped his can upon hers.

"There's something strange about following you into battle," he said. "Now it's so far removed from everything. Here's to lost horizons, mysterious one! I don't even know what fogbank you and your cycle came out of, but here's to it!"

She looked at him with her brown eyes, and tapped *his* can back. "To *Brigadoon*," she said. It made the toast intimate and she looked at him all the time they took the first thirsty gulp.

"I don't want to know anything, anyway," he said. "I want this place and you to be like the Army. *Brigadoon* is a good toast. Appearing suddenly out of nothing, but only briefly. That *is* what the Reserve is like. Totally removed from anything real or anything you've ever known. The only difference is the difference between pleasure and pain."

"Sometimes you can't separate them," said Joanne.

"I know," said Eros. "I secretly like the dentist's drill. And I like to beat my head against the wall, too . . ."

"Because it feels so good when you what?" knowing that

185

she didn't have to complete the phrase. It would have disappointed them both.

"Because it feels so good when you do this," said Eros, drawing her close to him and kissing her for the first time in the sunlight. She tasted of salt.

"Delicious," he whispered to her, and tasted her tongue as well, until the salt was all gone. "Make some more, please," he said, releasing her. "Juicy Fruit and you . . ." and she did her best while he kissed her forehead and her eyes and the base of her throat where the collar began. "You *are* getting better," he told her and turned to rip off two big sections from the bread loaf. From his pocket he took a dinner knife that he had stolen from the mess tent.

"Can you believe what a prize theft this was?" he said. "You know, they count every damn utensil in the mess and after two weeks, whatever's missing they charge to the mess officer. Everyone pleads not to be the mess officer. If anything *is* missing they forage or trade or steal from other units to make up the loss. Paper work involved for one goddam missing knife would take three clerks eight hours and twelve stencils to report. It's a great system."

"Good government *is* slow process," Joanne repeated, almost by rote. "At least now in Washington, everything is on microfilm. We can reduce it that far."

Eros handed her some bread with a slice of cheese, two pieces of tomato, and the ham.

"I know," he said. "And put examples of it in a time capsule to bury under Pennsylvania Avenue. Along with the original and eight carbons."

She couldn't help laughing, and grabbed at a few tomato seeds and juice that ran down her chin.

"You're an adorable slob," Eros told her. "What a fine piece of china to eat off," and he leaned over to kiss her chin with a smacking sound.

"You should rent yourself out as a human napkin at dinner parties," she told him. "From time to time, a shaggy dog will pass among you . . ." She felt fine, with the afternoon sun warm on her bare shoulders and legs. They had to talk loudly to one another to be heard over the racket of the dam, and the beer helped to ease the hoarseness of their effort. It was no problem at all to finish the six-pack. The sun had made them hungry and the ham and cheese disappeared, along with one of the bottles of wine. It was chilled nicely by the icy waters of the pool; they took turns pulling at the bottle and talking about their impossible meeting at Camp Cannon.

Eros had taken off his shirt. The sun and the wine had made him perspire. Joanne noticed the hardness of him, the smoothness of his skin, that was touched with tan from early summer days at the beach. She liked his arms and shoulders, muscular without being overdeveloped, moving down to his narrow hips and small bottom. She noticed that one pectoral was larger than the other and, being a seeker after truth, she asked about it. Eros flexed it obscenely for her, making it pop in and out.

"Comes from playing squash so much. Swinging the left arm with a racket in your hands. Builds up that side more. Logical?"

"Why squash?" She was trying to justify, as she had to, the activities of a man she was interested in. He obviously had no ambition; did no work; sneered at anything sincere.

"Why?" he answered. "Because you can count on it, if you're good. I can count on it and I *am* good. You know where you can place that ball every time. White, white court, brilliantly lit, with a black, black ball. Hard. Fast. One opponent at a time. Gladiatorial. Plus I can make a passable living hustling it."

"Why hustle anything?"

"Because everyone hustles," Eros told her. "The whole of life is gladiatorial: marriage, business, school, children. I want to be in a position to pick my own arena. Otherwise I don't play.

"And I have an ulterior motive. Ten years ago the best golfers in the world could only make about twenty-five thousand a year. Now the vast middle group of pros make that easily, with endorsements of balls, and jockstraps and God knows what. And they do public appearances demonstrating their swings and their grips. I have a feeling that squash is growing like that. Money is made by foresight."

"What are you going to do, Mr. Svengali," she said, "if you're back in the Army?"

He laughed. "This is a stupid little Mickey Mouse diversion to break up their own monotonous lives. Why do you think these old doctors and sergeants stay in the Reserve? It's their only escape from reality. Brief as it is, it helps them. But they've got no intention of turning it into reality. Any more than I do."

"You could be wrong, you know," she said, and saw a shadow pass over his face.

"Unthinkable," he said.

It was too nice a day to get wound up and he had waited

long enough. She was close to him, leaning her side against his side; his arm was cradling her shoulders around her back. She felt very warm and protected and indulgent of his positive ideas. All the free spirits she had ever known, all the liberals and believers in causes, were much too nervous to be taken seriously.

Eros crinkled up his nose and blinked innocently at her; she could see his green eyes rimmed with red from the beer and the wine. Since he noticed things also, he asked her, "Why is it that one of *your* pectorals is bigger than the other? See, we've got more in common than most people—"

She looked down in sudden disbelief, but he was kidding her; all she saw when she checked was his hand, which felt very safe and good over her McMullen. His hand covered six little blue and white flowers over her right breast; then suddenly his hands covered twelve little blue and white flowers. It felt doubly good. He didn't breathe hard or demand, and she couldn't refuse him. Very slowly he kissed her and she didn't want to let him go. He eased her down on the concrete surface of the dam top, and she didn't mind the little bits of gravel that she could feel under the bottom of her shorts; he unbuttoned her blouse all the way to her waist and pulled it out of her Bermudas.

She kept thinking silly things from books she had read and the phrases she could see in black and white that had always tickled her, like: "His mouth traced patterns of fire down her body and she could feel the nipples of her breasts stiffen with excitement and desire." She had always laughed at the descriptions; but she found it difficult now that *her* nipples were stiffening with excitement and desire.

It wasn't all at once, but slowly and after a long time that they lay naked on the top of the dam. He stopped touching her; he hadn't made love to her, but he stopped and rolled over on his back and held her head up from the concrete. They both looked up at the sky and saw in the distance the dark clouds that come up so quickly from over Lake Ontario. But directly above them it was blue, with the sun tilting down in its journey to the west. It warmed their tummies and chests and Joanne glowed inside and out. Her stomach waited to be touched again and knotted against the moment.

"It's beautiful up there, kitten," Eros said to her.

"Why isn't it beautiful down here?" she thought to herself, desperately wanting him to say that.

As if in answer, he rolled over and looked at her, up and

down. It was hard for her to lie still and not cover herself. "I want no shame, Joanne," he said very seriously. "I want to know everything and have you know it and see it and not be afraid." He looked straight down at her and she relaxed and opened up her mind to him. The rest was easy, and he took his time.

She knew that people said strange things sometimes when they made love and she wondered if he cared that, except for her quickened breath, she was outwardly silent. But she felt him inside her, moving it seemed in all directions; when he was gone for a moment she thrust up instinctively, wanting him back entirely. His whole weight pressed her into the concrete and she could feel the small loose stones grind into her skin; but she opened her eyes and saw his mouth moving and the clouds moving and she smelled their sweat and the shagbark hickory and the yellow poplars and the spray from the roaring waters and she thought she knew what it was all about.

Eros was glad that she was the one on the concrete. It was nice for him because it was so unexpected; but no different in his eyes than a dozen other career girls, all ready to shoot their ideals on a concrete dam, or a beach, or a back seat. That was part of Eros's way of getting back at the modern woman.

He watched two big red ants crawl over her shoulder and followed their progress around her back while he continued to observe *her* progress as well. "Amazing game," he thought. "It's a goddam amazing game," and, in order to wait, he found himself chanting, "Mama no want no peas, no rice, no coconut oil," in his mind in time to their rhythm. When she finally released and had to say, "I love you," out loud, he saw no need to wait any longer and, trusting in his incredible luck, filled her with millions of his sperms; little swimmers moving upstream.

"Oh, you have the smallest, most delicious bottom in the world," she said after a minute. "Do all men have bottoms like that?"

"No, baby, just me," he said to her before kissing her long and hungrily and holding her to make it memorable. Then he patted and stroked and kissed some more until she purred and patted him back, happily unafraid.

But knowing that she had told him that she loved him and that he had said nothing, Eros led her down the stone stairs to the trout pool. They waded in naked, laughing and splashing until they fell down in the cold water and giggled uproariously at nothing. They dangled their legs down into the white water and felt the pull of the river.

The clouds from Lake Ontario were now over them and Joanne felt cold.

"I'll get a towel, baby, and the corkscrew to tap this next bottle. Then I'll warm you proper," he said in a cockney accent.

She tossed her puppy dog haircut and watched her lover climb the stairs to the top of the dam. "What now?" she asked herself, seeing him run two steps at a time. "Life is so complex," she sighed, running her hands through the water and cupping them; then letting it run through her fingers, back from where it came.

Eros was up on the dam, bending down to pick up the towel, when the second bottle of wine crashed an inch from his head against the concrete, splattering bits of glass and Chablis over his face. He jerked around and there below him was Rufus Soule standing next to Joanne, his pants dark to the knee with water stain, his face twisting with emotion, the cords in his neck knotted.

"Stay here," he said furiously to her, looking at her naked body with horror and disbelief. Then he came after Winter.

"Just a simple picnic, sir," Winter yelled down at him, terrified, and then stood rooted to the spot as the agent ran toward him.

He found out fast. Soule, too angry to smash him, which would have been easy, grabbed for his throat and pushed him to the edge of the concrete, over the rushing white water pouring from the sluice gates. Joanne screamed, and cursing the fact that she didn't have on her fatigues and combat boots, ran to the battle to save her man.

"Let him go, Rufus," she yelled. "I love him."

But Soule was in a trance and didn't hear Joanne or the gurgling noises from the throat of Winter. Eros jammed two thumbs into Soule's kidneys, but still the fingers tightened on his windpipe. He could see the agent's head jerking horribly and white specks of saliva flecking his mouth.

"You bitch, Joanne, you bitch—that I ever cared for you!" Soule panted, and Eros knew that he'd turn on her next. He jammed his knee up hard between the agent's legs and they teetered on the edge, but Soule only grunted and kept squeezing. Winter could feel himself blacking out.

"A memorable piece of ass," he remembered thinking to himself. That was when Soule was hit with the other wine

190

bottle and a push which sent him, writhing and choking, tumbling to the pool thirty feet below. He didn't even have time to pick his nose.

Joanne was the first to react. Eros, in his panic, wanted to beat it and leave him there. She was cool, and oblivious to the fact that she was still naked; she ran to pull the agent from the water, unconscious now, but calmed down and breathing. They got dressed and laid Soule over the back of the Lambretta.

"I've got to stay with him and explain, darling," she said to Winter.

"Fine, you do that. Just drop me at the crossroads before you go back to Cannon," he said. "I'll be all right." He couldn't believe it all had happened, but she was all efficiency; she had decided that there was definitely a place in her life for Eros. Her instinctual protection of him convicted her of that. She could make him use his talents constructively.

Eros knew the feeling. People had had it about him before. He hitchhiked into town and got himself good and drunk with some of the boys from the unit he found in one of the bars. He told no one about the afternoon.

"What a goddam waste of a bottle of ninety-nine cent wine," he muttered to himself, sorry that life was so complicated. It pained him that life should be so complicated.

SEVENTEEN

Colonels Beauregard, Harden, and Fruitman were uncomfortable in their civilian clothes. They huddled on the afterdeck of the MS *Rock of Ages,* a pleasure boat that toured the St. Lawrence in the Thousand Islands. Marjorie Stavropolis was with them in a belted peasant smock, which she insisted on wearing with high heels. She was taking notes from them and felt put out that they had to go on Army business for their afternoon off.

"O.K., we'll stay in a motel," Beauregard promised, as compensation for not taking her to Montreal as she had originally been told to expect.

"—One that has those feely finger machines on the beds, for a quarter," she said. "I always massage you; you never do a damn thing for me."

"Nag, nag," he countered. "You're beginning to sound like my wife. I made you a major, didn't I?"

"Major, smajor," she pouted. She had felt neglected during the first week of camp. Colonel Beauregard was so preoccupied with the upcoming operation. Her ambition smoldered; but she found it increasingly difficult to get him to discuss any further promotion. As an alternative, she encouraged the attentions of Colonels Fruitman and Harden, who brushed her whenever they passed. But Beauregard remained too self-absorbed to be jealous. Even if he had noticed, he felt too secure within his chain of command to be threatened. He knew why Stavropolis was available. It was *his* particular fortune of war; *his* spoils for being commander.

"Look at that," he yelled, rushing to the rail as they passed Heart Island and the voice of the tour guide broadcasted: "There, rising majestically as a symbol of love's constancy, Boldt Castle. Built as a love offering by millionaire George Boldt for his wife's summer playhome. Tragically never finished, due to the sudden demise of Mrs. Boldt; now on view for us all." Stone turrets commanded a view of the St. Lawrence; Beauregard's companions dutifully followed their leader's pointing arm, sucking in their breaths in a tripartite exclamation of wonder at man's adoration of woman.

"Magnificent architecture," they chimed. "Those flying buttresses, just like on the Rhine."

"Not the castle, you idiots," Beauregard blasted them. "There's the island we're going to hit!" He had detailed instructions and charts from Soule of the Operation's proposed site.

It was a small island, owned by the State of New York as part of the Manhattan group, four miles square, tucked in a cluster of five, a quarter of a mile from the New York side of the St. Lawrence.

"There, gentlemen—you have our objective," Beauregard continued, as the tour boat moved within four hundred yards of the beach. "We are to move the hospital, starting at 0030 hours Thursday morning, 19 August, with all but ten personnel left behind to guard the permanent equipment. All operating-room, X-ray, mess, surgical, and emergency equipment are to be included. We will strike our existing encampment under attack and blackout conditions, then move—via two-and-a-half ton truck and ambulance—the thirty-five miles to Alexandria Bay and the jumping-off point. This assembly should rendezvous by 0230 hours, when we shall have a formation and head count. At 0300 hours the 219th Engineer Battalion of the Minuteman Division is scheduled to arrive with large rubber rafts which can contain all of our equipment and personnel. At exactly 0330 hours we shove off for the island, using no light but the few infrared lanterns provided by the engineers. The rafts will be rowed, gentlemen. The instructions and further assignments for the officers and men I am leaving in your hands. They are to be carried out, and I am to be informed that all preparations have been completed prior to 1200 hours, Wednesday, 18 August, day before X. Clear? Good! We shall go over and over this until there is no margin for error.'"

Beauregard went on: "The reasons for the blackout conditions are twofold. For one if we do this as real Army forces and not as Reserve, we must expect full-scale war conditions. Two, we must expect resistance and harassment from so-called Aggressor forces all along the way. Their purpose is to hinder our landing. Not enough to prevent it, just enough to make the landing appear authentic and make the 229th look ultra-efficient to Soule. I don't expect miracles, gentlemen. But I do expect results *and* the nod from Washington. It should, if we are chosen, mean promotion for all of us," (he included Stavropolis in the blanket statement) "and the glory of doing something for our country, in these difficult times, something besides paper work and handing out APC tablets to malingering National Guardsmen."

Beauregard looked anything but majestic, clad in Bermuda shorts and high black socks, with patches of very white and skinny bare knees showing their knobs to the sun. He swayed with the pitch of the boat, which did no more than five unsteady knots, insuring that the tourists got a full four hours' tour of the islands for their three dollars and fifty cents. His voice became high-pitched as he warmed to his subject; and his audience, becoming fascinated with the plan, pitched and rolled with him.

"After landing is completed," he continued, "and another head count taken at 0400, erection of the hospital will commence. I want *full* erection, gentlemen: personnel tents, wards, administration, surgical headquarters and mess. Then, I figure, at approximately 0500 hours you may post the sufficient number of guards and the hospital may bed down until 0630, when we shall put in a routine working day according to military SOP. Not much time to sleep—but after all, we are protecting the sleep of millions of Americans by our watchfulness. Any questions?"

"Yes," said Colonel Fruitman, dressed nattily in a seersucker suit with white buck shoes. "Will there be any patients or casualties for us to handle?"

Beauregard nodded. "That Thursday morning after we have landed, we shall receive, by helicopter from the mainland, simulated emergency casualties, as if they were being brought back from the front lines to be treated. They will be wearing moulages, paste-ups of various injuries or wounds, and will have emergency medical tags attached to their uniforms. You will use all aid teams and doctors available to separate the patients and distribute them to the wards.

"The Agency leaves nothing to chance," said Harden thoughtfully, "very little room for failure." He spoke quietly, thinking of World War II and remembering how many similar offensives he had seen. He didn't like the efficiency of it. It was not matching his conception of the Jolly Reserve that he had remained part of purely for his own pleasure.

"National defense can allow no error. Just one means—" Beauregard drew a finger across his throat making a "zzzzzzzp" sound; they all became absorbed in their own thoughts. The Colonel gripped the rail and watched the island recede into the thick wake of the pleasure craft.

"Soule and I have agreed to call it Operation Nightingale, you know—after Florence. That's our major purpose: saving lives, right?"

194

His three associates paid little attention. They were concerned for their own lives. Their two weeks of dust and beer was becoming a lie. The Colonel was serious and they felt a big joke being played on them. The day was bright as they worried; the tour guide droned on, bored by his own presentation.

Many of the men of the 229th took the pleasure tour of the Thousand Islands that weekend. Anything to escape the confines of Camp Cannon, where at any moment they might be subject to the whims of the detail sergeant left on duty. They walked in twos, threes, and fives along the boardwalks of Alexandria Bay and Clayton. A few had taken buses, but most had hitchhiked the thirty miles from camp. Some of the men wore civilian clothes, self-consciously; not wanting to be taken for soldiers, but failing in their attempt. Most of the men were in uniform, and MPs from Cannon cruised the streets in their jeeps, looking for fights and AWOLs and warning the men to put on their hats and roll down their uprolled sleeves. Beer after beer after beer made the weekend no different from the off duty hours of the week. Men who loved beer drank it. Men who ordinarily drank whiskey drank beer. Men who ordinarily drank Coke, drank beer. They got blasted or high or silly or depressed and it was the accepted norm; chemical proof of the fact that they were soldiers, unable to adjust to a part-time civilian life without its help. The souvenir shops did good business in salt water taffy, Thousand Island T-shirts and funny postcard scenes of the town. But the bartenders were the most pleased.

Eldor von Liebert prowled alone, looking across the river at Boldt Castle, shutting his eyes hard to try and transpose it and himself to Munich. Lost in his own blues he barely heard the voice at his shoulder asking him:

"Lonely, von Liebert? It's a long way from everything." Skippy Dennis was resplendent in a narrow-lapelled double-breasted cotton blazer, narrow slacks, cuffless, and pointy Italian shoes. He wore a handsome foulard ascot at his neck, with matching pocket handkerchief. His shirt, open at the throat, was wide-striped, the collar high, with just the lightest hint of starch.

"Hello, Sergeant," answered von Liebert, startled. "I'm not lonely. Just thinking how much like Bavaria this looks. It is a strange feeling, more than anything else."

"Like to have a beer?" There was a tightness to Dennis's smile. He had fought the impulse to approach von Liebert,

195

watching him for some time across the street near the ferry landing. ("There's no reason not to talk to him, at least," he told himself. "He's isolated, just like me. It doesn't mean I want anything more than just talk." He was very deliberate about the way he stepped across the street. Every time one of his feet touched the ground, he repeated to himself, "I only want to talk.")

"I'd like a beer," said Eldor. "What soldier can refuse a beer, right? Besides, it's a special bond that ties a sergeant to his men, huh?" The soldier-on-leave swagger made him hitch up his pants and smile in his sergeant's face. It wasn't the smile of a clerk typist at all. It was the smile of an infantryman with an idea. They crossed the street away from the Pleasure Boat landing, the German feeling proud that a non-commissioned officer would invite him for a beer; Dennis wondering just exactly how to play it. They walked into the first bar.

"What would you like, von Liebert?" said Dennis trying to be the gruff sergeant.

"Genesee is fine for me, Sarge." Eldor's accent sounded foreign, even grotesque, in the air-conditioned bar. The two men made a strange contrast.

"Any more trouble with Baer?" Dennis asked for openers, knowing about the trouble but feeling his way along.

Von Liebert's face clouded. "Nothing that won't resolve itself."

Dennis knew that he had taken the wrong tack. Eldor was reminded of friends of his father from the war—smooth-shaven with tailored uniforms and slight lisps, who held their cigarettes or long, thin cigarillos carefully between narrow, manicured fingers. He recalled that they all smelled strongly of cologne. Dennis also smelled of cologne, the same bitter-sweet gin and tonic smell. The sergeant's studied blondness and careful costume were interchangeable with those men from Eldor's childhood.

They said nothing to each other until the first thirsty-hungry sips were thrown down, the coldness all the more delicious because savored during off duty hours. Von Liebert broke the silence first, wiping off the malt moustache with the back of his hand. "What are you doing so—you know, all done up?"

"It's merely my way of maintaining some sort of touch with the real world," Dennis replied.

Eldor nodded and sipped, thinking how right Dennis was.

The decorator felt that he had to make the breakthrough. Nothing pained him more than silence. He decided to be direct. "Do you know that ninety-nine and forty-four one hundredths per cent of everyone on leave this weekend must be sitting down right now wherever they happen to be in this area and talking about one of two things."

"What's that?" said Eldor, knowing really, but wondering what Dennis would say.

"They're either talking about the Army or talking about getting laid."

Eldor agreed, but said nothing.

"Do you know why this is?" Dennis pressed him.

"No, I never think about it," said von Liebert.

"It's because they're lonely and isolated and the Army and sex are the only things that unite them."

"Then why bother them, if they're satisfied with talking about it?" Eldor avoided what Dennis was driving at. He didn't want to be intense that early in the day.

"Because I understand people," Dennis said, "ordinary people, so well. It's why they bunch up in twos and threes and I'm here alone—a thinker, a loner. It's also why you're here alone."

Eldor was resigned. The beer and the cognac that Dennis had ordered after it were good and he said, "Nu, wenn schon!" to himself and joined the ranks of the serious.

"I like being alone," he said. "I need no one else. My nationality separates me and it is a good thing. I have a job to do. It does not include getting drunk or wasting my few free minutes on frivolity. I have time to think and be alone and visit and see what goes into your country and why Americans do as they do. I am detached and I observe."

"But you must hold out your hand to something, long for something you don't have here." Dennis ordered two more beers and cognac for them both. Von Liebert did not say no. He let himself be lulled by the conversation, even though he didn't like Dennis. He was someone to waste a few hours with, someone who was intelligent, and perhaps even sympathetic. If he wasn't really so, he pretended.

"I do hold out my heart," said Eldor. "I do long for something. It's home. This is not difficult to see."

Dennis looked beyond him, through the neatly arrayed bottles on the bar, through the miles to something far away. It was his wistful approach. Dennis was pressing.

"I was in Germany once, not so long ago, through the

197

Dolomites and Cortina into Garmisch and Innsbruck and up to Munich, along the quiet, winding Rhine. I counted twenty-two castles on a seventeen-mile stretch, and we stopped to lunch. Trout and Riesling at a gasthaus beside one of the castles. Cold wine and fresh trout."

Eldor broke in: ". . . and a teethy smile from the waitress that showed too much gum and you wondered if she, too, had been sampling the Riesling." He grinned at his own easy description, pleased that someone had seen and known something in his own life away from the United States.

Dennis watched the red-blondness of von Liebert's sideburns and the straight-up brush cut of his hair. He wanted terribly just to run his hand across the German's head, feeling the close-cropped bristles scratch his palm and then spring back into place. He wanted to run his finger down the straight sunburned nose and let it rub into the small depression between nose and upper lip. He drank his brandy quickly, chased it with a long swallow of the cold beer, and ordered another. They talked about Germany and Europe and the fact that one could wander the streets of any European country alone at night and fear nothing. In the United States one was nervous just walking to one's car after a movie.

"It's the American self-consciousness—Eldor," said Dennis, purposely using the first name. It rolled off his tongue like a love word and he found pleasure in its sound.

Von Liebert liked it also. First names in the service, he found, were a move toward friendship. It was something he had lacked in the Army except for the odd thing between Eros Winter and himself. But he thought he understood Dennis. He didn't understand Eros Winter at all. Dennis was educated and traveled. He had an interest in people other than himself. Von Liebert drank and half believed; he talked about his family and home and even the war. Once he began, it was easy, having a sounding board.

The German's voice was guttural and fascinating to Skippy Dennis. He listened to it, alternately sipping his drink and fingering his ascot. He bided his time, knowing that he was making a score.

Von Liebert conceded that he liked Brecht, which was something he never dared tell his parents. He drank and talked, until the colored lights across the street at the landing were turned on, and he paid no attention to the fact that the jukebox in the bar played only rock and roll.

Dennis was hoping that someone would play a couple of

Tony Bennett selections. "He usually works for *any* language barrier," he thought. When the time was right and Dennis noticed perspiration on the brow and thickening speech in the German, he decided to get to the point. He was calculating, detached from his objective, not feeling the need so much as a compulsion to be right about the nature of loneliness.

"Why not look for a girl this weekend, like all the others?" Dennis asked him.

"I might ask the same of you," von Liebert countered.

"In my case," the decorator answered, "my particular forte is people. I like to observe them, like to communicate with them, like to see what makes them individuals. One can't do that in a desperate hunt for female companionship. Very few of them around here, anyway. They can smell the soldiers coming."

"So you find the next best thing."

"What do you mean by that?" Dennis was a little taken aback.

"I know you are homosexual. It doesn't matter to me, as long as you are not offensive."

Dennis didn't count on the effect that alcohol usually had on von Liebert. It made him sweat and slur his words. But, with every cognac, it also made him sit straighter and straighter and made him more arrogant. Dennis was shocked. His drinking companion had spoken the unspeakable. It was like calling attention to someone who obviously wore a bridge in his mouth. It just wasn't done. His whole approach crumbled and the German smiled at him. Dennis could only wilt under the sneering smile. He let the knot slip in his impeccable ascot.

"Do not be concerned, my friend," said von Liebert, immediately assuming the dominant role. "I *am*, as we have said, isolated and sympathetic. What are you willing to offer me?"

Dennis couldn't believe it. His sensitive pigeon asking for a proposition. He said numbly, without thinking, "Ten dollars."

"Throw in a no-KP clause for next week and it's all right. But I shall do nothing to *you*. I don't share your need, or your desire."

Dennis agreed. He was excited and wanted the arrogant young man terribly. He paid for the afternoon of beers and cognac; he would pay for the dinner afterwards. He followed the German like a dachshund, out of the bar and down the end of the boardwalk towards the outskirts of Alexandria Bay.

"The Americans degenerate daily before my eyes," thought Eldor, hurrying along but wanting it to last for a long time, wanting to humiliate the fools, all of them. Dennis felt dirty and unloved and foolish in his double-breasted cotton blazer. He knew he'd probably get it spoiled, but he had gone too far to back down.

All the troops had returned for midnight bed check on Sunday evening. Except the cooks. They never made bed check, since no one could figure out their duty schedules except Marlon Pinto. And he didn't care, as long as the stoves were lit at four-thirty in the morning.

When the cooks finally rolled in, they were drunk. It seemed they were always drunk—unsure of what to do with themselves during their day off, and hating the kitchen when they were on duty; only staying with it because everyone else told them it was a good deal. They were very noisy when they came into the tents. They disturbed the intellectuals, already back from the weekend. The intellectuals all returned early. They saved their money and wished that the boisterous cooks would quiet down and let them think and continue their conversation as to whether Judaism was a race or a religion.

Cameroons Jackson finally had to heave his great bulk out of his coat and stand in the midst of the tent. He stood there long enough and silently enough for everyone to notice him and know what he wanted. It was enough. Though there were more jokes to laugh at, more subjects to discuss and a few stomachs to empty, the commanders had ordered proper rest for the men, to ready themselves for Operation Nightingale.

"I tell you, O'Brien, it's a *race*, O'Brien," came one last attempt out of the silence.

"Shhhh," hissed the more responsible. "Shhhh . . ."

EIGHTEEN

The rain was the clincher. Everyone felt out of it on the night of the Operation.

"The gods frown on our enterprise," murmured Chaplain Papps; then quickly realizing what he had said, he added, "I really didn't mean it; I really didn't mean it," with conviction.

It had been raining since nine that evening and no one could sleep. It pounded the canvas tents, rushing off the surface to pour into the slit trenches which had been dug to catch the drainage. No one could sleep because there was too much bitching to do and bitching took a lot of time. Officers in charge of various sections sloshed through the muddy ground from tent to tent, rain running off their ponchos. They checked gear, which in most cases was incomplete and poorly packed. They checked instructions, which in most cases were vague and imperfectly learned. They checked morale, which in all cases was nonexistent. The 229th was willing to do nothing more than go through the motions. The rain was the clincher.

"How sweet this is!" said Kenny Keohane, ripping down the highway in his ambulance, squinting through the clicking windshield wipers at the darkness. Eros Winter sat beside him in the cab, his carbine resting between his legs. They had rubbed charcoal on their faces and hands, darkening everything but two white circles around their eyes. It made them look like end men in a minstrel show. Eldor von Liebert and three others rode in the rear with their equipment and weapons: smoke bombs, flares, boxes of blank cartridges, and tear gas grenades.

"Couldn't be better," continued Keohane; "did you see the look on Beauregard's face when it started to rain? Constipation and disbelief. All those bastards that want to activate us are going to have good tight assholes for a long time after we get them busted back to lieutenants." He laughed a loud, mad laugh and put his foot down farther on the accelerator, causing them to skid around a corner. The ambulance righted itself and continued into the rain, loaded with the six Aggressors, uniformed in the Lincoln green and the space-type helmets officially designed by the Army to indicate the mock enemy.

Keohane had maps and his own rubber raft for his Aggressor Team. They were to hit the island first and set up a few obstacles to the landing of the 229th. But Keohane had some ideas of his own. They left Camp Cannon at 1130, an hour before the unit itself was to start. Outside at the bivouac area they put up saw horses, painted white with black detour signs pointing to a road that in the rain would be a quagmire. If the unit emerged from that, the Aggressors sprinkled two- and three-inch nail studs along the entrance to the main highway that the convoy must cross. All Keohane wanted to do was delay the operation until they had time to go to work on the landing area at the island. Everything that would throw the 229th off schedule would help to assist Soule in preparing a negative report to Washington.

"Why the hell are you driving so fast?" Eros said, wary of anyone else putting him in jeopardy. Keohane eased up and lit a cigarette with one hand. He stuck it in the side of his mouth and dragged deeply, releasing the smoke from his nostrils.

"Look," he said. "I've organized this thing. Without me, only single, isolated guys would be able to spring themselves, maybe not even then. I'll be able to spring everyone. Who else would bother? You'd all let yourselves drift onto active duty, you stupid bastards! No one ever wants to take responsibility. I should let you all go to hell!"

Winter realized that Keohane was right, but still he was sitting in the death seat. Everyone was tense. "Go and drive any fucking way you want," he said, and retreated into his own dark silence, staring through the swishing wipers and droplets at the white line before them in the road. Keohane said nothing, but resumed his careening course toward the Thousand Islands, smoke streaming from his nostrils and happiness coursing from his adrenal glands as his opposition party bounced and cursed in the rear of the ambulance.

What they didn't know was that they were being followed. Another figure, alone and shrouded in a poncho over full battle gear, was bouncing along the highway, also scattering nails and broken glass from a big bag connected to the handlebars of a scooter. Joanne Moxie, astride her Lambretta, was determined to follow her lover into battle. She was as anxious as Keohane that they not be called to active duty. If she wanted him at all (and she did), she wanted him intact and in the country, not on a mission inspired by national security.

"Long-distance loves are so abortive," she reasoned. "I want him around. I want to smooth out the relationship." So she followed the fleeing red lights of the ambulance, bound to hook up with the others at the jumping-off point.

Soule had been sleeping when she left. He had recovered from his fall and calmed down; but he brooded about it. He had said practically nothing to her since the incident; but she knew that he blamed Winter and wanted to get him into the service and away from her. Since Soule himself was registered as a deadly weapon he could do nothing physical to Winter, but he prepared to give the 229th a Superior rating on their mission. Joanne tried not to think about it. She downshifted to avoid a skid on the wet pavement. Then, on the straightaway, she gunned the scooter, throttle open full.

Awakened by the assembling troops, Rufus discovered that she had gone. He fumed and raged, slashing at canvas and tent ropes, tables and lister bags—anything within reach of his lethal hands. He flailed away until the built-up calluses on the edges of his hands blistered over again and bled in several places. Then he gave himself a pep talk: "The Agency teaches me self-control. The Agency teaches me discipline. The Agency is my mother; I shall obey her ten commandments." He fingered his sterling string-tie holder for consolation, and popped a square of Hershey into his mouth for energy. He grabbed his rating pad and left the tent, determined to forget by throwing himself into duty. "Emotion is the weakest emotion," he repeated over and over, trying to force the image of Joanne, naked and washing herself in the sun, out of his mind. But all his training in self-discipline did him no good and he reveled in the rain which soaked him to the skin as he muttered at the night: "I'll get him. He'll get his, slowly—unhappily."

But Eros Winter was too frightened at the moment of Keohane's driving to care very much about any hate generated somewhere to his rear. The rest of the 229th, as Keohane tore towards the objective, stood in ranks, sullen, sleepy and wet until Colonel Beauregard verbally moved them out to their jobs. It was easy to goof off in the rain. Everyone looked like everyone else, ghostlike in the darkness with ponchos and field packs, faces shrouded in the night. That's why it took an extra hour to tear down all the tents and get them loaded onto the convoy trucks. Cords stood out in Beauregard's little neck from the screaming he was forced to do over the wind and the rain. When the men folded the tentage it retained the water, soaking it through and adding tremendously to its weight. Half the tent pegs were left in the ground as everyone kicked and kicked to loosen the embedded stakes. When they wouldn't give, the impatient Reservists, improvising, razor-bladed the ropes and threw one fold over another, backed the deuce-and-a-half up and threw the canvas on helter-skelter. It was a great opportunity for the Aggressors to attack, but Keohane and his men were halfway to the objective. Everyone else, soaked to the skin, cursed and laughed and coughed and dragged their ass, unwilling to do more than anyone else.

"Why am I surrounded by idiots? Why am I plagued by incompetence? Is this a conspiracy?" Colonel Beauregard raged, while Major Stavropolis tried to calm him down by stroking him in a very private place, and raising her fatigue shirt to give him glimpses of the ample gourds underneath.

"Not now, for Christ's sake," he piped, his voice getting higher-pitched in his excitement. "Oh Lord," he said, looking up at the rain, "even You are pissing on my Operation," and he leaped in back of Stavropolis when a tremendous thunderclap indicated to him that his blasphemy might have been overheard. Marjorie crossed herself and thought unconsciously, *"Hubris*—what danger he is in." She had her oracular moments, harkening back to Delphi and Megara, Piraeus and Mt. Pentelikon.

Truck motors ground over the noise of the rain; wheels spun and screeched in the mud as the men hurried to load. Phosphorescent white tape had been laid along the ground in strategic places, indicating where imaginary barriers had been erected around the encampment.

The nurses and WACs huddled in one of the covered latrines, waiting for the whistle to get under way. "We better wee-wee before the trucks leave," one of the more practical nurses recommended, and, while the others gathered around for warmth, six women squatted on the wooden boxes with the splatter-splatter of the storm for their inspiration. Just as they were seated, the canvas was jerked away, revealing a bizarre scene in tableau, frozen in the attitudes of a timeless concentration. The enlisted men sent to demolish the latrine stared stupidly and listened to the shrieks.

"Put up that latrine," said their lieutenant. "We'll come back for it later. Excuse us, ladies," he said gallantly. He had spent three days in Atlanta once, selling a premium stamp program to supermarkets, and had acquired a touch of Dixie politesse.

Most of the women continued unperturbed. They were

combat veterans of doctors' anterooms and hospital broom closets. "Didn't waste a drop," one of them said, and the others all laughed obscenely as the khaki cover once again sprang up around them.

Although the rain was a spur to confusion, it also caused a military double timing in the preparation of the trucks, with the officers goading, screaming orders, and pitching in themselves to help. All the gear was packed and loaded, the men steel-helmeted and ready within an hour of the scheduled time. They moved out of the encampment area in convoy, with Beauregard's jeep darting back and forth along the line with instructions and threats. Sergeant Baer drove skillfully, imagining himself in battle, dodging imaginary shell holes, avoiding imaginary machine gun fire, one hand on the wheel, one hand on the imaginary forty-five at his hip.

Rufus Soule was with them, writing violently on his rating pad, while Marjorie Stavropolis attempted, through the bouncing and the jouncing, to peek over his shoulder and check the efficiency marks the 229th was receiving. She couldn't believe the "Superior" ranking she saw in the columns already marked.

Their jeep was in the rear when the first truck hit the detour blockade thrown up by Keohane. The driver almost plowed right through it, as his vision was obscured by the rain, and the sawhorses were below the level of the truck's grill. But he stopped and swung to the left, leaving the blacktop and proceeding down the unpaved narrow road which was one and a half miles of mud and ruts. It rejoined the highway outside of Camp Cannon and the driver, knowing this, did not question the detour. He dropped his traveling speed to ten miles an hour and, almost like a dumb elephant parade, he led the convoy, tail-trunk, tail-trunk into the muck. Half the column had bogged down before Colonel Beauregard realized the error.

"I'll skewer that Keohane on a Q-Tip," he roared. "I'll pour hemlock in his ears." He felt like crying and giving up, until he noticed Soule, still writing furiously, silent and observing. It goaded him on. "Where's my adjutant? Where's my executive officer?" and Baer spun the jeep again to the head of the column, while his commander yelled into his battery-powered bullhorn for Harden and Fruitman, missing chief officers.

Colonels Harden and Fruitman heard him and whispered to

each other to be silent. The rain pounded the flat roof of the ambulance as they stilled their cavorting in the rear with one of their steadies.

"Man deprived of woman," Harden had told Fruitman, "is like artichoke deprived of hollandaise. It is not right for soldiers to build up pressure like this. Especially bad for officers in command. We need clear heads to think, and bodies free of poisonous overflows."

"My medical knowledge informs me that you are correct, trusted colleague," answered Fruitman. "My poisonous overflows, now threatening my entire mental health picture, confirm the diagnosis. What do we do about it?"

They sought out the immediate companionship of one of the nurses who believed, and commandeered the rear of a nondescript ambulance in the middle of the convoy. They made her keep on her steel helmet while she relieved their pressures.

"A steel pot to a military man is just like black silk stockings to a civilian," they told her. "It heightens your attractiveness, my dear, in these times of national emergency."

"For St. George and the Dragon," said Fruitman, preparing for his second round, when suddenly the speed of the ambulance dropped, as it hit the mud road.

"For God, country and Yale," echoed Harden, discreetly turning his back on his friend and ignoring the demands of the bullhorn that thundered outside.

Beauregard removed the detour signs himself, flinging them to the side of the road and kicking them where they lay, helpless and wooden. He halted the convoy and re-routed the half that hadn't hit the mud yet, ordering them to park and wait on the macadam. Then he moved the men out of the parked trucks to assist in freeing the bogged-down column. Spinning wheel sounds filled the early morning dark as men shoved boards and burlap under the tractionless wheels of jeep, truck and ambulance. Finally, the tentage was unfolded and shoved under the wheels, making it even wetter and more filthy. It took an hour and a half of exhausting labor before they were back on the road, and Beauregard was limp with the effort. He saw his longed-for star slipping ever faster into the recesses of everything except his imagination. It was a disaster, but he pressed on, hoping for a break in the weather and a miracle to restore Operation Nightingale to order.

Only one ambulance was put out of commission by the combination of broken glass and nails. The right front wheel popped, sending the vehicle careening out of control and ending on its side in a ditch. Again the column stopped and Beauregard's jeep came dashing to the rescue. He and Sergeant Baer threw open the rear doors and discovered the missing officers. There were Colonels Harden and Fruitman fully clothed in field uniform, but only from the waist up. Fruitman even had on his combat boots. The nurse was lying on the wall of the ambulance which, due to the new juxtaposition, was suddenly the floor. She wore only her steel helmet.

Harden spoke first. "Uh, we must have come disarranged in the accident." The nurse tried to cover herself with her headgear. It was a losing battle.

Colonel Beauregard spoke slowly; he was smoldering. "Move out, gentlemen, and attend to your commands. This incident deserves no comment; but hear this, it shall not be forgotten."

Soule wrote on rapidly and Marjorie had come up to look. Her mouth hung open and she stared at Harden's nakedness. Something about it fascinated her Attic mind. She stared until a sharp "Major Stavropolis!" came at her from Beauregard. She turned away reluctantly. But Harden had caught the look and filed it away for future reference.

"O.K., let's snap to and right this vehicle," he ordered, slowly pulling on his fatigues.

No other damage was done by the booby-trapped road, and the convoy rendezvoused at the Thousand Islands only two hours behind schedule. The Engineer group was waiting for them, irritated and tired, but with rafts inflated, at the ready. It was 0430 hours.

Keohane had encountered no problems. The island was small and easily found in the cluster of five. The beach had been marked with orange dye and the Aggressor force landed, pulled their raft up into the trees overlooking the large beach, and waited. The rain had almost stopped. Only an intermittent dribbling, like a loose faucet, kept things uncomfortable.

The storm hadn't done anything to the St. Lawrence but calm it down; the guide provided by the Engineer Battalion thoughtfully supplied them with lanterns, blankets, and jiffy hand-warmers. They put up a hasty shelter between two trees near the beach and lay down to wait for the lights of the pontoon rafts to move toward them.

"We've got plenty of time," Keohane said. "I expect them to be delayed." He checked the waterproofing of the tear gas grenades and, satisfied that they were in working order, he pulled out his deck of cards and a box of wooden matches to use as chips. He handed the cards to Winter and signaled the others to join him.

"Riffle 'em," he said to Winter. "Payday Friday. Let's not waste the free time."

When Keohane tapped the deck, refusing the cut, Winter checked the edges of the pasteboards for nicks or marks of any kind. Satisfied that everything was kosher, he started to deal.

Von Liebert didn't like cards. He was too impatient. He thought it was a waste of time. He sat aloof, using Keohane's sniper binoculars to scan the mainland. The infrared lenses picked up nothing but emptiness and the naked trees alongside the highway, which was itself bare of anything but closed hamburger stands and silent Dairy Whips. He tried to imagine himself in a concrete and steel bunker off Omaha Beach, running his eyes across the English Channel on June 6, 1944, waiting for invasion. He heard no comforting sounds from his low-growling German shepherd dogs—only the guttural noises of his G.I. companions, betting and raising, laughing and calling. Suddenly he picked up something in the glasses, at first quite faint. Then, as he focused, it moved clearer and closer. He made out a solitary figure, paddling a kayak with a double-bladed oar. It was Joanne Moxie in pursuit.

"Winter," he called sharply, "kommen Sie here."

"What do you want? I'm in a pot for a change."

"You've got a visitor, who looks relentless. Did you invite anyone for the weekend?"

Winter came up beside him and grabbed for the glasses. "Son of a bitch," he said. *"There's* a woman for you. Either that, or it's Nanook of the North." The rain had stopped completely and he ran down from their tree-lined hiding place across the beach to meet her, while von Liebert laughed and continued to watch through the binoculars.

"What do you think you're doing, you nutty broad?" Eros asked her, pulling the kayak up onto the shore, then grabbing her and kissing her the kind of kiss the occasion demanded.

"I wanted to help you, Eros. No time to see you since Saturday. No time to talk. No time to see how you felt."

"Are you all right?" he had to ask.

"Yes. Except I miss you. It's silly to be alone, so I came."

"Then leave the boat here and let's move. Come and meet

208

Keohane and his desperados in our mountain retreat." He led her to the concealed place where the leader was raking in a pot of twenty matchsticks. "Deal her in," said Eros.

She spoke to them all: "Rufus wants to activate the 229th. It would have to take a major botch of things for him to recommend that you return to civilian jobs. I'm afraid he's jealous." She looked at Eros possessively. He tried not to pay any attention.

"Thanks, miss," said Keohane, and they all gathered around the lantern, serious-faced. Their hands grabbed carbines, checking the clips loaded with blank cartridges. "We know what we've got to do. There's an old saying—'Look at an infantryman's eyes and you can tell how much war he has seen.' We want our eyes containing nothing but conjunctivitis. Winter, get those gas grenades ready. Those men don't know it, but they ain't raising no hospital on *our* beach. We'll drive 'em into the sea. Let's go to work!" They cheered briefly and went to work.

In the distance, with the sky just beginning to show sly hints of dawn, the 229th General Hospital pushed off from the shore. All their equipment had been loaded into the deep rubber rafts. The river was calm and conditions were perfect for the crossing. Beauregard sat in the forward raft with the charts spread across his knees. Harden and Fruitman attended him, along with Sergeant Baer and Marjorie Stavropolis. The Colonel pointed to the island in the midst of the cluster, dimly seen across the dark quarter of a mile.

Almost immediately the rain started again, heavy and insistent, drenching the men in the rafts, who had removed their ponchos. The river began to flow faster and the Engineers, at the oars, strained to keep the rubber vehicles on course. Dawn seemed to be nipped right in its beginnings and darkness closed in around them.

"Lash these rafts together," ordered Beauregard; they tossed each other lines and dragged the boats near enough to touch. There were only four hundred yards to go when Beauregard heard the noises of blanks being fired; then a big boom like artillery beginning a barrage.

"Make for the noises. Make for the mortars," he yelled into the rain. "It's the Aggressors putting up a withering simulated fire onto the beach." He stood up in his raft and stared into the rain, like George Washington. His fire was up; his juices were flowing; the rafts moved on their objective, toward the firing of the blanks which they could hear over the steady lapping "thwunk-whirsh" of the oars.

Cameroons Jackson held on tightly to the guy rope in his lap. He didn't like being on the water, even for the fifteen minutes it was supposed to take them to cross. He and the men with him huddled close to the bottom of the raft, pulling their ponchos tight around them and drawing near to one another for warmth. "What the hell old Jackson let himself be tampered like this?" he muttered to himself. But he heard Beauregard yell to get ready for hitting the beach and he raised himself up from the bottom of the raft. Just then they collided with the raft next to them. "I'm undone," is all he had time for, before he lurched into the swiftly flowing current of the St. Lawrence, with all his gear to weigh him down.

"MAN OVERBOARD," four or five voices yelled at once, and hands reached from the nearest raft. The Engineers changed course to effect a rescue; but it was difficult maneuvering the craft, all lashed together as they were. Jackson came up again, floundering, and grabbed for an outstretched oar. He missed and went under again. The second time he emerged choking and cursing and held onto the oar; they dragged him aboard.

Sonya Faust hauled him in like a great tuna and, desperate to be a heroine at last, turned him on his back. She put aside her carbons and portable typewriter and, while the vessels turned in the rain and resumed their course, she lifted his head and clamped her big lips over the gasping mouth of the sergeant. She blew into his lungs, seeing his cheeks fill with air. Then she released. Everyone in the raft watched with wonder as the grotesque clerk typist worked with dispatch, giving life-giving oxygen via the approved method.

"Oh, how exciting," she thought, feeling herself grow moist all over. "Think of what I'm doing. His mouth feels so warm and strong—I'm doing something terribly evil." But she thought it was also terribly nice and continued, even though Jackson was visibly conscious. "Is this carrying civil rights to its logical conclusion?" she thought, maintaining the mouth-to-mouth rhythm all the while. "I hope I can meet him in Boston. Maybe after drill meetings at the Army Base. Maybe even during coffee breaks."

As if reading her thoughts, Jackson pushed her gently away and grinned up at her, his wide smile brightening the storm. "Take it any way you can get it, baby," he said softly and only for her ears, as the others in the raft offered their congratulations for her quick thinking and courageous action. Sonya Faust cradled his head in her arms, protectively clinging to him as the armada approached the end of their crossing.

"Get those tents up as quickly as possible," Beauregard told his assistants. "If we finish by 0800 we can still salvage a Superior rating. They've *got* to give it, considering the elements we've faced."

He stood on the top of his rubber raft, flashlights pinpointing him as he waited, posed against the now-lightening sky. Sounds of gunfire reached their ears from the beach.

"Men of the 229th, get this new hospital operational and ready to receive casualties. Who's with me?" Without waiting for any sort of answer, Beauregard threw himself into the water and began to wade ashore, slapping a green stick against his leg. He was the first of his company to land.

Sergeant Lennie Baer, no longer the Tootsie Roll man but the complete soldier, poised himself at the edge of the raft right behind his commander, heady with emotion. He leaped out without hesitation and, motioning "double-time" with his arm, yelled: "Come on, you sons of bitches, do you want to live forever?"—and then was gone. Baer fell into a deep shelf of water and was up to his neck in the river. His comrades poured over and around him in their rush to be the next to the beach. They dragged him to his feet and then ashore, while they pulled their rubber conveyers loaded with tentage, surgical equipment, stoves and bedding. Officers, enlisted men, nurses and WACs, all in one wave, moved through the knee-deep water, some looking furtively about for the expected attack of the Aggressors.

They formed into ranks on the beach and Colonel Beauregard addressed them, proud and confident. "You've done it. Oh, I love you. You've done it," he said, his voice filled with tenderness.

That's when the tom-toms began suddenly and a huge noise of firing burst out from the trees above the beach.

"HIT IT, AND DIG IN. IT'S THE AGGRESSORS!" he yelled, flinging himself face down in the sand.

Over the hill ran seventy-five Indians of various shapes and sizes, some firing cap pistols, some beating upon small drums. They ran helter-skelter up to the soldiers as the sun broke through at last and dawn streaked across the sky. Seventy-five little boys dressed in loincloths with their faces painted, carrying toy carbines and wooden tomahawks, gathered around

211

the entire complement of the 229th General Hospital which lay groveling with faces in the dirt, avoiding the expected tear gas attack. When Beauregard finally looked up, he saw a tall Indian with a whistle around his neck and a T-shirt that had "Camp Webfoot" stenciled on its front.

"Who the hell are *you?*" Beauregard asked.

"I'm Uncle Henry. Who the hell are you?" the big outraged Indian demanded. "Camp Webfoot starts its Color War today at dawn. You've interrupted the entire totem ceremony."

Beauregard saw, up beyond the trees, permanent cabins, a flagpole with the American flag, and the camp staff all staring down at the beach. On a large wooden building that must have been a recreation hall, he could see a loudspeaker connected to a porch corner where the sun hit it full. A tape recorder was playing through it the strains of "Hava Nagilla." Beauregard knew they didn't really look like Indian children. He jerked his head to his left at the next island two or three hundred yards away and saw, to his horror, Kenny Keohane, Eros Winter, Eldor von Liebert and the others, in their green uniforms and helmets of the Aggressors. They were jumping up and down, and he felt his sphincter muscle begin turning to jelly. He had hit the wrong target.

"Bang, you're all dead," yelled the campers at the soaked and tired Reservists. "We take many scalps for Uncle Dave and Auntie Ann," they yelled at the soldiers. Uncle Dave and Auntie Ann beamed down the hill at their boys.

Beauregard felt his pants filling; but he could do nothing about it. He tried very hard to think of home and fluoridation and lowered his head into his hands so as not to see Soule advancing on him with his clipboard, or Marjorie, who was inching away, step by step, toward the rafts and Colonel Harden, who was wondering if he still had that bottle of Metaxa stashed in his duffel. It would come in handy when they celebrated becoming civilians again. For good.

212

"Hut ho, hut ho, hut hut hut ho," chanted the Special Forces Reservists as they double timed by Entry D of the Boston Army Base. Eros Winter grinned to himself as he went in to catch the elevator to the sixth floor. It was the first Wednesday drill since summer camp and he felt pretty good about it. His squash had been coming around beautifully, despite the two-week layoff, and he had nothing to do for the rest of the summer but hustle. He had thought about Joanne only once, before the buses had pulled out of Camp Cannon for Boston.

"No need confusing the summer with anything that can spill over into football season," he reasoned. "Shame she had to get in the way of a boring camp. It had to be *someone*. But she was much too dangerous. Too time-consuming. *Much* too neurotic." He felt free and his skin was pleasantly tightened from a warm afternoon's swimming in the sun.

"At least she can think I'm a bastard and leave it at that. Washington is a big space between us. Soule will be attentive, at least. More than I would ever be."

He had finally written her a goodbye with the classical description of Eros that he had used in the past:

"Evil his heart, but honey-sweet his tongue.
No truth in him, the rogue, he is cruel in his play.
Touch not his treacherous gifts. They are dipped in fire."
An application of mercurochrome soothes all, kitten.
There's a comfort station in my bus and trailer hitch on
 your scooter.
These are the real things and they're moving in opposite
 directions . . .

—EROS

He liked the touches. Nothing too meaningful. He put summer camp from his mind and moved in on the more pressing problems of adjusting civilian life to his soft game.

"Winter!" von Liebert called, as Eros was about to push the elevator button. He held the doors for the German.

"Wie geht's?" he asked.

"I'm going home," said the German simply. "Summer camp decided me. The whole fouled-up mess, with its politics and

213

foolishness. And that thing with Baer . . . you Americans are unreal. Children, with your toys."

"One thing you should've learned, if you learned nothing else by living here," Eros told him. "Without a sense of humor, forget it. You want to get the big bleeding U; take yourself too seriously. A sense of humor might not help you in the Ruhr Valley, but you need it here. It's something you'll never understand . . . probably best you go home," Eros agreed. He had forgotten about a lot of people; von Liebert would be just as easy to forget. He had other things to do.

"But I *did* come here to work," Eldor insisted. "No one seemed to care about that. A coat salesman playing Hitler. Baer was just like Hitler for two weeks, then returned to the road with his vicuña. A dentist commanding clerks and schoolboys and lawyers. Then you all put aside your little masquerade and go back to drilling teeth and filing and exams and torts. Madness!"

"Forget it," said Eros. "It doesn't mean a thing. Just a joke."

They got off at the fifth floor and walked into the NCO club for a pre-meeting beer. Everyone of the rank of corporal and above had at least three beers before the first formation. The officers all had whiskey sours or martinis at the base officers club down the hall. Hardly anyone signed in for the meetings completely sober. Unless they had been tied up at their business and forced to come in late. In that case, they waited for the eight-thirty break, and made up for lost time by ordering doubles. It made the last hour bearable and quite social.

They ordered a draught beer and Eldor persisted. "We've had war in our backyards for five hundred years. It's part of our jobs as adults and part of our lives to be prepared."

"Things have changed," Winter laughed. "What's the biggest influence on mid-century Europe? The United States. And what's our best-known export? Rock and roll or Coke. With the bomb in the background, we're finding new uses for bananas. What's next? Make it with the madness, Baron, or get a job."

"That's what I intend to do," Eldor said sullenly, sipping at his beer.

Winter was bored by the friendship now. Eldor was like a grammar school friend; they had nothing in common but the Army.

214

But von Liebert wouldn't quit. "I'm not frightened at all," he continued; "what I am is disgusted. I had to be a man when you and your friends were still wetting your pants. You're still not a man now. None of you! That's why I'm going home."

"Horseshit! Have another beer and don't bug yourself."

"None of you stand and face anything," Eldor pressed on. "I even admired Beauregard. At least he tried. The rest of the unit, all of you, just stabbed him in the back."

"You're going to make me feel real bad," Winter answered. "Where the hell were you when they hit the wrong island? Seems to me you were standing with a tear gas grenade ready to take Keohane's orders."

"I was only interested in getting Baer. That's what I cared about. Suddenly, I don't care any longer. The poor bastard is trapped in both his lives."

"You've got it all figured out, wise guy," said Eros. "Now you'll go home and tell your friends what a pushover the United States is. Next generation, we'll have to teach you all over again. I'm glad I'll be too old."

Eldor von Liebert got off his stool.

But Winter fired a parting burst: "Go scurry home to your Deutsche Kredit Gessalshaft, or whoever you're going to work for, and enjoy your liberal American education over a knockwurst or two."

The German turned on his heel and walked by Sergeant Lennie Baer who was coming in the door. They walked past each other without hiding; without making any sign at all.

Everyone registered for pay on the IBM sheets. Then a casual formation was followed by Major Fugue leading the professional complement off to classrooms. He would have one of his captains lecture on the causes and symptoms of granuloma inguinale, while *he* attended an investment club meeting conducted by an ambitious PFC who worked for Merrill Lynch.

Butcher Beanstock led his administrative complement back to their wire-enclosed offices where they cared for personnel records, payroll, supply and the thousands of pages of paperwork necessary each year to a Reserve unit. The men chattered and gossiped and drank Cokes and smoked; they did almost fifteen minutes of actual work in the two and a half hour meeting. Butcher Beanstock had time to kill, and played

215

gin rummy with Colonel Fruitman for a nickel a point. He had made parley in pork bellies that day and felt particularly flush. He was paid twelve dollars and forty-four cents per meeting by the government and did nothing for it but put in an appearance.

Eros Winter, as a second-year specialist fourth class, was paid four dollars and eighty-eight cents per meeting by the government and did nothing for it. It more than paid for the beer he drank, beer being only a quarter a glass. "Uncle Sam takes care of his troopers," he said, flipping a ball at the ten plastic bowling pins of the NCO club bowling game.

Warrant Officer Kenny Keohane was paid eight dollars and fifty cents per meeting. He was absent, interviewing a claimant for twenty-five thousand dollars on a jaywalking accident claim. The government would pay him for his time, since he had one of his motor pool boys sign his name on the roster. The IBM machine wasn't programmed to differentiate between signatures. It only verified the presence of ink.

At the final formation, where a cursory attendance was taken, friends answered "Here!" for friends that had bugged out after signing in for the night's drill. The following week the departed friends would then be present to return the favor for the ones who had stuck it out the week before.

"HOSPITAL!" sounded Fruitman, the adjutant.

"HOSPITAL!" countered the individual complement commanders, echoing the cry throughout the huge enclosed assembly area on the sixth floor.

"ATTEN-HOOT!" and the unit waited to be dismissed.

Colonel Beauregard looked stooped and tired. His moustaches sagged and his scrambled-egg hat was not at an angle, but straight and pulled down low over his eyes. "I have an announcement to make," he said, "one that does not please me; but, in view of the preceding weeks . . . necessary." His wife Margaret and his children, Raymond and Harriet, stood against the wall, morally supporting their husband and father. The ranks grew silent.

"Knute Rockne," he said, "once told his boys, his Notre Dame Football team, to go out there and win one for the Gipper. They responded with spirit. I asked you to go out there and win one for yourselves. You responded by letting me down. But what you probably didn't consider is that you let yourselves down even more. It's something that remains on

216

each individual conscience. I can't live your lives for you. But at some point in those lives, each of you has got to come to some crossroads, some decision that, in effect, says—'I'm a man of my word. I'm going to do a job, even a distasteful one, because it is my duty.' I'm merely a dentist, not a soldier. None of you are really soldiers, either; just ordinary men.

"But you are also citizens who are free and in a democracy. You won't be going on active duty. The 229th will not be chosen. I wish I could hold my head up and say it's not because we didn't do our best. You had no pride, men. You had no pride in yourselves or your Army or your country. I hope you are better civilians than soldiers. You didn't show me a damn thing! I'm turning over command of the unit to Colonel Harden and retiring fulltime to my practice, my family, and public politics. At least do me the favor of voting for fluoridation in your respective communities. If I can't lead you properly, at least I can keep your teeth free of cavities, your gums free of tartar deposits.

"HOSPITAL!" Colonel Gayle Beauregard boomed out for the last time, standing erect now with the old bristle back in his moustaches. The men stood tall, their backs arched, their chests out. "DISMISSED," he cried, and they broke for the exits, not caring about anything but getting to their cars and moving home.

Colonel Beauregard shook hands gravely with his staff and smiled wistfully at Marjorie Stavropolis, who had moved next to Colonel Harden and slipped her arm through his. She wanted to make absolutely sure that her new commander got the picture.

Colonel Gayle Beauregard turned and walked away with his family smiling, allowing his thoughts to stray to the next summer. "Two weeks with no training camp. Maybe we'll all take a cottage on the Cape. A little swimming, a little fishing. A man needs his ease after the long haul," he thought.

"I'm tired, Peggy," he said aloud. "Let's take that elevator down. If I tell Mrs. Fazer tomorrow that she needs her wisdom teeth out, she'll go along with it. A hundred and fifty dollars will go toward a color TV. Give her a better jawline, and I can watch football in color. It's getting more perfected than it ever was. Color, that is—"

The men ran by them in their rush to leave the Army Base. Everyone avoided talking with the Colonel. They had their own problems.

Doctor-Colonel Harden was holding his pill clinic the following evening, writing prescriptions in a large-charactered flowing script. He held his clinic for college girls once a week to praise that particular method of birth control.

"Stay on them, girls," he would leer. "It doesn't matter if you've got a steady boy or not. Keeps you more regular than not taking them. Besides, you never can tell when you're liable to get lucky and discover someone. Why wait thirty days and take a chance he'll slip away? He'll love you for it and you'll be thankful you cared enough to take the very best."

His nurse buzzed him. He had given instructions that he was not to be interrupted during clinics. "What is it?" he snapped at the intercom.

"Call from Washington—a Mr. Soule," came the answer.

"Oh, Christ! What does he want? Put him on."

"Colonel Harden," said the voice. "Rufus Soule here."

"Yes, Soule. What can I do for you?" said Harden. "We did find some shoes of yours. You want them shipped to you?"

"The 229th is being activated," Soule retorted. "Washington wants you on alert and down to the Army Base tonight. Now!"

"WHAT?" roared the shocked Harden.

"Orders are already out. You've been chosen as the support hospital for a military operation in the Caribbean."

"But our landing—our screw-up—" cried Harden in disbelief.

Soule hesitated. "That's precisely it. I couldn't believe it myself. The Agency took my report, which, due to the 229th's efforts, or shall we say, lack of them, was a highly negative and critical one. Seems they've decided to use you as a diversionary force in an island assault. You and your hospital are to serve as decoys. They hope, actually, that you'll make enough noise and cause enough confusion to divert attention from the actual point of attack."

"You mean we're being taken *because* we screwed up?" Harden asked.

"That's the word."

Harden felt the energy drain from his body. He listened dumbly while the voice from Washington continued. "My assistant is in Boston now with instructions for you. After the alert tonight, which will commence as soon as our conversation terminates, you'll have two weeks to get affairs in order. The unit will then report to Fort Devine in western Massachusetts for training; thence, wherever you are needed. A year is to be the period of duty. That's what the orders say. Harden—are you there?"

"Yes, sir," said the soldier. "Yes, sir, I'm here," said Harden, and he hung up the phone.

Turning to the girls who grouped around him, waiting for guidance, their faces shining, hands outstretched for prescriptions, he said: "Take these and go, girls. I'm going to have to refer you to one of my associates for the next year or so. Don't sigh. Be regular! I'm going to war—"

They left; he allowed himself three uninterrupted minutes of sobbing before he picked up his phone to call Colonel Fruitman and set in motion the chain of command for the alert. The calls took everyone unaware, but they responded.

"God can't always be everywhere, so he invented mothers," said Lennie Baer's wife to him after supper.

"Look," said Lennie. "Forget the philosophy and pack my goddam bag. If I'm not in Syracuse in the morning, God's gonna have one less mother to worry about."

"Are you threatening me?"

"Doris, please pack my suitcase while I figure out how many places I have to stop tomorrow. Don't aggravate me."

"You've been impossible ever since you came home from camp," his wife said. "You know that? Short with me and short with your daughter and short with who knows how many people I don't even know about."

"Can I have some more of your fresh-ground instant coffee?" Lennie snapped. "And tell Regina to answer the phone, for Christ's sake. I'd like to know what all those boys see in that slob of a daughter. I think she's going to turn into a hot fudge sundae one of these days."

"You're no Fred Astaire yourself."

"Look who's talking Fred Astaire. Last night I couldn't find it to make love to you. There's nothing but flesh."

"I hid it on purpose. Look in the bureau drawer. But next Purim, please!"

"Wise guy," Lennie said. "All the time, wise guys."

"Daddy," the voice called. "For you."

Baer got up from the kitchen table. "Probably tell me to hit Utica and Albany on this trip, too. Shit."

219

When he came back into the room he was smiling. "I'm going to war," he said, sweeping his appointment papers off the table. "Hot damn, I'm goin' to war! Drag out my Class A's, mother, and let's get our asses in gear."

"What are you talking about?"

When he told her, there was relief and jubilation on both sides.

"You'll send me allowances every month, won't you, dear?" she asked. Doris Baer was thinking ahead, thinking of the salesman in the Chevrolet agency. The Italian one with the slicked hair who had flirted with her when she brought the Impala in to have the differential adjusted.

Lennie was out the door, off to the Army Base.

"So when we're ready to storm down the beach," Kenny Keohane was telling his cronies at Downey's Bar in South Boston, "with our rifles blazin', what do they do but land in the middle of a boys' camp! You shoulda seen the Colonel with his nose buried in the sand. Thought I'd bust. Here, Mike," he handed the bartender a quarter. "Clancy Brothers—'Risin' o' the Moon,' 'Finnegan's Wake,' and 'Courtin' in the Kitchen.' Wet yer whistles, lads," he said to all around him. "Keohane's home to stay!"

"Call fer you, Kinny," said Mother Flaherty, the old woman who sipped beers every night until closing and was the best dart player in the ward.

"Proba'ly the Prudential, tryin' to lure me away from me job, mither," he mocked. "They've offered me everythin' but yer eyes, as blue as Galway Bay."

"Go on with ya, Kinny Keohane," she said, whipping a dart into the bull's-eye.

He returned ashen and shaken. "They need me, mither. I'm goin' to war," was all he said, and he left the bar without another word. His mind was moving; his thoughts carrying on to his return and perhaps a triumphal parade through Sullivan Square with ribbons on his chest. Who knew what could be next? A city council job! School committee! A piece of the action from the downtown parking lots! Anything was possible, with a little imagination. The air felt stifling in the late summer night, but he had resigned himself.

"How do you like it, Mr. Lassick?" Skippy Dennis asked the king of the decorators. It was the first time he had invited

220

Lassick to his new apartment; a special moment in his career. Skippy had done the place himself in blacks and reds, with Chinese screens and ivory figurines on black mahogany tables. He put up pieces of corduroy fabric on the wall in strategic places, giving the entire living room a checkerboard effect. He explained it to Monk Lassick, hoping to impress.

"I think of my life as a great chess game—slowly, inexorably moving toward checkmating anyone's king who opposes my progress."

Mr. Lassick was impressed. "How would you like it if I were your queen? Or you mine?" He wanted the dark-haired boy with the flair.

"Let's have a brandy and discuss it," said Dennis, thrilled to be taking the dominant role. They toasted.

"I love the bouquet of Grand Marnier, Skippy. It sets off your lovely apartment and your lovely manners." Mr. Lassick's jacket felt tight on him. His heart beat very fast under the fitted material. It would have beat directly under the lapels if the jacket had been made with lapels. Which it wasn't.

Dennis was about to swoop in when the phone rang. They both breathed in semi-relief and Skippy went to the bedroom to answer it. Lassick removed his jacket and unbuttoned his ruffled shirt.

Dennis returned quickly and headed for the door. "Party's over, Monk," he said.

"What do you mean?"

"Emergency. I've been called to active duty."

"What? You can't leave me like this! Darling!"

"It'll keep for the duration," said Dennis the soldier, suddenly disgusted. "Wrap it in wide wale, you fairy. I'm going to war!"

Eros Winter was playing doubles. The squash court at the Harvard Club was big and high-ceilinged and very bright. The doubles ball bounced high and stayed up for a much longer time than a singles ball. Eros had been roped into the match. He didn't like to play doubles. "It's a game for old men," he said, "after their legs go on them. Don't like to depend on a partner where my livelihood is concerned." But the stakes were small and he agreed. He had even fallen off his routine enough to have a drink and a small dinner of London broil before the match. It didn't bloat him and he had nothing bet-

221

ter to do with his early evening.

Behind two games to one, Eros looked up onto the balcony above the court. A single spot lit a corner where sat a gallery bench. There, dressed all in white, was Joanne Moxie, with a white ribbon like a halo spinning its bright way through her dark hair. She smiled at him.

"Match over, boys," Eros said. "I forfeit and pay all bets. Sorry, but I've got to have words with the lady." They all looked and approved and left them alone.

She leaned over the railing. "Hello, Eros, how is thy sting?" She seemed too happy.

"Joanne, what are you doing here, kitten?"

"Came to see you," she said. "Your parting shot was clever. But I wasn't satisfied. Did you think I'd let it go at that? A few bon mots and a kiss-off?"

"I lead a strange life, baby," he defended himself. "It wouldn't do to force anyone to share it. Not till I've got something to offer. What is all this for a woman?" He indicated the doubles court, his racket, and the ball, which had fallen in a corner and remained there.

Joanne smiled. "Let's say I've decided to take a chance on you."

"Kitten, you're a wonderful girl. And you potentially make love beautifully. You're smart and independent. What's your problem?" Eros asked her.

"No one ever left me like that."

"Naturally. Only your curiosity brought you back. You're all alike, you and your seven-sister cousins. Dump all over you and you break your backs for more. Let a nice guy offer you love and pay attention and it's goodbye, sucker. The best of you are crazy. Is your curiosity satisfied? I still ain't buying."

"Not quite," she said, getting up and coming down onto the court where he waited. She came very close to him and held out her arms. He pulled her even closer, his leg jamming between her legs, making her breath go faster. He kissed her and touched her and made her get to her knees with him, still kissing.

"Are you satisfied yet?" he asked her.

"Not quite yet!" she answered again, and he tilted her to the floor and when she didn't stop him he took off all of her white clothes, strewing them crazily about the floor. And he made love to her until she cried out, two naked bodies twisting, one on top and the other, across the tightly boarded, brilliantly lit squash court floor. It was blazing white with two off-white bodies and the only blackness, the only dark to mar the clean lines of the scene, was the hard black doubles ball. Stuck in the corner. Blind, without any eyes to watch.

"We've never made love in the dark," Eros said, kissing her neck. "Are you satisfied now?"

"I'm satisfied. But you better hurry," she said. "I've brought your orders from Washington. They're in my bag. You'll have a new career now, baby," she smiled at him. "I do believe you're going to war."

Eros knew, and he grabbed his shorts and ran for the steam bath. Her laughter filled the court, bouncing off the ceiling and swirling around her, carrying into Eros's ears as he fled downstairs, away from the brightness. He even forgot his racket . . . and the ball.

Mothers and wives and little girls marched in front of the gates of Fort Devine. They carried placards as they picketed, bearing sayings like. "U.S. UNFAIR TO RESERVISTS!" "WE'VE SERVED OUR TIME ALREADY, GIVE US OUR HUSBANDS AND FATHERS!" "LET THE PROFESSIONALS FIGHT THE WARS!" They marched back and forth, back and forth, into the evening while their men, waiting for training to begin, dug trenches and latrines. They peeled potatoes and carrots. They painted barracks; they cut the General's lawn and private putting green.

The men not on detail moved out of chow, bored and sullen under posters which reminded them that: "I am an American fighting man. I serve in the forces which guard my country and our way of life. I am prepared to give my life in their defense." They had no specific assignment the first three weeks of activation. Only details. They could watch their women as they picketed, day by day, back and forth.

Cameroons Jackson and Sonya Faust were having coffee in the company dayroom, content after a day of filing and stencils, morning reports and rosters.

"There's one thing about this, Jackson," Sonya said. "Everyone can really say, 'Sleep secure, your Reserve forces are awake.' "

"You can bet your ass on that one, baby," he answered, and she laughed because she was ready to bet *just* that. . . .

223

YOU WILL ALSO ENJOY . . .

DANGER! MARINES AT WORK! by Robert G. Fuller
The dizzy story of a wildly ingenious battalion of para-
marines—bemedaled heroes all—who are sent to a New
Caledonia recreation area to overcome their battle fatigue,
and how they overcame nearly everything else in sight!
(63-028, 60¢)

SEE HERE, PRIVATE HARGROVE by Marion Hargrove
The hilarious story of what happened to the Army when
Marion Hargrove joined in response to a letter from Washington! ". . . Rates a medal." —*New York Herald Tribune*
(53-755, 60¢)
